The
SIXTH VICTIM

Center Point
Large Print

Also by Tessa Harris and available from Center Point Large Print:

Dr. Thomas Silkstone Mysteries
The Lazarus Curse
Shadow of the Raven
Secrets in the Stones

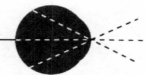

This Large Print Book carries the Seal of Approval of N.A.V.H.

The
SIXTH VICTIM

A Constance Piper Mystery

Tessa Harris

CENTER POINT LARGE PRINT
THORNDIKE, MAINE

This Center Point Large Print edition
is published in the year 2017 by arrangement with
Kensington Publishing Corp.

The text of this Large Print edition is unabridged.
In other aspects, this book may vary
from the original edition.
Printed in the United States of America
on permanent paper.
Set in 16-point Times New Roman type.
ISBN: 978-1-68324-438-7

Library of Congress Cataloging-in-Publication Data

Names: Harris, Tessa, author.
Title: The sixth victim : a Constance Piper mystery / Tessa Harris
Description: Center Point Large Print edition. | Thorndike, Maine :
    Center Point Large Print, 2017.
Identifiers: LCCN 2017016520 | ISBN 9781683244387
    (hardcover : alk. paper)
Subjects: LCSH: Jack, the Ripper—Fiction. | Whitechapel (London,
England)—History—19th century—Fiction. | Clairvoyants—Fiction |
Murder—Investigation—Fiction. | Large type books. | GSAFD: Mystery
fiction.
Classification: LCC PR6108.A768 S59 2017 | DDC 823/.92—dc23
LC record available at https://lccn.loc.gov/2017016520

In loving memory of my father,
Geoffrey Pennell, who "passed over"
while I was writing this novel

AUTHOR'S NOTES

First of all, I know that when I decided to write a novel set in Whitechapel at the time of the Jack the Ripper murders, I was inviting scrutiny from the many thousands of experts on the subject, also known as Ripperologists. I would like to say from the outset that, although I have read extensively, I do not pretend to be anything other than an amateur in this field and I have no wish to contribute to any debate as to the identity of the killer, or killers, in Whitechapel of the late 1800s. My aim in this novel is purely to explore the grisly episode in a fictitious context.

I would also like to acknowledge that the title of this novel is, in itself, controversial. It is historically "generally accepted" that there were five victims of Jack the Ripper, largely attributed to a report by Sir Melville Macnaghten, assistant chief constable of the Metropolitan Police Service and head of the Criminal Investigation Department (CID). In 1894, he stated, with hindsight: "[T]he Whitechapel murderer had 5 victims—& 5 victims only." They were, in order: Mary Ann "Polly" Nichols, Annie Chapman, Elizabeth Stride, Catherine Eddowes and Mary Jane Kelly. They are often referred to as the "canonical" victims.

Contemporaneous newspaper reports were, however, less certain. For example, in both the *Daily News* and the *New York Times*, Annie Chapman, the Ripper's second victim if we stick to the canonical five, was actually referred to as the fourth victim. That's because there had been two brutal, unsolved murders in Whitechapel earlier that year (1888). Some commentators believe that the second of these victims, Martha Tabram, may also have been the Ripper's first victim. In my fictional account, I take hers as the first Ripper murder. The "sixth victim" in the title of this novel refers to what has become known as the Whitehall Mystery—the headless torso of a woman, discovered in a vault on a building site of what became New Scotland Yard. At the time, sensationalist accounts claimed the murder to be the work of Jack the Ripper, but this was soon ruled out by police. Her identity remains unknown to this day.

England, 2016

I stood within the City disinterred;
And heard the autumnal leaves like light
  footfalls
Of spirits passing through the streets . . .

—Percy Bysshe Shelley,
"Ode to Naples," 1820

CHAPTER 1

London, Saturday, September 8, 1888

CONSTANCE

There's blood in the air. Again. They've got the scent of it in their nostrils and they're following it, like wolves honing in for the kill. Only the killing's already done. It's the third in a month here, in Whitechapel, and the second in little more than a week and everyone's in a panic. We're heading toward the scene, to Hanbury Street. There's a big swell of us and it's growing every minute as news seeps out. Shopkeepers gawp, arms crossed, on their steps. Barrow boys are spreading the word. Commercial Street's always busy at this time of the morning, but now the world and his wife seem to be funneling along the rows of old weavers' houses in Fournier Street.

Near me, a big man shouts over my head to a friend on the opposite side of the road, cupping his hands round his mouth. "By the cat meat shop!" he yells over the traffic's din. Past the tight-packed rows of dwellings I go, through Princelet Street, until I reach the place. Sure enough, a big cluster has gathered outside Mrs.

Hardiman's Cat Meat Shop. More and more people are pressing around me now, slavering and baying. They're craning their necks to see. Some men are even hoisting their little ones on their shoulders to get a look. There are a few newspaper hacks here, too, dressed better than the rest of us, all trying to snuffle up the juicy details.

In the crowd, I spot people I know. There's Widow Gipps and her creepy half-wit son, Abel. I wouldn't trust him as far as I could throw him. And Bert Quinn, the knife grinder, skin like a roasted chestnut—he's here, too. And Mrs. Puddiphatt. She lives on our street. Where there's trouble, there's Mrs. Puddiphatt. Sniffs it out, she does, with her big nose. There's Jews, too. Plenty of Jews. They're selling jellied eels from a barrow like it's a carnival, not a killing we've all come to see. But I'm looking for Flo, my big sister. I lost her somewhere down Wilkes Street. I bet I know where she's gone. She's friends with Sally Richardson, whose ma has a lodging house that backs onto Brown's Lane. She'll blag a favor and hope to get a good view of the backyard where they say it happened. Them that lives here are charging sixpence a pop, just for a gander. You can't blame the poor beggars, but you won't catch Flo parting with her money when she can get a good view for free.

Truth is, I don't want to see it. The body, I

mean. If it's anything like the last one, I know I'll want to retch. I read about Polly Nichols in the papers, see. What did the *Star* say? She was " 'completely disemboweled, with her head nearly gashed from her body.' " What sort of maniac could do such a thing? I ask you. And now this one.

A shout down our street woke us all up this morning, Flo and me and Ma. Dawn it was. Barely light. Nippy too. Flo stuck her head out the window. A moment later, she's back.

"There's been another!" she tells me, eyes wide as saucers. So she drags me out of my bed, all bleary, and says we're going to see what's what. That's how it is around here. We look out for each other. Everyone knows everyone's business in these parts, so when one of your neighbors is murdered, then it's your business, too. And this, this madman—well, he seems not to care who he picks on as long as they're on the streets.

Maisie Martin was in the Frying Pan on Brick Lane the other night. Flo told me that her friend had been sleeping with her babes not five yards away from where the fiend did his work on poor Polly. She'd heard a scream, then thuds, like someone was hitting her front door. But she froze. She didn't even dare to look out the window; she was *that scared* for her little 'uns. And, well, she might've been. They found Poll a few paces away, her throat slit and her guts ripped from her body like tripe on a butcher's block.

Now there's four women dead since April and the last two've been filleted not three streets away from us. When that happens, then you sits up and takes notice, don't ya? No one's been done for them, so **he's** still on the prowl. There are suspects, of course. They say a Jew did both of the latest ones. Or that it's the Fenians, them Irish blokes. After Polly, Old Bill started asking us all questions. Did we see anyone acting funny? Did we know them that was done for? But no one's behind bars, waiting for the hangman. And I don't mind telling you, that no woman round Whitechapel feels safe.

Anyway, Hanbury Street and Brick Lane is crawling with coppers. There's a ring of dark blue round Number 29. They're telling people to keep back. One or two of the rossers are even waving truncheons about, showing they mean business. There's an ambulance, too. The horses don't like the crowd. They're getting restless.

Rumors are racing round like fleas on a dog's back.

"It's Dark Annie," I hear someone growl.

"Annie Chapman?"

"So they say."

It's no one I know. I'm feeling relieved when I hear someone yell my name. "Con!" I switch round. "Con!" It's Flo, a few feet away from me, standing in a doorway. She beckons me to come quick. I break free from the huddle around me.

"Did you see anything?" I ask, scuttling across the street.

She shakes her head. "All I sees was a pair of laced-up boots and red-and-white–striped stockings. Sticking out of a piece of old sack, they was. Then they came to take her off." She jerks her head over to the waiting ambulance. Her voice is flat, like she's missed the star act at a variety show. Then, as if she's trying to make up for her own disappointment, she adds with a cheery shrug: "I 'eard 'er innards 'ave been ripped out, too."

I cringe at the thought. "You reckon it's Leather Apron again?" I ask, but before she can answer, a roar goes up. I wheel round to see the crowd craning and pointing. Old Bill's telling everyone to move back. They're sliding the body on a stretcher into the ambulance to carry it off. We watch as they shut the doors and slowly the cart pulls off down the street. It takes a while. There's idiots who cling onto it. Lads mainly. But a few sharp blows with a copper's truncheon soon sort out that problem and off the ambulance goes to the mortuary.

"Come on," says Flo, taking my arm. "We've seen all we can, for now."

I'm glad she's not going to try and sneak another peek of the yard. I've had quite enough excitement for one day.

15

EMILY

She has not seen me. I wanted to reach out and touch her from here, in the cold shadows, but I did not. Not yet. I've been away, you see. Not for long. Five weeks and three days, to be precise. But much has changed since I left. The district is in the grip of a new terror. The horrors that I knew were different in nature, but daily: the starveling in the gutter, the homeless old man dying of cold, the young widow poisoning herself to death on gin. But, unlike poverty, this new horror is not slow and insidious. It's swift and brutal. It's barbarous and depraved. It's murder of the most vile and visceral kind. And, what's more, it is happening on the streets I know so well. It's happening in Whitechapel.

The rumors among the crowd are true. Annie Chapman—or Dark Annie as she was known because of her hair color—is the latest victim. I knew her in life. She was a harmless soul. She used to scrape by doing crochet and making artificial flowers. But when she didn't have enough money to feed herself, she did what most other women in her position had to do, she took to the streets. And, like most women in her position, she also took to the bottle so that the next day she might not remember the sunless alley or the stairwell, nor the grunting and the thrusting and the insults that so often came her way.

Yes, I knew Annie Chapman and I knew she was not well. I could tell by the pallor of her skin and the cough that she so often stifled with the back of her hand that she was suffering from a serious malaise. A few weeks before she was murdered, she came into St. Jude's. She just sat in a pew at the back and took in the beauty of the place and then she bowed her head. It was hard to tell if it was in prayer or because she felt unwell. Either way, she found a sanctuary in the church. I hope she took away with her a little of the tranquility that she seems to have enjoyed that day. I wish I could have shared that peace with her, too. But it was not to be and the early hours of September 8 were to be her last on earth.

And I witnessed them.

I was in Hanbury Street as dawn was breaking. A stiff wind helped chase away the dark clouds, but still poor Annie had not had a wink of sleep. Turned out of her lodging house because she did not have enough money to pay, she'd roamed the streets all night, touting for business. None had come her way, so far. Barely able to stand because of the giddiness she felt, she'd lurched from one corner to the next. Her poor hands were numb and the nausea was rising in her throat. Little wonder she'd had not a single customer—until then.

From out of the shadows, **he** appeared and approached her. Of course, she did not know him. To her, he was just another lusty man whose urges needed satisfying. But I knew. I saw her nod in agreement at his words and I saw her being led through a doorway down a long passage. I followed with dread in my heart. I was powerless to help as I saw her walk down the steps into the yard beyond. I watched as she bunched up her skirts and leaned against the fence, splaying her legs in readiness. It was then that he loomed over her and then that I think poor Annie knew something terrible was about to happen. I heard her call, "No!" But it was too late. His hand was already pressed against her mouth. She flailed her arms and scratched at his hands as they tightened round her throat. She must have felt the cold steel on her neck then, because soon the warm syrup of her own blood was coursing through her fingers. I pray she fell insensible immediately. I pray that she was spared any knowledge of what he did next when he lifted her skirts and ripped her with his knife.

After that, I only stayed long enough to see a man open the back door of his home and stumble across the body in his backyard. Wild-eyed, he turned, shambled down the passage, then staggered out onto the street to summon help. And I? I had seen enough, too. But the questions that swirled around in my head reared up once more, just as they did after Martha Tabram and Polly Nichols. Could I have done more to stop this? Should I have done more to stop this? Sometimes I wonder if my own weakness has betrayed my sex, my own cowardice condemned these women? The answer to these questions is that, despite all that has happened to me, I am still powerless to change the minds of evil men. I can only guide those who are willing to listen and through them hope to exert an influence for the good.

The first policeman had been summoned as I took one more look at poor Annie Chapman, her blood still pooling on the ground. There was no more I could do.

CHAPTER 2

Friday, September 14, 1888

CONSTANCE

"Roses is red. Violets is blue. Three whores is dead. And soon you'll be, too."

They're leering at me, in their ragged clothes, with snotty noses and grins on their dirty faces.

None of the draggle-haired nippers can be more than twelve, but I'm scared as hell. I know I shouldn't be, but their stupid rhyme sends me all ashiver.

"Get away!" I growl through clenched teeth.

"Three whores is dead, and soon you'll be, too," they repeat.

"Bugger off!" I lunge at them and shout so loud I startle a passing gent. His monocle pops out of his eye socket in surprise. Anyway, my bawling does the trick. The mangy urchins turn and scuttle off like the sewer rats they are.

This may be swanky Piccadilly, where the ladies and gents dress up to the nines, and it could be a million miles away from Whitechapel, but still my heart's beating twenty to the dozen and my mouth's dry as sandpaper. Bold as brass they were, all cocky and brave. And they can be, 'cos they're not the ones *he's* after. *He's* after girls and women who work on the streets. The ones who are out at night, drinking their gin by the gill, so they don't feel the pain as much; so they don't have to think on what they've become.

You've got to pity them. I do, at any rate. Miss Tindall's taught me that. Most of them were once wives or mothers and fate's dealt them a cruel hand. They've all got their hard-luck stories to tell; how their masters had their way with them and landed them with a bun in the oven—I mean, with child—or how they lost their husbands or were beaten by them and forced to leave their homes. Men, eh? Can't live with them, can't live without 'em.

I don't go with 'em, myself. My ma says we're not that desperate . . . yet. I can tell you there are plenty of poor souls that do round here. Amelia Palmer, Mary Kelly, Pearly Poll. I know 'em all. Salt of the earth, by and large, they are. Granted, some of them are out to fleece their gents for an extra bob or two, but then I can talk. That's what we do, see. Well, when I says "we," I mean Flo, really. I don't like helping her out, only I do, 'cos thieving's not as bad as selling your body. But I'm still out at night, earning a living, of sorts. That's why I'm outside this theater tonight with my basket of posies.

In March and April, I sell oranges. They're the best. You don't throw them away like you have to with the blooms sometimes. This late in the year, it gets harder. There's not much left. I managed to buy the last of the lavender today and tied some up in bunches. The ladies like them, they do, to sweeten their cupboards and chests. Moss roses too. Make them up nice myself, I do. I get the rush to tie them for nothing; then I put their own leaves round them. The paper for a dozen costs a penny, sometimes only a ha'penny, if Big Alf's feeling kind. He's a gentle giant, he is. Used to work on the railways till his accident, but he'll do me a deal if I flash my pearly whites.

And rosebuds. They always go down well with sweethearts—and when they come to buy from me, Flo slips her hand in their pockets, and relieves them of a few pennies, or of their watches or anything else we can sell. Once or twice, she's done it too brown and been rumbled. The coppers have gone after her, and almost nabbed her, but somehow she's always managed to dodge them at the end of the day. She's slipped into a front room or a shop doorway and just disappeared.

Me? I don't like that sort of thing. I'm keeping my head down right now. But 'cos—sorry, I should say *be*cause; I know my letters, Mr. Bartleby—he's Ma's beau—he buys a penny dreadful of an evening and we all sit round and I read out the latest news from the *Sun* or the *Star*. I'm the only one in my family who reads proper, you see. My old man, God rest his soul, he taught me how when I was no more than seven. I'd sit on his knee and he'd make the sounds of the letters and point to the page. By nine, I was reading to him; by twelve, I was off with the *Pickwick Papers*. I used to have a good giggle at that Mr. Pickwick, I did. Miss Tindall, at the church mission, loaned me her books each week: *Pilgrim's Progress* and *Gulliver's Travels*. I didn't care for them too much. The words were too fancy, but then she gave me a dictionary and taught me how to look up what I didn't understand. Then it was like someone switched on one of them big electric lights in the theater and everything became crystal clear. Soon I found books about girls, *Clarissa* and *Vanity Fair*. Becky Sharp—now, there was a gal who knew her mind. Miss Tindall said that although I oughtn't to praise her behavior, it was good for a woman to have—what was the big word she used?—espir . . . aspiration. Yes, that's it. She told me I've been given a great gift and that I'd "set foot on the path to betterment." She said there's some that's happy to stay in the gutter, but there's a few, like me, who's looking up at the stars. So I started to help out at Sunday school, teaching the youngsters their letters, and, in return, Miss Tindall, well, she's been helping me to be more of a lady. You can always tell a lady, Miss Tindall says, and not just by her clothes. It's the way she walks and holds herself and the way she talks, too. So Miss Tindall started to teach me to talk proper. Or should it be *properly?* There are all sorts of rules about how you ought to speak if you've any hope of being a lady, so I try and follow them. Well, some of the time.

I think I'm doing well. Of course, I slips back to the ol' Cockney when I'm with my own kind; but when I've a mind, I can put on airs and graces as good as Sarah Siddons and the like. The thing is, I ain't—I haven't—seen Miss Tindall these past six weeks. She's not taken Sunday school and no one will tell me where she is. Anyhow, that's why I pronounce my aitches and say "them," instead of " 'em," like Flo, when I remember. She says I'm getting stuck-up, but I'm not. I just want a better life, and someday I might get to be a shopgirl and work in Piccadilly at Fortnum & Mason, or at Harrods, and leave Whitechapel behind. Of course, Miss Tindall says, I should set my sights even higher and aim to study at her old Oxford college, Lady Margaret Hall. Well, you've got to laugh. But she reckons I can make something of myself, and that means a lot to me. It means I can get out of the East End for a start.

Well, I can tell you, it's a scary place to be right now. It gives me the creeps, reading out loud 'bout what *he* done to them poor souls; the last two have been the worst. Some call him the Whitechapel Murderer, or Leather Apron, because he was a nasty piece of work already known round these parts. Everyone thought it was that Jew, John Pizer, but the coppers nabbed him earlier this week and let him go again because he had good alibis. Anyway, I have to read out to Flo and Ma and Mr. Bartleby how *he* slit Polly Nichols so deep that his knife ripped through her stomach. And, Lord help me, how he made off with Annie's womb. Imagine that! And I says this out loud and everyone listening goes "errgh" and "aargh," and then they says "go on" and I'm expected to read it like it was a nursery rhyme or a fairy tale. But it's not. It's real and it gets in my head, it does, like a bad dream, and I can't shake it off.

So that's how these rascals manage to terrify the living daylights out of me. That's why I hate walking all the way to the West End to pretend to sell flowers to ladies and gents outside the theaters when all I really wants to do is stay at home with the door bolted. But tonight's different, because tonight, now I've got rid of my flowers and my basket is empty, we're going to the theater ourselves. I'm just waiting for Flo, you see. Her sweetheart, Danny Dawson, is the doorman at this here Egyptian Hall. He's greasy as an old frying pan. His hair's slicked back with oil and his moustache is waxed sharp at the ends. He's always trying to steal a kiss from Flo—and from me when he's had a few too many—and I don't like him. The Lord knows what Flo sees in him. She could have her pick of any man she flutters her peepers at. She's that pretty. But Flo says she and Danny'll get wed next year, once they've put a bit aside, and then he'll be family. I'm hoping that means she'll give up thieving. Ma'll have one less mouth to feed, at least. Her eyes aren't good with all the sewing she takes in. She needs to rest them or she'll go blind.

Anyway, that's why I'm standing on these theater steps in the West End, under the glare of the streetlamps, surrounded by crowds of people packing the pavements before they go in to watch the show. We're going to see a famous American illusionist. Mr. Hercat is his name, and we're in for an evening of *Mirth! Mystery! Music!*— at least that's what the poster says. There's a nip in the air and I pull my shawl around me. But I'm still shaking, not with the cold, or with excitement, but with fear. Them boys have reminded me that afterward Flo and me have got to walk back through Whitechapel in the dark.

"Come on, Con!" Flo says, grabbing me by the arm. She gives me that much of a fright that I gasp. I forget, too, that I usually tell her not to call me that. I always says to her: "My name is Constance." And she always goes: "La-di-da, fat cigar!" and pulls a face, telling me I've got ideas above my station. She says I'm silly to have my dreams and silly to let Miss Tindall turn my head so. She can upset me sometimes. But tonight I'm just glad to see her. I'm glad when she puts her hand in mine, and I'm even gladder that when we go round the back of the hall to the stage door in the alley with all the rubbish and the rats, that it's Danny waiting for us, his face glistening in the lamplight, and not a man with a knife stepping out of the shadows.

EMILY

The streets of Whitechapel have been much quieter this week, since the murders. Few respectable women venture out after dark and even men seem more cautious, a little too eager to accompany one another in an unspoken show of solidarity, yet not wishing their eagerness for companionship to be misconstrued as weakness. Into the stead of the common throng step the policemen, the men of the Metropolitan and City of London police forces. They do their shambling best, but it is really not good enough, and at the Whitechapel Workhouse Infirmary the business of life—and death—continues as usual.

It is Friday evening and every Friday evening Terence Cutler, an obstetrician and fellow of the Royal College of Surgeons, pays his weekly visit. Tall, in his midthirties and with sandy-colored hair that is thinning slightly, he possesses—on the surface, at least—an air of calm efficiency, which is so often mistaken for arrogance. Normally, he appears a gentleman who is confident of his own professional abilities, although his personal qualities are a little more precarious. His youthful activities with the women he was later to treat have left an unfortunate legacy. On this particular evening, it is evident to me that he is deeply troubled, although not by irksome symptoms of a purely physical nature. The room is cool, verging on cold, but there is sweat on his forehead.

"Just the one tonight, Mrs. Maggs?" he asks as he steps away from the shivering girl lying on the table. Her skirts are rucked up around her waist and her bent legs are spread wide.

The midwife, a solid, woman, with a frizz of gray hair escaping from her dirty cap, is disposing of the contents of a chipped enamel bowl down the sluice.

"Aye, sir," Mrs. Maggs replies in her brusque Scottish manner. She returns to the girl and lowers her limbs onto the table, one after the other, restoring a vestige of dignity to someone who has lost all else. And there, the patient remains motionless, either too drugged or too afraid to make a move. It is not clear which.

The surgeon glances back, rather wistfully, I think, and studies his charge as she lies submissively, like a sacrificial lamb on an altar. She is a waif and her blond hair, made darker by sweat, is plastered around a small head. Her complexion is almost as white as the wall tiles.

"She's but a child," I hear Cutler mutter. His voice is despairing, almost tremulous. I know he is wondering how it ever came to this.

"Aye, sir," replies Mrs. Maggs, cheerful as a housewife at a market stall. "She's a wee one. They seem to get younger every year," she replies, leaning over the girl. She tilts her head in thought, then adds: "It'll take more than a change in the law to stop it." A large flap of loose skin hangs down from her jaw, hiding her neck and reminding me of a turkey. It wobbles as she speaks again. "Another drop o' laudanum'll see her right." She produces a dark glass bottle from her apron pocket, jerks round to make sure the surgeon is occupied, then takes a swift swig from it herself before offering it to the girl.

Cutler, his back turned on such misdeeds, shakes his head and glances at his hands. The lines on his palms are red with blood, as if someone has taken a pen and drawn them in ink. The rims around his nails are red, too. He reaches for a brush and begins to scrub them, taking even more than his usual care. It is as if he is trying to slough off something particularly vile. The trouble is, he knows he has become as corrupted as the diseased flesh he so often treats. He had started off with such high ideals. He would rid the world of the scourge of syphilis. But the French malady, despite its Gaelic soubriquet, is not fashionable, at least not among the moneyed classes who could further his career.

Meanwhile, the old midwife pats the girl's clenched hand as it settles on her chest. "Och! But you'll live, won't ya, dearie?" She switches back to the surgeon with a smile. "And you'll be able to get on your way sooner tonight, sir."

"What?" replies Cutler, deep in thought.

"You're finished for tonight."

"Yes, indeed." His reply is halfhearted. He does not bother to turn round to address her. Why he would want to go back home sooner defeats him at the moment. There is nothing and no one for whom he needs to return. A well-connected wife had been necessary at the time, so his research into venereal disease, while not stopping, needed to be conducted in secret. Upon his marriage, his papers and the lurid photographs of infected patients, so vital to his research, suddenly became incriminating to the lay eye. He was forced to keep them under lock and key, as if they were pornographic—a guilty and perverted secret.

The midwife's gray brows dip in reflection as she turns away from the table to busy herself. "No one wants to hang around Whitechapel at the moment."

"No, indeed," Cutler agrees. He nods at Mrs. Maggs over his shoulder, then turns back to finish washing his hands with carbolic soap. As he does so, I see his large moustache twitch as if his features have relaxed a little. He seems relieved that he will not be called upon again this evening.

The midwife takes another surreptitious swig of laudanum as if to give herself courage. "These terrible murders are making all of us fret," she continues. Her tone remains cheerful and I suppose the laudanum is having an effect on her mood.

"I am sure," Cutler replies without conviction. He is clearly humoring the woman out of his innate politeness. Shaking his hands over the basin, he turns to take the towel left out for him on a nearby rail. The chipped enamel dish has been deposited nearby. I see his eyes collide with it accidentally, then deliberately veer away, his face registering an expression of mild disgust. Next he divests himself of his spattered apron as if it is riddled with plague. Throwing it into the nearby laundry basket, he strides toward the frock coat that is hanging from a peg on the back of the door. He waits a second to allow the midwife to do him the service of passing it to him.

Mrs. Maggs continues unabashed: "Och! The women are all beside themselves with fright." This time her tone is more measured, as if even the laudanum could not expunge the threat that hung over the district.

"We must all be vigilant," replies Cutler as the midwife suddenly realizes what is expected of her and helps him ease on his coat.

We are in a long, narrow room. The light from the gas lamps bounces off the white tiles on the walls. A large, low cabinet with a marble top sits to one side. On it, various implements lie—a curette spoon and leather tubing—while a row of bottles is lined up neatly on a shelf above. The acrid smell—a sharp tang that might usually sting the nostrils and claw at the back of one's throat—was quite over-whelming at first. Now, however, it seems to have dissipated.

"Thank you, sir," says the midwife, handing Cutler his case. Her cheerful tone suddenly reemerges and her jowls wobble.

The surgeon is just about to gather his things when the girl on the table draws up her legs, pulling them toward her, and lets out a little moan. Cutler pauses at the sound. Turning around, he casts a concerned look at his young patient. "She will need plenty of rest," he tells the midwife.

The woman nods smugly. "Her guardian is sending a carriage for her later," she replies, folding her arms across her stained apron. "He'll be sure to see to her care."

I can tell Cutler has to force down his feelings on the matter. I see him bite his tongue. He manages an ironic smile. "I am sure he will," he mutters as he reaches for his medical bag on the marble-topped cabinet. As he does so, the sleeve of his coat rides up to expose the blood on his shirt cuff. He pauses for a moment, as if to study it.

"I almost forgot," chimes in the midwife. It is clear that she did not, but she intends to appear nonchalant. She reaches into her apron pocket and waves an envelope under the surgeon's nose. The handwriting appears educated. *Mr. Cutler, for services rendered*, it reads. "From her guardian," she tells him. Her eyes flick to the table and back.

Cutler relieves her of the envelope. "Of course," he replies, taking out a coin from his own pocket and handing it to the eager midwife. "Thank you, Mrs. Maggs," he says, opening his case and dropping the envelope into it, as if it were a fetid rag. As he picks up his hat, he glances at the girl one final time, and his shoulders heave from an audible sigh.

"Do we know her name?" he asks, not really expecting a reply.

The midwife snorts. "Best not to, sir," she tells him, covering the shivering child with a coarse blanket. He accepts the wisdom of the drink-addled old crone. But from the table, the girl stirs.

"Molly," she croaks through chattering teeth. "My name is Molly."

The surgeon pauses. It is clear he hadn't expected the child to speak for herself. He walks forward a couple of paces and leans toward her. Her eyes flicker as she regards him through a blur of tears. Cutler's mouth opens, but then words fail him. He had intended to offer her some morsels of comfort, but he can find none. It's as if his breath has suddenly deserted him. He simply pats her cold arm and turns away.

I follow him out into the corridor. It is dark by comparison. Only a single lamp burns. The smell is different, too. The walls of the Whitechapel Workhouse Infirmary are damp with mildew and the plaster is crumbling. The surgeon knows where to go. He turns right toward the main entrance, past the woman's ward, where the constant coughing seems to drown out all other noise. Just as he comes to within a few yards of the door, however, he hears a familiar voice.

"Cutler!" It is James Holt, the infirmary's medical director. He appears at the doorway of his office. His dark hair is disheveled and his eyes are bloodshot. Here is a man who has fallen from grace. An unfortunate mis-judgment with a scalpel as he performed surgery on a society heiress has led him to his present position. He's found comfort in the bottle, but very little elsewhere. It seems to Cutler, and to me, that he has just woken from a deep sleep.

"Good evening, Dr. Holt."

The director clears his throat and beckons Cutler into his office, glancing furtively down the corridor to ensure they are not seen. He shuts the door behind them.

"Have the police spoken to you yet?" he asks anxiously.

Cutler can smell whisky on his breath and his eyes stray to the half-empty bottle on his desk. *He doesn't even try and hide it anymore,* he thinks. He shakes his head. "They've been here?"

Holt nods. "Oh yes," he replies emphatically, slumping back onto the edge of his desk. "They've been here, all right, questioning some of the women and all the staff."

I see Cutler's jaw start to work a little. "Did they ask . . . ?"

"Yes, of course."

"And . . . ?"

"And, naturally, I told them you treated women's diseases. No more."

Cutler's expression relaxes. "I am grateful to you."

"I'm sure I'll have cause to call in the favor ere too long," replies Holt, raising one of his brows.

There is an awkward silence as both men consider their own predicaments. For a moment, the labored coughs from the women's ward are all that can be heard.

"Polly Nichols . . . ," Cutler blurts suddenly, as if a thought had just hit him.

Holt raises his hand. "There is no record. I made sure of that."

Cutler nods and lets a pent-up breath escape through his mouth.

"Drink?" Holt holds up the bottle of whisky.

"No," replies Cutler sharply, then adds as an afterthought: "Thank you."

"Ah," says Holt with a smile. "The lovely Mrs. Cutler. Do give her my regards, won't you, old chap?"

"I will," answers the surgeon with a nod. What he neglected to say was that he has neither seen nor heard from his wife, Geraldine, in over a month. He opens the office door and walks the few paces down the corridor toward the main entrance, where an elderly porter presides at a desk.

"Good night, Mr. Cutler," chirps the man with a nod of his bald head.

Cutler acknowledges him, but almost reluctantly, it seems. Can he trust him to stay silent? The trouble is, he is known to too many people in these parts, he tells himself. Plumping his top hat on his head, he is just about to cross the threshold out onto the street when his progress is halted by the sudden approach of two women. One, quite young in appearance, is leaning on another, obviously in considerable distress. Blood is flowing freely from her mouth and she is clutching her jaw.

"A doctor, please! Help 'ere!" squawks the older woman as soon as she sets foot in the infirmary. She flaps her free arm frantically. Cutler notes her sleeve is covered in blood.

The porter answers her call immediately. "Let's be 'aving you," he says, ringing a bell behind his desk to summon help. He is clearly used to receiving such visitors and there is little urgency in his actions. But as soon as the young woman lifts her bruised and bloodied face, he shakes his head disapprovingly.

"Well, well. If it ain't Mary Jane Kelly . . . again." The resignation in his voice is verging on disdain.

At the mention of the woman's name, Cutler, who has been standing motionless watching the drama play out in front of him, seems to hone in on her. Just as the porter is directing her toward the wards, she, too, looks up and sees the surgeon's gaze clamped on her face. There is a flicker of recognition in her eyes. For a brief second, I think she might say something. Her swollen lips part, but her companion tugs at her arm.

"Come on, my girl," she urges. "You're making a mess on the floor." She points to the blood dripping on the tiles.

It is a good moment for Cutler to leave. He sidesteps the women and makes a dash for the street. Outside, it is a crisp evening and his own breath suddenly wreathes him in great whorls. He surveys the thoroughfare. There is still traffic—several carriages and four or five carts, but few pedestrians. And those who venture out on foot seem to be walking faster than usual. He has no wish to join them. He will hail a hansom cab and in less than an hour he will be a world away from this violence and squalor, back in his comfortable home in Harley Street. But few cabs will answer his whistle in Charles Street. He knows it will behoove him to walk a few hundred yards toward Whitechapel Road. Stopping under a gas lamp, he flips open his pocket watch and strains his eyes to look at the face. A quarter past nine. He pulls up his coat collar against the creeping cold and sets off, just like everyone else it seems, at a fast pace.

I, on the other hand, remain a moment longer. I linger where others would not. You see, Terence Cutler has failed to notice what I have remarked. In his haste to leave the infirmary, he has not spotted a carriage parked directly opposite the entrance. Or, if he has noticed it, he has not given its presence a second thought. I, however, have and am just about to peer inside when I hear two loud taps on the roof. In a trice, the driver tugs at the reins and moves off. Whoever is in the carriage was keen not to be discovered.

CONSTANCE

So Danny leads us in through this tatty-looking door and into a dark passage inside. It's so narrow that when we meet a stagehand coming the other way, we three have to press hard up against the wall to let him pass. I suddenly feel Danny's hand clamp my thigh. He's like that, but then I catch a whiff of the lad as he jostles past. I wrinkle my nose and he lets his hand drop when he cops a load of it, too. But there's another smell in the air. Flo clocks it as well. She sniffs.

"What's that pong?" she asks as we squeeze along the passage backstage.

It's like there's been a fire, just how our grate smells in the morning when we've had enough cash to buy coal, that is.

"Ashes," mutters Danny. He's speaking in a low voice and puts his finger to his greasy lips to tell us we should do the same. "It's part of M . Hercat's act." He makes his eyes look bigger and goes all leery. *The Mystery of She,"* he whispers hoarsely, raising his arms like a ghost. Flo lets out a giggle.

The musicians in the orchestra pit are starting to tune up. The violins sound like strangled cats. There's a hum, too, as the audience begins to spill into the theater. Up ahead, we can make out the stage. The curtain's down and Danny says we can stand just at the side, in the wings, but that we're not to make a sound. If we do, he'll be out on his ear. If anyone asks, we're to grab a broom and look busy. So, as the noise grows louder from the stalls, we stay quiet and wait. We're excited, so it's difficult to keep still. Flo's a fidget at the best of times and she strays once or twice to look round, but I pull her back again. It's then we see a funny little bald man with a big moustache, in a tailcoat, just in front of us. Looks like a penguin, he does, or maybe a walrus. He's standing on the side of the stage, pulling at his cuffs. Flo nudges me and lets rip one of her cackles and my hand flies up to cover her big mouth. She's got away with it this time, but a second later the lights dip. The noise from the audience dies down and the air is electric. It feels like something fantastic is going to happen. And it does. The orchestra strikes up and the big red curtain rises. And the little man strides out into the center of the stage and the spotlight shines on him, making him look bigger. I think he's grown at least six inches.

"Ladies and gentle*mane*," he says. Not "men," but "mane." When I sees Miss Tindall again—if I ever do—I'll ask her if that's how I should say it. Anyway, he welcomes everyone and says that this amazing Mr. Hercat will be performing his new and startling illusion tonight, when the ashes of Ayesha will be burned in the presence of the audience, and "She" will rise from the flames.

40

Ayesha, we are told, will be played by Miss Fay Rivington. So he gets us all excited, winding us up like clocks, and then he says: "But first for your delectation . . ." My heart sinks. There's a warm-up act. We've all been secretly wishing the trick will go wrong and Miss Rivington, or whoever she is, to get singed, at the very least, and we're that pumped up that we don't want no one else to get in the way. "Boo!" shouts a few of the audience. But no.

"Ladies and gentle*mane,* I give you Mesmer the Magnificent!"

For a moment, I feel let down, like a burst balloon, but most of the punters don't seem to mind too much. There's loud applause as this Mesmer bloke sweeps onto the stage like a great colored bird in a long, flowing robe of yellow-and-blue silk. He flaps his arms like they're wings. The orchestra plays a tune that's a bit creepy and you can tell nobody knows what to expect. When everything settles down, the magician, or whatever he is, asks for volunteers to come on stage.

"Greetings!" he says loudly. He sounds foreign. "Greetings to you all. I am Mesmer ze Magnificent, and tonight, ladies and gentlemen, I will show you how I can control ze human mind wiz my voice." That raises a few eyebrows, I can tell you. But there's more: "Who, among you, will help me in my challenge?" He drops

41

his gaze and the people sitting in the front row hotch in their seats under his glare. "I would seek volunteers from among you," he says. He makes another great sweep with his arm. There's a murmuring in the audience, and, lo and behold, if Flo doesn't dart forward, waving her hands in the air, but I manage to grab her sleeve and pull her back again.

"What do ya think you're playing at?" I croak. She just doesn't think sometimes. She fends me off with a cross shrug.

Anyhow, we watch from the wings as two gents and two ladies go up on stage. Everyone is applauding them. The men, one lanky, the other with a mop of yellow hair, are laughing. Their faces are red and they look as though they've had a few. The women are more nervous and hold on to each other as if they're off to the chopping block at the Tower. By the looks of them, they're sisters.

"Ladies, please." Mr. Mesmer lines them up in a row, pointing like a sergeant major. Raising his arms, he calls for quiet. The orchestra goes silent and you could hear a pin drop, except for an old man who coughs.

"Face the audience, if you please," he tells them on stage. "Ze hands up, like zis." He raises his own and clasps them on top of his head, interlocking his fingers. The volunteers do as they're bid. Flo looks at me and titters; then she puts her hands on her head. I roll my eyes at her. But then she nudges me and says: "Go on." And I think, *Why not?* and do the same. All the time, Mr. Mesmer's doing his patter, like he's down the market at Spitalfields. But he's good and I'm hooked. And he tells the ones on stage to look up at their hands, and after a moment, a woman, the younger one, starts to blink and he's onto her, like a fly on horse muck.

"Your eyelids are heavy. You feel sleepy," he tells her in his scary voice.

You can see the others' eyes are closing, too. They're still standing, but I see a yellow head bobbing. Then I start feeling sleepy, too. My arms are heavy, like Mr. Mesmer says they are. But I still hear his voice. It's like it's in my ear. "Go to sleep," he's saying. "Go to sleep." And I want to. I really do. Then he tells them on stage to push their hands together as hard as they can, then pull them apart. Flo's hands come down straightaway, but when I try to unlock mine, they stay put. I shoot a look back to the stage. Both men and one of the women have taken their hands down, but one hasn't. Like me, she just can't pull her fingers apart. It's as if some invisible force is holding them where they are.

"Give them a big hand, if you please!" says Mr. Mesmer, and the audience applauds the other volunteers as they're ushered off stage, wreathed in smiles. But the woman, still with her hands clasped, is left there. Like me! Flo, meantime, grabs hold of my fingers and tries to pull them apart. "Hold still!" she tells me, but I jerk away from her.

Truth is, I don't remember any of it after that. I have to leave it to Flo to tell me what happened next as we start our journey back home. It's even colder now as we walk sharpish toward Leicester Square. Danny has stayed behind to clear up, so we're on our own. For now, there's plenty of people about.

"I know I felt hot and thirsty," I say as I try to remember anything about the evening.

Flo stops dead, her eyes big as owl's. "Well, I'll be! Mr. Mesmer told the lady she was in the desert; said to her that she was wandering about all forlorn."

"No!"

"She were that hot she tried to undo her blouse buttons!"

I can't believe my ears. "Then what happened?"

Flo starts walking again. "He circles her, and then from behind he asks her to stand with her feet close together and cross her arms over her chest like she's wearing one of them strait-jackets."

"Like what lunatics wear?" Now I'm the one who's stopped dead.

"Yes, that's it. And that's what you did. You

unclasped your hands, and put them across your front." She puts her arms around herself. "Like so."

As we walk down the Strand, I'm deep in thought, trying to recall the last thing I heard Mr. Mesmer say to the lady on stage. "When I count to three, you will wake up," I blurt out.

"That's it," she cries. "Shaking you, I was, for a good minute or so. Frightened the living daylights out of me, you did," she tells me. She lifts her hem as we jump over a large puddle. "You woke up when the bloke counted to three."

It's coming back to me now. I remember that strange feeling, like someone's been inside my house and rummaged around in my upstairs rooms. They've ruffled through my drawers, but they haven't stolen anything. Nothing's been taken, just rearranged a little. I feel different, but not disturbed. But I don't tell Flo that I've changed. I just smile.

"I'm fine now," I say with a nod, and I slip my arm in hers.

It's true. We've made it to Fleet Street and I'm no longer tired. I'm wide-awake, but still I'm nervous. We're leaving the safer West End, where there's gas lamps aplenty and wider pavements, heading for the shadow lands of the east. The landscape is changing. The buildings are closer together: lower and slanted, like drunken men leaning on each other. The sounds are earthier, louder. Voices boom; babies bawl; engines rumble; machines thud. Women's laughter doesn't tinkle like it does in Kensington and Chelsea. Instead, it scratches on the filthy air. The light is yellower, the shadows deeper. The street stink, always there, grows stronger.

We know we'll get propositioned; two girls like us, it's only normal. Three sailors standing outside a pub call out to us. Flo gives them a cheery " 'ello!" but I pull her away.

"Don't you know there's a killer out here!" I say. I bite my lip as soon as I say it. She only laughs at me, then pulls a serious face.

"Oh, Con! The world's not going to end!" she teases me. She bursts into laughter again and starts to sing. She's always one for a tune and strikes up with "Champagne Charlie." Well, as you can imagine, I try and hush her up. I tell her people'll think she's had a few too many; so, instead, she just hums.

There's another couple of smart alecs a bit farther on when we reach the Minories. "Evening, ladies," one says, doffing his billycock. He's swaying a bit and I catch the stink of beer on his breath.

His mate's the worse for wear, too. "Want to show us the sights, gals?" He belches loudly.

We pretend not to notice them and skirt around them, but they start to follow, calling after us.

"Playing 'ard to get, eh?"

When it's clear we're not available, they change their tune.

"Sluts!" the belcher calls after us.

We walk on, when suddenly something comes hurtling through the air, narrowly missing my right shoulder. In an instant, a beer bottle shatters on the cobbles nearby. We stop in our tracks and look back.

"Why, you little shit!" screams Flo, trying to break free from my grip. But I hold on to her.

"Don't be stupid," I hiss. "It's just what they want!"

She stops struggling, but growls at them, baring her teeth.

"Whores!" cries the one with the billycock. "I wouldn't give you one if you paid me!"

We're glad to see a copper up ahead of us as we turn down City Road. He's plodding along, twirling his truncheon. We follow in his footsteps for a while until we cross Whitechapel High Street and go down Middlesex Street. An old drunk moans in the gutter and a rat scuttles across our path. It smells different here.

"Not far now," whimpers Flo. She's changed her tune. I feel her squeezing my arm.

I know what she's thinking. I'm thinking it, too. Both murders were just a few hundred yards away from where we are now and *he* could be lurking nearby. Our eyes are darting like fish to the right and left, following any sound, any movement. A dog barks nearby and we jump. The bell at St. Luke's strikes midnight and we hurry our pace. It's then that we see two men cross the road up ahead of us. We stop. My heart is pounding in my ears. They both carry something long and thin in their hands. I'm thinking we ought to wait till they've gone. Flo looks at me and puts the brakes on, tugging at my arm, when one of the men calls out. "All well, ladies?" they ask, walking toward us.

Flo breathes again. "The Vigilance Committee," she says to me under her breath. And I remember the patrols they've just started in the area.

"All well, gents!" she replies. She can be too cheeky. "We're going home."

As they come nearer, I see it's Gilbert Johns. Big and stocky, he used to work as a slaughter man before the abattoir burned down last month. The other bloke—younger, with a loping gait like he's walking through mud—I don't know. Gilbert smiles and calls me by my name.

"Miss Constance," he says, touching his cap. He's looking at us like we're naughty school-girls. "You shouldn't be out at this hour. Let's walk you back, then." And he does.

Flo gets all skittish again. "Oh, Gilbert. You're a proper gent. And Mick, isn't it?" She leans across and touches the younger one on the arm. I see his eyes widen at the attention. She's a flirt, all right, is our Flo, but I just want to get to bed safe.

The lads stay with us just long enough to see us to our door a couple of streets away in White's Row. It's a two up, two down, and we're the lucky ones. Most gaffs our way are four or five to a room. Flo puts the key in the lock.

"Good night," says Gilbert Johns as we step over the threshold.

Mick raises his cap. "Take care now, ladies." By the sound of it, he's Irish.

"Thank you," says Flo.

"Good night," says I.

We shut the door behind us. Flo turns the key again, the bolt clicks in and we can breathe once more. We're safe for another night, at least.

CHAPTER 3

Monday, September 17, 1888

EMILY

Terence Cutler breakfasts alone as he has done every morning for the past few weeks. He takes tea, toast and thick-cut orange marmalade while seated at a large oval table in the first-floor morning room directly above his consulting room and directly under the gaze of his wife. A large, gilt-framed oil painting of Geraldine hangs over the mantelpiece. Cutler contemplates it. Her hair is dark and swept back into a low chignon, with the front curled and frizzled over her forehead. Her skin is quite pale, but the artist has taken rather flattering liberties, giving her high cheekbones, which are, in reality, only to be found behind plump flesh. Nevertheless, the artist has managed to capture that rather haughty expression of hers. *It's as if she feels she has married beneath her class,* he thinks. As if to emphasize the point, she is depicted in the grounds of the family mansion, where she lived before her marriage. Her father, Sir Roger Beaufroy, was an eminent surgeon, who regularly attended members of the royal family. He'd wanted sons; so when his wife presented him with their first daughter, the child was named Geraldine. When, much to his disappointment, another one came along three years later, she was christened Pauline.

Cutler has just finished eating his eggs and bacon while going over his correspondence, or more aptly bills. Such an exercise does not aid his digestion. There are invoices from milliners and drapers, from perfumeries and haberdashers. Bills and more bills. It seems that they are all his errant wife has left him. It is her way of repaying him. He knows that. On their wedding night, he had bestowed upon her a "gift," which has not only caused her endless suffering, but it seems to have rendered her infertile as well.

Dora, the maidservant, enters with more toast. She lays the rack on the tablecloth just in front of her master, steps back, then remains, nervously playing with her apron.

After a moment, Cutler, aware of her presence, looks up.

"Is something wrong, Dora?" he asks. He has never really warmed to the girl. She is scrawny and awkward and suffers from the most rampant acne. His wife engaged her as soon as they were married, six years ago. Since then, she has not progressed much. Her only virtue, as far as he can see, is that she remains fiercely loyal to her mistress.

"I've just 'eard there's been another attack, sir!" she exclaims. "A man pulled a knife on a girl, just 'cos she looked at him." Whether consciously or not, her eyes are fixed on the butter knife in her master's hand.

Cutler sets down the implement, takes up his napkin and slowly and deliberately wipes the corners of his mouth, one after the other.

"That is startling news, indeed," he replies without emotion. "But why should it concern me?"

The maid's pimply cheeks color quickly. "It's just . . . well . . ."

"Yes." He glowers at her.

"Well, it's just that . . ." She is looking at the neatly aligned slices of golden toast as she flounders for her words.

"Yes?" He is losing his patience, with both her and her acne. She really should have grown out of it by now. He knows exactly what irks her, of course, but he allows her to flap, sinking ever deeper into the quicksand of her own anxiety.

"It's just that the mistress has been gone such a while, and there's been no word." She lifts her head toward the portrait over the mantelpiece, then juts out her chin as if she's proud of herself for finally saying what she feels.

Cutler works his jaw again, as he always does when he feels it necessary to stifle his irritation. "Your mistress is staying with her family in Sussex, Dora."

"Oh" is all she can manage. He has taken the wind out of her sails, or so he thinks, until she retorts, "But she's not written, sir." Her observation sounds more like a protest and she realizes too late.

"So you are scrutinizing my post now!" Cutler's tone turns sterner.

Dora takes a step back. "No, sir. . . . I . . ."

He picks up the top letter from the pile of correspondence at his side. "Do you know the author of this letter?" he asks angrily, pointing at the writing on the envelope. He picks up another and holds it aloft. "And this one?"

The maid is on the verge of tears. "No, sir. I'm sorry, sir."

Cutler flings the letter back down onto the tray. "I think you'd better get back to your duties now, don't you?" he tells her through clenched teeth. "If, that is, you wish to be here when Mrs. Cutler returns."

There's a faint bleat of submission as Dora curtsies, then hurries from the room. Cutler waits until the door clicks shut, then slumps back in his chair. He glances up at the portrait and I see him hiss out a curse under his breath. "Damn you, Geraldine. Damn you to hell."

Geraldine, you understand, has put him in this predicament, even though he acknowledges she is only partially to blame. Their legion problems were already close to the surface when an unexpected visitor came into their lives. One morning at breakfast, Geraldine waved a letter about and presented him with a fait accompli. An old neighbor and friend from Petworth was in trouble. She and Pauline, he was informed, had practically grown up together, even shared a tutor. This woman arrived on the doorstep the following day while he was out. Apparently, she was in such dire straits that Geraldine had no hesitation in giving her the best bedroom, which happened to be hers. Naturally, his wife had called upon him to offer his medical opinion on their stricken visitor when he returned home later that day. He agreed and that was what set the disastrous train in motion. He'd hoped that his expression had not betrayed him; that Geraldine had not seen the glimmer of recognition in his eyes. This guest, this hapless woman, was, you see, a frequenter of the infirmary. He was safe as long as she was feverish. If she recognized him, he could put it down to delirium. But as soon as she started to feel restored, he wanted her out of his house before irreparable damage was done, before she could reveal his secret to Geraldine.

The surgeon balls his fist at the thought of it and brings it down on the table, setting the remaining cutlery and crockery clattering. *If only the smarmy little vixen had kept her mouth shut,* he thinks. *If only Geraldine had not been able to put two and two together and make a perfectly rounded four, then she would still be here, now.* With that infuriating thought, he rises. He will be late for work at St. Bartholomew's Hospital, or Barts as it is commonly known.

CHAPTER 4

Tuesday, September 18, 1888

CONSTANCE

"They've got 'im!" Flo shakes me awake. Her voice is urgent, almost gleeful. She pulls the blanket off my shoulder. I tug it back.

"What? Who?" Then I remember and sit up in bed. "Not . . . ?"

She's almost breathless as she rushes to tell me the news.

"He's been arrested. Threatened a girl with a knife, 'e did, on the High Street. Same one as scared the living daylights out of poor Lizzie Burns."

"And they've locked him up?"

"Yes!" She takes both my hands and pulls me toward her in an embrace.

Ma comes in all breezy. "We can all sleep easier tonight," she says. She perches herself at the foot of the big bed that I share with Flo and pats my feet through the blanket. She has a lovely, round face and must have been very pretty when she was younger. Of course, to me, she'll always be pretty, but other people might say she's looking a bit faded. There are lines round her mouth and she's lost a few teeth. Her hair is flecked with gray and she walks with a slight stoop, like she's battling against a strong wind. The arthritis has got to her hands, too, so she can't crochet no more to earn a crust. She still manages to make a few silk flowers each week. They come in handy, specially this time of year. But we love her no matter what, and so does Mr. Bartleby. I'm sure someday soon he'll put one of his fancy rings on her finger.

I lie back on my pillow and see the bedbugs have made a meal of my arms in the night. I take a deep breath and it's then that Ma asks me if I'm feeling all right. "Been a bit peaky these last few days, you 'ave," she says to me.

"Oh?" I reply, scratching my arms. I pretend I don't know what she's talking about.

"You're not ill, Connie dear?" Ma's the only person I allow to call me Connie. "Everything all right downstairs?" She points to my privates through the blanket.

I feel myself flush and sit up again, thinking I must make more of an effort. "Yes," I say quickly, almost too quickly perhaps. The trouble is, I'm not myself. Ever since we went to see Mr. Mesmer, I've felt a little bit queer, as if I'm not really here. There's a distance between me and the things around me. It's like I'm floating above it all, in a dream. "I'm fine," I tell her, and I force a smile. It seems to satisfy her and she grabs hold of the bedpost and hauls herself up off the mattress.

"Good." She nods. "Then I'll let you get dressed."

It's another ten minutes before I manage to rouse myself.

CHAPTER 5

Wednesday, September 19, 1888

EMILY

Happenings are afoot in Harley Street. It's late afternoon and a carriage is drawing up outside the Cutler residence. Presently its passenger alights. Dora answers the bell. The door opens wide and the cold blasts the girl's unsightly face. Despite the chill she smiles.

"Miss Pauline," she says, dipping a curtsy.

"Good day, Dora," comes the reply. Dark curls peep out from under the woman's hat, which is trimmed with a rose. Her cheekbones are high and the texture of her skin marks her out as quite young; yet her manner is self-assured. She is swathed in a warm wool coat of muted plum, which is not as brazen as crimson; but in a dull and drab autumnal London, audacious nonetheless.

"I wondered if your mistress was in?" she asks.

The question wipes away Dora's smile as surely as if a damp cloth has just been taken to her face. "I . . . I . . . ," she stutters. "I shall inquire, miss. Please." The maid ushers in the unexpected visitor, and leaves her to wait in the hall as she knocks on her master's study door.

"Yes," comes Cutler's voice from within.

"Miss Beaufroy is here to see you, sir," Dora tells him, skittering through the door. Her spotty face is screwed up in an anxious grimace.

The surgeon, who has been writing at his desk, puts down his pen. "Is she, indeed?" He frowns. "Very well," he replies. "Show her into the drawing room and bring us some tea."

Dora drops an agitated curtsy, but becomes even more anxious when she turns to see that the visitor is already standing behind her on the threshold of the study.

"Terence," Pauline greets her brother-in-law breezily. She has told herself to keep calm, that her arduous journey from Sussex was entirely unnecessary, and that all will be easily resolved. There will be, she has been assuring herself all the way from Petworth, a simple explanation for the fact that she has not heard from her only sister for several weeks.

Cutler leaps up from his chair as soon as he sees her. "Pauline." He manages a smile, although her arrival has clearly taken him off guard. *She shares a striking resemblance with her sibling,* he thinks, *only she is much prettier.* It is as if each of Geraldine's features has been fashioned with so much more skill and attention to detail by the Almighty before being placed on her sister's face. "To what do I owe this unexpected pleasure?"

His visitor smiles sweetly. "I was in town, running some errands," she lies. "And I was rather hoping to see Geraldine," she tells him with a disarming smile. She begins to pull her cream kid gloves from her fingers to signify she is staying.

Glancing over Pauline's shoulder, Cutler registers Dora's startled expression and thinks it wise to be rid of her.

"Tea, Dora!" he barks. And, as the confused girl scampers off, he continues his charm offensive. "Perhaps we would be more comfortable in the drawing room," he suggests, motioning toward the door. But Pauline will not be put off.

"So my sister is not here?" Suddenly there is a little sharpness in her voice.

Cutler's eyes scoot away from hers. When he had told the servants that his wife was staying with her family in the country, he had not bargained on a visit from her inquisitive sister. "I fear not." Just as a sailor trims his sails to suit the prevailing wind, he had adjusted his lie to cater to the circumstances. "She is staying with friends out of town."

Pauline's brows rise in unison. *"Friends?"* she repeats. "Do I know them?"

The surgeon is irritated. As if she has the right to know all their friends! He shakes his head. "No. No, I think not." He realizes he must do more if he is to convince her. "The husband is an old colleague of mine." Then to furnish a little extra detail, he adds: "They live up north."

"Up north?" echoes Pauline, with her gaze skimming the room. There is a cobweb in the corner by the window—a sure sign that her sister has been absent for a while. "It's strange she didn't tell me," she says nonchalantly. "But then, as I said, I haven't heard from her in quite a while."

Cutler nods. "She's been very busy."

Pauline fixes him with an unsettling glare. "Busy?"

"Yes. Good works and all that."

She lifts her dainty chin, but there is a barb underneath it. "I always say that charity begins at home, Terence. I'm sure you'll agree it is a sad day when a woman neglects her duties to her frail mother and her devoted sister and does not write for almost five weeks."

Cutler is slightly surprised by his wife's omission; he's slightly surprised by her behavior overall, in fact. He'd genuinely thought that she'd taken herself back to Sussex. Of course, this was not the first time she had walked out on him in high dudgeon. There had been that unpleasantness last year, when it all got a bit fraught. She had taken a leave of absence overnight and then reemerged the following day as if nothing had happened. He had not pressed her about it at the time. He was just grateful that she had returned safely. He shakes his head. If she wasn't with her family, he secretly agrees that it's odd his wife has no, at the very least, contacted them. "Geraldine would never slight you or your mother intentionally, Pauline," he tries to assure her.

I could tell by her expression that she stifled the urge to say out loud: "But you would, Terence."

The truth is, Terence and his sister-in-law have never seen eye to eye. He well remembers that wet June day in 1882, his wedding day. The carriage in which Pauline and her mother were traveling to the church had become stuck in the mud. They had been an hour late, necessitating the postponement of the ceremony to accommodate them. As it turned out, the unfortunate event had been an ill omen.

Clearly growing exasperated with her brother-in-law, Pauline finds it increasingly hard to hide her frustration. "When do you expect her back?"

Cutler shrugs. "She only left a couple of days ago," he lies. "She plans to stay at least two weeks, I believe." He tugs at the sleeve of his cuff as he speaks.

"Then I shall return toward the end of the month," Pauline tells him firmly. She nods, as if to underline her determination, then turns and heads out into the hallway. Just as she does so, Dora appears with the tray of tea.

"Sadly, Miss Beaufroy will not be staying," Cutler tells her. His frown conveys to her that he means business. "Show her out, if you please."

The puzzled maid deposits the tray on the hall console table and makes for the front door. Pauline pulls on her gloves once more as Dora opens the door wide. Cutler follows her into the hall.

"I shall be back," she tells her brother-in-law. Even though she is smiling as she speaks, there is a hint of a threat in her voice.

"I look forward to it," he rejoins, forcing a cheery tone, and he bows as she brushes past him.

Cutler watches as his visitor disappears out onto the hubbub of the street and Dora shuts the door after her. It is only then that he notices the maid's face, even puffier and redder than usual. She has been holding back scalding tears, which suddenly burst forth and cascade down her spotty cheeks. Without waiting to be dismissed, she rushes off below stairs.

CONSTANCE

As it's a Wednesday, we're expecting Mr. Bartleby. He always comes to supper on a Wednesday. And he always brings cake. He's good that way. We've never gone hungry since he and Ma began courting. She pays the rent and he manages to slip her a few bob each week for our food. Tonight it's a Sally Lunn. So after me and Flo have cleared away the dumplings and gravy, we get stuck in.

"You do the honors, Mrs. P," Mr. Bartleby'll say, and Ma gives a girly shrug and cuts up the cake. She always doles him out an extra-big portion and he rubs his belly when she sets it in front of him and declares: "I shouldn't, but I shall."

Flo swears that one day she'll tell him he can't. She'll take away his plate to see how he'll react to that. She doesn't rate him much. She says he niggles her—the way he hums to himself or strokes his whiskers. But I don't mind him and he seems to keep Ma happy enough.

Mr. Bartleby's shop is in Limehouse, near the docks, along with a lot of other rag and iron shops. And like most shopkeepers in that vicinity, Mr. Bartleby is a fence. When the place is home to so many water rats that steal from the ships, it makes sense, don't it? I mean, *doesn't* it?

We first met him two years ago, when Flo lifted a particularly fine gold timepiece outside the Bank of England, no less. Ma wasn't happy to take it to old Jan Kimski round the corner, like we usually do, so we headed off toward the docks and Mr. Bartleby's was the first shop we came to. He looked at the watch with one of them funny eyeglasses and said how fine it was, but it was clear from the start that he really only had eyes for Ma. And that was it. He took a shine to her, and she to him; and from then on, we saw them billing and cooing in the front room at least once a week. Like a pair of turtledoves, they were. They still are; only nowadays, I've seen them have a few cross words, too, like when Mr. Bartleby brought mud in off the street, or didn't notice when Ma wore her new bonnet for the first time.

So we're eating cake, and, as usual, talk turns to the murders.

"Mrs. Puddiphatt says she saw a man looking all shifty, with blood on 'im in the Prince Albert," divulges Flo.

"That woman would dob her own son in if she thought she'd get a reward," Ma declares with a shake of her head.

"He's a German," says Mr. Bartleby through a mouthful of dried fruit.

"Mrs. Puddiphatt's son?" queries Flo. We all ignore her.

"I 'eard he's a hairdresser," chimes in Ma.

"You can be both," says I, and everyone looks at me like I've gone cuckoo. "He's a German hairdresser," I tell them.

Mr. Bartleby shakes his head and strokes his whiskers thoughtfully. "Never trust a German, that's what I say. Or a Jew."

"He's that, too," Ma informs him.

"There's a surprise," says Mr. Bartleby sarcastically. He licks his forefinger and presses hard on a wayward currant on his plate. "Come to think of it, never trust foreigners, eh, Mrs. P?" He sticks out his tongue and flicks it at the currant, which disappears instantly from his finger.

Ma smiles and starts cutting him another slice of cake.

Once Flo's polished off her helping, she spies the folded copy of the *Sun* that Mr. Bartleby has brought with him. He catches her eyeing it. "Tell us what they're saying, Connie," he prompts.

I open my mouth to protest at him calling me Connie, but close it again. I let it pass and pick up the newspaper from the arm of the chair. Not surprisingly the arrest is on the front page. I read aloud what it says, " 'A German called Charles Ludwig has been arrested, in connection with the recent ghastly murders in Whitechapel.' "

Mr. Bartleby, stroking his whiskers, grunts. "What did I tell ya?" He nods at my ma. "A foreigner."

I lay down the paper on the table and smooth out the creases. I feel Mr. Bartleby's eyes on me. "Talking of foreigners, how was that American you went to see the other night?" he asks. He waves his hands and wiggles his fingers with his great gold rings on them and puts on a funny voice. "The ill*ooo*sionist!"

I feel uncomfortable. A pungent smell suddenly fills my nostrils as I vaguely remember the flames on stage that night. Through the haze of my memory, I see a woman rising up from them accompanied by a dramatic crescendo from the orchestra. But my recollection of what happened after Mr. Mesmer put that lady in a trance is fuzzy. It's all a blur to me now, and I'm not sure why.

Flo comes to the rescue. "It was a good laugh," she replies.

Mr. Bartleby raises a brow. "Was it supposed to be a comedy?"

Flo shakes her head. "No!" She giggles. "But there was this big red curtain around this woman, and by mistake, this geezer lifts it up, so everyone in the front sees the priestess, or whatever she was, scarpering down through a trapdoor!" Her telling of the tale makes me smile, even though I may as well not have been there. Then she puts me on the spot. "But Con was most taken with Mesmer the Magnificent."

"Mesmer the Magnificent!" Mr. Bartleby repeats in a haughty voice. "Were you, indeed?" He turns to me and his voice goes all upper class. "And what did Mesmer the Magnificent do, pray tell?"

Before I can say anything, Flo pipes up: "He puts people into trances." Mr. Bartleby frowns; so, by way of explanation, Flo adds: "Like Madame Morelli."

The knife clatters on Ma's plate. Flo's let the cat out of the bag.

"Madame Morelli?" he repeats. "Who's she when she's at home?"

My dear sister's gone and done it good and proper this time. Ma's been going to Madame Morelli's séances for the last few months—ever since she met Mr. Bartleby, in fact. She wanted to contact my pa to find out if it was all right to see another gentleman. Madame Morelli says her spirit guide is in touch with the Old Man and that he's happy for her. It's been three years since he's passed and it's time to move on. That's the message that he's sent to her. I know it comforts her to hear this, but Mr. Bartleby doesn't know about it.

He strokes his bushy, black whiskers. "A medium, eh?" He looks at Ma oddly, then shakes his head. "You can't . . . ?" And then he sees from the expression on her face that she can, and does, believe; he shakes his head. "It's a scam, my dear. A nice little earner, but money for old rope." He reaches for her hand, but she pulls it away, like an oyster shell shuts up. He smiles and carries on like he's talking to a little child. "Madame Morelli is no more in touch with the spirit world than Connie here." I feel a little slighted that I should be the one he singles out, and I feel I ought to stand up for Ma.

"You don't know that I'm not," I say with a shrug.

Instead of backing me up, Flo adds fuel to the fire. "That why you been acting strange of late?" she asks with her cheeky look.

"No, I ain't!" I protest. I forget I should've said, "I haven't," but my grammar goes out the window when I'm riled.

"Yes, you have," insists Flo, leaning across the table and pointing at me. I'm taken aback by her attack. "All weird, you've been. Dreaming all day long."

"Daydreaming, eh?" says Mr. Bartleby, ejecting a currant from his mouth as he speaks. "That's what girls her age do, don't they, Mrs. P?" He winks at her. "Dreaming about your sweetheart, eh? Who is he, then?" He nudges my elbow and I lean back in my chair, out of his reach. "She's gone all shy," he says, like I'm not in the room, then adds cheerfully: "We'll find out soon enough, I dare say."

Flo slides me a saucy sideways look as if to say she's won.

It's already growing dark outside and Ma tells me to draw the patched-up curtains to keep the heat in the room. We clear the table of the dirty dishes and it's then that Flo and I usually go into the kitchen to wash up. We leave Ma and Mr. Bartleby alone to talk, or do what they do. But not tonight. I can tell Mr. Bartleby's in a mischievous mood. Just as we're stacking the plates to wash, he calls us back through.

"Let's have our own séance, shall we, ladies?" he says, sticking his tongue into his cheek so that it bulges. "Come and join us." And he pats the chair beside him. The idea gives me the creeps at first. I look at Ma and I can tell she's miffed, but she nods gently.

Flo and me sit down and Ma tells us to put our hands on the tabletop, with our little fingers touching the person's next to us. I don't like the idea of touching Mr. Bartleby's digits, but I do. We blow out the candle and sit in silence.

Mr. B takes the lead: "Is there anybody there?" he asks in a creepy voice.

We wait for what seems like ages and then Flo

suddenly gasps and I think she's playing silly beggars, but she lets out a big sneeze and we all giggle.

"Serious now," barks Mr. B, and we're quiet again. After what seems like an age, I start to think that Mr. Bartleby might be taking it all seriously until, that is, the table starts to shake and lifts a little, and I can tell it's him that's moving it.

"Let's ask about Leather Apron," he suggests in the dark. I can't see his face, but I bet he's smiling. "Go on, Mrs. P," he cajoles, but Ma's floundering.

"What should I say?"

I hear him tut-tut in the darkness. "I'll do it, then," he says with a chuckle. His voice goes all ghostly.

"Spirits of the other world," he starts. "Will you tell us who Leather Apron is? One knock for 'yes,' two for 'no.' "

I feel him jerk his knee and tap the floor with his foot. Flo goes "ooogh" at the sound. She's encouraging him to make a fool of Ma, and I don't like it.

"Is it Aaron Cohen?" he asks. Silence, then two taps. "Is it Jacob Minski, the barber?" Two more taps. I knew they would be two of the Jews who've been hauled in by Old Bill. Then he asks: "Is it Charles Ludwig?"

The answer comes back again, only this time

there's just one tap. "Yes." Mr. Bartleby starts to laugh and we all lean back from the table and you can feel the tension melt away. There's relief in the air. We know it's only larking about, but in our heart of hearts, we all hope it's true. We all hope they've caught *him*.

EMILY

At Brown's Hotel, in fashionable Mayfair, the bellboy places the leather suitcase onto the stand, takes a step back and flattens his palm. His gesture sends Pauline Beaufroy reaching for her purse.

"Ah, of course." She pulls out a sixpence and hopes it's enough. She does not wish to seem too mean, but she really cannot afford to be overly generous. This room, with its sumptuous drapes and elaborately dressed bed, is costing her enough. Her father used to stay here regularly when he came up to town, and her mother insisted that she should continue the custom. The latter, however, has no idea that the family is not as well-off as it used to be since Sir Roger's death.

"Thank you, ma'am." The boy, seemingly satisfied, whips round and closes the door behind him, leaving Pauline alone to survey the luxury that now surrounds her. Her eyes wander over to the walnut dressing table to

feast on the array of treats for her delectation: a silver dish of bonbons, a small mirror
in a mother-of-pearl frame and a bowl of
potpourri, which she holds up to her nose.
Lily of the valley—her favorite.

Standing in front of the cheval mirror, she
unpins her hat and lays it on the silk bedcover,
before she unbuttons her coat and it joins
her hat. Next she sits on the edge of the bed.
There are several perfectly comfortable chairs
in the room, but she eschews them, choosing
instead the bed on which to perch. Sitting in
that inviting armchair might lower her guard
and she is on a mission. Terence is such a
poor liar. It would be bad enough if he were
covering up his wife's whereabouts, but she
has the distinct impression that he has no idea
where she is, either. She puts her arms around
her torso, hugging herself, as if she is feeling
a chill. However, the room is quite warm.

How I long to put a comforting arm around
her, too. Then, as if she knows that I am
thinking about her, she delves into her reticule
and brings out a letter. As she unfolds it, I see
the signature on the bottom of the brief note.
Dated July 15, it is from Geraldine. It reads:

My Dearest Sister,
I write, albeit hurriedly, to tell you we are
about to welcome a very special guest

into our home. Yesterday I received a wholly unexpected communication from our dear friend Emily Tindall. As you know, she has been living in London for the past few months, based at St. Jude's, in Whitechapel. However, I fear she has run into a spot of bother and is most unwell. I have offered her accommodation until she is recovered. I am hoping that you will take this opportunity to come up to grimy old London within the next few days to visit us. We can reminisce and enjoy each other's company, just as we used to.

I do hope to see you soon, dearest Pauline.

Yours ever in sisterly affection,
Geraldine

The single sheet is refolded. Pauline sighs deeply. Naturally, she replied to Geraldine's letter straightaway. She almost found herself wishing to point out that I had always, in fact, been her dearest friend, not her sister's. Ah, I have let it slip, but you have probably realized already that I am Emily Tindall; the Emily Tindall whom Constance seeks and the Emily Tindall who is a close friend to Pauline Beaufroy. In fact, if you were to pry a little deeper into that reticule of hers, you'd

73

find a bookmark I gave her a decade ago. I embroidered it myself with my favorite quotation from Lord Byron. It says: *Friendship is love without his wings.*

During our childhood, Geraldine, as the older sibling, was always a little aloof from Pauline and me. She expressed no desire to join in our silly games, preferring instead to read her father's anatomy books. However, the bond between Pauline and me lasted into adulthood, until it was broken, or rather loosened, two years ago when we finally went our separate ways.

Pauline replaces the letter in her bag. Unfortunately, she could not accept Geraldine's invitation at such short notice. Such impetu-osity was, she believed, typical of her flighty sister. As she well knew, their mama was recovering from yet another severe bout of bronchitis and could not be left for the time being. *Please pass on my fondest regards to dear Emily,* she had written. *I am so sorry to hear that her health is poor and I wish her a speedy recovery.* She finished her reply with the assurance that she would come up to London: *as soon as circumstances permit.* As fortune would have it, however, she has left it far too late.

CONSTANCE

Flo and me are both in bed and I'm thinking about the rapping game we played with Mr. Bartleby, and I says to her: "What if there is such things as spirits?"

"What?" Flo's head is at the bottom of the bed. We sleep top to toe. I lift my head and look down to see she's lying on her side. "You mean ghosts? Like in *A Christmas Carol*?" I'd read it out loud to everyone last year.

"Yes," I reply. "What if you can really talk to people who've died, like Ma thinks you can?"

I see her shoulders move, as if she's shrugging under the covers. "You mean like the Old Man?" She goes quiet. She's thinking, but after a moment she says: "Well, that wouldn't be such a bad thing, would it?"

I am thinking, too. My eyes are closed and I suddenly see a picture of my pa, bathed in a bright light and he's smiling and holding out his hand to me. And it gives me a warm, comforting feeling, like I'm sitting in front of hot embers in a grate with a mug of cocoa in my hand, and I say: "No. No, I suppose it wouldn't be bad at all."

Chapter 6

Thursday, September 20, 1888

Emily

The notion is in her head. Tentatively, I have reached out to Constance and she has accepted my approach, albeit unconsciously. Only a few are chosen, you see. And she is one of them. She is the reason I have returned to this place—the place where I used to trudge around the streets for hours, going from one reeking doss-house to the next, or stopping at corners to talk to the poor benighted souls who let themselves be used for the price of a large glass of gin.

Whitechapel. They knew me in these parts. They called me Lady Emily, although I had no real title. I just had a vocation. I'd heard about the poverty and the suffering in the East End from the Reverend Samuel Barnett and his wife, Henrietta, while I was at Oxford. Such a fine, upstanding couple, with noble ideals and hearts so full of compassion. I wish I could have made them proud.

The need to reach out to these poor unfortunates was what brought me here in the first instance and perhaps that's why I've returned, although really it feels as though I've never been away. It's only been a few weeks, but I thought something might have changed. The streets are still filthy, the urchins still beg barefoot and the lost women still ply their trade. I suppose I'd hoped for too much. It takes someone to care to change a place like this. And nobody cares for Whitechapel.

CHAPTER 7

Friday, September 21, 1888

CONSTANCE

The cold fingers of an easterly wind rattle the window frames and set the threadbare drapes of the front room all aquiver. I'm edging my way to the door, tying my bonnet ribbon under my chin as I go. I'm so intent on being quiet that I don't see Flo on her hands and knees about to brush the hearth. "Where you off to?" she asks, giving me the once-over.

I stop dead in my tracks and feel my heart leap in my chest. She leans back on her haunches, and as my eyes grow accustomed to the light, I see her twitch a little smile to show she's quite pleased about giving me a fright.

"To St. Jude's," I tell her. Lying don't come natural to me, not to Flo, anyway. She looks put out and her mouth droops at the corners.

"But it ain't Sunday. I thought we was doing the West End today."

Of course, I know it's only Friday. I shake my head and hear a sigh escape my lips. "I need to see Miss Tindall."

Flo dips her brows and grabs hold of the arm of a chair to heave herself up. She just looks at me and it's enough to make me crumble.

"I have to talk to her," I say. What I want to tell her is that I feel like I'm carrying this terrible weight on my shoulders and my heart is really heavy, but I don't know why. My voice sounds all vexed and breathless and I feel I'm drowning. But I don't think she'll understand.

"Why don't you sit down and I'll make you a nice cup of tea?" she suggests, walking toward me. Her voice is all singsongy, like she's talking to a little 'un, like she's not taking me seriously. She doesn't get how I feel. How can she? Whitechapel is her world, but it's not mine anymore. It's my prison. Miss Tindall has shown me what lies beyond its walls. She's told me about a better life and I need to escape this miserable patch of squalor to find it, but how can I tell Flo? That's why I can't wait until Sunday.

"What's amiss?" Ma suddenly shouts down

from the top of the stairs, her chamber pot cradled in her arms.

I tense, thinking Flo will give me away. She'll say something like "Connie's come over all queer" or "Connie fancies skiving off today." Only, she doesn't. Our eyes lock and it's as if she suddenly realizes how badly I need to see Miss Tindall.

Flo pads over to the foot of the stairs and cranes her head around the door. "Nothing!" Ma's chest is all tight again, so she's kept to her bed a bit longer than usual. "Stay there and I'll bring you up some tea." Then she looks over her shoulder at me and whispers, "Back by nine, you hear."

My mouth bursts into a smile and I hurry on my way, careful to close the door quietly. I have to be quick if I'm to be home before Ma misses me.

Even though it's not yet eight o'clock, the streets have long been stirring. There are cartmen heading for Pickford's warehouse and brewers' drays are leaving the breweries. Errand boys weave in and out of the workaday folk and nothing seems amiss, only I know it is. My legs are feeling like lead. They're slowing me down. The moment slows, too, and as I look about me, I try to swallow, but my throat seems all tight, like I'm being choked. I shiver and retreat into my shawl, until, in less than five minutes, I emerge from the side lanes, from White's Row onto Commercial Street. It's broad here, but the highway's a mess. All the traffic's been diverted for the next few weeks. Navvies are swarming everywhere, digging up the road for the new tramway. But I feel safer here. I start to walk toward St. Jude's. I always see Miss Tindall when I help out with the little kids at Sunday school. We have our chats after that. I miss them. Course she hasn't been there the last few weeks. Come to think of it, she was a bit out of sorts the last time I saw her. I'm praying she'll be there today. I know she often works outside of the church with the Reverend and Mrs. Barnett on the streets sometimes. One of their Oxford ladies, she is.

Now I'm half running, half walking down the street, past Spitalfields Market and the Ten Bells and the old weavers' houses with their glass lofts that let in the light. But there's not much light today; only a sky the color of watery gruel. The gloom licks at walls and doorways and water stands cold in pools between cobbles.

I glance into a shop as I pass and see a butcher, sharpening his knife on a steel. Ham hocks and sides of bacon hang from the ceiling and I think of Annie Chapman's body from the other day. Further on, a one-armed bootblack, with a hook for a hand, is polishing shoes. I imagine him plucking out Polly Nichols's guts with it. He looks up and ogles me and I see his teeth are as black as his polish. I wince at the sight and he catches the fear on my face and raises his hook to me. I break into a run. That's how I arrive at St. Jude's with my bonnet slumped to one side of my head and my breath so hot that it burns in my chest.

The church door creaks open, sending me all aquiver, but the darkness inside is pricked by the light from dozens of candles. *He* can't be in here. Not even *he* would venture into the Lord's house, I tell myself. I feel safer.

The air smells damp and musty, like a coal cellar. I catch a whiff of tallow, too. My eyes quickly adjust to the gloom and on either side of the aisle I can see there are two ladies laying out the hymn books on the pews for the morning service. From the way one is bobbing up and down, I can tell it's Mrs. Le Bon from Wilkes Street. They say she was run over by a carriage when she was a girl and now her left leg's a full three inches shorter than the other. No wonder she's up and down like a Jack-in-the-box, but she manages well enough. The other woman, that's Mrs. Parker-Smythe. She's got airs and graces, she has. All prim and proper. I call her Mrs. Snooty. She doesn't like Miss Tindall, because she's rumbled her. Emily, I mean Miss Tindall, can see that she's all show and not a real lady at all. She says real ladies are always sympathetic to the needs of those less fortunate. So Mrs. Parker-Smythe may have a fancy double-barrel name, but I know she's not well-bred 'cos she always squints at me as if I'm a dog turd on her shoe. And there it is again—that look of disgust as she turns. She's just caught sight of me and her nostrils flare and her thin lips purse and she pretends she hasn't seen me. I clear my throat. She carries on laying out the hymnals. I cough again, only much louder. This time, she can't ignore me. Mrs. Le Bon has heard and bobs over to where we're standing by a big fat column. She's a nosey old beggar.

"Well, girl?" Mrs. Snooty speaks in a loud whisper. She smooths her skirts and tugs at her cuffs, like she's work to do. It's almost as if she's spoiling for a fight. Well, she's met her match in me. I'm in no mood to take stick from her.

I square up to her. "Please, missus, I'd like to see Miss Tindall," I say in my best voice.

"Miss Tindall?" she repeats slowly as one of her eyebrows shoots up.

"Yes, please," I say.

I can tell she's working hard to stop a scowl spreading across her face. She answers me through unmoving lips. "Miss Tindall is not here," she says. Her voice is raised so that Mrs. Le Bon, who's hopped over quick as she can, has heard. She's wearing a frown like a scared rabbit. She sidles up to Mrs. Snooty, who tells her what she already knows, that I want to see Miss Tindall. "But she's not here, is she, Mrs.

Le Bon?" There's something snide in her voice that grates on my nerves.

Mrs. Le Bon gets a fit of the jitters and shakes her head. "No, no, Constance," she tells me, all flustered.

"Then I'll wait," I tell Mrs. Snooty, and I start to sit down.

"You'll be waiting a very long time, my girl," she comes back at me, like a wasp on the attack. "Miss Tindall has gone away."

I straighten my bent legs with a start. *"Away?"* I can't believe what I'm hearing. "Where?" I blurt. "She never said . . ." Suddenly I'm angry and hurt at the same time.

The two women swap knowing glances. "We are not Miss Tindall's keepers. She is free to come and go as she chooses," says Mrs. Snooty, her hands crossed over her waist. She wears a large gold cross and chain at her neck and I suddenly want to yank at it. I know she's not telling me the whole truth. A smile lifts her lips. It's so forced that I wonder at her gall. She expects me to swallow that?

An old man struggles up the aisle and plonks himself down in a pew on the other side of the aisle. He leans forward and bows his white head in prayer. I know I can't make too much noise. "Has she gone back to Oxford?" I hiss through my teeth. Then, to soften my cheek, I add: "If you please."

Mrs. Snooty shakes her head. "As I said, I have no idea." I glance at Mrs. Le Bon, as if to plead with her, but her eyes are planted to the ground. She wants to avoid my gaze.

"I need to see her. I . . ." But I can tell from Mrs. Snooty's expression that she's as cold and unmoving as the big stone pillar that looms up behind her. I feel my shoulders suddenly droop, like my body is admitting defeat. I swallow hard and feel my lips tremble slightly, but I say nothing. I simply turn and start to walk back down the aisle.

There are more people coming inside now. I suppose they must be arriving for the morning service, which starts in twenty minutes. I look at the draggle of men and women, mainly old and bent. I suppose, like me, they're all looking for something. I hope they find what they want, but I certainly haven't. I'm coming away confused and frustrated. Why would Miss Tindall leave without saying good-bye to me? I thought we was friends, but maybe I got it wrong. Why would someone like her want to be friends with me? After all, I'm only a Whitechapel flower girl. Course she doesn't know about Flo's pickpocketing. Or does she? Maybe she's asked Mrs. Snooty to tell me she's gone away because she's found out about our thieving. Maybe that's it, but she always says that God forgives sinners as long as they repent. And I always feel bad after Flo's lifted a wallet or a watch. So, surely, she'd have said something to me, if she knew. Wouldn't she?

I'm walking back down the aisle, trying to stifle my tears, when I suddenly feel something brush my shoulder. I lift my head to see I've bumped into a lady.

"Sorry!" I say out loud. I think she's going to be angry with me, and I wouldn't blame her. I wasn't looking where I was going. But she smiles. It's a kind smile, the sort that can melt a bad mood, and I like her face. It's pretty and smooth and framed by dark curls. And I can tell she's a lady by her silk hat with a rose in it and her plum-colored coat. And she says to me: "The fault was mine." She tilts her head, all gracious like, just how Miss Tindall does. For a second, our eyes meet and it's like we're connected in some way. I get this strange feeling that I know her, but then she moves on and I go on my way, out under the steel press of a gray autumn day, onto Commercial Street, heading toward home.

EMILY

Ah, St. Jude's—the scene of so many of my small triumphs and joys, and, of course, the seedbed of so much evil. I well recall my first briefing there with the Barnetts. With their support, I was going to change the world—the world of Whitechapel, at least.

It was a chilly spring day when I stepped out of there with a tread as light as thistledown. However, my mind was clearly not on where I was going because that was when I bumped, quite literally, into Robert Sampson for the first time. Raising his hat, he apologized, as any gentleman would, even though, like Constance's encounter in the church, the fault was entirely mine. I remember he had a mane of dark hair, but it was his eyes that caught my attention. They were deep blue and quite piercing. His smile was wide and unaffected, too. I could tell this, even though his lips were half-hidden under a dark, well-trimmed moustache. I abandoned my normal composure and started to flap and fluster a little.

"I should've been looking where I was going," I rejoined. And that, I thought, was that. He dipped his head in a courteous little bow and bid me "Good day." He continued on his way and I went on mine. And yet there was something about him . . . but that is a story another time for the telling.

CONSTANCE

I can't really remember much about the walk from the church because I'm close to tears. The fog doesn't help, neither. It's closing in.

The outlines of buildings that line the street are blurred. Rooftops and spires dissolve into the gray that envelops the city. The weather matches my mood.

I can't believe that Miss Tindall would leave without a word. Where would she go? Back to Oxford, I suppose. Or to her parents' home in Sussex, perhaps? She told me all about them: how her pa was a good man, a solicitor, she said, and that he was always championing the underdogs, the tenants against the big landowners. She chuckled when she said how his conscience was the bane of her mother's life. I remember her saying to me: "Yes, my mama always fancied me married to the local squire's son." Once she referred to her daughter as a bluestocking, too. That's an insult, a name for a lady who prefers her books to men.

I'm lost in my thoughts when, up ahead, I hear a familiar cry from a street seller.

"Chestnuts. Hot chestnuts."

Then I remember. We stopped there once on the way back from a class. Miss Tindall bought me a bag of them and I ain't never tasted nothing so good in my entire life. I stop by the brazier that glows red against the dull street and hold up my hands to feel its warmth. The seller—he's chirpy with a peak to his cap that he wears on the back of his head—he shoves a bag in front of me.

"Penny for 'em," he says. I must have looked at

him all queer because he repeats himself. "Penny for 'em," he says again, and thinks it necessary to explain: "For me nuts. Not your thoughts." He gives me a cheeky grin.

I return his smile. "I ain't got no money," I say with a shake of my head. I see his face drop. The smile disappears and I'm about to move on when I feel myself pull back. "You seen a lady lately? That tall." I raise my arm just above my head.

The seller stokes his brazier as I talk. "Lady, eh? You don't get many of them round these parts."

I persist. "She's a regular. She told me." I search my memory for something that makes Miss Tindall stand out; then I remember her umbrella. "She carried a brolly. A green brolly," I blurt.

The seller stops poking the coals and looks up. "The Brolly Lady, I call her," he says with a nod. I tense before he adds: "Nah. I ain't seen her these last few weeks." My shoulders droop. "She your mistress, or some'at?" he asks, looking me up and down. "Run off without paying your wages?" He thinks himself a real clown.

I cast him a haughty look. "She's my friend," I say huffily.

"Yeah, right. And I'm Mr. Gladstone!" he chuckles.

I walk on, trying to think of any other places that Miss Tindall used to visit on the regular. I call in at the stationer's, where I know she sometimes bought paper and pencils. No luck.

Then, of course, I recall the mission: Sir George's Residence for Respectable Girls, in George Yard.

I remember Miss Tindall used to teach there sometimes. I quicken my step. I make a detour and cut through the archway off Whitechapel High Street. The road itself is teeming with people, a lot of them Jews. You can hardly move for them here these days, but they don't give any trouble. Away from the street, it's quiet. The covered passage into George Yard is empty. It's like I'm walking into another world, all dark mysterious, like Alice going down the rabbit hole. Beyond is the warren of slums and rookeries. And there it stands: the ragged school for "respectable" girls. It's a stern brick building that was only opened a couple of years ago and I feel like a little child again as I gaze up at its front door. There's a long metal chain attached to a bell and a sign that says, VISITORS' ENTRANCE. I ring and my stomach churns as I hear footsteps coming toward me from behind the door. It creaks open, like it's never been used in years.

A red-haired matron stands there and raises a monocle to her right eye to study me like I was a specimen in Dr. Frankenstein's laboratory. After a second she sniffs and says, "Girls round the back. This entrance is for visitors." She points to the sign, then adds churlishly, "Or can't you read?" She's about to shut the door in my face, when something tells me to stand my ground.

"I can read," I say. My cockiness surprises even me.

The matron raises one of her brows. "Well, that is something, I suppose," she replies, but she still makes to close the door.

"I'm looking for a teacher!" I cry.

The matron sets her face into a scowl. "All potential pupils need to register around the back," she hisses, pointing with her gnarled finger to the left.

"But I don't want to register," I protest. "I'm eighteen and I'm looking for one of your teachers. I'm worried about her."

The door stops moving. "Worried about her?" The matron is frowning. "Is it really your place to worry about a teacher at this establishment?" There's a spiteful catch in her voice.

I gulp down any fear I felt before. I know I'm getting somewhere. "She's gone missing."

"Missing?" The matron tilts her head.

"No one's seen her these past few weeks."

"And how, may I ask, is that any concern of yours?" She's straightened her back and gone all puffed up again.

"She's . . . she's . . . ." I want to say that she's my friend, *my best friend,* but I can't. "She's my teacher," I tell her. "And I know she teaches here sometimes and what with that Leather Apron about and that—"

The old woman suddenly lets out a sigh and

rolls her eyes as if saying the fiend's name irks her. "Very well," she says, finally opening wide the door. "You better come into the office and I shall ask the secretary if we can find her."

She leads me into the hallway, as grand a hall as I've ever been into, with a stone floor and a wooden staircase that goes up as far as the eye will reach. A gaggle of girls in pinafores walk past us in silence and go through another door into a classroom. I follow the matron into a large office off the main entrance. The room is lined with ledgers and books, and the smell reminds me instantly of my copy of *Little Dorrit*, only a thousand times stronger.

At one end sits a stony-faced lady, all angles, with sharp shoulders and a pointed nose with a pair of spectacles balanced on it. The matron explains my business to her; and in her surprise, the secretary's face lifts and her specs take a tumble.

"Most irregular," she declares. I think she'll tell me to leave that instant, but instead she rises slowly and turns to pull one of the large ledgers off the shelf. She's quite frail and I, for a moment, fear she'll drop it. It wobbles slightly in her grip for a second, then lands safely on the desk.

"The teacher's name?" she asks, finally opening the pages. I can see the book is full of lists.

"It's Miss Tindall," I tell her, arching my neck at the upside-down text.

She jerks up her head and looks at me over her specs. *"Tindall?"* she echoes. I may be imagining it, but I think she's just lost what little color she had in her wizened old cheeks.

"Miss Emily Tindall," I repeat, nervously, like I shouldn't be saying her name at all.

It's then that she shuts the ledger with a thud. A cloud of dust flies into the air. She shakes her head. "Miss Tindall left us a few weeks ago."

"Oh" is all I can manage for a second or two; then I pull myself together. I was half expecting it, to be honest. "Did she give a reason?" I know I'm out of order, but I don't care.

That arching of her brow again. She thinks me impertinent and her tongue lashes me again. "Young woman, it is not for the likes of you to ask or know matters of a disciplinary nature."

Disi . . . what? She's talking gibberish. I've not come across that big word before, but I can tell from her face that it's not a good word, not an easy one. I don't tarry.

"Begging your pardon," I say, and I dip a surly curtsy, like I don't think she deserves it.

The matron, who has been watching silently, rings a bell and stares at me until, a moment later, a girl appears.

"Show this young woman out," she instructs in a voice as sour as vinegar.

This time, I don't protest.

EMILY

Constance is on the right path. She grows closer to finding me, dear girl, but before I let her, I must tell you a little more about how certain events came to pass. As we are standing outside the ragged school, I shall relate to you how it was here, on this very spot, that I met Mr. Robert Sampson, quite by chance, for the second time.

It was a pleasant afternoon in early May; the sun was shining. After lessons had finished for the day, many of my freed charges remained outdoors, kicking stones down the street or playing hopscotch on chalked squares on the road. Lines of washing, strung across the cobbles, swayed in a gentle breeze, and women, often with babes on their hips, took a moment to feel the sun on their faces.

I glanced down the narrow row of houses. There was hardly a windowpane that was not cracked, nor a door not loose on its hinges. In these near-derelict dwellings, families would be crammed, sometimes a dozen or more in two rooms. Water was fetched from a pump at the end of the street and there was a privy in the backyard, if they were fortunate. This was the area chock-full of rookeries. A stranger took his life into his own hands walking in this area at night. Daytime was only marginally better, and that is why I was most curious to see a fine carriage parked down at the far end of the street. Two men, one clearly a gentleman, stood on the other side of the road. I assumed the vehicle was theirs, for no resident round these parts had ever even ridden in one, let alone owned one.

I fear I found myself gazing at them, wondering what on earth they were doing in such an area. It took a moment for me to realize they were going from house to house, speaking to the residents, by which time they had grown much closer. It was then, when he was but a few feet away, that the gentleman turned, looked at me, then raised his hat, not through familiarity but out of courtesy. In an instant, I realized where I had seen him before and my look sparked his own memory.

"Good day to you, again, Miss . . . ," he greeted me.

I confess I was a little nonplussed at seeing him again. I think I smiled. "Tindall. Miss Tindall," I replied, feeling the color rise in my cheeks at being taken off guard. There was an embarrassed, yet cheerful, silence between us, both of us smiling at each other, but not really knowing what to say. In the end, we both blurted out the most obvious question in unison. "What brings you here?" Then we both laughed nervously.

"I teach, here," I said, turning and waving at the austere building behind me. I waited for him to volunteer his own business, but in the end, I needed to prompt him. "And you?"

"Me?" he asked self-effacingly. He was wearing a formal gray frock coat. "Robert Sampson, at your service." He gave a gallant bow. "I'm here on some business for my father."

"Business?" I asked, having no inkling as to what business a respectable gentleman could possibly have in these parts.

"Yes. He insists that I should learn the ropes. Start on the bottom rung, as it were." His tone was jovial, but I remained in the dark. It was only when I turned to the man standing next to him, who was clearly no gentleman at all, that I understood. They were collecting rent. It also accounted for the slight embarrassment I detected in Mr. Sampson's manner, for his companion seemed, in fact, more like a henchman. Heavily built and with a thick neck, around which was tied a kerchief, he appeared like a brute, no more or less. He was bareheaded and his pate was as bald as a boiled egg, while his face seemed to be set in a permanent scowl. I dipped my eyes to his belt to see what might even have been a cosh dangling from his waist. Then, as if Mr. Sampson felt my curious glance deserved some sort of explanation, he added: "Mr. Butcher, here, works for me."

The brutish-looking man gave a shallow bow. Even then I wondered if his name was a soubriquet; but despite that, my naivety still had the better of me. I wanted to see righteousness in everyone. There were good landlords and bad landlords—weren't there?—even though I was yet to find a good one in Whitechapel. With hindsight, I confess part of me was a little taken with Mr. Sampson. But then, as I have discovered to my cost, I fear I was a very poor judge of character.

CONSTANCE

The first thing I see as soon as I arrive back home from the ragged school is Flo, on her hands and knees on our front doorstep. She's been scrubbing it and it's covered in suds. She's looking flushed as she brushes a wayward strand of hair back from her face with the back of her hand. "So?" she sneers, like she's expecting me to deliver some choice nuggets of news.

I look at her and wonder how she can seemingly take such pleasure in other people's pain. "So," I repeat, if only to bait her.

"What did your fancy lady say?" She springs

up and stands in front of me, barring my way. She shifts from one leg to the other, but she keeps her voice low. I hear the clatter of pans in the kitchen and know that Ma is up and about.

"She wasn't there." I suddenly bite my tongue. Something stops me from telling Flo that she might've gone away. I feel my chest tighten and I'm not sure why. Maybe it's because I'm worried. Something isn't right. Maybe I'm afraid I've lost the only person whoever made me feel that there is more to life than Whitechapel.

Flo senses my hesitation, but instead of goading me and trying to prize out my anxiety like a pearl from an oyster, she leaves me be. Perhaps she has seen something in my eyes that tells her I might burst into tears if she presses me.

"She'll come back," she says encouragingly, letting me pass.

I nod my head and start to untie my bonnet ribbons from under my chin.

"I hope so," I reply, even though the bad feeling inside me has grown a whole lot worse.

EMILY

Molly Deakin is sleeping now, albeit fitfully. She lies in a comfortable bed, but goose down and cotton sheets do not assuage a fever. The heavy drapes are drawn and a single oil lamp burns at her bedside. An elderly nurse sits by her, dozing, but her nap is interrupted as the door is pushed ajar and a gentleman looks in. I recognize him from that fateful night. His chestnut hair flows from his crown like a romantic poet's. He is proud of it, and clearly vain. Yet his business is anything but the stuff of love poetry. It is dark and dirty; a business so vile that most right-minded people shut their eyes and ears to it. Yet, oddly, I no longer feel the sense of outrage that propelled me into my current state. That is because I am certain in the knowledge of what lies beyond for him and his kind.

"Any change?" he asks in a low rumble, his gaze not even straying to the child herself.

The nurse, stirred from her light slumber, looks at him with rheumy eyes. She shakes her head. He glances back to the girl. He will give her another week. If she is not available after that, then he will have to turn her out, just as he has the dozens of other young girls before whose maiden wares are now too soiled to be of any use.

CONSTANCE

Later that evening, when Flo and me are in bed, I snatch the dictionary, which I keep on the little bedside table. By the light of my candle, I thumb through the pages until I find the *d*'s. It takes me a while, squinting at all the words. At first, I can't find one that fits the sound—*"disi"*—then I imagine what Miss Tindall would say.

"Break down the word into parts."

"I've done that. It don't work," I say.

"Doesn't work," she corrects me. "Does it sound like any other word that you do know?" she asks.

Quick as a flash, I come back at her: "Disciple." I scan the pages and, sure enough, in the same column I find the word *"disciplinary."* Eagerly I read the definition: *concerning or enforcing discipline.* I'm really still not much wiser, then I read the example they give in a sentence: A *soldier will face* disciplinary *action after going absent without leave.* Once again, my guts start to roil.

"That can't be," I mutter under my breath. Miss Tindall would never do anything bad, I tell myself. *Never.*

"Blow that bleeding candle out, will ya?" mumbles Flo, tossing down at the other end of the bed and pulling the blanket over her face. "Go to sleep."

She's right, of course. It's past midnight, but I know there'll be little shut-eye for me tonight. I won't be able to rest until I know what's happened to Miss Tindall.

CHAPTER 8

Sunday, September 30, 1888

EMILY

The night is as black as pitch, although, of course, that no longer troubles me. I can read the poster clearly as it flaps forlornly in the wind. It's nailed to a warehouse door on Berner Street, but there's a jagged tear down the middle. Whether or not it was torn deliberately, I cannot say. Perhaps it was an accident, or even a sick joke. Perhaps someone has taken a knife to it, just as they did to Polly Nichols and Annie Chapman. I read it. Ghastly Murder, it says. Dreadful mutilation of a woman. The words cause me to ponder. It seems that this, now, is my task: to see things done in the dark, executed in the shadows; acts that are so terrible that they are perpetrated in secret. I must shine a light on them, expose calumny and sin. That's why I am in Berner Street tonight. I am come to see another slaughter.

Once again, it is cold and rainy; once again, we're in the early hours. It is the sort of night that seems interminable: a night where the damp penetrates your bones and chills your marrow and you long for it to be over. And for Elizabeth Stride, it soon will be. I know that before it is out, she will lie dead, her throat slit and her blood spilling out over the cobbles.

We join her as she stands in Dutfield's Yard. **He** is already with her. They are facing each other, arguing. Above the din, however, I detect footsteps. I switch round to see a man approaching from Berner Street. Hearing the cross words rise into the air, he looks in the couple's direction. To his horror, he sees him grab Elizabeth and hurl her to the ground. She lets out a scream, and then another, and, for a second, I think the passerby might act. I think he might at least challenge the attacker, but no. He simply quickens his pace and keeps on walking, crossing over the street. My eyes follow him. I want to call after him, but, of course, I cannot. But wait! There's another man, standing on the pavement nearby, smoking a pipe. I glance back. Elizabeth is still struggling, although her screams are being stifled. Suddenly **he** bolts up and shouts at the two men as they glare, transfixed by what is happening. "Lipski!" he cries. It shocks me to hear his voice, and shocks me that he should be so audacious as to berate the men. I know that Israel Lipski, who'd been executed last year for the murder of a young woman, was a Jew. If his intention is to frighten them away, he achieves his goal. The two men make off in haste, one breaking into a run to escape any further threat. Swiftly he resumes his gruesome work. Elizabeth has become insensible. The one chance that she'd had to be rescued has now gone. And so he begins. I cannot watch.

A stiff breeze has got up and is whipping the rain, slashing it diagonally. Yet despite this, I still hear the clatter of hooves. A pony and cart is being driven down the street. It turns onto Dutfield's Yard. Then something strange happens. The pony suddenly veers to the left, shies and refuses to go any farther. I hear the man cuss, then watch as he leans forward in his seat, his whip in his hand. He is prodding something on the ground, but still the pony will not budge. That's when I see him shooting away. The driver doesn't spot him. But I do. I see him slip silently back out of the yard and disappear into the night just as the driver jumps down to investigate what troubles his pony. The murderer has been interrupted and I know I have to follow him.

I am about to leave when I see the driver strike a match to get a better view. The squally wind blows the flame out almost immediately, but the second or two of flickering light is enough to tell him that what he sees is a woman lying crumpled by the wall. I know her throat has been cut. The flower that she wore pinned to her jacket is now drenched in blood.

"My God!" I hear the cartman mutter, before I see him hurry into a nearby building to call for help from friends. I do not stay around to wait for their arrival.

They say this woman was his fourth victim: Martha Tabram, Polly Nichols, Annie Chapman and now Elizabeth Stride. But Long Lizzie, as she was known round these parts, has remained relatively unscathed. She's escaped his evil artistry to a large degree because he's been interrupted. There's been no time to lunge and rip and rearrange. That is why I'm afraid there'll soon be another. And I'm soon proved right. A few minutes later, I catch up with him in Duke Street, two miles away. This time, I'm afforded a better view. He's of medium height, with a moustache. On his head, he wears a peaked cloth cap. He's already talking to a prostitute. This time, there are a few other men around. I see three of them leaving a nearby club. I tell myself it's too public. Surely, he won't do it here? I am right. As the other men disappear from view, he leads the woman by the arm along Duke Street. Her name is Catherine Eddowes, and she is wearing a black straw bonnet and a black jacket trimmed with fur. She seems to go willingly and the pair turns onto Mitre Square. It's then that he strikes so quickly even I am shocked.

There is a soft gurgling sound and the woman falls where she stood. Immediately he sets to work, lifting her muddy-hemmed skirts over her head, then taking his fiendish knife to her, slashing and hacking and disemboweling with such inhuman brutality that I am thankful no one else witnesses it. Not content with drawing out her intestines and placing them over her right shoulder, he takes his knife to her face, slashing it with such savagery that I can no longer bear to look. Despite this, his vile work is completed in just a few short minutes. Forcing myself to look once more, I discover, to my horror, that he's even taken trophies—a kidney and part of her womb. And the rain keeps falling, sluicing the blood off the flagstones and into the gutters of the human abattoir the courtyard has become. Even though I am now above such things, I can stand no more.

CONSTANCE

When I do finally drift off, it must be the early hours and there's a nightmare waiting for me in the shadows of my sleep. I'm walking along Duke Street. I know it's Duke Street, 'cos there's the synagogue on my left. It's a nice-enough day, and there's people about, but suddenly a cloud covers the sun and it goes dark and I start to feel afraid. I'm afraid because I'm all alone.

Everyone's gone and then I hear footsteps behind me. I glance round, but there's no one there. Then I look in front of me and I sees this man, dressed from head to toe in black and he's blocking my way. And when I try to pass, he raises a great dagger and I turn and run, but he starts chasing me. I run onto Mitre Square, but he's still after me. I'm trapped and I cry out. And then I wake up, but I'm too afraid to move. All I can hear is the sound of my own heart pounding in my ears. It takes me a long while before I dare close my eyes again.

EMILY

It is still dark when I return to Catherine Eddowes's body an hour or so later. I feel compelled to be with her. Even though I had been powerless to help her in the yard when she was being so brutally attacked, at least now she would know that I was there. My presence, I thought, might be some small comfort to her as she lay on the slab at the City Mortuary in Golden Lane.

They've already gone through her pockets before the doctor arrives. The search has yielded a bewildering array of tins, fragments of material, chunks of soap and a small-tooth comb. Dr. Brown, a portly man with an efficient manner that brooks no dissent, walks in and takes charge. He orders her poor body to be stripped and washed down. To the muted disgust of one of the morticians, a piece of Catherine's ear drops from her clothing as he undresses her. He retrieves it from the stone floor and holds it at arm's length before depositing it in a kidney dish for later examination. Resuming his task, he removes layer upon layer of clothing from her blood-soaked body. First a black cloth jacket trimmed around the collar and cuffs with imitation fur, next a dark green chintz skirt, then underneath a man's white vest. Below that Catherine has worn a brown linsey bodice. There are more undergarments: a gray petticoat, an old green alpaca skirt, another ragged skirt with red flounces and a white calico chemise. It's like watching the layers of an onion being peeled away. Each time something different is revealed, and each time Catherine becomes smaller and more vulnerable, until there is only her bloody corpse lying like a cut of meat on the slab.

Looking at the forlorn collection on the table and the sodden clothes, it occurs to me that these were all the possessions she had in the world. She had carried all that she owned around with her, like a nomad, never knowing where she would lay her head that night. She wore all her clothes not simply because she needed protection from the cold, but because she had nowhere else to put them. Like so many of the women of Whitechapel, she never knew when, or if, she might earn her doss money; and, as so often happened, even when she did have a few pennies in her pocket, she'd spend it on gin rather than a bed for the night.

As they uncover her bloody nakedness, I try not to look on the tangle of intestines that the fiend has placed over her right shoulder. I try to ignore the fact that her ear has been cut off and her nose severed, and the slits that have been carved into her sad, weather-beaten cheeks. I find my gaze hovering over strange, inverted *V*'s. They bring to mind . . . I blink, suddenly reminded of the place and the symbols on the walls. Surely, not the compass and set square? I banish all thoughts of that night and push them to the back of my mind, where they must remain until later, until it is time to tell you and, of course, dear Constance.

I return to poor Catherine, and for an instant, I feel my own heart wrenched out of me, just as he had yanked out part of her womb, as I ponder on not just how she died, but how she had lived, too. Once she was a daughter, a sister. Once she was a wife, not a pile of scarified skin and bone, stripped of what little dignity the streets of Whitechapel had left to her. But I pull myself together and make myself focus, instead, on the person she had been, less than two hours before, and I seek out a place that he had not mutilated. My eyes find the palm of her left hand as it lies facing upward on the slab. When I touch it, it is still warm and limp. The death stiffness has not yet set in. But there is something else, too, although Dr. Brown is yet to discover it. I peer closely as they take the sponge to her other side. When he comes to examine Catherine's right side, he will turn her over and note that on her forearm, tattooed in blue India ink, are two letters. Together they make up the initials *TC*.

CONSTANCE

I wake to the sound of church bells. It's a Sunday. I'm thankful that the Lord's come to my rescue. This morning, the market's closed. But, try as I might, I can't put that nightmare out of my head. It's still there, in the back of my mind, hanging around like a bad smell from Fleet Ditch, and I'm thinking about lying low today, bunking off church and saying I'm sick. The Almighty'll understand, won't he?

Flo, on the other hand, never goes to St. Jude's, like Ma and me, although Ma says she needs to start going, otherwise the vicar won't let her wed her Danny in church.

I'm just about to stir my stumps when suddenly

there's a hammering on our door. Flo throws off the blanket from over her tousled head. "Who the bleeding hell is that? Don't they know it's the Sabbath?!"

Then we hear an urgent voice. "Flo! Flo, it's me, Sally!"

"What the f . . . !" Flo scrambles out of bed, pulls up the sash and sticks her head out of the window. "Sal!" she cries as soon as she sees her friend waiting outside. "What the fuck you doin'?"

"I'll have none of that dirty talk, my gal!" Ma calls through.

I join Flo at the window. Sally Richardson can't stand still. She's dancing around like a Hottentot. "There's been two more!" she shouts up.

A sash on the opposite side of the street is thrown open. "Two more murders?" shouts Mrs. Puddiphatt.

Sally, liking the attention, cups her hands to her mouth to proclaim the news. "Two more bleeding murders overnight!" she yells at the top of her voice.

"Wait up!" hollers Flo. "We'll be down in a jiffy!"

Soon Flo is a tangle of stockings and petticoats and laces and pins. She can't find her boots and her hair's a right mess, but she gets dressed as if her life depends on it, and then she sees me. I'm just sitting on the bed, watching, and she gets angry. "Hurry it up, Con!" she snaps.

"What if I don't want to come?" I reply.

She's got one arm in the sleeve of her coat, but she stops, like she can't believe her ears. "Don't want to come? But, Con, why ever not?" She's looking at me with those puppy eyes of hers that she sometimes uses on Danny.

My objections suddenly melt away. I can't tell her that I don't want to come because of a nightmare. I shake my head. "If I must," I tell her, and her face splits into a broad smile before she rushes to the window.

"Give us another tick, Sal!" she tells her waiting friend. But she needn't worry. Sally's being kept busy by the neighbors who are huddling round her, wanting to be kept up to date with all the momentous news.

It's another five minutes before I'm ready and we make our way toward Duke Street. I can tell straightaway that something's wrong. I count four or five coppers and see there's a huddle of people standing by Church Passage. Flo's eyes are open wide and I just feel sick. She grabs hold of an old woman passing.

"Where's the murders?" she asks her.

The old biddy throws a look over to Duke Street. "One of them was in Mitre Square," she says, showing the blackened stumps of her teeth. "Cut her guts out, 'e did," she says, beaming.

Her words break my dream. I feel like I'm

going to swoon and stagger a little on the pavement. My legs start to buckle and I have to steady myself against a wall.

"You all right, Con?" Flo asks. "You look ever so pale."

"My dream," I gasp.

"Yer what?"

I mumble my reply: "I had a dream there was a murder, right here in Duke Street." Luckily, she does not hear.

The murders are the talk of Whitechapel. With it being a Sunday, there's no newspapers, but word has spread, all right. And not just round the East End. By the afternoon, there's omnibuses and carriages coming in from the West End and beyond, disgorging hundreds of people at a time to see where *he's* claimed his latest victims. It's like they're tourists, all eager for a good day out. The Jews have set up their stalls again, only they're not happy. It's said that they found a piece of Catherine Eddowes's apron in an alley off Goulston Street and above the spot, written on the wall in chalk, was something against the Yids: *The Juwes are not the men who will be blamed for nothing.* That's what it said, or something like that. Anyway, the coppers rubbed it off before it caused any trouble. No one wants the Jews to riot. But it makes you wonder, don't it? He's so sick and twisted. They've got to catch him soon, haven't they?

CHAPTER 9

Monday, October 1, 1888

EMILY

I find myself in Whitehall, just by Big Ben. I can hear its chimes, but I cannot see the tower. It is barely light and a ghostly mist is rising from the river, making it even harder for ordinary people to see. But, of course, I see everything. I am standing on the banks of the Thames at Whitehall. My grandfather was a member of Parliament, so the vicinity is well-known to me. The plot where I find myself was originally earmarked for a new opera house, and I remember how excited Grandpapa had been at the time. Then later, how angry he was to hear that cultural excellence was to be sacrificed to the more mundane require-ments of the Metropolitan Police. The building site is to be their new headquarters.

I watch the burly man, a carpenter by trade, and his companion as they collect their tools from their usual hiding place. They're behind some boards that have been laid across one of the many vaults that run like veins below ground on the Scotland Yard plot. Theft is all too common on the building site and the men often come up with ingenious ways to conceal their precious hammers and chisels from the errant grasp of their fellow workers. On this particular morning, as the carpenter reaches into the blackness for his tools, he feels something soft on the ledge. Striking up a match, he squints into the half-light and can just about discern a large parcel wedged up tight in a niche against the wall. He scratches his graying head in thought and glances up toward his waiting companion, who is whistling tunelessly through gappy gums. He needs to get on, so he grabs his bag and sets off to start work on the floors above, giving scant thought to his discovery. Little does he know that the parcel's contents are about to put all of London, if not the entire country, into even more of a frenzy.

CONSTANCE

We stay close to home today. Two murders within an hour of each other! *He's* the Devil Incarnate! Our nerves are rattled and jangling like a jailer's keys. I wasn't keen on flogging all the way to Covent Garden, and Ma says we needn't go farther than Farringdon. So I'm not selling and we're just biding our time. I distract a geezer and Flo lifts his wallet early on and the two notes inside will keep us going till the end of the month, so we're feeling pleased with ourselves. But all that changes as soon as we see the *Daily News*. The newsboy has arrived at the corner of Farringdon Street not two minutes before. He's laden with the first edition. Soon he's donning his sandwich board and pacing up and down the pavement, shouting at the top of his lungs. At first, we can't see what it says on his board, or hear what he's calling. The clip-clop of hooves drowns out his cries, but whatever it is, it's drawing in the punters. Soon people are jostling to buy their copies and I look at Flo with a frown. Without a word, we join the scramble and soon I catch sight of the headlines and realize what all the palaver is about. Flo glares at me and I know what I must do. With my basket braced like a shield, I barge into the throng and bump into a clerk who's carrying a folded newspaper under his arm.

"Will you mind where you're going?" I says, all hoity, and I sniff the air like a French poodle. Meanwhile, Flo has relieved the gentleman of his copy without him catching hide or hair of her and it's mission accomplished.

"Well?" Flo is ratty. She gets ratty when she's nervous and she's registered the look of panic on my face.

"It's full of it," I tell her. I call out the headlines as if I'm reading from a menu card in a fancy restaurant. " 'Shocking mutilation of a body. Exciting scenes.' "

"Exciting scenes?" Flo raises an eyebrow and gives a long whistle. Danny has taught her how. Even she thinks that's a bit rich when two women have been butchered for some sick pervert's pleasure.

My eyes race down the columns, over the residents' lurid accounts and the paper's own opinion on the matter, to read about an arrest.

"An arrest?" echoes Flo.

I clear my throat to read the first sentence aloud. " 'Yesterday morning a tall, dark man wearing an American hat entered a lodging-house in Union-street, known as Albert-chambers.' " I tell her that his fellow lodgers thought he was acting dodgy, so the duty keeper called the cops. " 'On the arrival of the officer the stranger was questioned as to his recent wanderings, but he could give no intelligible account of them, though he said he had spent the previous night on Blackfriars Bridge. He was conveyed to Stone's End Police-station, Blackman-street, Borough,' " I say. But the account doesn't fool us.

"Don't prove nothing," Flo says with a shrug. Despite a moment's hope that the fiend was behind bars, the respite is short-lived.

"Oh, my Gawd!" I blurt out a second later.

"What is it?" Flo crowds in on me, shoving her head in my view. I push her away, but my mouth's so dry the words are like ashes on my tongue. I'm trying to read what it says. "He's sent a letter," I tell her.

"A letter?" She looks back at the newssheet and I notice my hands are starting to shake. "Sent to the Central News Agency, it was. Written in red ink." *Or is it blood,* I ask myself.

"What's he say?" She's as keen as mustard to know what he's written. They've published all of it, every word of evil, every syllable of hatred. So I read it out loud, and as I do so, I hear my voice is spiked with shock.

" 'Dear Boss,' " I begin. " 'I keep on hearing the police have caught me, but they won't fix me just yet.' " I look up and see the fear creep across Flo's face as I read the rest of the sick diatribe. But there's more. "He's given himself a name, and all," I tell her.

"A name?" Puzzled, Flo stiffens her neck.

"Signs himself Jack the Ripper, he does."

"Jack the Ripper," she wheezes, as if repeating the name robs her of her own breath. In our heads, we can both hear him say it.

EMILY

So today, murder has a new name. Of course, it's nothing new around Whitechapel. It lurks down pinched alleys and in dark court-yards. It lies on the cobbles in the fetid slums,

116

and crouches behind locked doors and in filthy rented rooms. But now it's been given a macabre immortality. Thanks to Scotland Yard's publication of the letter, the Whitechapel murders will live on in the imagination of the public for many years to come. From this day forth, the name Jack the Ripper will strike fear into the hearts of everyone who hears it. And that is exactly what **he** wants.

CONSTANCE

We're not late home that night. Early, in fact, and Ma, peering out at us from under a rag over a hot bowl of friar's balsam, is glad to see us back. She frets for us a lot these days.

"Thank the Lord," she says when she sees us, patting the condensed steam from her face. "I don't like you two dillydallying." The balsam eases her breathing, but the moisture's made the front of her hair all frizzy. "Worries the life out of me, it does, you being out with that monster on the streets."

Just then, there's a knock at the door and she jumps, even though she's expecting Mr. Bartleby again. He bumbles in, all wrapped up against the cold in a big brown coat, with the collar turned up, and a bowler hat.

" 'Evening, ladies," he says, wiping his feet on the doormat and his nose with the back of his hand. His gold rings flash in the lamplight.

Flo and me smile politely. Even though he's got his faults, we're glad he's come. It makes us feel safer having him in the house. We're all on edge and Mr. Bartleby knows it. There's a copy of the *Star* under his arm, but he looks at the table and sees we've already got one.

"Couldn't wait, eh?" he says.

Ma shakes her head. "Such a terrible business. It's just not safe round here, Harold." She hardly ever calls him by his Christian name in front of us. She's rubbing her thumb with her forefinger, making it sore. It's a sure sign her nerves are getting the better of her.

Mr. Bartleby, on the other hand, looks like the cat that got the cream. He's grinning from ear to ear. He says: "Have no fear, ladies. All will be well."

So Ma blurts out: "Have they caught 'im? Have they?"

Mr. Bartleby shakes his jet-black head, but he's still beaming. He takes off his hat and coat and hangs them on the peg near the door and replies like he owns the place. "It won't be long now, Mrs. P. Not with me on the case," he says.

"You?" cries Flo. There's scorn in her voice, more than is seemly to show.

Ma scowls at her, and Mr. Bartleby suddenly looks like a nipper that's been punched in the playground.

"What's happened?" asks Ma, trying to rescue his pride.

It seems to do the trick. He draws himself up and clears his throat, like he's going to make some big announcement. And he does, of sorts. "I've only been appointed to the Whitechapel Vigilance Committee."

That's the committee formed by George Lusk, the builder, after Annie Chapman copped it. They set up the patrols on the streets. There's other tradesmen that are members, too—carpenters and grocers, all full of their own self-importance. Mr. Bartleby's in good company there, all right. He's with his own kind.

"How come?" Flo says, although I'm pleased that this time her tone is a little softer. Even so, his face drops. He turns to us. He's waiting for Ma and me to say something. The silence makes me want to cringe, but Ma steps up after a second or two.

"That's wonderful news," she says. I can tell that smile of hers is forced. "Congratulations, Harold." Her voice is all funny and stiff.

Mr. Bartleby's face has lifted a little now and he sticks out his stomach and pulls back his shoulders. "They, or should I say, *we,*"—he throws Ma a gleeful smile—"want to offer a reward."

"A reward?" echoes Flo.

"They want to put up fifty quid for information that leads to the butcher's arrest."

"And they asked you for the old spondulicks?" Flo has the measure of him.

He huffs a little. "Indeed, they did." He seems proud they touched him for a quid or two. "George Lusk, he says to me, 'How about a pound, Harry?' And I says, 'I'm willing, George, just as long as you'll let me on your committee.'" He chuckles.

"So you bought your way in?" Flo just can't leave it alone.

"Now, look here. . . ." Old Bartleby's at the end of his tether.

"Hold your tongue, young lady!" snaps Ma.

Mr. Bartleby stiffens his neck and nods by way of thanks. "My first meeting's tomorrow night, and I'll get on this evil maniac's trail." He throws Ma a smile and hooks his thumbs under his braces. "I'll have the fiend behind bars in no time at all." He rocks back on his heels, wanting to look like a copper. But Flo and me know he's just a plonker. A well-meaning one, maybe. But a plonker, nonetheless.

Ma returns the smile a little awkwardly as he draws close to her. She doesn't have as much faith in him as he has in himself. None of us does.

CHAPTER 10

Tuesday, October 2, 1888

CONSTANCE

Today we're in Whitehall. Jim Dylan, the old joker, said he'd a load of timber to take to a building site at New Scotland Yard, so Flo and me got a lift on the back of his cart. We had to listen to his terrible jokes all the way there. "I had a thought the other day, ladies," he said, all serious like. "Then it got lonely!" He cracked up laughing and Flo giggled. I just smiled politely. It was like that all the way there.

You can't go to the same patch too often in our line of work. Old Bill always keeps a lookout for our sort, but maybe now with the murders, he'll have his eyes open for Jack the Ripper, too. Still, you can't be too careful.

It was a right bumpy ride from the City, I can tell you. The Strand was busy, too. A wagon had shed its load of barrels and that didn't help, neither. It's a good job I've put my Pa's old vest on, too. Winter's arrived early this year and I'm wearing my mittens for the first time. And the cold doesn't do Flo's chest no good, neither. Ma says she'll cough her guts out one of these days. She's a fine one to talk!

Anyway, it's after midday when we arrive and we plant ourselves by the Houses of Parliament, near the river. We reckon the toffs round here might buy a flower or two for their wives—or mistresses—and be touched for a few shillings, or a pocket watch, while we're about it. We get to work.

Business is slow at first, but it soon picks up and Flo's nimble fingers are kept very busy. There's an old dear, blind as a bat, with her butler, who stops to sniff my roses. So while she's making up her mind about which one smells the sweetest, Flo gets to work and relieves the geezer of a bob or two from the butler's purse. He doesn't even notice anything's missing when he comes to pay. After them, there's a young couple. So in love, they are, that they only have eyes for each other. They don't see Flo helping herself to a crown when the girl's choosing her bloom. Sometimes I wonder how she has the heart.

EMILY

I have returned to Whitehall, to the Scotland Yard building site, to watch events unfold. The carpenter I saw yesterday, who goes by the name of Frederick Windborn, happened to mention his strange find to his foreman, one William Brown. Mr. Brown is a curious fellow, so during a break for lunch, he asks to be shown the parcel. Together the two men stoop low into the vault and Brown is immediately struck by the smell.

"A bit of old bacon?" ventures Windborn, reaching for the large packet. He hauls it down from the shelf, disturbing a few feasting flies as he does so. Brown is not so sure. He watches with growing anxiety as the full horror of the contents slowly reveals itself to them. Wrapped in old newspaper and material and secured by various lengths of string, it soon becomes apparent that the "old bacon" is, in fact, human flesh. The two men have accidentally stumbled upon the naked torso of a woman.

I do not follow them after that. They leave the site in all haste to report their grisly find to the police. Not long afterward, a detective and two uniformed constables are on the scene. It is this commotion that attracts the attention of Constance and her sister.

CONSTANCE

I always keep my eyes open for rossers, so when I clock three of them together, it puts me on edge. And when I watch them pushing a handcart, it makes me curious.

"See them?" I ask Flo, nodding in the peelers' direction. "What d'ya reckon they're up to?"

"Let's go 'ave a butcher's," she grins, nudging my arm.

I glance at my basket. It's almost empty except for one measly posy and my feet are freezing. I fancy a change of scenery. "All right," I reply.

So we follow the rossers with the cart. A man is with them, but he's not under arrest. He's showing them where to go, leading the way through the high gates on Cannon Row. He's wearing a cloth cap and he's all dirty and it looks like he's a workman. After a few moments, we know that he is. He's taking the three policemen toward the river, to the building site that'll be the new police headquarters. Mind you, you'd need a good imagination at the moment to see how it'll be when it's finished. Today it's all cranes and scaffolding and mud. The ground is dug out to make tunnels and channels, like some mad mole has run amok in the soggy dirt.

"We best go back," I tell Flo, the mud sucking at my boots.

"Wait," she tells me, tugging at my sleeve. Her gaze is fixed on the men's heads as they bob up and down, breaking up great clods of earth with pickaxes and shovels. I'm assuming they're digging the foundations for the new building. I want to go back.

"There's nothing to see here," I tell Flo. "It's just mud." But again, she tugs at my sleeve as I turn.

"No. Wait," she tells me in a hoarse whisper, and I notice her eyes are on stalks.

It's tricky to make out what's so caught her attention, but I strain to see. There's a little cluster of men waiting for the coppers as they fast approach. Faces smeared with mud, they're scrambling down into the mire like mudlarks, but you can still catch their grim expressions. They're taking turns to jump down into a pit to look at something. One skinny lad has to be hauled back up by the others and breaks away to bend double and throw up in a nearby trench.

"Christ Almighty!" says Flo, and she grips me tight. I feel her breath hot on my cheek. "I think they've found another one."

"I don't like the look of this," I say, swinging my basket round. "We've got to get out of here." Back through the gates, we go. We've scarpered a few yards away from where we saw the coppers. I'm hugging myself, wrapping my own fingers round my arms against the cold and against the fear. "It's like he's following us," I whisper.

I wait for Flo to tell me not to be so stupid. Only she doesn't. She's out of breath and her nose is running. She wipes away the snot with the back of her sleeve, giving me a look at the same time. Barely have I stopped speaking, then Big Ben starts to chime. We both raise our gazes to the clock face that looms in the distance and see that it's five and it's getting dark.

"Jim'll be here soon," Flo says, trying to be cheerful. "He'll put the smiles back on our faces."

It'll take more than a few stupid jokes to lift my mood, I think.

EMILY

A crowd of laborers has gathered like flies around the spot where the torso lies. They jostle to get a better look, but many of those who manage to also double over and retch. Gilbert Johns is one of them.

"Move away! Away will you. This is a crime scene!" A bowler-hatted detective and two uniformed constables arrive on the scene. The detective, a clean-shaven young man, with sharp eyes, tries to swat the onlookers away. He and his hapless men do not relish their task. They know, from the ghoulish account that Windborn has just delivered at the nearby King Street Police Station, that what they are about to view will be unpalatable, to say the least.

The foreman has accompanied the policemen to the site. As the constables clear the path to the vault, Windborn remains anxious. He shakes his head. "The gaffer's not going to like this," he tells the detective.

"*The gaffer?*"

"Sir William," replies Windborn. "Sir William Sampson. Him what's the head of everything. Him that pays our wages. He'll not like this holdup. If we can't work, he'll stop our money."

The detective—Hawkins is his name—has only recently been promoted. It's clear to me that such responsibility sits heavily on his young shoulders. He shrugs a little too much and his cough is caused by nerves rather than any physical congestion. Any inconvenience caused to these leering laborers is of little consequence to him. There is much more at stake.

I feel nothing but pity for him and his men as they gaze with a mixture of disgust and horror at the maggot-infested torso, with its breasts exposed for all to see. While his men keep curious eyes at bay, Hawkins crouches on his haunches, a handkerchief clamped to his mouth. He has seen decomposing corpses before. It was part of his training, but this . . . this was something else: a dismembered hunk of rotting meat, foul and fetid and, most shockingly, human.

He waits for what must seem to him an age for the medical officer, who joins them perhaps half an hour later. Dr. Bond is an elderly man, with silvery hair and a large moustache, and his arrival is clearly welcome. He seems to bring a semblance of order to the proceedings.

"So," Bond begins, staring at the torso that presents itself to him on the mud. The newspaper in which it is half wrapped rustles slightly. He stills it with the cane he carries. He will examine the remains more closely later. For now, he is keen to see where it was found.

"In here, I assume?" he asks Hawkins, pointing to the large slab of stone that's been heaved across the entrance to the vault to keep out prying eyes.

The young detective nods. "Sir."

The doctor frowns and takes off his topper, handing it to a waiting policeman.

Two constables roll away the slab to allow the doctor access. Bond ducks down into the vault and begins his inspection immediately. I follow just in time to see his fingers spider along the ledge. He is holding his breath, shutting his mouth and nose to the sickly sweet smell that pervades the vault. The second constable was ordered to follow the doctor into the catacomb and now holds up a lantern so that Bond can inspect the shelf. He examines the wall, holding up a magnifying glass to it, before returning to the torso itself. He notes the maggots and the advanced state of decomposition, but pays particular attention to the twine used to bind the parcel.

"Well, sir?" Detective Constable Hawkins is waiting outside, thankful to be in the open air. The stink of the Thames is as perfume compared with the stench in the vault.

Bond takes out his pocket handkerchief and blows his nose in an attempt to rid his nostrils of the foul smell. He is highly regarded by the police force, and he is aware he has not been summoned to the grisly scene by chance.

"You want to know if this is linked in any way to the other, I presume, Hawkins?" He is wiping his hands with his handkerchief, paying particular attention to the webbing between his fingers, as if he is about to conduct an operation.

The younger man dips his head and looks away, as if too embarrassed to admit it. "The thought had occurred to me, sir."

Of course, I knew he was referring to the arm, the one that had been found in the river mud near the sluice off Ebury Bridge Road not three weeks before. Bond had examined it shortly afterward.

The doctor flourishes his handkerchief before secreting it in his pocket once more. "It is a possibility. The string," he says with a sniff. It is clear to me that he is recalling the twine he had found when he was called to examine it. It had been used as a ligature to prevent the blood draining from the cut end.

The older man looks up and fixes the young detective with the measured gaze that comes with years of experience. "But I'll wager you also want to know if this is the work of the dastardly fiend who is stalking Whitechapel, eh, Detective Constable?"

"I . . . um. Well, I . . ." Hawkins's manner can lurch from being upright and bold to slouched and unsure in the blink of an eye.

Bond shrugs and snatches his hat from the waiting constable. "And that, I fear, I cannot say," he tells him, clamping it down on his head. "Not yet, at any rate." He picks up his medical bag and glances back down at the unsavory parcel. "See to it that the remains are removed to Millbank Street. I shall examine them there."

"Yes, sir," replies Hawkins, almost standing to attention. As soon as the medical officer is out of sight, he orders his reluctant men to load the parcel into the undignified conveyance. He turns his back on them so that he does not have to witness their repulsion as they manhandle the torso unceremoniously into the cart. And as he does so, facing toward the slow flow of the slate-gray Thames, I see his lips move as he asks himself the question that Dr. Bond was unable to answer, at least for the time being. Could this poor, unfortunate woman—with neither a head, nor legs, nor arms—be Jack the Ripper's sixth victim?

CHAPTER 11

Wednesday, October 3, 1888

CONSTANCE

My poor old feet are killing me. I'm walking back home after a long day that's left me with three bunches of wilting herbs. I think they're past saving and that means money down the drain. Flo's running some chores for Ma, but I can't wait to sit down in front of the fire.

The light's fast fading, even though it's just after four o'clock, so I'm not loitering. I'm coming down Fournier Street when who should I spot but the Irish lad with the funny walk called Mick. He's the one who saw us home safe the night we came back from the Egyptian Hall. He's pushing a cart that's covered in tarpaulin. I'm not sure I want to speak to him again, so I look the other way, pretending not to notice him. The trouble is, he notices me.

"Hello!" he says cheerily.

I turn and feign surprise. We're standing quite close to each other and it's then that I catch it on the air—a foul stink that makes me want to retch. My eyes instinctively dart to his barrow. Flies buzz around it. He sees me pull a face.

131

"Meat for the cats," he tells me. "Don't 'alf stink!"

I nod. "I'll say." He's wearing a leather apron that's smeared with blood as well. I think I'm going to be sick. I offer him a vague smile, then walk on.

"See you around some time!" he calls after me. I pretend I don't hear him.

Later that night, Flo and me sit by the fire, watching the dying embers and holding our hands out to them now and again, making the most of the warmth. Mr. Bartleby's come and gone and Ma's long been tucked up. Neither of us is in much of a mood for talking. We're too wrapped up in our own thoughts. It's Flo, as usual, who breaks a long silence.

"You 'eard that physick went to the police?"

I look up at her. The candle went out a while ago and the only light in the room comes from the fire.

"*Physick?*"

"Yeah. One of them that says they can see into the future. Speak to dead people and all that load of cobblers." She wiggles her fingers.

"You mean a *psychic*."

"*Physick. Psychic.* Don't matter what name you give 'em, they're all balmy, if you ask me. Anyway, this bloke reckons he knows who the Ripper is."

132

I want to say that nobody did ask her. But I don't. "Robert James Lees," I tell her.

She shrugs. "Couldn't tell ya his name."

"So what happened?" I'm curious to know for my own peace of mind.

She shakes her head. "What d'ya think? He pipes up and goes to the rossers and they say they'll look into it. They didn't tell him he was off his rocker to his face."

I know why she's telling me this story. She's testing me. I'm waiting for the question to come and, sure enough, it does. "So you reckon you're physick. . . ."

"*Psychic!*" I snap.

I've wounded her. "All right. Keep your hair on!"

I take a deep breath. "I'm sorry," I say, adding: "And, no, I don't. I'm not psychic. It was just a dream, that's all."

Flo lifts the poker and jiggles the last few embers. A lone flame suddenly bursts into life, then dies down just as quickly.

"You got an idea, though."

"*An idea?*"

" 'Bout who this Jack might be." Flo's suggestion stuns me. "You must have thought about it," she goads.

My mind flashes to Abel Gipps, all jumpy and excitable the morning they found Annie Chapman, the bootblack with his hook on

Commercial Street and then to Mick and his bloody apron and the cart full of stinking meat. What if there was another body in there, all chopped up and ready to feed to cats?

"Not really," I reply. Even though she can't make out my expression in the shadows, she knows I'm lying. "What about you?" I ask, keen to take the attention off myself.

I see her head nod in the dying glow. "I've got my suspicions," she tells me, tapping her nose with her forefinger.

"Oh?" She seems quite sure of herself.

"Yes. And he's known to us all."

I'm shocked. "Who?"

"A regular visitor, he is." She lifts her gaze to the ceiling, to where Ma sleeps, and the light catches the whites of her eyes and I read her thoughts.

"No!" I cry out, all breathy.

She nods and lifts a hand to count on her fingers. "Always wants to know what's going on, keen to blame the Jews, all cocky about the Vigilance Committee."

What she says is true. But, of course, it's no proof that Mr. Bartleby is a murderer. Nevertheless, I think of his fingers touching mine at the table when we held that séance and the way he looks at me sometimes and I feel my flesh creep.

"Yes," says Flo. "I think, from now on, Con, we

should watch our mutual friend, as Mr. Dickens would call 'im."

I think, perhaps, she's right. Every man in Whitechapel is under suspicion.

CHAPTER 12

Thursday, October 4, 1888

EMILY

Of course, it suits the press to maintain the fiction that all the murdered women have died by the same monstrous hand. A mania is taking hold of the city—indeed, the whole country. It has even spread as far as America, where various near-hysterical newspaper reports even point the finger of suspicion at their own citizens.

I, therefore, wonder how much publicity will be given to the letter that is being held firmly in the hands of Chief Constable Adolphus Williamson. I am in his office at Scotland Yard. Because of the chief constable's years of experience, Chief Inspector John Shore has called upon the services of Dolly Williamson, the name by which the officer is known. Sadly, however, the chief constable's heart condition and subsequent failing health have meant he can no longer pursue a very active role within the force. He cannot take personal charge of the investigations and direct operations, as some think he should, but his expertise is still much prized.

As I watch him read the missive for the first time, I can see the beads of sweat emerge on his forehead, even though away from the fireplace, the room is really quite cool. He takes out his handkerchief to mop his brow. He is experiencing palpitations.

"What do you make of it, Dolly?" asks Shore, after an anxious wait. He is leaning forward. His voice is low.

The chief constable looks up, then tosses the letter on the desk as if it repulses him. "The man's obviously depraved," he says, pulling at his collar in a vain attempt to loosen it.

"Obviously," replies Shore. "But is it genuine?" He jabs the letter with his fore-finger. "Are we dealing with two mad killers?"

Williamson scoops up the sheet of paper again into his sweaty hands. He reads out loud: " 'I swear I did not kill the female whose body was found in Whitehall.' " He pauses and shakes his head before carrying on: " 'If she was an honest woman, I will hunt down and destroy her murderer. If she was a whore, God will bless the hand that slew her.' "

"A religious maniac?" suggests Shore. "The references to the women of Moab and Midian . . ." He points to another sentence, written in an educated hand.

Williamson nods slowly. "It certainly looks like there's two of them on the loose."

Shore lets out a sigh and slumps back into his chair. "Well, at least we can tell the press that the Whitehall body might not be the Ripper's sixth victim, eh?"

The chief constable shrugs his shoulders in a gesture of resignation. "Tell them what you want. Whether they believe us is another matter," he says.

It is clear to me that the police are in disarray. They are beginning to look like fools in the eyes of the increasingly anxious public. And there is more bad news to come.

CONSTANCE

Flo's talk of Mr. Bartleby being Jack has unsettled me even more. I haven't seen him since, but I know that when I do, I won't be able to act normal round him. And now the papers are full of letters about psychics. They're coming forward in droves, all wanting to help solve these terrible crimes. Mediums calling on the victims, or tracking down Jack; clairvoyants seeing him in their mind's eyes; spiritualists in contact with the other side—they're everywhere, and I know that means Mr. Bartleby'll be after me, like a dog with a bone. I just don't know where to turn. *Miss Tindall, where are you?*

EMILY

I hear her call, but I cannot answer. Not just yet. Poor, dear Constance is not the only woman feeling threatened in Whitechapel, and even farther afield, at this time. From the length and breadth of London, and beyond, anxious people are coming forward with their suspicions: errant lodgers, absent husbands, oddly-behaved employees. Every man has become a suspect; and if they are foreign, or Jewish, it seems they are even more likely or capable of committing fiendish atrocities. It does not surprise me in the least, then, to learn that this Robert James Lees, a self-styled spiritualist and medium, has come forward to offer his psychic services to the police. I fear the man is a well-meaning fool. He claimed he could attempt to get in touch with the victims, no doubt for a fee. Wisely, the police have declined. There are too many at the moment who fancy themselves blessed with such supernatural powers. Either they are poor, deluded dupes, or simply eager to make money on the back of a fear that is verging on mass hysteria. The true ones who are chosen do not put themselves forward. They are sought out and they are few. I am eternally thankful that I have been given the power to find them.

CHAPTER 13

Sunday, October 7, 1888

EMILY

I'm in Green Park in Mayfair, watching poor, dear Pauline. If only she knew. If only I could tell her. The autumn leaves are starting to fall and now and again a gust of wind sets them in a flurry. There's a bite to the air. It's not the time to loiter, but she sits on a bench, clutching one of the last letters I ever sent her. Despite the cold, she's reading it and smiling and crying at the same time. Past events, both happy and not so happy, meld into one long memory, like a photograph in a frame, to make a complete picture of a life. She remembers me with deep fondness. It is important for us to be remembered, as if the very act of remembrance keeps us alive. The trouble is, when what has happened is uncertain, then the picture becomes blurred.

"Emily." She whispers my name in a long,

deep sigh. When she inquired about me at St. Jude's the other day, she was told, like Constance had been, that I had left without leaving a forwarding address. She has evoked my name out loud, and I feel her thoughts reach out to me, like a gentle breeze that ruffles reeds. I know what I must do. But before that, there is so much more to impart, not to Constance, not yet, nor indeed to Pauline, but to you.

I'll take you back to April of this year. Sunday in Whitechapel could by no means be regarded as a day of rest; although for most, it still held religious significance, even if not a Christian one. As there were barely any parks or open spaces in this part of London, its inhabitants would take to the streets on a Sunday. Since all the shops were closed, too, there was little to do but stroll in the open air. The roadway was filled with horse-drawn vehicles and the footways were crowded with huddles of people talking. However, if you passed by, you would notice that the language they were speaking would, in all probability, not be English. Whitechapel to the average Englishman was becoming a foreign land. It was evolving into a refuge for Jews. They came from all over Europe: from Poland and Galicia, from Russia and Germany. In fact, they come to Whitechapel from every country where they have been persecuted and hounded out because of their race. For the most part, they are welcomed here, blending in with the indigenous population, while strictly observing their own customs. Their behavior is generally good. Drunkenness among the men is not common and there is little aggression toward women. On the whole, they are a sober, industrious people. Being aliens in faith and speech they are, of course, not under any obligation to observe the Christian Sabbath. Yet, they take this opportunity to see to it that their children are even better versed in the ways of their religion. The attendance at Jewish Sunday schools is fast becoming the envy of many a Christian parish. Thousands of Jewish boys and girls regularly attend these classes and their promotion is rightly seen as ensuring the future of Judaism in London, at the very least.

As I mentioned before, by contrast, our own Sunday school at St. Jude's was a paltry, halfhearted affair. Attendance was declining and, it seemed to me, there was a general antipathy toward the religious education of young girls and boys. For years, the Sunday school at St. Jude's had been run by a small committee headed by one Mrs. Hilda Parker-Smythe. I'd had some success running a literacy group for women, and Reverend

Barnett felt that my experience might bring fresh impetus to the classes. He, therefore, asked Mrs. Parker-Smythe to allow me to take a regular lesson. By reputation, she was a prickly woman and very set in her ways; and although the committee passed my appointment, she, herself, seemed most reluctant to accept me. Our first meeting certainly reinforced the rumors I had heard. Politely and gently, without wishing to tread on anyone's toes, I began my classes in March.

I first became aware of Dr. Melksham's presence after a class in April. Mrs. Parker-Smythe had told me of his arrival. He was the representative of a great benefactor—a titled gentleman, I was told, and had come as his agent to see that the money he'd donated was being well-spent. A dapper-dressed man, in late middle age, his silver hair was brushed back from a thin, narrow face, which was cut in two by a razor-sharp moustache, waxed at the edges. That first Sunday afternoon he was greeted, very cordially, I noted, by Mrs. Parker-Smythe and directed to take a pew at the back of the church. From here, he could watch my pupils recite various passages from the Bible. Constance and I were teaching them about St. John's Gospel and the children took turns to deliver the particular verses they had been asked to study. They did so with different degrees of ability—some hesitant and shy; others, like Molly Deakin, with a pleasing confidence. Anxious that our guest should be impressed by my students' efforts, I was glad to see a smile on his face at the end of the lesson.

As the pupils filed out of the church past him, under his watchful gaze, I approached him, hoping to be introduced by Mrs. Parker-Smythe, who was standing nearby. When I caught his eye, he granted me a polite nod, but that was all. Mrs. Parker-Smythe clearly had no intention of introducing us. Instead she guided him away from me and into the vestry, closing the door firmly behind her. I was put in my place. Now I know why.

CHAPTER 14

Monday, October 8, 1888

CONSTANCE

They're burying Catherine Eddowes today. She was the one they found in Mitre Square with the tip of her nose sliced off and slits cut into her eyelids. Only the other night, an artist took it upon himself to chalk pictures of the victims' bodies on the pavement. Drew a big crowd, they did. For a few halfpence, you could round off your Saturday night's entertainment with the sight of women's innards all ripped out. It's not my idea of a good time, but Flo was all for it. She and Danny were there, elbowing their way to the front to catch a butcher's of the squalid cartoons in all their ghoulish detail.

So it's no surprise that while Ma wants to go and pay her respects, Flo just wants to see the crowds and lap up the atmosphere. If they still hanged criminals in public, she'd have been at the front of the mob. But this is a funeral—the funeral of Jack the Ripper's fifth victim—so the world and his wife will come out, and Flo is never one to miss the chance to lift a few souvenirs of the occasion. I decide to go with her, not to ogle and gloat, but to mourn in a dignified way, the way Miss Tindall would mourn.

Miss Tindall. She wasn't at church on Sunday, neither. I asked a few people if they knew where she was—old Mrs. Grimthorpe and Timmy Porter, who's always got his grubby fingers on the pulse, but no one had seen her for the past six weeks, not since just before Martha Tabram was murdered, come to think of it. Not since Jack chose his first victim. A horrible thought suddenly lands in my head. No, I tell myself. I'm just being foolish. My mind flashes back to the vaults near the Thames and to the wheelbarrow with the remains in it, and a terrible wail rises from somewhere deep inside me. It catches in my throat, but I manage to cough it back.

"You all right, Con?" asks Flo. I stare unseeing into the speckled looking glass I'm polishing above the hearth in the front room.

"Yes," I say quietly. I see the girl in the mirror give a tight smile. "Yes," I repeat, more convincingly, I hope, this time. But I am not.

Later that morning, we dig out all the black clothes we can muster. Flo says she wants to show willing. Ma and me—or rather Ma and I—have got black bonnets and Flo's in her black jacket with its fake-fur black trim. She flings a black boa over her shoulder as well. It's too showy, but my lips remain shut tight. I think she knows that I find her ways a bit vulgar at times. When I see her act like that, it's as if there's a stone in my shoe and I want to be rid of it. Her manners are beginning to irk me. I don't want us to grow apart, but I fear we are.

Just after one o'clock, we join a steady stream of people heading for the City Mortuary in Golden Lane. Everyone's keen to give poor Kate a good send-off as the cortege leaves for the cemetery at Ilford. I glance up to see the windows and roofs of the buildings on the route rammed with gawpers. It's a big do. There's a fancy hearse, a mourning coach with her relatives and friends inside, and a brougham with the newspapermen. One of her sisters lays a lovely wreath on the polished coffin as it's placed in the hearse. Real touching, it is. Course I didn't know her, but it don't stop me from welling up. I just hope she didn't know much about it when it happened. Let's pray she's in a better place now, away from the dark, dirty alleys of Whitechapel, enjoying the light.

Even Flo is quiet when we arrive back home later that afternoon. It wasn't the big party she was expecting. It was quite sad, really; just how a funeral should be. No one deserves to die like that. Catherine Eddowes might have been treated like scum in life, but at least in death, people gave her a bit of dignity. Miss Tindall says that every human being should have certain rights, no matter their religion or the color of their skin, or whether they're rich or poor, man or woman. It seems to me that a good few politicians haven't heard that yet. Maybe it's time they did.

EMILY

What a sad affair these funerals are: an earthly show of both pomp and sorrow for those departed. Better to bury our bodies under trees so that we can at least feed the soil as we decay. In death, we should nourish those still in life.

Reflecting today on Catherine Eddowes's

short, tragic time on earth has inevitably led me to think about my own. Do I regret what I did? Of course. I was shortsighted, selfish, if you like. But I was also desperate. I could see no other way. Hindsight is a wonderful thing, but even now—now that I have the gift of it—I am not certain how I could have done things differently. I felt like a cornered animal. I suppose I could have put my head in the sand. I could have kept quiet, not raised questions. But it was not in my nature to remain silent when I suspected that something was so terribly wrong. As it turned out, my initial suspicions were grounded. I was right all along, but no one would believe me; or if they did, they were too afraid to add their voice to mine and speak out about the wickedness that was being perpetrated under their very noses.

I know Pauline would've believed me. As Constance watches a funeral procession a few miles away, Pauline Beaufroy sits straight-backed at the Sessions House in Westminster. The place is packed to the rafters. The great, the good and the darn-right evil are all eager to hear the lurid details of the Whitehall torso at the opening of the inquest. It does not surprise me to see Pauline amongst them. Her visit to her brother-in-law has done nothing to allay her fears about her sister's whereabouts.

If anything, it has compounded them. After she had drawn a blank at St. Jude's, she decided to return home to Sussex, but with the discovery of this new victim in Whitehall, her fears for Geraldine have turned into anguish. So she has returned to London and I watch her as she sits, notebook and pencil in hand, jotting down various facts.

The coroner, John Troutbeck, seems capable enough, given that his witnesses are of very little help. They are comprised of the workmen on the site; the foreman and several laborers can add nothing of any value to the proceedings. In fact, it is only when Dr. Bond, the medical examiner, takes the stand, that evidence of any import comes to light. Pauline starts scribbling frantically as he speaks. His examination of the torso has uncovered several interesting facts. For example, he estimates the woman was well-nourished and of mature age—twenty-four or twenty-five years, perhaps. She would have been tall, with fair skin and dark hair. The date of death would have been from six weeks to two months ago, and the decomposition occurred in the air, not the water. Most crucially to the press, her uterus has been removed. Jack has struck again, or so it seems.

"Was there anything to indicate the cause of death?" asks Mr. Troutbeck.

Dr. Bond shakes his head. "Nothing whatever."

"Could you tell whether death was sudden or lingering?" presses the coroner.

The doctor pauses thoughtfully before his reply. "All I can say is that death was not by suffocation or drowning. Most likely, it was from hemorrhage or fainting."

Next the coroner asks about the woman's possible height.

"From our measurements," replies Bond, deferring to his colleague Mr. Hebbert, seated nearby, "we believed the height to have been five feet eight inches. That opinion depends more upon the measurements of the arm than those of the trunk itself."

Ah, yes, the arm. This limb, I should tell you, was uncovered several days previously on the shore of the Thames at Pimlico. Once joined to the torso, it was, according to Dr. Bond, "a refined hand" and one not used to manual labor.

"Was the woman stout?" asks Mr. Troutbeck.

"Not very stout, but thoroughly plump; fully developed, but not abnormally fat," comes the reply. She has not borne any children.

I listen intently to what he has to say. He impresses me. Yet, it is not enough. He also states that the adhesions to one of the dead woman's lungs indicate severe pleurisy at some stage. Despite such helpful analysis, however, Mr. Troutbeck seems just as baffled as everyone else as to how the torso arrived on the scene in the first place. Exasperated, he adjourns the inquest for two weeks.

No doubt Constance will be keen to read an account of this initial session, news of which will be plastered all over tomorrow's scandal sheets. Their accounts, I'm sure, will only fuel her fears.

CONSTANCE

So we're sitting by a fire that's just clinging onto life like a sickly child. We haven't lit the candles and the room's all gloomy, like our moods. Flo's made us all a brew. We sip the tea in our own wordless worlds, and no one mentions food. For once, none of us is hungry. It's like the sorrow of the afternoon's events and the fear that lies below it have hollowed us out inside, and we're not ready to be filled again. We're just lost in our own thoughts. Ma's chest is bad. It always is when she's upset or tense; and for a little while, the only sound to be heard is her wheezing, like a kettle on the hob, and the odd tinny rattle.

Eventually her breathing steadies and after a while she says she'll go up to bed. Flo and I are left alone. It's that cold that we're still wearing our coats and Flo draws her chair closer to mine.

At first, I think she just wants to keep warm, but then I see her reach into her jacket pocket.

"I heard two old fellas talking about the body in Whitehall," she tells me in a half whisper. She cocks her head over to the door to make sure Ma isn't there. "The Whitehall Mystery, they call it," she says to me, and she pulls out a square of newspaper. She draws the lamp near so that its faint light falls on her hands and starts to unfold a page of today's *Star*.

I don't bother to ask where she got the bit of newspaper from. All I'm interested in is the headline: WHITEHALL DISCOVERY.

"Well," she says, nudging me impatiently after a moment.

I look up at her with a frown. "It says they're looking for a toff," I tell her.

"A toff," she repeats, then scans the newspaper again, as if she can understand the letter.

I read verbatim, as Miss Tindall would say: " 'Rumor at times like these invariably gets in advance of truth, but in what are known as Government circles highly sensational revelations are anticipated.' "

Flo is staring at me, openmouthed. "What's that mean?"

"It means they think someone important did it," I tell her, but my eyes are already straining to read the next few sentences. "They've found more bones at Guildford," I say. My voice dips as I conclude: "But they belong to a bear." My forefinger flies up: " 'and therefore have no relation to the human remains found at Westminster.' "

Flo's shoulders slouch. She seems disappointed. She thought she was onto some juicy new revelation and she turns her face to the shadows. But it's the last sentence in the report that suddenly catches my eye. I don't bother to read it out loud. I read it only to myself. It says: *A feature in the case of the discovery of the mutilated body at Whitehall is the number of missing women brought to the notice of the authorities by persons making inquiries respecting the remains.* A cold shiver again. How can it be that so many women are missing? The terrible thought seizes me by the throat once more. Could Miss Tindall be one of them?

CHAPTER 15

Tuesday, October 9, 1888

CONSTANCE

We're up with the larks as usual. But today our plan is different. Because they're digging the tramway along Commercial Street, it's causing chaos on the footways, especially in the mornings when everyone's rushing to work. All herding together like cows, they are. Some carriages are even dropping off their well-heeled passengers at the end of the road to avoid the diversions. Therefore, Flo and I have been and got some white carnations for gents' buttonholes. We reckon they'll go down well with City types. "A bloom to brighten your day, sir!" I say with a smile. Some of the swells fall for it. They think they're only parting with a penny, but there'll be a fair few bankers who find they've "mislaid" their wallets before they get to work if Flo has her way. They'll be so distracted by the navvies and the cranes that they won't notice her fingers in their pockets.

After market, we come back home for a brew before we start work. That's when Ma asks me. Wheezing like a steam train, she is, and I see that she's been rubbing her thumb again to make it bleed. She sits down with us at the table. I pour good, strong cups for us all and Flo slices the bread, which has already started to go moldy. The tea soon seems to perk the old girl up, and after a moment or two, she's back smiling again when we tell her our plan for the day. Then I see her fixing me with her weather eye. She looks a bit cheeky, more like Flo than usual, and she says to me, "Madame Morelli's holding a special do tonight."

I put down my cup. "What sort of *do?*" I ask.

Ma leans forward, her bosom propped on the table. "She's hired out the concert room at the back of the Frying Pan. She's going to try and contact the dead women."

Flo slaps a thick slice of bread onto a plate and pulls a face at Ma. "*What?* You're having a laugh!" she snorts.

I know she's not. There's lots of phonies jumping on the bandwagon at the moment. Only in yesterday's *Star*, I read of a séance up north in Bolton, where the medium described Jack as looking like a farmer. She says he'll be caught in the act of committing another murder.

For a moment, Ma looks a little wounded; then she shifts in her seat and gazes into her teacup. "Madame Morelli says that if anyone can reach the dead gals, she can, so she's going to try and get in touch with Dark Annie and Long Liz Stride and the others."

Flo's expression suddenly turns and she nods thoughtfully. "She'll make a killing out of that," she mutters. Then realizing what she's just said, she lets out a little laugh. "If you'll pardon the pun," she adds.

Ma turns to me and reaches for my hand that's holding my cup up to my mouth. "You'll come with me, won't ya, love?" I feel her fingers, cold and rough against my warm skin.

She's not quite pleading, but I couldn't say

"no" to her, could I? I forgo my sip of tea for a moment. "Of course, I will," I say with a smile, but I immediately regret it.

EMILY

The Whitehall inquest has left Pauline in a most fearful state. She decides, therefore, to pay a second visit to her brother-in-law—only this time, she is in a less forgiving mood. I can tell from the set of her jaw and the precision of her gait as she climbs the steps to his Harley Street home that she means business. She yanks at the bell.

Dora answers. The door opens wide and the cold of a foggy October day blasts the girl's face. Despite the chill, she smiles. "Miss Pauline," she says with a curtsy.

"Good day, Dora," comes the reply. This time, she does not wait to be invited in. Rather she steps over the threshold, crosses the hall and heads straight toward Terence Cutler's study. Dora does nothing to dissuade her. The only concession the determined caller makes to privacy is that she knocks resolutely before entering.

"Yes," comes Cutler's voice from within. He is shocked when he looks up from his desk to find his sister-in-law striding into the room to stand in front of him. Her expression tells him she is spoiling for a fight. He leaps up from his chair.

"Pauline!" He is almost standing to attention. "Geraldine is still not returned."

Pauline Beaufroy tugs at the fingers of the glove on her left hand, one by one, as she faces her brother-in-law. "Please don't play me for a fool, Terence. I wasn't born yesterday. Tell me where she is. Mama and I are worried sick. We've heard nothing from her for more than six weeks now. And what with these terrible murders—"

"*What!?*" He stops her midsentence and regards her with incredulity. "You think your sister has been murdered?" There is derision in his tone.

"Do not mock me, Terence. I have just been to the inquest into the latest murder. The one at Whitehall."

His expression suddenly changes. "The torso?"

She nods and bites back the tears, which she feels welling up from somewhere amid her anger. "Precisely. They're saying the victim was not like the others."

"Oh?"

"They're saying she was well-nourished, not a working woman." She tries to remain calm, but finds it increasingly difficult. "They think she was in her twenties, Terence."

Cutler suddenly understands her unease and lifts up his palms in a gesture of surrender. He can no longer keep up the pretense. "You need to know the truth," he acknowledges with a sigh. "You'd better sit down." He points to a chair and Pauline smooths her skirts. He returns to his own seat and leans forward, his elbows on the desk. "Geraldine has left me," he begins, almost apologetically, then adds, "but I assumed she'd gone to Sussex to be with you."

Pauline scowls. The news is not well-received. "Then why on earth didn't you say before?" She sticks out her chin defiantly and slaps the desk with her palm. "So where is she now?"

Cutler shakes his head. "I'm afraid I have no idea." His eyes dart around the room as if he is looking for inspiration. He's playing for time, I can tell. "I thought, perhaps, she was making you tease me. You know she can be so cruel."

Instead of rising to her sister's defense, Pauline lets out an odd little laugh and nods. "I know she can be very strong-willed," she concedes. "But twisted? I think not, Terence." She shakes her head and allows her eyes to wander over the study at the bookshelves, a large framed etching of a woman's uterus and a somewhat unnerving human skeleton in the corner. Unlike her sister, she has always felt uncomfortable in the presence of such objects. She forces herself back into the moment. "Had you quarreled?" There's an icy silence as even she realizes she has overstepped the mark. "I'm sorry, Terence." She rolls her eyes. "I should not be so harsh on you, but I am so very worried."

Cutler leans back in his seat and tents his fingers. He is feigning a look of offense. Would you like a tea?" he asks in a conciliatory tone. He reaches for the small bell on his desk to summon Dora.

Pauline ignores his question. "You see, I know," she tells him before he has the chance to ring.

"You know?" Puzzled, he tilts his head and sets down the bell. "What do you know, pray?"

Suddenly losing a little of her bombast, Pauline dares not look at him. "I know that Geraldine could not give you the child you both so desperately wanted."

"Ah." She has come to the crux of the matter and Cutler seems temporarily stunned. He studies his fingernails for a moment. He scrubbed them so hard with carbolic soap the other day that he has grazed the skin. He starts to pick at the scab that has formed. He is grateful that his sister-in-law has no notion as to what caused Geraldine's barren state. "It's true it has caused a certain"—he searches for the word—"tension between us."

Pauline knows that "tension" is an understatement. Her sister had so often written to her bemoaning her apparent inability to bear Terence a child. But more recently, her deep disappointment had manifested itself in a resentment of other women, too. In one of her latest letters, she had highlighted the irony of her situation. Silently Pauline recalls her words: *"I have a gynecologist for a husband who helps women conceive, and yet he cannot help his wife, because I am beyond all hope."* In a subsequent one, she had even admitted that she envied all those women who were mothers because of Terence's expertise. The cruel irony of the situation was lost on no one. At the very least, she might try and harm herself; at the very worst, she might have fallen victim to a crazed murderer. The thought seizes Pauline violently.

"I fear we need to notify the police." They are the words she has dreaded hearing herself say for days, but now say them she must. Yet, she is not prepared for Cutler's reaction.

"No! Not the police. I beg you, no!" The words come tumbling from his mouth far too quickly. He continues to shake his head.

"But we must!" she protests. "Geraldine could be roaming the streets, confused." She pauses and gulps hard, thinking of the inquest. "She may even be . . ."

"No," Cutler says again, more calmly this time, but with desperation in his eyes.

"Why ever not?" asks Pauline, frowning in disbelief.

Cutler slumps back in his chair. "My work," he says, his eyes flicking to the nearby bureau, where he keeps his unsavory images of diseased female parts.

"What about it?" Pauline snaps. She is losing patience.

"Sometimes it takes me to Whitechapel." He squares up to her, as if bracing himself for her reaction.

"*Whitechapel?*" she repeats. The name clearly tastes bitter on her tongue."But I thought you worked at St. Bartholomew's."

He works his jaw again, then looks at his grazed fingers. "I sometimes treat women . . ." His eyes swivel in their sockets.

She looks at him in an odd way. *He is ashamed,* she thinks. "Women," she says slowly, as if trying to make sense of what he has just told her. "You treat . . . ?" Then the realization dawns and a look of shock scuds across her face. Her eyes widen. "You treat *fallen women?*" The color rises in her cheeks, but she manages to keep her emotions in check. After contemplating this newfound information for a moment, she asks him: "Does Geraldine know?"

Cutler nods slowly. "She found out about six weeks ago." He sighs deeply. "We had a guest in the house."

She stops him. *"A guest?"* She recalls Geraldine's letter, informing her about my arrival. Her brother-in-law is corroborating what she already knows. He will try and pin the blame on me. Yet, I am blameless. I had no idea when I mentioned to Geraldine that I'd seen her husband at the infirmary, that it would cause such a terrible rift between them.

"Yes," he goes on. "A do-gooder . . ."

Pauline springs to my defense. "I will not have you speak about my dear friend so!" she protests indignantly.

Cutler is checked, but only for a second. "Of course, I was forgetting you knew her," he says, but, nevertheless, he remains unrepentant. "When she recognized me, then Geraldine discovered, well . . ."

"So you'd kept your work there a secret from her?"

"Of course, I had! You know what she's like," he sneers. "She would have tried to put a stop to it instantly. As it was, she was disgusted at the thought of my treating 'fallen women,' as you call them. What would people say? That would soon put an end to the dinner parties and the coffee mornings. We had an almighty row. And that's why she walked out on me."

Pauline shuts her eyes for a moment to try and regain her composure. "And you haven't seen her, or heard from her since?"

"No." Again he shakes his head at the recollection of the incident and a pulse suddenly throbs in his temple. "No. I have not."

Pauline eyes him incredulously. "And you do not fear for her safety?" She shakes her head. "There is a maniac on the loose in London, possibly even two, and you are not out on the streets looking for your wife? What sort of a husband are you, Terence?"

The question is left hanging in the air for a moment before Cutler calmly replies: "Your sister is a strong woman of independent means. I have every confidence she can take care of herself."

What he fails to tell Pauline, of course, is that Geraldine, while going through her husband's correspondence, as she often did, had come across an envelope addressed to *Mr. T. Cutler, Whitechapel Workhouse Infirmary.* In it was a sum of money and a note assigning the cash, *For services rendered.* She knew that could only mean one thing. She had confronted her husband and found out her darkest suspicions were well-founded. Terence Cutler was an abortionist. The following day, she left.

Pauline rises from her seat. "Keep me informed of any new developments, won't you?" She is telling her brother-in-law, rather than simply asking him. She does not share his confidence in her sister's ability to look after herself.

Chapter 16

Thursday, October 11, 1888

Constance

My carnations went down well today and Flo's fingers went down even better. We made five shillings and threepence. To celebrate, Flo suggests we pop into the pie shop down the road. I agree, even though I've not the appetite. I've been thinking about the excursion to Madame Morelli's this evening and that feeling has come back again: that awful sense of foreboding I felt after I'd had that dream about another murder and it turned out to be true. It's like I foretold the future. So maybe Madame Morelli really does have a special power. Maybe there are people who can see into the future or speak to the dead. I know that Mr. Bartleby says that Madame Morelli's out to make a quick tuppence, just like we all are. But what if it's not a scam? What if some people know what's going to happen before it does or talk to them in their graves? The very thought of it scares the living daylights out of me, because I just might be one of them.

I watch as Ma wrestles with her coat. "Give us a hand, then, Con," she gasps, and I walk across the room and help her. "That's it," she says, fumbling with her buttons. "We mustn't be late, must we?"

There's a queue outside the side door of the Frying Pan. It stretches all the way round the corner into Thrawl Street. It's a colorless draggle of people, mainly women. The men that are there have been coaxed along by their wives, or else they've come to heckle. You can tell that from the banter.

"Polly Nichols! Polly Nichols! Are you there?" calls a joker in a shrill voice.

A couple of clever Dicks have clearly downed a few pints to pump up their courage. While some of the other punters chortle, the women nearby tell them to shut it and one of the older ones clocks the joker with her bag.

There's a bruiser on the door, stopping people from entering. He reminds me of a bulldog, his nose all flat and his jaw sticking out from beneath his baggy lips. It's cold and I can see my breath rise like fog on the air. I'm stamping my feet to keep warm as we shelter in the lee of the building when I spot a familiar face.

" 'Ere," says Ma, suddenly nudging me. "Ain't that Peggy Johns's boy? Mr. Bartleby says he's one of the lads helping out with the Vigilance Committee."

Ma's outburst makes Gilbert look our way. He's one of the bouncers, hired to keep order. They had a few problems last month when they had some gals wrestling in the altogether, and Pat Collins, the fiery Irish publican, don't want the same thing happening tonight.

Despite the cold, Gilbert's wearing shirtsleeves that are rolled up so that he seems ready for fisticuffs if anyone gives him any lip. I'm thinking he's a bit of all right, but he sees me looking and tips me a wink. I feel myself blush before I turn away.

We don't have much longer to wait, thank goodness. Bulldog is soon opening the double doors into the concert room and the queue piles in. We follow suit and find ourselves in a room that's not much bigger than the saloon bar itself, only there's a raised platform at one end. On it stands a table draped with a red plush cloth, but it's hard to see much else. The candles are lit, but there aren't that many of them, so my eyes strain into the gloomy corners. I suppose that suits Madame Morelli.

The seating is a free-for-all, but Ma manages to nab a couple of chairs at the front. I'd prefer to be at the back, out of Madame Morelli's creepy glare, but Ma says she's expecting us and she wants her to know she's there.

So everyone finds a seat. Those that don't, they have to stand at the back. Despite the temperature outside, it's soon stuffy inside, and sweat and smoke and beer hang heavy on the air. We number no more than fifty, but we've all paid our sixpence and we expect a good show. There's still a bit of jostling and elbowing from those that clearly don't take the séance seriously; the smart alecs and the nay-sayers. And me? Well, before my nightmare and the murder of Catherine Eddowes in Mitre Square, I'd probably have been with them. I held no truck with such music hall gimmicks. Granted, Ma's sessions with Madame Morelli have brought a lot of comfort to her, but I always thought the wily old Italian to be a bit of a charlatan. I doubt that she can speak to the dead any more than Mr. Bartleby can, but there's this feeling inside me that makes me think there might be something—something beyond. It's nagging like a pain, but I can't put my finger on it. Miss Tindall would know what it is, I'm sure of that. It's like there's this ache inside me that's growing and spreading and taking me over, as if someone is trying to get into my very soul and share it with me. And I'm very much afraid it has to do with *him*.

Someone starts to snuff out the candles, one by one. It's a signal for the audience to be silent and the noise fades with the light, although there's still the odd snuffle and giggle in the back seats. A moment later, Pat Collins—his red hair sticking out in wild tufts from both his head and his face—strides to the front of the platform. He clears his throat, like there's a growling dog at the back of it. I'm so close to him I can hear the phlegm rattle and smell the spilled beer down the front of his apron. Red Pat, as we call him, looks real serious.

"Ladies and gents," he says. I catch his expression in the candle glow. I can see something in his eyes and he's tugging at his fat hands. If he's putting it on, then he's a better actor than I thought he'd be. "Now there'll be no need for me to tell ye that tonight'll be a special one," he tells us in his singsong Irish jabber.

"It better be, or I'll be wanting my money back!" barks a wag standing at the side. But the audience turns on him and he's told to shush in no uncertain way by some old matrons in front of him.

Red Pat isn't put off his stride. He goes on: "I don't need to tell ye that the monster that calls himself Jack the Ripper is terrorizing our streets. None of us can sleep sound in our beds at night as long as he's roamin' Whitechapel."

All around me, heads are nodding in agreement. He's got them eating out of the palm of his hairy hand. "Six women is dead now, if you count the one at Whitehall the other day." Ma gives me a quick glance and I swallow hard. "And I don't need to tell ye that his sort won't stop at six. He's got a taste for the killing and the blood." He's getting more worked up now and a fleck of spittle arcs from his mouth and hits me on the cheek. "Many of ye will know that Madame Morelli is a respected medium about these parts, so she is." I stifle a snigger. "She's in regular contact with those who've passed. May God rest their souls." A few heads nod knowingly. Red Pat goes on: "That's why tonight she has agreed to try and contact one of the victims." There are a few loud gasps in the audience—as if they didn't know that that's what the evening is all about. "That's why tonight, ladies and gents"—his voice is rising—"we may walk away knowing the identity of this fiend that stalks our streets." There are even more gasps from the audience. "Ladies and gents, I give ye Madame Morelli," says Red Pat, waving his hand and retreating to the side.

So Madame Morelli glides onto the stage like a stately swan and it's all eyes on her as she sits behind the table. She plays the part well, I'll grant her that: a black veil and gloves, the very picture of a fragile woman in mourning. When Ma goes to visit her for her reading, she's always in black, too. Older Italian women wear it all the time, so I've heard. She's quite a pretty woman with olive skin and dark hair, flecked gray at the temples, although it don't show tonight. Tonight she's all in shadow. She's pulled out all the stops for her audience, all right. I'm expecting quite a show. We all are. You can hear a pin drop in here. It's like we're holding our breaths. Then she speaks. Her voice is quite low; but like all Italians, she sings instead of talks. Normally, it's quite gentle on the ear. But tonight, she's putting on a special voice for the punters. She knows that if she plays her cards right, she'll have them as putty in her hands, so she goes all out to impress.

"Ladies and gentlemen of Whitechapel," she says, moving her head slowly, scanning the gloom. "I ask you to be silent as I endeavor to make contact wiz zose who have died at ze brutish hand of ze murderer who calls himself Jack . . ." She pauses for effect. "Jack ze Ripper."

Ma suddenly reaches for my hand and holds it tight. She's scared, or excited, or both. I am too. Silence falls once more like a thick blanket on the room until another clever Dick shouts out: "Get on with it!"

He breaks the mood and I turn to the door to see Gilbert dispatch him quickly, amid all the cursing from the audience. It takes a few more seconds for everyone to settle again, but once Madame Morelli has composed herself, I can see that she closes her eyes and lays her palms flat on the table.

"Spirits, we mean you no 'arm," she sings out.

"We would speak wiz Martha Tabram, or Polly Nichols, or Annie Chapman. We would speak wiz Liz Stride or Catherine Eddowes, or wiz ze unknown woman in Whitehall. We would speak wiz any victim who 'as died at ze 'and of Jack ze Ripper."

It's still and quiet as the grave. No one dare move.

"Spirits," Madame Morelli calls out again. "Rap ze table if you are zere."

We catch our breaths; then after what seems an age, it comes. A knocking from the table. I suspect it's Madame Morelli stamping her foot, but, judging by the breathless squeals, most of the audience thinks it's for real.

"You are a victim of Jack ze Ripper?" asks Madame Morelli. "One knock for 'no,' two for 'yes.' "

One knock. Silence. Another. More gasps.

"You will speak to us?"

Two knocks.

From out of the corner of my eye, I see there's movement. Suddenly one of the women who had been standing swoons. Gilbert comes to the rescue again and carries her out. The room is all aflutter, anxious and unsettled.

"You will speak to us?" repeats Madame Morelli, as if to make sure the spirit hasn't been put off by the fainting woman.

Two knocks.

"Who are you, spirit?" she asks. "Reveal yourself to us."

So, by this time, everyone's nerves are on tenterhooks. I'm tight as a drum myself. Then, just when I think I can't take it no more, there's something moving in the darkness. And then I see it; we all see it. A white figure coming from the shadows that seems to hover on the stage. There are screams as the shape approaches. It's a woman, I can see. Or rather a girl. She is swathed in white, and her face is pale. She seems to be floating in the air just behind the table.

Madame Morelli is undaunted. She doesn't even turn to look at the ghostly specter that's suddenly appeared on stage. She lets the din die down before she asks: "Make yourself known to us. What is your name?"

The girl whimpers something and I smell a rat. All the dead women were at least in their late twenties. Even I can't make out what she says in the front row.

"We mean you no harm," repeats Madame Morelli. "You are among friends. Speak up."

The figure does as she is bid. "I am the one they found in Whitehall," she says shakily. Her voice is a breathless whisper.

A sigh escapes from my lips and the penny suddenly drops. It's a clever move to have the mystery woman appear to an audience of people who knew all the others. Polly Nichols was a regular at the Frying Pan and the others were well-known in these parts. "Welcome," greets Madame Morelli. "Step forward, and tell us your name, please."

So the spirit makes to move forward when suddenly there's this terrible renting sound, like a great tearing of material. There's a sharp intake of breath from the audience and a squeal from the spirit as the white floaty drapes that surround her are pulled tight and fall to the ground.

"Oh, my Gawd!" wails the girl, suddenly doubling up like she's naked. Only she's not. She's wearing a tatty old dress and her dark hair hangs down in straggles. She dares to look up for a second, then dashes off the stage. Before anyone has the wit to grab hold of her, she's out of the door, quick as you like, screeching like an alley cat. She's left the room in an uproar. There's people leaping up and down like Jack-in-the-boxes. Some are shaking fists, calling for their money back; a few are chuckling. Some go after poor Madame Morelli. The bulldog bouncer appears from nowhere and puts his big beefy body between the old fraudster and a couple of fishwives, who want to knock ten bells out of her. Someone lights a lamp or two, so that the commotion becomes clearer for all to see. Gilbert is ushering people out as fast as he can, and Red Pat is calling for calm while being buffeted by angry punters.

Ma gives me a sheepish look, as if to ask me how she could ever have been so stupid as to put her trust in such a fake. I squeeze her hand, then pat it with my other. She don't need to say nothing. It's not her fault she was taken in and fleeced. And, as I said, it gave her some comfort regarding courting Mr. Bartleby.

"Home?" I ask her.

She nods and coughs a little. I worry that the shenanigans might bring on one of her nasty attacks.

We're walking toward the door, past all those calling for their money back. Old Bill's got wind that something's up and Constable Tanner appears to see what all the fuss is about. This is his beat and he knows Flo and me and what we get up to. He's never caught us red-handed, but we know he's a mind to, one of these days. Ma's ahead of me and I tug on her sleeve. She hasn't noticed our lanky copper friend.

"Hold up, Ma," I says to her, as more people press toward the exit.

My words cause the woman standing by the door to look at me. I say woman, but as soon as I see her, I can tell she's a lady. I know from her bearing and from her hat—the hat with a rose on it that I've seen before, in St. Jude's. She's the lady I bumped into in the aisle, the morning I was asking after Miss Tindall. So she's standing by the door, having a word with Mrs. Puddiphatt, who nods at me when she sees me, as if she's been waiting for me; then she shuffles off. The lady looks up. Our eyes latch onto each other and she smiles at me. For a moment, I don't know whether I should curtsy or scarper.

"Miss Piper?" She's saying my name in her lovely voice with her consonants crisp as linen sheets. "Miss Constance Piper?"

I want to come back at her: "Who wants to know?" But I hear Miss Tindall's voice in my ear, telling me that would be rude. Instead, I say: "How can I help you, ma'am?" She's in her midtwenties, I'd guess, so she's likely married, although I can't see a ring because she's wearing gloves. There's something else she's wearing, too—a worried expression.

"I am so very glad to have found you," she tells me. She's leaning forward, and if I let her, I swear she'd give me a hug. I can see relief on her face as her lips widen into a smile. "Mrs. Puddiphatt pointed you out to me. It's about . . ." She hesitates. "I understand that you were in Whitehall the other day."

"Whitehall?" I croak. It's like she's just gone for my jugular. I can barely swallow. *How the hell does she know? Has she been following me?* I frown and switch round to see Ma. She's stopped to talk to Mrs. Bardolph, the fishmonger's wife, and hasn't seen my strange encounter. I'm glad of it.

"What if I was?" Suddenly finding my voice, I give up all my polite intentions, but my expression betrays me.

She nods and slides her eyes toward Ma. "I understand," she says in a low voice. "Tomorrow? Can we meet?"

My heart's in my mouth. I don't want Ma to see. I think quickly. "Christ Church. The graveyard. Eight in the morning, sharp," I say through gritted teeth. I don't know what she wants, but I need to find out. Quickly I spin round to see Ma approaching. I put my arm through hers to shepherd her away from this place, and as I do, I realize that I don't even know the name of the stranger I've just agreed to meet again.

As we make our way home as fast as we can through the ill-lit streets, the trussed-up torso, writhing with maggots, flashes into my mind for the second time this evening. Even though it's cold and our own breath wreathes around us like smoke, my fear makes me break out into a sweat. Neither of us says a word. We're both paying heed to the night noises of Whitechapel: the trains rumbling, the carriages clattering, the doors bolting, the babies bawling, and the cats mewing. But most of all, we're listening for the footsteps behind us, the heavy breathing at our shoulder and the knife being drawn.

I know I won't be able to sleep tonight.

CHAPTER 17

Friday, October 12, 1888

CONSTANCE

As luck would have it, Flo started her monthly early this morning. Rolling on the bed like a loose barrel, she is. So I seize my chance.

"Don't you worry about the market. I'll go alone," I tell her.

She looks at me, clutching her belly, then suddenly dives over the side of the bed and throws up into the pot.

"Bless you, Con," she says a moment later, heaving herself back onto the mattress. "You're a proper star."

Of course, I feel bad. I haven't told her about this mysterious lady or my secret meeting. She'd warn me off. She'd tell me not to go. But I have to. I need to. I've got this odd feeling worming away at me and I won't be able to rest until I know what this lady wants.

So I do my business at Spitalfields Market with Big Alf. He's got a few winter pansies and some bunches of herbs, but there's not much round at the moment. I buy a sprig or two of sage and a dozen roses he's put by for me, and just as I'm about to be off, he says to me: "Did the lady find you, then?"

The question stops me in my tracks. "Lady?" says I, all innocent like.

"Nice red coat. Hat with a rose in it." He pats his own bald head. "She says you weren't in no trouble."

I can't look him in the eye. "Yes," I reply; then I add: "It weren't nothing important," just to get him off my back.

So that's how she tracked me down, I think to myself as I trudge over the road toward Christ Church with my full basket. But it still don't explain how she knew to look for me at the market and how she figured I was at Whitehall when they found the body.

The church is over the road from the market and I'm not the only flower seller standing outside. There's a girl, can't be more than six, shivering barefoot by the railings. She gives me the eye and I bend down to reassure her.

"Don't you worry, sweetheart," I tells her. "I'm not here to steal your trade. Just to meet someone." She smiles nervously, then cheekily offers me a bloom. I'm just about to give her a mouthful for her sauce, when I hear a voice behind me.

"I'll take that." And there she is, my mystery lady, bending low, delving into a black dolly bag and offering the little urchin a sixpence for her rose. And so she lifts it from the girl's grubby hands and gives me a smile as she slots the stem behind a brooch that she's wearing on her lapel. "Shall we sit?" she asks, gesturing her gloved hand toward a bench in the churchyard.

There's an old drunk sleeping it off, not five feet away on a tombstone, but she's not put off. Leastways she doesn't show it. I look at her properly for the first time as she brushes away the golden beech leaves that have fallen onto the bench before she sits. She's pretty. She's got high cheekbones and a small, neat nose. Peeking out from under her large, black hat, the sweep of her chestnut hair is visible, and her delicate earlobes have little pearl droplets hanging from them.

"So," she says finally, smoothing down her skirts as we sit side by side. She's looking friendly, but I'm still wary. She knows she owes me an explanation. I can tell it from the way she looks at me, as if to say: *I'm sorry, but . . ."* So I let her do the talking.

She takes a deep breath and begins. "This is all about my sister," she starts. "She's missing, you see." The tight feeling in my stomach loosens a little, but I still don't understand. "She's been missing for nearly two months. No one has heard anything from her and I'm so very worried."

I shake my head and shrug. "I'm sorry, but . . ."

"Please"—she stops me and lifts her hand to show me her palm—"hear me out." She takes a deep breath. "Then, when these terrible murders began, I naturally grew more anxious. I knew, everyone knows, that this terrible man, this Jack, only kills . . ." She hesitates. "He kills ladies of the night." Her words make me open my own mouth to protest. It's like Polly Nichols and Annie Chapman and the others don't count as much as ordinary women 'cos they're on the streets, but she gives me another of her looks to tell me to be quiet. "But then, I heard about this Whitehall murder and that the postmortem had found that the"—she pauses again—"that the victim was not . . . was not . . ."

"A prostitute." I say the word that tastes so sour on her own tongue for her.

"The postmortem said that they thought the woman was about five and twenty years old and that she was well-nourished."

"And that she had fair skin and dark hair and had never borne a child," I add.

Her mouth opens slightly in wonderment. "You know of the report?"

"Yes," I say, not bothering to tell her that I've read every word of it, over and over again, in the *Daily News* three days back.

"Then you'll know the medical examiner also believes the victim had been dead for between six weeks and two months before she was found."

"And that's when your sister went missing?"

"Yes." She looks up and into the distance. "When I heard about this latest atrocity, I decided to come to London, to Whitehall, to see for myself the scene of the discovery. My late father was a good friend of the police commissioner, you see, and so I was allowed access to the site. And that's where I found this."

Her hand's back in the dolly bag and she brings out a small enameled box this time. When she opens it up, I feel my eyes pop out of their sockets.

"Blimey!" I blurt out. It's the remains of one of the posies I made for the Whitehall toffs.

She doesn't take it out because she's knows it'll fall to pieces. The petals are wilted and dirty and the paper's all soggy.

"It was crushed underfoot in the mud nearby. I picked it up, and the constable with me told me he remembered seeing two girls near the site at the time of the body's discovery. There'd been reports of pickpockets in the area and so he'd been sent to investigate. Apparently, up until he was called to help retrieve the body, he was watching you and your sister very carefully." The tone of her voice has suddenly changed. It's like she's got one up on me and she knows it. I squirm a bit on my seat at the thought that Old Bill might still be after us. But as if she can read my mind, she goes on: "The Metropolitan

Police have limited resources, but my time is my own. I went to Covent Garden and asked the traders if they'd sold any yellow rosebuds to a couple of young flower sellers and, in particular, any of this." She lifted a corner of wet paper with its blue edging. "They couldn't recall two girls fitting your description, but told me to ask at Spitalfields Market. My inquiries soon paid off. From there I went to St. Jude's, where I found someone who knew you."

"Mrs. Puddiphatt?" I ask, wanting to break every bone in that nosey old crone's body.

"Yes," she replies with a nod. "She told me you would be attending a public séance at the Frying Pan public house. It all came together so easily." She shrugs and shakes her head at the same time. "Remarkably easily," she says, as if she can't believe her luck.

I'm still in the dark. "So now you've found me, what do you want to do with me?" I hear myself ask. I sound anxious. I worry she might even try and blackmail me.

She raises her head and fixes me with an odd look. *"Do with you?"* she says, as if I've just asked a really stupid question. "I don't want to *do* anything with you, Miss Piper." It's odd being called Miss Piper. She smiles and says: "I am asking for your help."

"Oh" is all I manage at first.

"You see, you were at the scene. You saw

181

where she . . . where the victim was found. And you clearly know all about the case. You know, too, about the other women. You are interested, engaged in it all. You went to the séance, you want to see this monster behind bars as much as any woman—"

"Hold up!" I say. This time, it's my turn to put my palm between us. "Some people say that this Whitehall woman isn't one of Jack's at all. Didn't you see the letter to the chief constable?" From somewhere at the back of my memory, I recall the finding of a torso in Rainham, in Essex, the year before, too.

My words seem to knock the wind out of her sails, but only for a second.

"That may be," she says, looking at me with glassy eyes. I think she may burst into tears any moment. "But I firmly believe that you are the one who can tell me if this . . . if the Whitehall remains are those of my sister."

I'm confused. "I don't understand," I say.

"Nor do I," she replies.

I'm none the wiser.

She takes a deep breath as if to gulp down her emotions. "This may sound strange, but all I know is that I have been led to you—the flowers at the murder scene, the policeman, the market trader, Mrs. Puddiphatt. It's all been so easy, as if . . ."

"*As if . . . ?*"

"As if someone has been guiding the way, showing me where to go. I know it sounds strange, but . . ."

I stop her. This time, I feel myself reaching out to her, as if someone's telling me to comfort her. I can't fight the urge to lay my hand on her sleeve, and when I do, she looks at it, wide-eyed. "It's not strange," I say softly. "Feelings like that . . ." I search for a way to tell her that I have them, too: odd, unaccountable stirrings that make you think someone is trying to tap into your mind and your soul. "We all have them," I tell her with a smile, like I'm trying to say it's the most normal thing in the world. Only I know it's not. Nor do I tell her that she's not the only one who's been fretting over the body in Whitehall. For all anyone knows, it could just as well be Miss Tindall's torso. I feel sick at the thought. And that's just it. Everyone is on edge. Everyone's fears about their missing loved ones are climbing out of the woodwork.

"So you'll help me?" She's suddenly a little brighter.

I shake my head. "No," I say firmly. "I'm sorry. I'm a flower girl, not a detective. I don't want no part of it." I try to think quickly of a good excuse. "Besides," I tell her, "I'm looking for someone myself."

She frowns. "You are?"

"Yes." I swallow hard. I've started, so I need to

go on. "My teacher," I tell her, thinking of Miss Tindall and where she might be, even though I know she's just probably gone back to Oxford. "My friend," I add forlornly. "She left without saying good-bye."

The lady nods. "I am sorry," she says, then adds out of the blue: "I know what it's like to lose touch with a good friend."

"You do?" I ask, as if I'm the only one in the world who's ever felt this way.

"Yes. I do. We grew up together. She gave me this." She delves into her bag and brings out a scrap of embroidered material to show me. " 'Friendship is love without his wings,' " she says with a smile.

My eyes suddenly widen at her words. It's a line I know well. "It is a precious thing," I say, as if someone else is moving my lips.

She tilts her head and frowns slightly. "You know Lord Byron?"

"He was my teacher's favorite poet," I reply with a faint smile.

"Then you had a very good teacher," she says softly. "I hope you find her."

"And you had a good friend." Have I spoken out of turn?

"Yes." She suddenly becomes reflective again, like she's gazing back at her own past. "Yes, I did." In another moment, she's rallying and her jaw sets firm. "But, of course, you have your

own worries. I must not burden you with mine."
She leaves me feeling quite guilty, but not before
her hand plunges into her bag once more. "If
you change your mind . . ." She leans forward.
"Here's my card. I shall be staying at this address
for a few more days."

I take the card with what Miss Tindall would
describe as "good grace," but I don't intend
to get in touch again. Instead, my eyes follow
her as she glides along the paved path of the
churchyard and out onto the street. Only then
do I glance down at the calling card. On it
is written the name of where she's staying,
Brown's Hotel, and underneath it says *Miss
Pauline Beaufroy.* I pop it into my apron pocket,
even though I don't plan on contacting her.
She's right. I have enough worries of my own.

EMILY

The niggling suspicions that had taken root
after my first encounter with Dr. Melksham
certainly grew most exponentially when
he returned again the following Sunday to
observe my lesson, just as he had done
before. I watched him nod his approval as,
one by one, the pupils recited their various
verses. I thought little of it, until the end of
the class, that is. As before, all the pupils
filed out past him, but this time, Mrs. Parker-

Smythe beckoned to Molly Deakin. She was such a fair child and a promising student, too. She'd never missed a class in the past two years and her reading was coming on well.

"Molly," said Mrs. Parker-Smythe, laying her hand on the girl's shoulder. "This is Dr. Melksham and he'd like to have a word with you, in private."

I was close behind. "Is something wrong?" I asked. But my inquiry was given short shrift. Mrs. Parker-Smythe eyed me disdainfully, but the gentleman appeared charm itself.

"On the contrary," he replied with that disarming smile of his. "We would like to reward . . ." He broke off and glanced at Mrs. Parker-Smythe as he fumbled for a name.

"Molly," she prompted.

"Molly," he continued, "for her excellent efforts."

I felt myself relax. As I recall, I was even aware that my lips lifted in a smile. I regarded my star pupil, a sense of pride blooming inside me.

"That is good news," I heard myself say.

"Yes, indeed," replied the gentleman; and with that, Molly was ushered into the vestry and the door was shut.

The following Sunday, she was absent. The one after that, too. The gentleman still sat at the back of the class, still paying great attention to the pupils. But it was when Gracie Arden stood up to recite a poem she had learned that he seemed to take particular note. Her delivery was poor and her stance self-conscious. She twisted the corner of her pinafore between her fingers and mumbled her words to the floor. Nevertheless, the gentleman leaned forward and bent his ear toward her. When she had finished, I watched him give a self-satisfied nod. It was not until the end of the class, however, that a worm of discomfort started to wriggle its way into my brain. Once again, Mrs. Parker-Smythe beckoned the child as she walked down the aisle toward the door of the church. For some reason, she had been singled out for a reward, even though her recitation was not good. I wondered if it was because, like Molly, she was a particularly fair child, with large, brown eyes and perfect teeth.

"Excellent diction, my dear," the gentleman told the bewildered girl. "Your efforts shall be rewarded."

Constance and I had been gathering books and had just bid the last of the class stragglers good-bye when, from out of the corner of my eye, I caught what was happening. The next thing I saw was little Gracie being shepherded into the vestry, just as Molly had been two weeks before.

When Gracie didn't return to Sunday school the following week, nor the week after that, the worm of suspicion resurfaced once more. Up until then, I had kept my concern to myself. I made no mention of it to Constance. Now, however, I decided to ask Mrs. Parker-Smythe if she knew why both Molly and Gracie were absent. I plucked up the courage to mention the fact the next Sunday, while we were setting out the hymnbooks.

"Molly Deakin and Gracie Arden haven't attended class for a while now," I told her. "Do you know if they are ill?" I asked casually.

For a moment, I saw her tense, then she shrugged. "Goodness knows," she said, cradling a pile of books. "These waifs and strays are a law unto themselves," and she continued doling out the hymnals.

It was true. In Whitechapel, you could never count on full attendance. Children fell ill, or had to work, or mind their younger siblings, all the time. There was always a good excuse not to learn. That was why I had begun to keep a register. It listed the name, age and address of every pupil in my class and recorded their attendance. I checked. Molly had only been absent once when she had the chicken pox, but Gracie had never missed a Sunday lesson since she started coming five months ago. Both their absences were totally out of character.

The following Sunday, Dr. Melksham appeared once more, sitting at the back of the class, and once again the children were asked to recite for him. This time, he singled out Libby Lonergan for special treatment. Mrs. Parker-Smythe shepherded the child toward the vestry, ostensibly to reward her for her recitation. Once again, I followed behind Dr. Melksham, biding my time, in the hope of an introduction. My chance came as I followed him down the aisle. From out of his pocket, something fell onto a pew as he passed. I bent down to retrieve it with the intention of reuniting it with its owner. It was a glove, a gentleman's white glove, but it was the smell of it that suddenly hit me—a sickly-sweet tang. I lifted it to my nose and sniffed it. I felt a little light-headed and then it struck me.

Chloroform.

Clenching the glove in my hand, I watched dumbfounded as the gentleman proceeded to head for the vestry. He must not know I have it, I thought. I stuffed it in my pocket. Nausea was rising in my throat, but it wasn't the chloroform that made me feel queasy. It was the thought of what it might be used for and on whom.

CHAPTER 18

Wednesday, October 17, 1888

EMILY

Before I continue relating the story of my missing pupils, I find myself returned to the New Scotland Yard site. It's shortly after eleven o'clock in the morning on another miserable day. Before me, I see a bowler-hatted gentleman accompanied by a large terrier. The man, a London journalist named Jasper Waring, is with two police officers and his young assistant, a Mr. Joshua Pugh. Somehow he has managed to persuade officials that his hound might be of assistance in the search for more evidence. As they light their lanterns, I join the party in the mire and mud at the entrance to the vault where the torso was discovered.

The dog is let off its leash and darts straight into the vault. Those who accompany it duck low and strain their eyes in the gloom. They can see very little and have to be guided by the animal's snuffling. The rest of the party remains in anxious silence outside. They do not have to wait long, however, before the hound starts sniffing suspiciously at a mound of earth.

"He's got something," says Waring, turning on his haunches.

The announcement sends the small party into a flurry, but it is Mr. Pugh who suggests the next action. "A spade," he shouts. "We need tools over here!" He signals to a couple of workmen who are nearby and they offer shovels and a pickax, as well as their labor.

As the work proceeds, the terrier becomes even more excitable, flailing the soil with its front paws. More and more earth is flung out of the vault, until, at length, the dog seizes upon an object that is caked with damp soil.

"Here! Bring it out here!" the officer in charge calls into the vault. Mr. Waring duly obliges, laying the object on the muddy ground outside.

"My God!" cries the policeman as soon as the daylight illuminates the grisly discovery. It suddenly becomes startlingly clear what has so excited the hound. It has found, buried under several inches of thick Thames mud, a portion of a human leg, severed at the knee.

CONSTANCE

Mr. Bartleby supped with us this evening. He brought four nice chops, which we served with gravy and mash. I managed to eat mine, even though I didn't feel like it. Afterward, Flo and I cleared away to leave Ma and her beau alone. Flo's keen to be off to see Danny tonight. There's something special on at the Egyptian Hall, so I'm left to my own devices. Mr. Bartleby's given me a penny classic—the first installment of *The String of Pearls*. It's about a barber called Sweeney Todd, who kills his customers and puts their meat in his pies. I'm not sure about his choice. He laughs out loud when he sees the look on my face as he hands it to me. Nevertheless, I take it and settle myself down in the kitchen, when I hear them talking. Ma's voice is raised slightly; then she coughs. It's clear she's getting tetchy. So I put my ear to the door and I don't like what I hear.

"Is it true, Harold, what they say about George Lusk?" Ma's known Mr. Lusk for years. They grew up on the same street. Although she'd never say it, she's always had a bit of a soft spot for him.

There's a pause. I imagine Mr. Bartleby drawing on his pipe and crossing and uncrossing his legs while he thinks. After a moment, he says: "That depends what you heard, my dear."

There's a small crack in the door and I squint to peer through it. I can just about make out Ma, looking all fidgety. She's up from her chair and pacing back and forth across the hearth.

"I heard a box was delivered to him yesterday

evening in the post and that when he opened it . . ." She takes a great gulp of air. "When he opened it, inside there was . . ." She stops and brings her hands up to her mouth, unable to bring herself to utter whatever it is she wants to say.

I tense and my mind starts racing. *What in God's name was inside the box?* The answer is every bit as bad as I'd imagined.

"Part of a kidney." Mr. Bartleby puts her out of her misery. His voice is flat and I wonder at his calm. "He showed it to some of us this morning."

"So it's true?" A horrified look pelts across Ma's face, like a freight train hurtling toward her.

Mr. Bartleby nods his head. "George thought it was another prank." I knew poor Mr. Lusk has had many cruel hoaxes played on him since he fronted up the Vigilance Committee. He even felt himself being watched by an odd man with bushy whiskers. Mr. Bartleby shakes his head: "But the doctor we contacted thought it was half a human kidney."

My mother lets out a gasp that ends up in a wheeze. She collapses into her chair.

Mr. Bartleby's put out. He leans over her. "Don't fret yourself, Patience. It's being examined now and there are some that still say it's a practical joke. Medical students having a bit of fun, eh?" He pats her on the arm.

I pull away from the door and bring my shawl close round my shoulders. The bile's risen in my throat at the thought of a kidney—a human kidney. I'm wondering if it once belonged to Catherine Eddowes, who was found missing one of hers. I lean my head in once more.

"What do you want of me, Patience?" Mr. Bartleby's asking. Along with his tobacco smoke, his voice is thick with frustration. He's taken his pipe out of his mouth and he's pointing the stem at Ma. His big, gold ring catches the candlelight and glints. "We're doing all we can, but the police . . ."

Ma nods. "I know," she snaps, her hands held fast between her clenched knees as if to stop them hitting him. Then, after a moment's thought, she switches back at him, her eyes wide. "Will this Ripper have your address, Harold? Will he?"

"Ummgh." Mr. Bartleby seems taken aback by this terrible thought. I am too. He sucks thoughtfully on his pipe again. "My name's out there for all to see, I suppose," he says finally. "But you're not to worry. You hear, Patience?" He raises his gaze and shoots her a look like a stern father. "Ya hear?" Then he breaks into a smile.

Ma looks at him and reaches out her hand to him. He kisses it. I ain't seen them being tender together before and it feels queer.

"I couldn't bear it if anything happened to you, Harold," she tells him.

I'm feeling more afraid than ever.

EMILY

Was I wrong not to involve Constance in the whole affair with Melksham? I think not. Dragging her down into the mire that eventually enveloped me would have served no purpose other to ruin her reputation as well. Yet I was soon to discover that no one can ever feel more alone than when they are concealing a most shameful secret.

I decided to pay a visit to Commercial Street Police Station as soon as I could, while the stink of chloroform was still strong on the glove. It was evidence, I thought, if not proof, of some suspicious deed.

The sergeant on the desk raised one of his bushy brows when he saw me, perhaps because he was not used to seeing women of my class visit his station unless they had just been robbed or assaulted. I was determined to be quite rational in the face of his skepticism.

"I wish to report something suspicious," I began.

He leaned closer to me, elbowing his counter. "Do you, indeed, Miss er . . ."

"Tindall," I told him. "Miss Emily Tindall." I began to spell out my surname. "*T, I, N . . .*"

Instead of taking down my name, however, he was quite brusque. "Hold up, miss," he told me, lifting his forefinger. "Perhaps you'd like to tell me what worries you before we proceed."

I found his attitude irritating. I made certain he heard me sigh before I took out a paper bag from my reticule and presented him with the glove. I laid it on the counter. Sniffing it, I was relieved to satisfy myself that it still smelled of chloroform, albeit weaker than before.

"A glove." The sergeant was obviously seeking to be deliberately obtuse.

"Can you not smell it?" I snapped. I held it up and flapped it under his nose. He did not appreciate the gesture and I immediately regretted my impetuosity. I decided to cover my foolishness by telling him the whole story straightaway, rather than play any more ridiculous games with him. "I am a Sunday school teacher. I teach children up to the age of twelve, and recently three of my female pupils have gone missing."

"*Missing?*" I thought the sergeant was suddenly interested.

"There is a gentleman who watches the class. It has become his custom to single out girls to interview afterward—the pretty ones—then they seem to disappear. I never see them again. I—"

I was in full flow when the sergeant stopped me. "This is Whitechapel, miss. Girls go missing all the time." There was a smirk on his face.

"But I worry they have been abducted," I told him. "The chloroform on this glove . . ." I picked it up and waved it in front of him once more. He would have none of it.

"Perhaps you haven't heard, miss, but five women have been murdered round these parts in the past few weeks. I'm afraid my men are too busy to investigate a crime that may or may not have been committed when Saucy Jack's still out there." He pointed to the door as if to signify that there was an awful lot going on outside in the real world and that I should rejoin it as soon as possible.

I could see that I would make no further progress in the face of such derision. I returned the glove to its bag and walked away.

CHAPTER 19

Thursday, October 18, 1888

CONSTANCE

Flo didn't half give me a fright just now. I was kneeling at the grate in the front room, brushing up the ashes, when the front door flings open and in she rushes, all out of breath. For a terrible moment, I thought *he* must be chasing her; but when she gets her breath back, she says: "House to house. The coppers! They're at number twenty-nine already."

Ma's come through from the kitchen, wiping her hands on a tea towel. "Did I just hear right?"

Flo nods and lurches toward the stairs. "I've got that pendant, remember?" she shouts.

I do. It was a nice one, heart-shaped with a ruby in the middle. She got it from a young lady in Mayfair last year and didn't want to give it over to Mr. Bartleby, so she put it in the upstairs chest.

Ma's wiping her hands harder now, even though they're dry. "Anything else you can think of, Con?" she asks, casting her eyes around the room.

"The clock!" I cry, lunging at the mantelpiece. It was so obvious I didn't think of it at first. Mr. Bartleby gave it to Ma last Christmas. It sits all grand and stately among our other lowly nicknacks, like a gold ring in a magpie's nest, and, of course, it'll have been lifted from someone else's home.

I chase up the stairs with the clock clasped tightly to me. Flo's looking out of the front bedroom window, craning her neck to peer down the street. I can hear a knocker being rapped. Old Bill must be close.

"They're asking about the Ripper, ain't they?" I say, opening the lid of the chest.

"Yes," she replies curtly.

"They're not interested in stolen stuff," I tell

her as I hide the clock under a pillowcase and an apron.

She turns round and looks at me as though I'm a half-wit. "If it's easy to nab us, they will," she says. "So best not give them a 'and, eh?"

Her words put me back in my box, good and proper. I wind my neck in as she passes me and walks back downstairs. I glance, once more, into the chest and spy the corner of a leather-bound book. I reach in and bring it out, the copy of *Little Dorrit* that Miss Tindall gave me. It's one of my favorites. Like little Amy, I fancy one day that I might discover I am the heiress to a vast fortune. I open up its leaves and the smells of leather and paper dance in front of me. I turn to the inscription on the flyleaf, where Miss Tindall has written in her neat hand:

> To dear Constance
> Always know I am never far away, should you need me.
>   Your faithful friend,
>   Emily

I remember the day she came to deliver it to me here, in person. It was her first visit to the house and I hadn't expected her. It was one evening this spring and still light. Ma and Flo were out buying the leftovers at market, but I stayed behind. I was in the middle of *Pride and*

Prejudice and couldn't put it down. I was so surprised to see her standing there, I can tell you.

Of course, I panicked. I bid her sit in one chair, then realized its leg was broke, so I bid her move to the other. I offered her a cup of tea and found we had none. I looked down at my feet and saw I had no shoes on. Yet, through all my awkwardness and eagerness to impress my teacher, she remained calm and polite and that saintly smile of hers never left her face.

"Please don't fuss on my account, Constance," she said, looking at me direct. "I am come to see you, not your house. And I am come to give you this." She held out the book.

These words put me more at my ease and I sat down beside her on the chair with the wobbly leg and took the book from her.

"Thank you, miss," I said, studying the cover in delight.

"I thought you would enjoy it. It's a romance, but a witty one," she told me.

As I thumbed through the volume, my eyes snagged on the dedication. My head darted up and I saw that she was looking at me, as if to gauge my reaction.

"You are very kind, miss," I said.

"Nonsense," she replied. "You deserve a reward for all your hard work at the Sunday school."

We talked then, about the lessons and what we might study in the next class; then she began to mention some of the pupils by name. "Charlie Phipps is coming along nicely, isn't he?" she said. I recalled the sad little urchin who first appeared last year, who now knew his alphabet. "And the girls," she said suddenly. "Molly Deakin and Gracie Arden." I thought of poor Molly, delicate as a twig, then of Gracie, pretty as a picture, with golden ringlets and large, brown eyes. "Come to think of it, I haven't seen Molly for a few weeks. Have you?" she asks me.

I give a little shrug and think for a moment. "No," I say. "No, I haven't, miss."

EMILY

I will have to tell Constance soon, although I know she has a notion. I recall the look on her face when I visited her in her own home and questioned her about the missing girls. Yes, I must tell her the whole story very shortly, but not before I have finished telling you.

After my abortive visit to the police station, I consulted the school register. I found Molly Deakin's address easily enough. Flower and Dean Street. It was a notorious hangout of criminals and prostitutes. A girl from there stood little chance of ever making anything of herself. That was one of the reasons I was so eager for Molly to continue to better herself, so that she could escape a life of squalor that seemed preordained for her because of her family's impoverished circumstances. I vowed, there and then, to get to the bottom of her disappearance. I would visit her home and speak with her mother.

The Deakins lived in a narrow row of blackened brick cottages just off Whitechapel Road. I remember the cold rain, funneled by the wind, stinging my cheeks as I turned into their street. I was thankful for my trusty green umbrella that shielded me from the worst of it. From beneath the cover of my brolly, I searched for number 23. I found it halfway down the street, with a scuffed wooden door and a broken pane in the front window that had been patched with a square of wood. Two ragged children brushed past me as I waited for someone to answer my knock. I am ashamed to admit that for a moment I feared they had snatched my reticule. They had not.

The door was answered by a woman. She looked old. Her face was crumpled like a worn shoe; yet I was sure she was no more than in her midthirties.

"Yes?" Her dull fish eyes were suspicious. Perhaps she thought I had come to collect her overdue rent.

"Mrs. Deakin?" I said with a smile. I tried not to seem threatening.

"Yerrrr . . . s." The suspicion in her voice

remained. "You ain't from Mr. Sampson, is ya?"

Sampson. The name was familiar. Then I remembered.

"No, I'm not here to collect your rent, Mrs. Deakin. I am come about Molly." I kept my voice light and made sure that the smile did not leave my face, even though my cheeks were tingling with the cold. It had the desired effect.

"You'd best come in, then," she told me, opening wide the door.

The front room was dingy and damp, like a dozen other such homes into which I had ventured during my time in the East End. There was black mildew in the corners and the wallpaper had peeled to reveal bare plaster. There was no one else in the room, and for that, I was grateful.

Mrs. Deakin limped toward a chair with a sort of rocking gait and, using her apron as a cloth, wiped the seat. I thought it rude to refuse her after she had gone to so much trouble, so I sat down, even though I feared the chair so rickety that it might break beneath me.

"It's just that she's not been to Sunday school lately and I was worried she might be unwell." I was circumspect, hoping against hope that there was some reasonable explanation for her absence.

Mrs. Deakin remained standing, her hefty

weight supported almost entirely on her left side. "I thought they'd've told ya," she said, raising her brows.

My heart beat a little faster. "Told me what?" I managed to retain my smile.

"That she's gone into service."

"Service?" The word almost stuck in my throat.

"That teacher of 'ers, Mrs. P . . ."

"Parker-Smythe?"

"That's the one. She found her a place at a big house in Mayfair last month." The woman seemed proud to tell me of her news.

"Ah!" I said. Perhaps my fears were misplaced. "And how is she getting on?"

Mrs. Deakin shrugged. "I've no idea, miss. . . ."

"Forgive me," I replied. "I am Emily Tindall. I taught Molly."

The woman nodded. "She spoke fondly of you, Miss Tindall." A smile flickered across her cracked lips. "It's thanks to you she can read." I felt a little shot of pride well up inside me, but it was short-lived. "It's thanks to you she might make a lady's maid."

I tried to hide my disappointment. Molly could have gone far—certainly much further than a lady's boudoir.

"Do you have an address for her?" I asked, adding: "I would like to write to her."

It was then that my fears resurfaced. Mrs.

Deakin shook her weary head and sucked in her flaccid cheeks. "I'm sorry, miss," she replied. "I was told I weren't to contact her. It's up to her to get in touch."

I felt my stomach knot at the news. Perhaps Molly had gone to Mayfair to be a lady's maid, but there was also a chance that she had been pressed into service of a very different kind.

CONSTANCE

I'm just about to close the lid of the trunk when I notice something in the pocket of the apron that's hiding the carriage clock. My hand reaches inside. It's the calling card the lady gave me. " 'Pauline Beaufroy,' " I whisper to myself.

Just then, there's a loud rap on the door. Even though I'm half expecting it, it makes me jump. Quick as you like, I shove the card back into my apron pocket. Miss Beaufroy will have to wait.

It's PC Tanner, our local bobby. He keeps his eye on Flo and me and it's not the first time he's set foot in our front room. I'm thankful I remembered the clock—although, as the constable looks around the room, my own eyes settle on the telltale ring of dust it's left on the mantelpiece. Luckily, he doesn't notice it. We're all lined up like the proverbial three wise monkeys and he just asks us if we've seen anything suspicious lately. We shake our heads in time.

"No, Constable. We ain't seen nothing," says Flo, all coy. "But we're very afraid." She flutters her lashes.

"I'm sure you are, miss," he says, his cheeks flushing slightly. Flo's the mistress of her art. He wants out as quick as possible. "We're doing everything we can to find the killer," he says, all flustered and heading toward the door.

Ma opens it to let him out, and he's just about to step over the threshold when I suddenly get this terrible urge. I don't know what comes over me, but I have to ask him.

"Any more news on the Whitehall Mystery?" I say, out of the blue.

PC Tanner stops dead and fixes me with a frown. "Why d'ya ask?"

Flo stands on my toe and takes over. "We read about it in the papers. He's getting everywhere, this Ripper fella!" she says with a little roll of her head.

"As a matter of fact," replies PC Tanner, his back stiffening with his own self-importance, "there was a new development just yesterday."

"Oh?" says Flo, now genuinely keen to know.

"Yes. Between you and me," he says, leaning forward all confidentially, "they found a leg to go with the torso."

"No!" gasps Flo.

I instantly think of poor Miss Beaufroy and clamp my hands over my mouth.

"You all right, miss?" asks PC Tanner.

"She's fine," Flo comes back at him. "Just gets upset easy, that's all." She points to her head as if to signify I'm a little soft, and the copper understands her straightaway. He takes his leave without further ado.

As soon as Ma shuts the door behind him, Flo's down on me like a ton of bricks. "What you want to do that for?" she scolds.

"I'm not sure," I say. And I'm genuinely not.

CHAPTER 20

Friday, October 19, 1888

EMILY

Terence Cutler sits alone by a sickly fire. In his hand, he cradles a brandy. It is his third this evening. His sister-in-law's visit has rattled his nerves even further. He was worried before, but now he is constantly on edge. So much so, that the sound of rapping on the door past eight o'clock at night makes his stomach lurch. He holds his breath as he hears a man's voice; then Dora's light footsteps approach. A knock and she enters.

"Sir, there's a Mr. Troutbeck to see you."

"Troutbeck," repeats Cutler. He wonders what on earth the Westminster coroner could possibly want with him. He was a friend of his late father's. The prickly middle-aged gentleman was even a guest at his wedding, and he knew that in his professional life he did not suffer fools gladly, especially journalists. Yet, he doubts his visit is a social one.

"Show him in," he orders. He stands, grabs his jacket from a nearby chair and hurriedly pulls it on to add a formality to the occasion, just before his unexpected guest appears in the doorway.

"Mr. Troutbeck." Cutler offers his hand. The coroner, a somber-looking man, with curly, gray hair and spectacles, steps forward and takes it.

"I am sorry to call on you so late, Cutler, but I felt it a matter of urgency."

"Oh?" The surgeon motions to a nearby armchair.

Troutbeck seats himself on the edge, as if he is about to conduct important business. "I shall come straight to the point," he says, flapping away a proffered glass of brandy. "You will know I am presiding over this most ghastly business in Whitehall."

"The torso?" Cutler seats himself opposite.

"Precisely," he says with a nod. "Well, as

if that weren't enough, they've found more remains."

"What?" Cutler frowns and reaches for the brandy decanter. "Do you mind?" He lifts up his glass.

"Go ahead," says Troutbeck. "Yes, another leg. A bloody journalist, it was. He set a dog on the site and the bally beast uncovered it!"

Cutler shakes his head in disbelief. "And it belongs to the torso?"

Troutbeck nods. "Bond says so." He eyes the brandy decanter. "Damn me, I'll have one."

Cutler jumps to it, pouring the coroner a glass and giving it to him. He hopes he doesn't notice that his hand is shaking.

"Makes a mockery of the police, of course. They were supposed to have searched the site thoroughly after the discovery of the torso." He takes a large gulp of the brandy.

Cutler agrees. "Of course."

Troutbeck, his eyes playing around the room, has spotted a framed photograph of Geraldine on a nearby console table. Suddenly the coroner rises and stalks across the room to study it.

"Fine-looking woman," he pronounces, picking up the frame.

"Yes," Cutler agrees. Only that morning, I know, he toyed with the idea of placing it in a drawer. Troutbeck's intrusive manner surprises him.

"But I digress," says the coroner, placing the frame gently back on the table. "The leg's not the only thing Scotland Yard seems to have overlooked, either," he says, resuming his place on the chair.

"Oh?" Cutler's curiosity is piqued.

"No." The coroner hotches to his left and reaches into his waistcoat pocket to produce a small paper packet. He sets it down on the low table in front of him and unwraps it. "The bally journalist found this, too."

Cutler stares wide-eyed at the object. It is a gold bar brooch, studded with three rubies. His expression gives him away.

"It is familiar to you?"

"Why, yes," says the surgeon, his voice registering alarm. He reaches for the jewelry to inspect it. Turning it over, he looks at the back.

Troutbeck nods. "As soon as I saw the inscription, I feared it might be your wife's."

Cutler stares at the inscribed words: *To dearest Geraldine on the occasion of our marriage, 3rd June 1882. Forever, TC.*

"Where was this found?" Cutler feels the bile rising up in his chest. He sets down the brooch before him.

"Just by the leg. The journalist handed it to an inspector, who thought I should see it."

Cutler reaches for his handkerchief from his pocket and holds it to his mouth.

The coroner looks at him anxiously, but presses on. "Of course, I told the pencil pusher I'd make inquiries straightaway. I'm assuming your good wife is about."

The surgeon has turned an odd shade of gray. "I fear not."

"Out then?" The coroner grows more wary. "Away?"

Cutler is silent.

"When was the last time you saw your wife, Cutler?" The coroner grows impatient.

The surgeon can barely breathe. "A while ago," he wheezes. "She went away."

"*Away?* How long ago?"

"Eight weeks, ten weeks perhaps." He thinks a lie may be called for. "We quarreled. She went to stay with friends, but I have not heard from her."

Troutbeck's stern expression relaxes. He does not pry further, for the time being. A man's relationship with his wife is a private matter. "And this is hers?" He points to the brooch.

Cutler simply nods at first, then finally manages to find words. "Yes. It is Geraldine's." He pauses, as if steeling himself to ask the question that burns his mouth. He bows his head. "So you think the body is hers?" he mumbles.

The coroner purses his lips. "It is the obvious

answer, dear boy, and the one that you least want to hear. I hate to be the bearer of such awful news." He pauses before adding: "But I shall say nothing, of course."

Cutler's bowed head shoots up. *"What?"*

Troutbeck looks grave. "What has passed here this evening shall remain between you and me for the time being. Neither of us wants the press on our doorsteps, do we, eh? If it was up to me, I'd ban the whole bally lot of them."

The surgeon takes a slug of brandy. "So no one will know?" He fingers the brooch.

"Not for the moment," says Troutbeck. He drains his glass. "It shall remain between us two until there is a positive identification."

Cutler's face pales again. *"An identification? You mean . . ."*

Troutbeck nods. "I'd make every effort to contact Geraldine, if I were you, Cutler. If you can't . . ."

". . . I will be called upon to identify the remains."

The coroner nods. "Precisely. But in the meantime . . ." He lifts the brooch from Cutler's grasp—and with it, any hope that the surgeon might not be implicated in a murder. "I shall need to return this to the police."

Cutler's jaw drops. "Can I not keep it, sir?" He is pleading innocence, faking the worried husband, even though he is genuinely at a loss as to how the brooch might have arrived at the building site in Whitehall.

Troutbeck brooks no nonsense. " 'Fraid not. Evidence, dear fellow. Evidence," he tells him firmly, pocketing the brooch, then adds ruefully: "I'm sure it will be returned to you in due course."

CHAPTER 21

Saturday, October 20, 1888

CONSTANCE

Last night, I had another dream. I was back at the building site at Cannon Row in Whitehall and the torso was on the ground. Lying next to it was the leg. A woolen stocking clung to part of it and the rest was crusty with dirt. Miss Beaufroy was at my side, weeping, and I was comforting her. I was sad, but then my sadness turned to terror when a great black dog suddenly came bounding from nowhere and started digging in front of our very eyes. It dug and slavered, flinging earth into the air, until suddenly it seized upon an object and began to growl and snarl. It had something in its jaws and it tossed it about like a plaything. Then I realized what it had in its grip. The beast was holding Miss Tindall's head.

I could see her features clear as day; her eyes were wide and her mouth moved, calling out to me. That's when I screamed. I screamed myself awake. Yet wakefulness doesn't seem much better.

EMILY

I cannot be certain how my investigations into the missing girls were uncovered. I think, perhaps, that someone must have followed me to Flower and Dean, to the Deakins' home. Of course, that is irrelevant now, but at the time, I felt betrayed and angry. It happened one morning in May. I had just arrived at the ragged school shortly after half past seven. It was my custom to be in my classroom half an hour earlier than my pupils so that I could further prepare for my lessons. On this particular morning, however, the principal, Mr. Antrobus, a stern man with huge muttonchop whiskers and spectacles so thick that everyone assumed he was half blind, was waiting for me. As I opened my door, I was shocked to see him standing on the raised dais at the front of the room. Hands clasped firmly behind his back like some sergeant major, he was looking out of the window. The children were not allowed such a privilege. Their desks were on a lower level and all that the fortunate ones who sat at the front could see were the gables of nearby dwellings and the occasional handkerchief of hazy sky. From my chair behind the desk, I, however, could view the tangle of squalid dwellings that surrounded the school like skeins of dirty wool. It was on this scene that Mr. Antrobus was now brooding through his jam jar glasses.

"Miss Tindall," he greeted me sharply, not bothering to turn round. "Shut the door, if you please." He was a man who rarely smiled, but sometimes his tone would be almost jovial. On this occasion, however, it was far from it. There was a gravity in his manner that delivered a sense of foreboding; on reflection; I might even dare to say a hint of menace. I felt the hairs on my neck rise.

"Yes, sir," I managed to blurt, closing the door and moving toward the headmaster. Suddenly I was a child again, forced to look up to my superior who loomed above me.

Clasping my own hands in front of my waist, I tried to stop them from shaking. I had no wish to show any weakness. As I said, Mr. Antrobus did not turn immediately, clearly preferring to allow me to stew in my own confusion and anxiety. I glanced at the large clock, placed at the back of the room. It was purely for the teacher's benefit, and out of the sight of the pupils, some of whom would gladly watch time tick past rather than pay attention to their lessons. After several seconds of silence, I decided to take the initiative.

"Is anything wrong, Headmaster?" I asked, my voice quavering in my throat.

Mr. Antrobus allowed another few seconds to elapse before he finally turned. Through his huge lenses, I saw him narrow his steely eyes. "I ask the questions here, Miss Tindall," he barked. "And it would seem that you ask far too many." From his high perch, he pointed an accusing finger at me. The sudden motion caused his glasses to slip down his bulbous nose.

I froze. Had someone reported my visit to the Deakins' lodgings? I kept my counsel. I must remain calm and not incriminate myself.

"Sir?" I played the innocent.

"Come, come, Miss Tindall." Clearly, my feigned ignorance would not wash. "We have received complaints."

"*Complaints?*" The news came like a thunderbolt, wrong-footing me. I had no idea what he was talking about. "I'm afraid I am at a loss, sir." My mouth was suddenly so dry that I struggled to form my words.

I watched Mr. Antrobus put his hand into his waistcoat pocket and retrieve a letter. Clearing his throat, he pushed his spectacles back up the bridge of his nose, then unfolded it. He read out loud: " *'It has come to our attention that one of your teachers, Miss Emily Tindall, has engaged in conduct that is both unbecoming, and possibly even criminal, in her dealings with the parents of certain pupils at St. Jude's Sunday School.'* "

Mr. Antrobus peered at me over the rims of his spectacles. "Well? What have you to say for yourself, Miss Tindall? According to this"— he waved the letter at me—"you have been demanding money for your services from parents who can ill afford to pay." The shock of such an accusation must have registered immediately in my face. Suddenly I felt light-headed and had to put out a hand to steady myself on a chair. "So you deny you approached Mrs. Deakin at her home?"

My head was swimming. Mr. Antrobus's voice seemed distant. My vision began to blur. "I . . . I . . . ."

"Well?" He showed no mercy.

Leaning heavily on the chair, I forced myself to address him. "I did visit Mrs. Deakin, but never to ask for money. I was concerned."

"Concerned?" He pushed back his wayward glasses once more. *"Concerned?"*

"Her daughter, Molly, had been absent from my Sunday school class for several weeks. I wanted to—"

The headmaster broke into my explanation before I could finish it. "Enough, Miss Tindall!"

"But, sir . . . ," I pleaded.

"Enough. You can state your defense at the hearing."

"Hearing?"

"There will be a full disciplinary hearing when you will be given a chance to defend your actions. Until then, I have no choice but to suspend you from your post at this school." He may as well have delivered the news with a black square on his head. But there was more. "It goes without saying that you are also suspended from your teaching duties at St. Jude's by Mrs. Parker-Smythe."

The name echoed around the room and bounced off the walls. *Parker-Smythe.* I should've known that she was behind this, although I had no idea at the time that she would stoop so low. She was acting not out of sheer malice, but out of fear. She was afraid that I might uncover something and had been pressured to act. I suddenly suspected Dr. Melksham's white-gloved hand in all this, although at the time, as I stood under the great vaulted ceiling of my classroom, I could think of very little, save that it may as well fall in on me and crush the life out of me. My world had suddenly ended.

"But, Mr. Antrobus." I suddenly found the

218

strength to rush toward him, but, I am ashamed to say, that by this time my reason had deserted me. I tugged at the hem of his topcoat as he towered above me on the dais.

"Please. No. It's lies. All lies!"

I must have appeared to him as a demented woman, deprived of any vestige of sanity. I felt his cold hands reach down and prize off my grasping fingers, as if I were a yapping terrier. He swiped at me with the letter. "Control yourself! Have you lost all sense?" At that moment, I probably had. My mind was a maelstrom; my breast a seething cauldron. I was railing at the injustice of the situation, but my innocence was no shield and my impetuosity forced the headmaster to act. Suddenly he bent low and pushed me back with such force that I staggered, colliding with a desk as I struggled to maintain my balance. The jab to my chest momentarily robbed me of my breath, but it meant my sanity was restored. As I gulped down lungsful of air, my reason seemed to return. My racing heart steadied. My head cleared a little—just enough to compose myself. I picked up the chair I had just knocked over and set it straight, then tucked a lock of wayward hair, which had broken loose in the fracas, behind my ear.

"Forgive me, sir," I croaked. "I will leave this instant."

Mr. Antrobus regarded me warily, like a lion tamer might a wildcat that he has temporarily managed to subdue. I picked up the pile of books that I had earlier placed on a nearby desk, then bobbed a curtsy. He acknowledged it with a nod, his eyes appearing larger than ever through his thick lenses. Just as I was halfway to the door, however, I turned. From somewhere deep inside me, a little well of courage suddenly sprang forth.

"I am innocent, sir," I told him through clenched teeth. "There are powerful forces at work here—dark forces. I am certainly not the guilty one in all of this and I intend to prove it."

CONSTANCE

"Fancy a drink?" says Flo later. She knows the nightmare has rattled my nerves. I've been on edge all day. "It'll do you good. I'm meeting Danny later on. He's bringing a friend."

The thought of an evening with Danny Dawson fills me with dread, especially if he brings a friend along, and Flo tries to pair us up.

Ma looks up from her sewing and rubs her tired eyes. "Go on, love," she urges. "Mr. Bartleby's coming over soon. I'll be fine."

I picture her holding hands with Mr. Bartleby while we're out. It's clear she wants time alone with him. And Flo's right. I need to stop thinking. My head is whirring constantly and my mind is filled with horrible visions. Suddenly before me appear the faces of the girls Miss Tindall mentioned to me: Molly Deakin and Gracie Arden. There were others, too: Maudie Dalton, twelve going on twenty, and Libby Lonergan, face of an angel and a singing voice to match. What has happened to them? Are they missing, too? Are they missing just like all those other girls and women? Just like Miss Tindall? And there's this shadow. It's him. *He's* there, moving silent and unseen in the swirling fog, leaving no echo, leaving no trace but the bloody remains of his kill. *He's* looming over me the whole time, breathing down my neck, making my flesh creep. Maybe I do need a little escape. A little fun. A little tipple.

"You're on," I say.

In half an hour, we're linking arms down Brushfield Street like a couple of swells. It's just gone eight of the clock and dark. The week after the two killings in one night there was hardly anyone around. We all shut ourselves away. Nearly three weeks on, women are still avoiding the side streets and the dark alleys—unless they get paid to go there, if you get my meaning—but it seems that most are going about their normal business, or pleasure. I even heard gobby Mrs. Morton, from down our street, say the Ripper had buggered off up to Gateshead now, after a poor girl was found filleted there.

We cross Commercial Street, but I balk as Flo steers me toward the Ten Bells on the corner. I know that Annie Chapman drank in there on the night it happened and I start to panic.

"What's the matter?" asks Flo sharply.

"It's, well, there's brass nails in there," I hear myself say. Brass nails is what we call loose women, and I fix my eyes on an old pro propped up against the bar.

Flo snorts and tugs at my arm. "My, my, we are getting up ourselves these days!" she chides. "This is Whitechapel, there's brass nails everywhere."

Inside it's smoky. The thick fug of tobacco hits me like a wall. There's a fiddle player in the corner and all the tables are full. Flo pushes past a handful of dockers standing by the entrance, like she owns the place. There's a few comments and a whistle, but they soon stop as soon as they see that Flo's meeting up with her beau. Danny's already sitting down, but he gives us a wave and stands up like a real gent.

"No seats in the lounge bar," he tells us above the din. He's wearing his Sunday jacket and tie. There's another lad with him, but his back is facing us and it's only when I'm in touching distance of him that he turns round. It's Gilbert Johns. He rises and smiles at me and I feel myself blush. I shoot a look at Flo that says: *"You've set me up."* I'm embarrassed and a little cross with her, but I manage to nod my head politely.

"Miss Constance," he says, holding out my chair for me. At least he's not calling me Con, I tell myself, although if I let him take liberties, I know it'll only be a matter of time.

"You two know each other, then?" chimes in Danny. I slide a look at Flo again, but butter wouldn't melt in her mouth.

Gilbert smiles. He's wearing a tweed jacket, but the sleeves are too tight and cling to his bulging biceps. In the low gaslight of the pub, he's not bad looking, neither, although I still think his eyes are too close together. "Sort of," he says, keeping his gaze on me.

"Gilbert lives down our street," explains Flo, adding, "Saw us home the other night, didn't ya?"

Danny rolls his eyes knowingly. "The Vigilance Committee."

Flo nudges him, but addresses Gilbert. "I keep telling him he ought to join," she tells him. It's like she's playing one off against the other, but that's just her style. She reaches over to Gilbert and feels his forearms. "Right muscly, aren't ya!"

"Oi!" says Danny. I'm worried things could get nasty.

Gilbert manages to bring it back from the brink of a row. He stands up, scraping his chair across the sawdust: "My round," he says. "What'll it be, Miss Constance?"

Flo looks up at him and I swear she flashes her lashes. "Mine's a port and lemon," she butts in.

"I'll have the same," I say, but I add a "please," and it makes Gilbert smile.

We watch him elbow his way to the bar. There's plenty of seamen in tonight, all right: a rowdy crew from America by the sounds of them. They're banging on the bar and shouting at the tops of their voices. Danny waits until Gilbert is swallowed by the crowd before he starts in on Flo. I don't blame him.

"Some of us have jobs at night. We can't be going round the streets looking out for this Saucy Jack, or whatever he calls himself," he tells her, his face like thunder.

I'm feeling like a gooseberry and can't wait for Gilbert to come back with the drinks. Flo and Danny are sparring with each other, jabbing with snide remarks and sarcastic barbs. So I'm looking all around me, anywhere but at them. It's then that I think I see her—a glimpse, a flash in the corner of the room. Could it be? I leap up suddenly and crane my neck. I feel my pulse race.

"What's up?" Flo breaks off from her quarrel with Danny to look at me.

"Miss Tindall," I reply. "I've just seen her." I flap my hand over in the direction where I think I

224

spotted her out of the corner of my eye. She was heading into the lounge bar.

"Oh!" is all she says and turns back to Danny, leaving me free to go and see if I was right. I worm my way through the seamen. One of them puts his hand on my bum; another, with an earring, presses against me and I smell his beer breath.

"Leave her alone," booms a voice, and I look round to see Gilbert carrying a tray of drinks above his head. Earring moves away and I retreat back to the table with Gilbert at my side.

"You find her, then?" Flo asks me after she's taken a gulp of her port and lemon.

I shake my head. "I couldn't get to the lounge."

"If she's there, she'll have to come back this way," says Flo wisely.

"Who?" asks Gilbert. He's taken off his jacket and draped it on the back of the chair.

"A friend," I reply.

"Her old teacher," chimes in Flo.

"Teacher's pet, eh?" says Danny with a sneer.

The lads down their pints of ale quickly and Danny's soon getting in another round. Flo's acting merrier by the minute, but I'm feeling on edge. I keep glancing at the entrance to the lounge bar every five seconds. I don't want to miss her. From somewhere in the corner, the Yankees are making even more noise. They've settled round a table and are thumping it and braying like donkeys. Danny's away at the bar again and comes back with news.

"They're arm wrestling," he tells us as he hands me my third port and lemon.

"Arm wrestling?" Flo perks up at the words, then shoots a look at Gilbert. "I bet you could beat 'em," she says.

The ale has already flushed Gilbert's face and he shakes his head. "Naa," he says, shaking his curly head. "I don't . . ."

"Go on!" jumps in Danny. "You afraid, or somefink?"

"Look at them forearms," says Flo, patting Gilbert's sleeve again as he stands at her side. "Like ham hocks."

"You're not scared, are ya?" jabs Danny. He's laid down the gauntlet.

Gilbert can't back off now. His manhood's at stake.

"Right," he says. He downs his ale in one, then wipes his mouth with his sleeve. "You're on!" he cries, and we watch as he marches over to the Yankees and challenges one of them to a contest.

"He's done it!" Flo is clapping her hands. "Let's go and watch," she says to Danny. Like a sulky mongrel, he obeys. He's betting on Gilbert making a fool of himself, but I wouldn't be so sure.

"Come on, Con!" Flo's tugging at my arm, but I'm not budging.

"I'd rather sit tight," I tell her, lifting my drink up in a sort of toast.

"Suit yourself." She shrugs, downing the rest of her port and lemon. She hooks an arm around Danny and drags him over to the table where Gilbert is poised to start his arm wrestle. I'm left on my own. I just hope no Jolly Jack Tar fancies his chances with me. I glance over to the lounge bar yet again. The crowd has thinned and it's then that I catch sight of her a second time. She's wearing her usual dark blue jacket and matching hat, and, yes, there's her green umbrella dangling from her arm.

"Miss Tindall!" I call out, but she doesn't hear me over the racket. Chin up, she just carries on, not minding the men pressing around her. She's heading for the door. "Miss Tindall!" I have to reach her. I stand up from the table, but suddenly feel light-headed. The booze has made me a little giddy and I steady myself against my chair. "Miss Tindall!" I call again. My eyes follow the crown of her hat as it bobs along among the crush.

Over in the corner, there's quite a crowd. The Yanks are cheering on their man, but Gilbert's got his supporters, too. There's jeering and whistling and it's doing my head in. I need to get out of this place. I need to follow Miss Tindall. I elbow my way toward the door just as it opens. For a moment, I lose sight of her; then my eyes latch onto her hat again as it glides into the night. A moment later, I, too, am over the threshold and outside. The cold air hits me hard and stings my face. For a moment, I'm stunned and my eyes find it hard to make sense of the dark. I blink and in that second I've lost her.

"Miss Tindall!" I hear myself mew pathetically.

A couple passing by give me an odd look, then tut to each other, like I'm some slut. My head switches from left to right. The gas lamp on the corner is glaring, but I still can't see far ahead of me. I don't know which way to turn, until suddenly I see a brougham clopping up Fournier Street and there's a figure silhouetted in its lights.

"Miss Tindall! Wait! Please!" My arms fly up and I dash out into the road. The sound of neighing horses fills my ears and I turn just in time to see a cart swerve to the left to avoid me.

"What the bloody hell!?" The driver is shouting at me, cursing at me. I think I shall cry as he shakes his fists at me. My mouth trembles, and my guts roil, but I scuttle away toward the pavement on the other side of the street.

"Little idiot. Could've got yourself killed!" an old crone scolds, then shuffles on.

I look about me, then back at the lights of the Ten Bells. They're getting dimmer now. Pinpricks in the blackness. I turn again and there she is. It's her. I know it is. She's about to go down Wilkes Street.

"Miss Tindall."

She stops for a second. Has she heard me? My heart misses a beat. She'll turn. I know she will. I'm holding my breath. But, no, she walks on and I hear myself bleat as she disappears into the blackness once more. I quicken my pace in pursuit, but I keep my head down. There are two men leaning against a doorway in Hanbury Street. *Hanbury Street.* My mind flashes to an image of poor Annie Chapman, found with her guts hanging out just a few yards away.

I swerve to avoid a pool of vomit and pass a dark alleyway. A man's earthy grunts stab the cold air. They make me shiver. I won't think on what he's doing.

I'm at the junction with Brick Lane. *People, thank God.* There's a small crowd outside the Frying Pan. For a moment, I feel a little safer; then I hear someone shout and a punch is thrown. A scuffle breaks out between two men—sailors, I think—and it soon turns into a brawl. I look down the street and strain my eyes toward the brewery. The smell of hops fights with rotting cabbage. *She's there!* I break out into a trot.

"Miss Tindall!"

She's no more than ten yards away.

"Miss Tindall!" I call again, following her round the corner.

She stops and turns. I stop, too, my heart barreling in my chest. Then it's like someone takes a sledgehammer to me. It's not her. It's an old woman, dressed in shabby garb. Her blue hat's all battered and the brolly, I see now, is a walking stick.

"What you want?" she yells, angrily shaking her stick at me. Her face is all bloated by booze.

I drop back. "Nothing," I say pitifully. "I thought you was . . ." My voice trails away to a whisper. I'm feeling like a fool and the woman carries on her way into Quaker Street.

EMILY

I think her time is growing closer. I could tell from the outset that she was different. Her quick speech and willingness to engage stood her apart from the other bedraggled waifs. She was pleasing to the eye, but not so attractive to the opposite sex as to be a distraction. I did, however, find her large eyes quite captivating and her general mien intelligent and alert. She was older, of course, but at eighteen she was yet young enough to mold. I could still fashion her into a thing of refinement, sculpt her manners and her outlook. Yet, my task would have been futile, had she not been a most willing participant in her own transformation. She lapped up her education like a cat does cream. She devoured the books that I gave her to read, then sought out more—often less suitable ones—of her own volition.

Her elocution, at least when speaking to me, was much improved. Her deportment, too, progressed as if she grew an extra inch in my presence. But there was more, a change perceptible only to me—a connection, a synthesis, a synergy, if you like. Between us, there was an undoubted chemistry. Whenever she read to me, or showed me her letters, or, latterly, when we began to discuss politics to a small degree, she would look at me as if to seek my approval in a way that I found both exciting and inspiring. There was an electric charge between us; the spark and fizz in her expression and manner, which had initially attracted me toward her, became quite magnetic. I had not managed to mold her, not entirely, but I had knocked off the hard edges, smoothed out those telltale irritations that make more genteel persons cringe and wince. And now I see that her physical metamorphosis appears to have created a vacuum. She is a glass awaiting a good vintage, a clasp open for a pearl. She is a vacant space ready to be filled, a room ready to be occupied. I think I am pushing at an open door.

CONSTANCE

Suddenly I find myself quite alone and it's started to drizzle. The wind whips the rain right into my face, making my eyes sting. There's no one about. A dog barks in the distance, but that is all the sound I hear—that and my own footsteps, echoing down the deserted street against the pitter-patter of rain. An eerie darkness is pressing around me.

I should turn back. A cat leaps up onto a window ledge at my side and damn near gives me a heart attack. Yes, I should turn back. I'm about to pivot on my heels when I hear my own footsteps joined by another's. They're heavier. A man's. I'm too afraid to glance over my shoulder, terrified of what I might see. Could it be *him?* The cat leaps down again and crosses my path. It's black. That's bad luck, ain't it? I can still hear them footsteps. Someone's close at hand. I walk in the center of the roadway. I tell myself it's safer here. His arms can't reach out of the shadows to grab me. I'll have more of a chance. If I scream, will anyone hear me? Will anyone come? There are houses all around me, but does anyone know I'm here?

"Miss Tindall," I mutter under my breath. "Miss Tindall, where are you?" My words catch in my throat and I start to cry. I feel the hot tears scald my cold cheeks. "I need you, Miss Tindall."

The footsteps again! They're growing closer. Louder. I can hear him breathing. Feel his breath wreathe my neck. *Please, God. No!*

From somewhere up ahead, there's a great rumbling sound that rises into a thunderous roar and I realize I've come to the railway viaduct. The air fills with steam and I press my hands over my ears as a train screeches overhead. All I can think of in that moment is that no one will hear me scream if he strikes me now! I shut my eyes tight, waiting for the steel to rip into my throat. Waiting for *him*. But he does not come. He does not come. Instead, when I open my eyes, there's a bright light. It's so bright that it fills all my vision and then I see her. It's Miss Tindall. This time, it's really her. She's standing there clear as day and she's smiling at me.

"Miss Tindall!" I cry. I can't believe my eyes. "Miss Tindall!" I rush forward, but it's like my feet are glued to the cobbles. I can't touch her, but she's reaching out to me. Then she speaks. She opens her lips and she says to me: *"Constance, know that I will always be with you."*

And suddenly I'm not afraid anymore. All the fretting and the fear fall away from me, like someone's lifted a load off my shoulders and I feel as content and peaceful as a suckled babe. It's like I'm wrapped in a warm blanket, in the arms of someone who'll take care of me. And that's when I know. I know that from now on, everything will be all right and that *he* cannot harm me. From now on, I know I have nothing to fear.

EMILY

And so it is done. The terror has gone and in its place oblivion. She is lying on the cobbles now, in a swoon. The rain is driving down hard and it is a piteous sight to see her, crumpled like a pile of rags, in the gutter. She will not be alone for long. Help is on its way. A police constable is not ten yards yonder. Soon he will round the corner and come across her. He will stop in his tracks and, for a moment, may even dread that he has come across Jack the Ripper's next victim. With trepidation, he will edge forward and, with his boot, will gently prod her limp body. He will be praying that she will moan, that she is simply gin sodden, and not slashed and gutted by this madman who is terrorizing the streets. He will hold his breath until he realizes that she is alive and has simply fainted. Relieved, he will call for help and all will be well.

How do I know? I know because something happened underneath the railway arch tonight; in a flash, in a moment, something remarkable. Something supernatural. Constance Piper is now me, and I am her. We are one, but not the same. We are a whole, yet divisible. The change will not happen instantly. It will take a little while, but, from now on, she will know I am near. You see, I am present, but I am not. I am to be found underfoot in the cobbles of Whitechapel, on the panes of grimy glass, in the fabric of people's clothes, on wood and on brick, even floating on the air you breathe. There are traces of me all around—of what was, what is and what will come—but only the chosen few can sense them. And Constance Piper is one of them.

I will be her guide. I am the lamp in her darkness. I will lead and she will follow. I shall show and she shall tell. She shall be the one to bear witness to the truth, and she shall shine a light into the deepest, darkest corners to uncover man's direst misdeeds. This is why I returned. This is now my new mission.

CONSTANCE

"Con! Con! Can you hear me?" Is that Flo's voice I hear? It's all muffled, like she's talking through a blanket. "Con!" I feel a hand on my arm. I open my eyes and there are blurred shapes all around me. "Oh, thank God!" I hear someone say.

It's Flo. She's beside me in this . . . Where am I? It's cold and it stinks. I lift my head, but she presses me down gently. "Lie still. You've had a nasty accident." She shakes her head and looks worried. "What was you thinkin'?"

"Miss Piper." A man's voice. Gruff and stern.

I turn my head and suddenly there's a terrible pain shooting up my jaw.

"I . . . I . . ." I feel the spittle run out of my mouth and down my cheek.

"Don't talk, Con," says Flo, patting my arm. She turns to the man beside her. He's top to toe in dark blue. I suddenly realize he's a copper.

"What the . . . ?" Despite the pain, I raise my head; then, too weak to hold it up, I let it fall back down onto the hard wooden platform that I'm lying on.

The constable ignores Flo and leans right over me. "Miss Piper, I found you in the street. I could smell alcohol on your breath."

"Leave it out, will ya!" scolds Flo. "Can't you see she's hurt?"

I put my hand up to my cheek and feel a crust over my skin. I am grazed.

"I'll call the surgeon," says the policeman.

But Flo won't have it. "You'll do no such thing," she tells him. "She's coming home with me right now and we'll take good care of her there." She's like a mother hen when she gets riled, is our Flo.

I see the copper's eyebrows lift. He's not used to being bossed by a girl. All the same, he nods. "Very well. If you think . . ."

"I do." Flo cuts in like a boxer with a mean left hook, and she slides her arm under my shoulder and helps me up.

The room swims a bit before I can make sense of where I am; then the penny drops. The brick walls, the iron grille. I'm in a cell—a cell at the police station—and I don't like it. I try and heave myself up from the bed. "Get me out of here!" I bleat.

" 'Course, Con. You come on 'ome with your big sis." She takes hold of my arm and pulls me upright. There's a lamp dangling from the ceiling and for a moment I'm blinded by its glare. Then I remember. I remember what happened before.

"Miss Tindall," I mumble. It hurts to move my jaw.

"What she say?" asks the copper.

Flo flashes me an angry look. "Nuffink," she snaps. "She didn't say nuffink." And she takes me by the arm and marches me out of the cell.

"I saw her, I tell ya," I protest, suddenly feeling a little stronger.

Flo looks round, like she doesn't want me to be heard. She pulls me toward the counter, where the old duty sergeant has the discharge book ready for her to sign. Quickly she makes her mark on the paper. As she bends over, I see the door behind is ajar. Inside I can make out at least four rossers, but there must be more. They're all listening to a man who's talking. He looks important and he's waving a piece of paper about like it's a flag.

"So there you have it, lads. Saucy Jackie's

latest. He says there'll be more. It's our job to make sure there aren't."

It's the night shift—for all the good they'll do. *He's* too clever for them by half, but at least now they're taking him seriously.

"Be careful now," says the sergeant as Flo hands him back his pen. "It's not safe for you ladies out there this time of night."

Flo snorts. "And don't we know it," she replies. "Best get your boys on the streets, eh?" she tells him, jerking her head toward the room where the men are gathered. Then she puts her arm through mine and we're out into the night once more. I'm not sure how I'll manage to stagger back home, but somehow the streets of Whitechapel don't hold as much dread as they did before. Now it's as if there's someone looking out for me, watching over me. It suddenly feels very different.

CHAPTER 22

Sunday, October 21, 1888

CONSTANCE

Next thing I know, I'm waking up in my own bed and it's light. The sun comes streaming through the holes in the curtains and hurts my eyes. I screw them up and moan. The church bells don't help, neither, making such a racket. Then I realize it's a Sunday.

"It's all right, love." It's Ma. She's sitting on the bed. "You 'ad us that worried," she says. But she's not scolding me. Her words are soft and round, like a big hug.

Just then, Flo comes in, carrying a jug. There's a rag over her arm. "I'll say she did," she mumbles, pouring out a cup of small beer before setting the jug on the bedside table. "Here," she says, thrusting the cup in front of my face. It's plain she's not as forgiving as Ma.

I manage to heave myself up on my elbows and take the cup. My face still hurts and so does my head. It feels like a football that's been kicked from one end of Brick Lane to the other. Slowly I part my lips to sip the beer. It feels cool on my dry throat, even though it hurts to open my mouth.

"You came a real cropper, my gal," says Ma, shaking her head. "Catching your face on the curb like that." This time, there's a note of disapproval in her voice.

"I hope it learns ya," chimes in Flo, wetting the cloth. She reaches over and dabs my cheek. I wince. My hand flies up to the right side of my face and I push her away.

"But I saw her," I protest.

"Who?" asks Ma. She turns to Flo. "What's she on about?"

Flo and I swap looks. I can tell she thinks I'm off my rocker. "You know you can't hold ya drink, Connie," she tells me with a shake of the head.

I open my mouth again to gripe, but the pain reminds me to keep my own counsel. I slump back on the bolster. It's no use. I know what I've got to do and I'll just have to do it alone.

So I wait. I wait until Flo slips off to see Danny, and Ma goes off to church. They thought they'd left me sleeping. But I've more important things to do. I ease myself out of bed and pad over to the chest. My head still feels like someone's driven a coach and horses through it, but I open the lid and take out my old pinny. The card is still there in the pocket. I force myself to focus. *Brown's Hotel, Albemarle Street, Mayfair.* I know there is no time to lose.

EMILY

Before we rejoin Constance, I must take you back again to the day of my dismissal. I recall little of how I returned to my lodgings that day. I must have been too shocked and dazed to be able to record my journey back to Richard Street. Yet, return I must have, because some while later, I remember my landlady, Mrs. Appleton, banging on my door, asking me if I was unwell. Apparently, I had not emerged from my room for almost thirty-six hours and she was growing concerned about my welfare. I dared not tell her the truth. Kind as she was, it would test even her limits of generosity to give shelter to an out-of-work teacher with no prospects and no other means of supporting herself. I feigned illness, which, as it turned out, was actually prophetic.

It was little wonder that my health began to deteriorate. As my funds dwindled, I was forced to make economies in order to pay my rent. Soon I could no longer afford a fire in my grate, nor nutritious food to eat. Naturally, I looked for work, but without references, my options were severely limited. Then, one evening, I returned from trudging the streets, by now so desperate that I would take any form of employment, when I began to feel feverish. A great fire was burning at the back of my throat, and despite wrapping myself in three woolen blankets, I was unable to stop shivering like a wreck. My head began to throb and my chest tightened. Shortly after the coughing began, I took to my bed. I remember very little of the next four or five days. Only later was I told that dear Mrs. Appleton kindly lit a fire and kept a kettle boiling on the hob so that the room was constantly filled with steam to soothe my rasping lungs. I do, however, remember that on the fifth day my fever broke and I returned to the world, still coughing and wheezing like an engine, but out of serious danger. It was then that Mrs. Appleton asked me if I had any friends she might contact who may wish to pay me a visit. Knowing I was persona non grata at the church mission, Geraldine Cutler was the only acquaintance who sprang to mind. I had not paid her a visit since my arrival in London, but it had always been my intention. Mrs. Appleton sent her a telegram and on the very same day a carriage called at my meager lodgings and the driver delivered a note. I was invited to convalesce in the comfort of the Harley Street home Geraldine shared with her surgeon husband, Terence. She would refuse, she wrote, to take "no" for an answer, and I was in no position to shun her generosity. And that is where I spent the next seven days, being cosseted in a large bed with duck feather pillows and blankets that were not coarse against my skin. I was fed chicken broth by the bowl and feasted on sweet black grapes. My sore throat was soothed with honey and lemon, and my persistent cough assuaged by a foul-tasting linctus. With such care and attention being lavished upon me, my recovery was undoubtedly hastened, but this unbridled hospitality was, I later discovered, offered freely by only one side of the matrimonial partnership. I was still far too ill to remember much about the first few days of my confinement. My fever came and went. I slept for much of the time, and it was only later that I recognized Terence Cutler—although, at first, I was not entirely sure where I had seen him before. Naturally, I mentioned to Geraldine that her husband's face seemed familiar and then it came to me.

"Whitechapel Workhouse Infirmary," I said out loud. "That is where I have seen your husband." I regularly escorted sick and injured women there.

Geraldine raised a brow. "I think you must be mistaken, dear Emily," she told me. "My husband works at St. Bartholomew's."

From her reaction, I could see she was not happy about my remark and so I let it lie. That night, however, I heard raised voices downstairs; the following day, I became aware of a frostiness between the pair of them. Shortly afterward, it was apparent to me that my presence was an increasing source of friction between Geraldine and her husband. I began to feel ill at ease and I was certain that my days in the Cutler residence were numbered. I knew I would have to vacate that capacious bed in favor of more modest accommodation. I had been forced to leave Mrs. Appleton's for good, but Geraldine recommended another lodging house just a few streets away and supplied me with an excellent reference. More important, she also gave me money, although I preferred at the time to think of it as a loan, as a deposit for the new room. Just how I would be able to pay back the money, I was not sure. All I knew at the time was that I would be forever in her debt. If only I knew then, what I know now.

CONSTANCE

Don't ask me how I drag my sorry carcass all the way from Whitechapel to Albemarle Street in the West End, but I do. It's like someone is egging me on, telling me I need to get there, that I *have* to get there. I wrap myself up in my old shawl and pull my hat down as far as it'll go, so my scabby cheek won't show. As I reach the hotel and see the doorman all togged up in his fancy livery, with his top hat and his gold brocade, I want the ground to swallow me. I'm just about to turn round and bolt for home when I hear this faint voice somewhere in the distance. *"Have courage,"* it says. *"Have faith."* So I stick out my chin, take a deep breath and march right up to the front door.

"And where do you think you're going?" asks the doorman. He sidesteps so quick to bar my way that I very nearly bump into him. "Trade round the back." I don't like the look on his face.

His nostrils are flaring and his lips are curling in a smirk. It's like I'm a bad smell.

It's no use. I step back and put on my best speaking voice. "I am here to see a guest," I tell him. I sound such a toff that I surprise myself—and him.

"A guest, indeed?" He tries to mimic my fancy talk.

"Yes."

He scowls and bends low so his face is peering under the brim of my hat.

"The likes of you still need to go round the back. Who do you think you are?"

"Go on, Constance. Be brave." It's that voice again, only louder.

"Be brave," I says to myself.

"What?" barks the doorman.

"Please allow me to pass," I say in my best voice. "I have urgent business." I lunge to the right, but again he blocks my way.

"Oh, no you don't!" he says. "Try that again and I'll call the guards." That's when he starts to manhandle me. He grabs hold of my wrist and I let out a cry.

"No! Please! I need to . . ."

So he's bending my arm behind my back and is about to pull me away from the door when someone calls out.

"Miss Piper!"

The doorman stops in his tracks. I stop

245

wriggling and we both switch toward the door where an elegant woman is standing, glaring angrily.

"What is the meaning of this?" she asks the doorman. Her voice is all cold and it cools his hot head in a moment, I can tell you.

"I . . . Forgive me, miss, I . . ." He's lost for words, and when she says: "Miss Piper is a friend of mine. Let her pass, if you please," well, you could rub his nuts with a wire brush, if you pardon my French. He's that dumbstruck.

That's what I call making an entrance, and as I tug at my ruffled sleeves, I beam at him before following Miss Beaufroy back into the hotel foyer.

There's a porter nearby and he's just put down the trolley he's been pushing with a small trunk on it. He looks bemused. The hoity-looking man behind the desk asks Miss Beaufroy if everything is all right. She slaps her gloves in the palm of her hand, takes a breath and says: "Tea for two, if you please. We shall have it here." She gestures to the comfy chairs clustered around a low round table. "And take my trunk back up to my room. I shall be staying on." Her voice is calm but firm. The porter flashes a look at Mr. Up Himself behind the desk, who nods. It is settled, so I follow Miss Beaufroy and let her sit first before I sink, giddy and exhausted, into the sofa.

As I wilt opposite her, she catches sight of my cut jaw and grimaces.

"But your cheek!" Her eyes are wide. "The doorman . . ."

"No," I reply. I finger my bruise. "It happened last night. I fell in the gutter and hit my face on the way down."

She looks worried. "You poor thing." She seems concerned, but she checks herself. We both look at each other, as if each of us has got some explaining to do. She wants to know why I'm here, I'm sure of that. And I want to find out how she knew to come to my rescue outside. An odd silence hangs between us, but it's not frosty or awkward. It's as if we've known each other for a very long time and it's comfortable, like an old armchair that knows the shape of your body. Suddenly I get that same warm feeling that I felt last night when I was all alone in the street, except for Miss Tindall, as if someone's stroking my soul.

Finally she's the one to break the silence. "I knew you would come," she tells me straight. "I'd planned to leave today, but then I felt I shouldn't. Something stopped me." She's smiling gently as she fixes me with a look that bores straight through me. "Yes. I knew you would come."

I return her smile, even though it hurts me to move my mouth. I want to tell her that I knew I had to see her, too, but I don't want her to think I've lost my marbles. I smooth my skirt and notice the hem's all caked in mud. No wonder the doorman didn't want me to be seen in the foyer! Yet, here I am, in the company of a lady at a top hotel. I don't care if the porters are muttering in the corner, or that Mr. Up Himself is so clearly put out. It don't . . . It shouldn't feel right and yet somehow it does.

A couple of flunkies suddenly appear from nowhere. One carries a silver tray, with a silver pot on it and china cups. They pour out the tea and ask us if we take milk and sugar, then bow and leave us alone again. No one's ever bowed to me before. I'm not sure I like it, but I suppose it's different if you're born to it.

Now we're alone again, there's another silence. I study her face. It's beautiful, but there is sadness in her eyes and worry lines crease her brow. Her words flash through my mind again. She knew I'd come, she said. How did she know? I didn't know myself until I woke up this morning that I had to find her again.

I take a deep breath and begin. "You said, miss, that you knew. . . ."

She is nodding and looking at me oddly. "It may sound strange, but I believe you have been sent to me." She sips her tea as if she's just asked me the time. She returns her cup to its saucer and fixes me with earnest eyes. "Is there someone you loved, and who loved you, who has passed away recently?" she asks.

I'm that taken aback by the question that for a second or two I can't answer. It's like my tongue won't work till my brain tells it what to do. Then I remember.

"My pa," I say. "He died three years ago."

She gives a little shake of her head. "*Died* is such a final word," she says. "Don't you think? It's like a sharp flint."

I suppose she's right. I'd never really thought of it that way before. In the East End, people die every day. Young, old and all stops in between. It's something that happens, like eating or sleeping.

She tilts her head. "*Passed over* is how I like to think of it, of dying," she tells me softly. "Death can't be the end. Everyone leaves their trace here on earth. Everyone leaves something of themselves, don't you think?" She's suddenly all wistful, but I know exactly what she means. I keep my pa's old clay pipe in a drawer upstairs and run my fingers over the stem and bowl every day, just to feel closer to him.

"Yes, I suppose they do," I reply.

"I firmly believe so," she says, but there's a catch in her voice. "That's what makes these brutal murders so awful." She switches back to me so sudden that she scares me. I feel my blood suddenly run cold.

"And you've still had no word from your sister?" I say in a whisper, careful that we're not overheard by the flunkies standing nearby.

She, too, is mindful and leans in toward me. "Geraldine? None, but I have found out more."

"More?"

Her eyes dart around the foyer before they settle on me again. "My sister's husband . . ." She pauses, trying to think how to frame her words. "He is a gynecologist and a surgeon."

The first big word she uses means nothing to me, but I know what a surgeon is right enough, and I know that Jack can find his way around a woman's innards like a true professional. My eyes open wide. "And?"

"Naturally, I have asked him where my sister might be and he told me they'd quarreled and she left him." *Even toffs have their tiffs,* I think, but I let her carry on uninterrupted. "But he says he does not know where she has gone. At first, he assumed she would return to my mother and me in Sussex, but when I told him she had not, he became agitated. When I said that we needed to inform the police . . . Oh, God, help me!" She suddenly closes her eyes and bows her head.

I look around, hoping no one has seen her. She pulls out her handkerchief and dabs her nose. "I'm sorry," she says. "It was such a shock."

"What was?" I ask clumsily, like a bull in a china shop.

She gulps back an angry sob. "I discovered that my brother-in-law treats women in Whitechapel with certain disorders."

"Ah," I say as her words sink in. I need to be sure of exactly what she suspects him of doing, so I sit tight and let her carry on.

"If Geraldine found out that her husband regularly goes to Whitechapel and consorts with these women and threatened to expose him, then he might have . . ." She can't say it out loud, but I know what she means and her accusation shocks me to the core.

I gasp and the sip of tea I'd just taken suddenly sprays out of my mouth. A flunky's head turns and he frowns disapprovingly. I dab the front of my dress with a napkin. "You're saying your brother-in-law . . . ?"

She nods and her face contorts into a painful grimace, as if she really doesn't want to believe what she has just confided in me. "I know there are witnesses who say that Jack the Ripper is a gentleman. I pray it is too much of a coincidence, but I need to be sure. That's why I need your help." She reaches out and places her hand on my knee, and the fear and confusion I felt a moment ago suddenly dissipates.

"How?" I ask calmly.

"I believe you are in touch with the other side."

251

"The other side?" For a second, I'm shocked. Confused too. It must show in my face.

"You seem to know things that most people can't possibly know."

I feel my guts churn. She's right: the dreams, the bright lights, the strange feelings. I look at her with wide eyes.

"I want you to hold a séance," she says.

If she'd asked me last week, I'd have laughed in her face. I suddenly think of Madame Morelli at the Frying Pan and perhaps I should feel insulted. But not today, not now, not after last night. I nod slowly, as if she has just asked me to accompany her on a shopping trip or to go for a walk in the park.

"You want me to find out if your sister has"— I pause, recalling her exact phrase—*"passed over."*

Her eyes are suddenly bright and she's nodding her head as she speaks to me. "I knew the moment we met that we had a connection. I know you are special."

"Yes, I am special," I want to say. *"I've been given a gift."* I can see things, feel things, know things that other people can't; and last night, in the brilliance of that bright light that nearly blinded me and exploded in my brain, I finally understood. I should use it, this gift. I should use it, as Miss Tindall believes everyone should use their talents, for the benefit of others. I will find

252

her, too. Sooner or later. But for the moment, there is someone who needs me more.

"I will help you," I reply to Miss Beaufroy, adding most assuredly: "But it won't be easy." The truth, I'm learning, is never obvious.

CHAPTER 23

Monday, October 22, 1888

EMILY

Once again I'm in the Sessions House at Broad Sanctuary for the resumption of the inquest into the Whitehall torso. The hall is overflowing with the common horde and the press. And among so many morbidly curious voyeurs, I spot Pauline and Constance. Seeing them seated, side by side, fills me with a certain pride. I have brought them together, and I find much consolation in that. And what a young lady Constance looks. She has been decked out in a close-cut jacket and a skirt with a frilled hem. She even wears kid gloves and sports a fashionable hat. I beam as I watch her converse with Pauline just before Mr. Troutbeck enters the room to begin this, the second session of the inquest.

Pauline, present at the first session two

weeks ago, takes out the same notebook in which she has recorded all the salient points. She does the same again, listening intently to the evidence given by Mr. Brown, foreman of Messrs. Grover, the builders of the new offices, and several men connected with the works. She notes the fact that in their opinion the remains were not in the vault on the Friday or Saturday before the discovery.

Toward the end of the day, it is Dr. Bond who takes the witness stand once more. Mr. Troutbeck questions him closely. The former declares that the leg and foot must have been lying among the debris for several weeks. A careful examination, he assures the coroner, revealed the leg had been severed from the thigh at the knee joint by clean incisions. Perhaps most important, he says he has no doubt that the limb belonged to the trunk discovered a fortnight before.

Constance has sat attentively throughout, with her back straight, her expression alert. I am sure that razor-sharp intellect of hers is mentally processing all that is being said. And now it is time for Mr. Troutbeck to sum up the evidence. He tells the jury that after the verdict has been found, the police will be left to make inquiries, and, if possible, elucidate the mystery. "For it most certainly is one," he quips. There is a ripple of laughter among the crowd, but they are quickly brought to order once more. Mr. Troutbeck continues by conjecturing that most probably the other parts of the body will turn up someday. And he adds: "For, so far as I can see, the aim has been to destroy the possibility of identity rather than to destroy the body."

At his words, Constance and Pauline swap wary looks. Nothing that either of them has heard today has helped allay their fears.

"Gentlemen of the jury, have you reached your verdict?" asks the clerk after the men return from their deliberations ten minutes later.

"We have, sir."

"And what did you find?"

The rather obvious, but unsatisfactory, reply is unequivocal. "Found dead, sir."

CONSTANCE

Today I am not myself. I do not mean I am ill, although I may be. I simply feel different. It's as if all the nerves in my brain have suddenly connected and I can make sense of things that held no meaning for me before. I suddenly know things, too. I know how to deport myself, how to hold a teacup, how to be a lady.

I am also in a different place. Another world, peopled by fine ladies who hold their shoulders back and titter politely and say things like, "Oh, my goodness" and "Simply marvelous." There are potted palms and long mirrors and a string quartet plays in the corner. I know I should feel like a fish out of water, surrounded by all these toffs who are savvy about minding their p's and q's, but I don't. I feel right at home.

We—that is Miss Beaufroy and I—are sitting in the elegant Victoria Tea Rooms, just round the corner from Westminster Abbey and a few paces away from the Sessions House. The tables are covered in starched linen cloths and the bone china is the very finest. All about us, people are nibbling chocolate cake or smothering scones in jam and cream, but we're in no mood to eat. Not after what we've just heard. Miss Beaufroy orders a pot of Darjeeling.

I don't just feel different. I look different, too. Instead of my usual woolen shawl, I'm wearing a smart jacket, and my old linsey dress has been replaced by one made of taffeta, with a frill round the hem. I'm even trying to get used to a bustle, although it's hard to sit down. And I'm wearing gloves, like every other lady in the place. Miss Beaufroy has kitted me out so that I look like a fitting companion for her, on the outside, at least.

I catch sight of myself in the mirror and I hardly recognize me in my new attire. I appear older, more self-assured, and, of course, I am no longer marked out by my clothes as a working girl. For a moment, I even think I have a look of Miss Tindall about me—the way I hold my head, the way I smile. But then I dismiss the thought—how foolish I am.

The notebook lies open on the table between us, and Miss Beaufroy is glancing at it and frowning. "The description is of Geraldine," she says, shaking her head. "Over twenty-five years of age, a well-nourished woman, fair skin and dark hair. No indications that she had borne a child, tall, not used to manual labor." She steels herself to say it. "It is she."

I, on the other hand, am not convinced. I glance around me before I pipe up: "It's her and at least a thousand other ladies in London." She seems a little taken aback by my forthrightness. I still have a long way to go to be a real lady, I know.

She pauses for a moment, as if she's just thought of something important, then reaches for her portmanteau.

"Here," she says, handing me a small photograph.

I see a round-faced woman with a strong jaw. Her hair is dark and curled over her forehead. She reminds me a little of Miss Tindall—similar eyes, that same faraway look. I smile and hand it back after I've saved the image in my head. "There is a certain likeness with you," I tell her, although I don't say that Miss

Beaufroy is by far the prettier of the two sisters.

"May I?" I ask, politely this time, as I point to the notebook. She slides it over to me and I scan the neat writing. As she sips her tea, I thumb through the notes she took at the earlier proceedings. She watches me inquisitively; yet there's a calm acceptance in her manner. It is as if she is confident that I will find the needle she has missed in this haystack of evidence. She is putting her faith in me. I read Dr. Bond's detailed description of the woman's torso. It contains words that are new to me: "incisions," "debris" and "preservation," but somehow I understand their meaning. It's as if someone is translating them for me in my head. Less than a minute later, something strikes me.

"No uterus," I say. It's a word I've never said before. It sounds queer bouncing off my tongue.

Miss Beaufroy looks shocked and glances about her, hoping no one else heard me.

Not to be put off, I jab at the page. "Annie Chapman and Catherine Eddowes had theirs cut out, too." There is no refined way of putting it.

Miss Beaufroy whispers her startled response. "So you think the same maniac, this Jack . . ."

"It's possible," I reply.

Another minute passes. She's jotted down the ramblings from some of the workmen. Most of them swore the torso was not there the day before, but Dr. Bond disputes that. He said that "decomposition" must have happened in the vault. And I know, for a fact, that it was crawling with maggots. It's then that I suddenly hunch over the page and my eyes latch onto a word in the notes, and it's as if my finger is being guided toward a certain passage: *The victim had suffered from severe pleurisy.* I point to the phrase, then look up.

Miss Pauline meets my gaze with wide eyes. "I quite forgot."

"So, did she?"

"Have pleurisy?"

"Yes. Did your sister have pleurisy?"

"No. I don't believe so." Miss Beaufroy shakes her head. "She had a slight cough the last time I saw her, but then don't most people who live in London?"

Of course, she was right. My own dear mother and my sister were testament to that. The smog was no respecter of age or class.

I feel excited. "Then this is good news. The woman in the vault did suffer from pleurisy. Look here, it says, 'one lung was healthy, but the other lung was adherent.'" My mouth widens into a smile. "Don't you see? It's a negative proof. It's not your sister." I hear the words coming from my mouth and I can't believe I am saying them. I'm talking like a scientist now.

Miss Beaufroy smiles, too. "You're right," she says excitedly. "She is so like the description given in every other respect, except in the most telling of all."

"Exactly!" I cry.

She lunges forward and grasps hold of both my hands.

"I can't tell you how happy this makes me," she says, her eyes clamped onto mine.

"Me too," I say, and suddenly we are united in a shared moment of relief and joy.

I fear, however, it is short-lived.

CHAPTER 24

Tuesday, October 23, 1888

EMILY

Terence Cutler is taking his weekly clinic in the Whitechapel Workhouse Infirmary. It's toward the end of the evening and he's craving a brandy. He's seen the usual string of unfortunates with their repulsive complaints— their rashes and warts and chancres. There are those who regularly poison themselves, too, sluicing out their intimate and much-abused orifices with warm water mixed with alum and sulphate of zinc. They come to him when all else fails; these poor, pathetic creatures are so utterly without hope. Young and old women alike lift up their skirts and splay their legs for him as if they were simply opening their mouths so he can examine their tonsils. His mind sometimes drifts to that young girl, Molly. He regrets asking her name. It comes back to haunt him far too often.

Now that Jack's stalking Whitechapel, however, the women come to him with a new ailment. Fear. Many of them are worried sick. Yet, sometimes he's tempted to think they deserve all the ills that befall them. He knows of some men who even applaud this Ripper character because he's helping to rid the streets of such filth. They certainly agree with that sentiment at his club, despite the fact that several of its members often avail themselves of the women's services on a drink-fueled evening, then complain of burning groins a few days later. But then, he tells himself, it's far easier to appear to have principles than to live by them.

So he's tended to the usual stream of wretches and is about to tell the midwife that he'll only see one more, when his next patient causes him to say her name out loud. "Mary Kelly!" he exclaims, his voice tinged with surprise, or is it delight?

Certainly not many of his gentlemen acquaintances would turn their noses up at Mary Jane Kelly, given the chance. Whereas most of the women Cutler treats wear the scars of the street on their drink-bloated faces, Mary Kelly is still pretty enough. With her fair hair, large blue eyes and clear skin, she's the darling of the whores. Despite her Irish name, she's spent years in Wales and speaks with the singsong dialect of the Valleys. She'd married a miner, but her husband had been killed in a pit accident and she'd eventually found her way to London and into the mean streets of Whitechapel. Earlier in the year, she'd come to him, asking for an abortion. He had duly obliged—for a fee, of course. Then, last month, he had seen her again; her face all bloodied as she sought help at the infirmary. He assumed that her common-law husband, and the one she claimed was responsible for her unwanted child—although she could not possibly be certain—was to blame for her injuries. Like most men of his ilk, Joseph Barnett—no relation, of course, to the Reverend Samuel—is a bully and a brute whose idea of sport is to beat a woman until he draws blood. And for some reason, Mary Kelly tolerates him, although not for much longer. But tonight, at any rate, sees her back at the Whitechapel Workhouse Infirmary once again.

"Miss Kelly," he says more formally. Instead of her usual jaunty air, however, her shoulders are slumped and there's a sheepish look on her face, he notes. "Take a seat."

Her movements are slow, labored even. She nods by way of acknowledgment, but does not speak at first.

The surgeon regards her face with a professional eye. "Your injuries have healed well," he remarks. She never wears a hat, so it is easy to see her cheek that needed dressing a little over a month ago.

Mary touches her jaw lightly. "Yes, sir," she mumbles.

Cutler leans forward over the desk and softens his tone. "But I dare say you have come to see me on another matter."

She swallows hard and bites her lips. "I'm in the club again, sir," she says, her cheeks flushing pink.

He'd guessed it the moment she'd walked in, of course.

"I see." He pauses. It is not his place to judge, but he does and he despairs. He waits for her to continue. He wants to make her feel uncomfortable, ashamed.

"The pennyroyal didn't work," she tells him, spitting out the words in a sudden show of panic. Her lips tremble. Her eyes dip to the floor.

"How far gone are you?"

"I ain't been on the rag for five months." A tear rolls down her cheek.

"*Five months?*" He tuts and shakes his head.

"You are too far, Mary," he tells her, abandoning all formality.

Her face puckers. "What? No!" She lurches forward and slaps her hand on his desk. "I can't be. You did it before!" Her voice is warped with anger.

Cutler is forced to retreat into his chair. "That is precisely why, Mary. Less than six months ago. It is too dangerous to do it again, so soon." He meets her gaze as she glowers at him over the desk. But then her shoulders heave in a sudden sob and she takes a step back.

"I've got the money." She pulls out a handful of coins from her tatty apron pocket. One by one, she counts them out on the desk. "Two, three, four shillings. There. I've got enough, see." Her voice is as bitter as aloe.

Cutler remains unmoved. He shakes his sandy head and strokes his moustache in thought. "The money is irrelevant, Mary." His tone is conciliatory. "We are talking about your life."

A curious smile curls her lips and suddenly she rises from her chair. "My life?" she snorts. "I know it's already over, either way." She punches her own belly with her fist. Her simmering anger mounts. "There's not enough to feed just me, let alone a babe. I'll die this winter, Mr. Cutler, and there's the truth of it." With a look of despair on her face, she pivots and storms out of the room without so much as a backward glance.

Cutler watches her bluster toward the door and slam it behind her. He rolls his eyes; then he slumps forward on his desk, hiding his face in his hands. He cannot blame her. He has seen it all before, but it never gets any easier. Time and again, he asks himself why he works among these godforsaken women without hope of redemption. It's hardly for the money, although the extra does come in handy to service Geraldine's extravagant tastes in French perfume and fashionable hats. He plunges back into his chair and strokes his moustache in thought. Perhaps it's because there is something deep within him that tells him he needs to leave a legacy to this wicked world. He cannot father a child with his wife, so he is compelled to compensate for such inadequacy in his own small way. And that is when the idea suddenly strikes him. I see his eyes light up, like an electric bulb. A thought has planted itself in his head and he drums his fingers on the desk. His plans will take shape over the course of the next two weeks. He will ruminate and procrastinate. And he will grab the opportunity when it arises. Yes, his idea is a small seed, but soon it will germinate. And it involves the desperate young woman who has just flown from his surgery in such mortal danger.

CHAPTER 25

Thursday, October 25, 1888

CONSTANCE

"Well, hark at you!" Flo sizes me up and down as I walk through the door and I wonder why. I freeze to the floor. "Aren't you the lady?" she mocks.

Ma squints up from her sewing by the hearth. She's wearing her spectacles and peers over the top of them to get a better look. "What nice boots, dear," she says.

I follow her eyes and look down at my feet to see I'm still wearing the pretty Tavistock button boots. My heart sinks. I thought I was being so careful, but I've forgotten to take them off. I'd left home that morning in my old clothes. I'd made up some excuse about helping Old Joe Marsden's wife shift some of her fruit and veg. Only I didn't, of course. I met Miss Beaufroy at a ladies' outfitters and she footed the bill for my new togs. On my return, I stopped off at St. Jude's and changed back into my old clothes, which I'd hidden at the back of the cupboard where we keep the Sunday school books. I wasn't ready to tell Ma and Flo, you see. It's probably because I don't really believe what's happened myself, but now I feel I owe them some sort of an explanation. Even if it is a lie.

"A lady at the church was giving them out," I tell them. "Fancy, aren't they?"

"I'll say," chimes in Flo. "Too fancy for Whitechapel, at any rate."

I'm saved by a knock at the door. We all jump, but then we hear a familiar voice.

"Have no fear, dear ladies!" It's Mr. Bartleby. I glance at the clock on the mantelpiece. Six o'clock. He's come for his weekly tea.

I'm nearest the door, so I open it and greet him. I even manage a smile.

"Come in, Mr. Bartleby," I say.

As he enters, he brings with him a cold, smoggy blast from the street, which sets Ma coughing again. He hands her the box he's carrying.

"Bakewell tart," he tells her with a wink. She titters and coughs even harder.

"Put it on a plate, there, Flo," she directs as soon as she gets her breath back. Flo obeys.

I help Mr. Bartleby off with his big coat and relieve him of the *Evening News* he's carrying under his arm. I catch sight of the headline: THE QUEEN AND THE EAST END MURDERS. He tracks my gaze.

"You signed the petition, didn't ya, Connie?" he asks tongue in cheek.

"I heard about it," I say, hanging his coat on

the peg. I know a group calling itself the Women of the East End has managed to get over four thousand signatures on their petition to close all brothels.

"Bunch of gospel-grinders, if you ask me," butts in Flo.

"Nobody did, dear," says Ma, waddling through to the kitchen.

"If they close all the knocking shops, then where will all the toffs go?" Flo carries on with a snigger.

The table is already set, so we bid our guest to sit and offer him a stout. I go and fetch the pot of a stew from the range. Flo brings the plates and ladles out the dumplings and gravy and a few scrag end bits of meat.

Our talk is of the murders, of course. The inquest into poor Liz Stride opened today. Then we get onto what Mr. Bartleby labels "the business." That's when we show him what we've pilfered over the week, but it's slim pickings tonight. He's looking at a gold watch, a cuff link and a bracelet.

"This all?" he asks, taking out his loupe from his waistcoat pocket.

"It's quiet these days. People don't loiter on the streets no more," protests Flo.

"Two shillings the lot," he says, flinging down the cuff link. Clearly, he's not impressed. He drums his fingers on the table as if to say what's next, then spies the newspaper he's left on the arm of the chair and draws it toward him.

" 'Suicide caused by dreams of Jack the Ripper,' " he reads out loud. "What's this?"

"Read it to us, will ya, Con?" urges Flo.

I clear my throat and begin. " 'An inquest was held at Sheffield, yesterday, on the body of Mrs. Theresa Unwin, who committed suicide on Monday morning by cutting her throat.' "

"Poor dear," says Ma, shaking her head.

"Go on," says Flo, elbows on the table.

" 'Her husband, a man of private means, said his wife had for some time been low-spirited, and on Monday morning she told him that she had had a nasty dream, and thought "Jack the Ripper" was after her. A little while afterward, Mrs. Unwin was found dead with her throat cut. A verdict of temporary insanity was returned.' "

I look up to see Mr. Bartleby with an odd grin on his face. "A nasty dream, eh?" He chortles; I frown. "You 'ad one o'them, just before the Saucy Jack downed two in one night, didn't ya, Con?"

My head darts to Flo and I feel betrayed. She glances down. At least she feels bad about it, I tell myself.

"Yes." I jut out my chin to show I'm not ashamed. "I did have a dream about the murders, as it happens. It's all this gruesome talk." I try to brush it off.

Mr. Bartleby cocks his head and fixes me with a stare. "You better watch yourself, my girl," he warns. "We don't want you ending up with your throat cut, un' all." He draws his forefinger across his neck and sticks out his tongue.

"Harold!" exclaims Ma. She's shocked by his behavior. I think we all are, even Flo.

That night in bed, I don't cuddle up to Flo as I usually do to keep warm. Normally, in autumn and winter, I put my feet on her knees, but not tonight. In the space between us lies a sense of betrayal. It's deep and it's cold and I'm so angry with her that I clench my fists under the covers.

After a few moments of icy silence, she finally speaks from the bottom of the bed.

"I know I shouldn't have said about your dream, Con."

I let her stew for a moment, then say: "No, you shouldn't."

There's another silence. "But you've got to admit you've been acting odd these past few days, thinking you saw Miss Tindall and—"

I jerk up onto my elbow, feeling the anger tighten my chest. "I saw her, I tell you. I did."

A shaft of light from the streetlamp illuminates her and I see her body shudder as she starts to giggle. But then she catches my expression and puts her hand over her mouth to stifle her laughter. She understands it's not funny.

"Let's get some sleep," she says.

It takes me a while to drop off, but when I do, I have another dream. I see a large room with drawn velvet drapes at the window. In the center is a large bed, a rich person's bed, and in it is a woman. At first, all I can make out is her outline. Her hair is dark and there are two men standing by her. One, a doctor I presume, is listening to her chest with a stethoscope; the other watches anxiously.

"As I feared," says the doctor. "It's pleurisy."

The other man is tall, with sandy hair and a moustache. He bows his head.

"But she will live?"

The doctor shakes his head. "I fear I cannot say for sure, Mr. Cutler."

I wake suddenly and find myself struggling to breathe. My forehead's damp with sweat. "No," I mutter.

At the bottom of the bed, Flo stirs. She turns over, then settles again. I know I need to tell Miss Beaufroy about what I've just seen as soon as I can.

EMILY

In the darkness of a Harley Street town house, something stirs. The fires have been doused, the doors bolted and the servants all taken to their beds in the attic, but someone, or something, is about. Terence Cutler is suddenly awakened from his slumber by a sound. A footfall on the stair? A step on the landing? A click of a lock?

At first, he lies still, listening, but all he can hear is the *thrum* of his heartbeat in his ears. But then, there it is again. He jerks upright and throws off the bedclothes. Thrusting his feet into slippers, he rises to investigate. There is a spill and some matches on his bedside table. He manages to strike one and lights a candle. Thus armed, he feels his way, bleary-eyed, toward the door. He opens it.

"Dora," he calls in a half whisper. There is no reply.

Holding up his candle, he squints into the gloom. Geraldine's bedroom is across the landing. He tilts his head and listens again. A rustle? A drawer opening?

"Geraldine?" he murmurs, shaking the sleep from his head. He feels his heartbeat grow faster as he pads across the landing. "Geraldine?" he says again, only louder this time, as if each of his footsteps brings with it a renewed confidence. "She has come back," he says aloud. "Thank God!"

In his eagerness, he flings open the door. Moonlight floods into the room from the open drapes. He sees the bed, the dressing table, the chaise longue, in perfect relief. He smells her perfume, too. But there is no one there. Everything is as she left it the day she walked out. The room is empty, and suddenly so is he. There is a longing inside him when he realizes he has been mistaken. She has not returned. There is no one there, and his hopes, wrought between sleep and wake, are dashed by her palpable absence. As he stands by the doorway, he misses her more than ever.

"Geraldine," he whimpers, unable to stem a tear.

He turns and slowly makes his way back to his cold and lonely bed.

Chapter 26

Friday, October 26, 1888

Constance

I have to see Miss Beaufroy again to tell her about my dream. Before, in the tearooms, we agreed that if I needed to meet her urgently, we should plan a place. She gave it a fancy French word. *"Renday-voo,"* or suchlike. She said that for the next few days she'd remain at the hotel and that she'd always take a walk in Berkeley Square at eight o'clock every morning.

"I'm off to Mayfair today," I tell Flo, slipping on my stockings under the bedcover. I try to sound like my old self, even though I know I'm different inside.

I sleep with my drawers and petticoat and stockings under the blankets so that they don't freeze over when it's this nippy. My own body heat keeps them warm, so that I'm not chilled to the bone when I pull them on next to my skin. As I slip my petticoat over my head, it suddenly occurs to me that I may never feel like my old self again.

"You was there the other day," she says, shivering on the side of the bed.

"It's good over there," I lie. "I sold a dozen oranges." Despite my best efforts to keep warm, I notice I'm still covered in goose pimples. I shiver, but I'm not sure it's only because I'm cold.

"Suit yourself," Flo says, making a dash for the chair where she left her skirt last night. She's gone all shirty with me, but I'll have to live with it, just as long as she don't follow me.

An hour later, I'm standing outside the railings of Berkeley Square gardens.

"Oranges, lovely juicy oranges," I call as soon as I see Miss Beaufroy strolling toward me, all carefree like. But when she draws close, I can see I've worried her. She looks about her, then at me with a frown.

"What is it, Constance?" she whispers as I hand her an orange from my basket.

"Last night, miss, I had a dream," I tell her.

I hear breath being sucked into her lungs. "A premonition?" she asks.

I don't like it when she gives what I see fancy names. "More a flash of something that happened in the past, I think," I say, biting my lip.

"About Geraldine?" She leans in as she hands me a sixpence.

I nod. "I saw a lady lying sick in a bed."

Her eyes widen. "Sick?"

"There was a doctor by her side and another man, tall he was with sandy hair and a moustache."

"Terence!"

"Terence?"

"Geraldine's husband!" she tells me.

I eye her, dumbstruck. How could I possibly have known what he looked like? Yet she seems unperturbed.

"What happened?" she urges me.

"The doctor looked at the gentleman and said: 'I fear it's pleurisy.' "

At my words, Miss Beaufroy puts out her gloved hand and has to steady herself against the railings.

"Oh, miss!" I cry, dropping my basket and reaching out to help her. I manage to guide her to a nearby bench. "I'm sorry, miss," I say as she reaches for her handkerchief from her bag. "I didn't mean to upset you."

She rolls her hankie into a ball and presses it against her mouth; then she bows her head. "Oh, dear God," she says, gasping for air. I think she'll pass out. After a moment, her breathing steadies. "Describe the lady to me, will you, Constance?"

I picture the scene again in my mind's eye. "She's in a big wooden bed carved with fish and shells and . . ."

Miss Beaufroy thrusts her handkerchief to her lips once more to stifle a cry. She's lost all the color in her cheeks. "But that is the bed my father gave Geraldine as a wedding present." Her face suddenly screws up and tears start to flow. I've brought her the worst news possible. She turns to me and there's horror in her eyes. "Don't you see? It must be Geraldine."

"Is this girl troubling you, ma'am?" Suddenly a shadow looms over us both and I look up to see a copper, slapping his truncheon on his palm.

Miss Beaufroy lifts her gaze. She's a bit confused at first, then says firmly: "No. Not at all, Officer. I have just had a nasty shock." She straightens her back as she dabs her eyes.

"Very good, then, miss," he says, giving me a sideways look. He walks off slowly, whistling.

Miss Beaufroy takes a deep breath as she watches him go. "You know what this means, Constance?" she says, turning to me.

"What, miss?" I play the fool, even though I'm fairly certain what's coming next.

As she fixes me with an odd look, I remain still, but a strange tingling sensation runs down both my arms. Suddenly she takes both my hands in hers. "Oh, Constance, we need to go to the police with our suspicions."

I know she is right. I nod, even though I'm afraid that I'm being sucked deeper and deeper into something so horrible that it threatens to draw all the life out of me, like sinking sand. It's taking me further away from finding Miss Tindall, too. I'm confused and tense and I really don't know which way to turn. I try to focus on the matter at hand. I ask myself what Miss Tindall would do.

"Don't we need to tell your sister's husband first?" I suggest.

Miss Beaufroy's brows arch in unison and she looks at me aghast, as if I've just suggested we consult Saucy Jack himself. It turns out I'm not too far off the mark. "Good heavens, no," she replies bluntly. "As I told you, it would not surprise me if he did have a hand in her disappearance." A fire burns in her eyes as she speaks. "I know Terence Cutler," she says between clenched teeth, but she can tell that I need to know more. "You see, Constance," she begins, "I went to Whitechapel Workhouse Infirmary yesterday to make discreet inquiries."

I picture her in that dingy, filthy building where no one ventures unless they have to. "I spoke to some of the women." She bites her lip. "I told them . . ." She finds it hard to relate. "I told them I was with child and needed help. They told me Mr. Cutler was the man who could help." A short pause allows me to take in her meaning. I can't hide my shock. She fixes me with a dark look. "That's how I know he is capable of terrible things." Then she answers the question that she must be able to read in my expression. "And, yes, I fear that just might include murdering Geraldine."

EMILY

Terence Cutler is readying himself for an afternoon at St. Bartholomew's Hospital. It's where he practices two full days and two afternoons a week. He has breakfasted and is gathering his papers in his study. Any moment now, his regular cab will draw up outside his home to convey him to his place of work. Or so he imagines. But the knock he is expecting is particularly loud this morning; there is an urgency about it, as if its instigator is the bearer of bad news. He hears Dora rush to answer the call and listens as the door opens.

"This is Mr. Cutler's residence?" The voice, a man's, is unfamiliar.

"Yes."

"Mr. Terence Cutler?"

"Yes, sir."

"We're from Scotland Yard. May we come in?"

In his study, Terence Cutler endeavors to steady himself. *The police.* He feels his guts rise and twist. He must remain calm. Dora knocks.

"Sir, there's the . . ." The girl is fretful.

"Show the gentlemen in, will you," he instructs. He looks in the mirror on the wall, straightens his cravat, smooths his hair.

The policemen enter. There are three of them—two detectives and a uniformed constable.

"Gentlemen, this is an unexpected pleasure. Normally, I would welcome you, but I fear you come at a rather inconvenient time. You see I—"

The senior officer, his face as gnarled and weathered as an old oak, lifts a hand. "Bad news never comes at a convenient time, Mr. Cutler," he pronounces.

Cutler swallows down his anxiety. *"Bad news?"* The papers he has in his hand suddenly slip out of his grasp.

The officer nods. "I am Inspector Marshall and this is Detective Constable Hawkins. We have been assigned to the case of the Whitehall torso. You are familiar with it, sir?"

Cutler suddenly feels the need to sit down. He slumps into the chair behind his desk as if he knows what is to come. The Sword of Damocles has suddenly appeared above his head. It is poised to fall.

"I am," he replies, trying, but failing, to remain impassive.

Marshall signals to Hawkins, who produces a brown paper packet from his coat pocket. "And you know that this brooch was found nearby. I believe you have already identified it as belonging to Mrs. Cutler." Hawkins, the younger detective, thrusts the jewelry under the surgeon's nose.

Cutler recalls Troutbeck's highly irregular visit to warn him of the brooch's discovery. He looks at it, lying on tissue paper in the palm of Hawkins's hand.

"Yes."

Marshall shifts his weight. "Then it is my duty to inform you, sir, that we have reason to believe that the remains found buried on the embankment, and those found both previously and subsequently, may be those of your wife, sir."

"Oh, God!" mumbles Cutler; then, more intelligibly, he adds: "Surely not?"

"I'm afraid we'd like you to come to the mortuary with us to make an identification, sir," adds Marshall.

The surgeon is silent for a moment. His eyes have drifted toward his wife's portrait above the mantelpiece. He hasn't been able to digest the possibility before. The thought has always stuck in his craw. Up until a few moments ago, he was still convinced that his headstrong wife, who'd walked out on him when she discovered he performed abortions for fallen women, was still living in high dudgeon somewhere. But now, it seems, this really is happening. These policemen are telling him she may be dead. He finds the prospect hard to swallow. He feels his lips start to quiver.

"Of course," he replies, still looking at Geraldine's framed face.

"We'd also like to conduct a search of Mrs. Cutler's bedroom, sir," pipes up Hawkins, seemingly buoyed by the senior officer's presence.

The surgeon suddenly switches back, frowning. "A search? Whatever for?"

"For anything that might help confirm the remains are Mrs. Cutler's. We have some fabric from a dress and—"

"Very well," snaps the surgeon, cutting off Hawkins in midflow. "The maid will take you upstairs," he tells the young detective. Trying to appear calm and dignified, the surgeon rises slowly and moves toward the door. As he opens it, he is not surprised to see that Dora has been hovering outside. Her pimply face is redder than usual and her cheeks are damp.

"I shall be going out with this gentleman, Dora," says Cutler, deferring to Marshall. "Meanwhile, you are to show the other officers into your mistress's bedchamber."

Dora's hands fly up to her face, but Cutler's disapproving look brings her back to the moment. "Pull yourself together, girl," he hisses sternly through clenched teeth. She drops a negligible curtsy and hands her master the hat and coat that were draped over her arm. "Ask Mrs. Jones to send word to Barts. I shan't be in this afternoon."

Marshall talks little in the carriage that conveys them to the mortuary located on Millbank Street. The journey seems to take an age, each second marked out by the clop of the horses' hooves.

The trip is well under way when the inspector displays a rare show of compassion. "I am sorry to ask you to do this," he says, staring out of the window.

Taken slightly aback by the remark, Cutler is not sure how to respond. When he does, it is a clumsy attempt at black humor, trying to shrug off the gravity of the situation. "It's a good job I'm used to seeing corpses," he says. The policeman is not amused.

The mortuary is a travesty of a building, no

more than a makeshift facility attached to a dwelling house and a shop. A few wooden partitions provide a little privacy, but there are three other covered corpses occupying tables that are clearly visible to Terence Cutler as he is shown into the room. The amenities are minimal, and if one judged by the stink and the flies, no thought has been given to sanitation, either. Even the surgeon, accustomed as he is to the unsavory detritus of the human body, is unsettled. The sight of a familiar face approaching him does nothing to calm him, either. The man with the walrus moustache who greets him is known to him. Cutler searches his memory. *Bond. Thomas Bond.* They were at St. George's Hospital together for a time.

Bond offers his hand. "I'm sorry about this, Cutler."

The surgeon takes it and gives a tight smile. "Let's get on with it, shall we?"

"This way, if you please." Bond makes an arc with his arm and stands back as an attendant leads them past the row of corpses. Marshall and Bond follow Cutler into the small area that has been portioned off, where a mound lies under a cloth on a table. The air in the immediate vicinity is pungent with preserving fluid. The tang fights with the underlying reek of rotting flesh.

"You may wish to make use of your hand-kerchief," Bond warns.

The surgeon, however, ignores his advice as he approaches the table. Dr. Bond signals to the attendant to pull back the cloth and Cutler steels himself to look. His features are set hard. For a moment, he is professional as his eyes examine the mutilated trunk, then carry on to the amputated leg that lies adjacent but separate. Seemingly oblivious to the stench and the maggots, he does not turn away in disgust as most men would, but he leans closer to inspect the jagged stumps and the dark chasm where the uterus once lay, before leaning back again. He takes two steps away from the table and lifts his head.

"That's not her," he says finally.

Inspector Marshall and Dr. Bond swap glances. "You are sure?" asks the detective.

Cutler seems unmoved. "I've never been more certain of anything in my life," comes his retort. "That is not my wife."

The cloth is returned over the mound and Bond leads the way out of the room and into the reception area again.

"You must be relieved," says the doctor. He allows himself a restrained smile.

"Naturally," replies the surgeon, even though his expression remains inscrutable.

The inspector stands close. "So, Mr. Cutler,"

he begins. "I must apologize for putting you through such an ordeal. My men will take you wherever you wish to go." His tone has changed. He is humble in his manner, even though humility does not sit naturally with him.

Cutler acknowledges the offer with a grudging nod. "Yes. I shall be very late for work." He proceeds to make his way to the main entrance, when Detective Constable Hawkins suddenly appears at the doorway. His eyes are bright as he bobs a telling nod at his boss.

"Well, if you'll excuse me, Mr. Cutler," says Marshall as Hawkins approaches him.

The surgeon allows himself to take a moment before he walks toward the open door, where a police officer awaits him to arrange his transport.

"I need to get to St. Bartholomew's," he tells him haughtily. "And quick as you like," he adds.

The constable is just about to do as he is bid, when a voice stops him short. "I'm afraid that won't be possible," calls Inspector Marshall from behind.

Cutler frowns and turns to see the two detectives regarding him in a very odd way. He suddenly feels disconcerted. "And why not, may I ask?"

Hawkins, newly returned from searching Geraldine Cutler's bedroom, lifts up a leather-bound black book. "Because of this, sir," he replies.

The surgeon screws up his eyes. "And what is that, pray?"

Inspector Marshall snatches it off his junior. "This, Mr. Cutler," he says, leafing through the notebook, "is your wife's diary. And it makes very interesting reading."

The surgeon jolts backward, as if he has just been punched in the stomach. "A *diary*? Geraldine didn't keep a diary!"

Inspector Marshall shakes his head. "Apparently, she did. And it seems there's enough evidence in here to make a conviction," he counters, holding the book aloft and glaring at the surgeon.

It's then that the younger officer steps forward and places his hand on the surgeon's shoulder. Cutler's eyes dart first to Hawkins, then to Marshall in disbelief, before the junior detective utters the dreaded words.

"Terence Cutler, I am arresting you for the murder of Geraldine Cutler. Anything you say may be taken down and used in evidence against you."

CONSTANCE

Much against my better judgment, I find myself at Miss Beaufroy's side in a carriage heading toward Mr. Cutler's home in Harley Street. A messenger came to our house late this afternoon. We were just sitting down to tea when there was this knock on the door. Well, when I was handed this message in front of Ma and Flo, asking for a meeting at Brown's, I had to come clean, didn't I? I had to tell them that I was helping Miss Pauline look for her missing sister and that she needed me urgently.

"I hope she's paying you for all this tommyrot," says Flo as she watches me tug on my old bonnet. There's no time to stop off at St. Jude's for my fancy clothes. I'll be a Whitechapel flower girl in a toff's town house. I squirm at the thought.

"Yes," I lied. "She'll pay me at the end of this week."

"Good," she'd said with a sneer. She's making her feelings very plain.

It's been nearly four weeks now since Saucy Jack last struck, but everyone's still on edge in Whitechapel. We're all on our guard and no respectable woman likes to be out after dark.

"You take care, now," warns Ma, pouring herself another cup of tea.

"I will," I say. It's strange, but ever since my

funny turn in Brick Lane, I've got this sense that Miss Tindall is looking out for me, wherever she is. Like she's my guardian angel, which is silly, I know, because to be an angel you have to be dead. And she's not dead. She can't be dead. "I'll be back by midnight," I tell them.

So, here we are on our way to Harley Street. Miss Beaufroy's right vexed, but she says she knows how to find out one way or the other if her sister is alive or dead. At first, I don't press her, but I can tell she's got something up her sleeve. And then, just as we turn down the street, it all comes out.

"You remember, dear Constance, we spoke about a séance."

"A séance?" I repeat. And then I do remember. Back in Brown's Hotel, it was. And now it doesn't seem such a good idea.

She's matter-of-fact. "We shall hold it in my sister's bedroom. We shall try and contact her."

I'm inclined to holler at the cabdriver to turn round and take me straight home this instant. If I was Madame Morelli, it wouldn't be a problem. I'd sit in a darkened room and say I could see Geraldine and even speak with her. But I'm not. I'm no charlatan. You won't catch me going into one of them fancy cabinets, or spewing ecto . . . ectoplasm, or whatever it's called. If it's theatricals she wants, she's best off going to the

Egyptian Hall, or paying her money to see the famous Florence Cook turn into Katie King. I don't believe in all that nonsense. Floating hands and heavenly voices, indeed! I can't perform like a circus pony, and I don't know any tricks like these fraudsters do. But how do I tell her that? I say nothing.

It's five o'clock and dark when we arrive at the Cutler household. Miss Beaufroy knocks and is answered by a maid she seems to know well.

"Dora, is your master in?" she says, blustering into the hallway. I follow behind.

It's clear for all to see that this maid, Dora, has been crying. Her eyes are red and underneath they're puffy as plumped-up cushions.

"Oh, miss!" she wails.

"What on earth is it?" asks Miss Beaufroy. "What has happened?"

"The police came, miss," she sobs. "They asked the master to go to the mortuary."

Miss Beaufroy gasps. "Oh, dear Lord!" she mutters. She closes her eyes for a second, then asks Dora: "Where is Mrs. Jones?" She looks at me. "The housekeeper," she explains.

"She went out," simpers the maid. "She's visiting her sick aunty and won't be back till late and it's Cook's night off."

"Good, so you're alone?"

The girl nods. "That I am, miss."

Miss Beaufroy nods. "It's probably for the

best." She darts a look at me. "Then we must get to work quickly." Suddenly she sounds feisty, like she's up for a fight, but I'm not ready for how she introduces me to the maid. "Dora, this is Miss Piper and she is a spirit medium."

She's never called me that before. I'm not sure I like it. *A spirit medium.* I roll the words round on my tongue silently: *"A spirit medium."* But they prickle, like so many thorns. They feel uncomfortable. I know what this "work" is, too, and I'm not happy about it.

"Come along, Constance," she tells me, motioning to the stairs. "Dora will lead the way."

We traipse up the stairs behind the maid, who's holding a lit candle. There are gas lamps on the stairs and on the landing. I've never seen them in a private house before. I think this Mr. Cutler must be very rich.

Dora stops outside a door and looks behind her for reassurance. Miss Beaufroy gives her a wordless nod and the girl opens it into a bedroom. The door creaks on its hinges, making me shudder. We stand on the threshold, our own shadows creep onto the floor, making us look like tall ghouls. Dora edges in farther, her candle aloft, and my eyes grow accustomed to the gloom. But as I look about me, a shudder suddenly darts down my spine, as if someone is running icy fingers along my backbone. It's because I've suddenly realized that this is the very room I saw in my dream. I clap eyes on the bed. It's the one—the one with the carved fish and shells. In a panic, my head whirls round to the window. There's the chaise longue under it. The dressing table, too, with a mirror stand on top. And the smell. *That perfume.* I sniff the air. Yes, I have been here before, in my mind, and it scares me.

"My dear Constance. Are you quite well?" I hear Miss Beaufroy's voice by my left ear, but it sounds far away, like she's in the next room. Quickly I shake my head.

"Yes. Yes, thank you, miss," I say.

"Good," she replies, and she takes off her gloves, lays them down on a nearby chest of drawers and begins to direct Dora.

In the diffused light from the gasoliers on the landing, the maid shifts a small table in front of the chaise longue. On it, she sets down the single candle in its holder. As the candle flickers, strange shadows leap into life around the room. There's another small button-back chair by the fireplace and I drag it up to the table, too. Miss Beaufroy bids us both to sit.

Dora's not happy. "Me, miss?" asks the girl in a strangled whisper. I can see her eyes are wide with terror. "But, miss, I . . ."

"Come, Dora. Surely, you want to help us find your mistress?"

"Yes, miss, but . . ."

"Then don't be so ridiculous and sit down. No harm can come to you."

Reluctantly the maid, trembling like a leaf, does as she is told.

"Close the door, Constance," orders Miss Pauline. I obey.

My action has plunged the room into almost complete darkness. I edge my way back to the table, guided by the light from the flickering candle. I take my place opposite them. I am so nervous that I think I will be sick all over the floor. I am not a fraud. Everything that I have felt and seen is real—to me, at least. I cannot conjure spirits from thin air any more than I can conjure a rabbit from a hat. I want to cry out, to tell Miss Beaufroy that this is a mistake. She's been reading too many novels by Mr. Poe and Mr. Collins; ghostly apparitions and disembodied skulls are not real. Instead, I bite my lip.

"Let us hold hands," says Miss Beaufroy. She leans over the table and I feel Dora's clammy fingers clasp mine. She's still shaking. Miss Beaufroy's hands, on the other side, are dry and her hold is firm, as if she's determined I won't be able to escape her clutches. "Constance, it's up to you now. You must make contact."

I feel my chest tighten. I have no idea what to do, other than close my eyes and think of Mrs. Cutler. I remember her photograph—her hair and the line of her jaw. I picture her in my mind's eye and hope an image might suddenly appear.

"Mrs. Cutler," I say. My voice sounds thin, like watery broth. "Geraldine," I call, only a little louder. Silence. "If you are there, please let us know." I hate myself for what I am about to say, but say it I must. "Knock on the table if you can hear us." I hold my breath. Dora lets out a little squeal. The candle flame sputters. Nothing. Outside a fox barks. It's an unearthly sound, like a howl from the grave. We sit firm. Still nothing. I try again. "Mrs. Cutler. Are you there?"

In the darkness, Miss Beaufroy lets out a sigh so heavy that she almost blows out the candle flame. Is she getting tetchy with me?

"Geraldine, it's Pauline," she says in a low voice. "If you can hear us, then please give us a sign."

I'm tempted to kick the table leg or crack my toe joints, like I've heard some mediums do, to fake a spirit visit, but I resist. Still, nothing, apart from the oppressive blackness of the room that feels like it's growing smaller by the second. I don't want to be part of this madness anymore.

"She's not there," I say a few moments later. "I can't feel her." My words slice into the darkness and break the spell. I uncouple my hands from Miss Beaufroy's and from Dora's and lean back.

Dora wastes no time in rushing to the door and opening it, letting the light from the landing flood back in.

"She's not there," repeats Miss Beaufroy. But she isn't angry. In the candle glow, I see she looks calm. "She's not there," she says again.

"I can't hear her," I say, as if I feel the need to explain myself again.

"But don't you see, that's a good thing," counters Miss Beaufroy.

"Is it?" I ask. I don't follow her. I can't understand why she's not angry with me.

"If you can't reach her on the other side, perhaps it's because she's not there," she says, patting my hand.

I pause for a moment, taking in what she's just told me. "You mean she's not dead?"

I see her lips curl in a smile. "Could not that be the case? Geraldine may not be dead."

The thought is such a relief that I hear a little laugh escape from my mouth. "Maybe not!" I seize on the idea like a hungry dog on a bone. "Maybe she's alive and well."

Miss Beaufroy nods, but then I see her expression switch suddenly. She turns away, picturing another scene. A moment later, she asks: "What if she has been kidnapped? Or tortured? Or both?"

Dora lets out another horrified squeal. I think Miss Beaufroy's imagination has been fired by those Gothic novels where brides are banged up in dungeons or locked in spiked coffins.

"Lord save us" is all I manage.

Miss Beaufroy rises from the table. "Perhaps we should resume another time. The conditions are obviously not right tonight," she suggests, as if she's just been chairing a business meeting that hasn't gone well.

I'm eager to follow her lead. "Another time," I say, even though I really hope there won't be another.

I start to make my way toward the door. Dora has already reached the landing and Miss Beaufroy is walking by my side when she suddenly grabs hold of my hand. "We will find her, won't we?" she pleads, her eyes so urgent they almost burn my face.

Yes," I reply, a little taken aback. "Of course."

From out of the corner of my vision, I see that in her haste to depart the room, Dora has left the flame burning on the table. As Miss Beaufroy continues onto the landing, I retreat once again into the gloomy room to retrieve the candle. Swiftly I snuff it out and begin to make my way back toward the door. Just as I do so, I pass the dressing table and glance into the mirror. Something makes me stop in front of it for a moment. My warm breath mists the surface; but then, just as quickly, it clears. As I stare into the dark glass, I suddenly become aware that it is not my reflection that stares back. Someone else is regarding me from inside the mirror. Someone I know. Instead of me, I see Miss Tindall gazing out. She's right there. Looking at me. I reach for her, trying to touch her. "Miss Tindall," I call, the glass cold beneath my fingers. I see her lips move, as if she is trying to tell me something, but then the mist returns. In the blink of an eye, she's gone and I'm alone again.

CHAPTER 27

Saturday, October 27, 1888

EMILY

I will have to tell her soon, although I know she has a notion. She was calm when I stared out at her from the looking glass. She neither took fright nor swooned, as I feared she might. I must tell her the whole story very shortly, but not just yet. For now, we must away to the headquarters of the Metropolitan Police's A Division in King Street. Or, more precisely, to a room within it. It is small. Deliberately so, I suspect. It enables the interrogator to skirt the small table with just enough berth so as not to touch the prisoner. But Terence Cutler can feel Inspector Marshall, all right. He looms over him, smells his stale breath on his neck and the reek of tobacco on his coat.

There is a single small window high up in the bare brick wall. Three vertical bars stripe the gray London sky. It is morning and the surgeon has spent his first night in a police cell, deprived of both freedom and sleep. He is a man of secrets. However, in this cramped space, where the walls are covered in mildew and the corners festooned with cobwebs, there is nowhere to hide. He fears his secrets will slip through his fingers like sand eels.

Seated opposite him at the table is a young constable who is taking down his words in a neat, but labored, hand. Inspector Marshall is relentless in his questioning. "So you had no idea that your wife kept a journal, let alone what she might have written in it?" He is wearing a heavy overcoat as he paces round and round, flapping the diary in his hand. The temperature in the room is barely above freezing; yet there are beads of sweat on Terence Cutler's forehead.

"I told you. None at all."

Marshall huffs, then nods. "It is hardly surprising, given the contents of it," he acknowledges. "Let me read you an extract. It is a sort of foreword, if you like, before she starts making entries." He produces a monocle from his waistcoat pocket and reads, " 'To whoever may find this diary: If you are reading this, then it is likely I am dead.'

"What say you to that, eh, Mr. Cutler?" The inspector closes the journal and bends low so that his face is no more than two inches away from the surgeon's.

Cutler lifts his red-rimmed eyes to meet his inquisitor's. His gaze is unflinching. "I'd say they are the ramblings of a poor, deluded woman who intends to take her own life, sir, and you and your men would be better off looking for her rather than detaining me here."

"Would you, indeed?" Marshall flips open the journal once more at a place he has previously marked with a length of string. "And what about this? 'Friday, April fifteenth: We lunched with the Pattersons. We saw their new baby son, Raymond, for the first time. He was adorable, but I must confess that seeing him upset me very much. I saw the look in Terence's eyes as he watched the child grasp hold of his father's forefinger and hold it tight. Then he looked at me and I swear I saw contempt in his expression.' " The inspector slams the journal shut. "*Contempt,* Mr. Cutler. It's a strong word. Did you have contempt for your barren wife?"

The surgeon shuts his eyes for a moment, as if to blink away this nightmare that he is living through. "Of course, I didn't," he hisses.

"It's ironic, is it not, that in your profession

you assist women to conceive and yet you are unable to help your own wife?"

The jibe is a cruel one. Cutler does not rise to the bait. "The irony is not lost on me, Inspector."

"And you don't deny that your marriage wasn't a happy one?" Marshall thrusts in the knife with an easy jab.

Cutler pauses, rather touchingly, I think, before he replies: "We were happy at first."

The inspector nods. "Ah, yes. The brooch." He signals to the constable to unwrap the small packet lying on the table. He picks it up and holds it to the window to catch what little daylight there is. He squints to read the inscription: *To dearest Geraldine on the occasion of our marriage, 3rd June 1882. Forever, TC.* He completes another circuit of the table in silence. "TC," he states. "That's you, yes?"

Cutler frowns. "Yes," he snaps. "Of course, it's me."

Marshall pockets his monocle and dips low again. Now he whispers into the surgeon's right ear. "Did you know that the initials *TC* were found on the arm of Catherine Eddowes, too?" Cutler is clearly riled. "Did you?" barks the inspector.

"No, I did not. I told you, I know nothing about these ghastly murders."

The journal falls open once more at a marked page. Marshall scans it. "And what do you do in Whitechapel every Friday evening, Mr. Cutler?"

Cutler rolls his eyes. "How many more times?"

The inspector slams the diary down on the table, almost catching the surgeon's fingers. "I ask the questions!" he shouts. He takes a deep breath and steadies himself. "What do you do in Whitechapel every Friday evening?"

Cutler sighs deeply in an effort to calm his growing exasperation. "I treat sick and pregnant women at the infirmary."

Marshall nods. "Ah, yes, the very model of Christian virtue," he says with a smirk. "And I'm sure you are rewarded for your good works."

Cutler swallows hard. "I receive a small stipend," he acknowledges with a nod.

"But you feel the need to supplement it from time to time?"

The inspector's eyes bore into the back of his head.

Cutler switches round. "What are you insinuating, Inspector?" I can see the hairs on his neck stand erect. He thinks of Polly Nichols and the girl Molly and the others. He fears his illegal activities may have been uncovered.

Marshall wheels round to face his prisoner. "Or perhaps you ask for favors from some of your patients?"

Relieved that it is merely his own morality that is being called into question, and not his other, more dubious professional activities, the surgeon keeps himself in check. "Of course not."

"Then perhaps you'd like to account for these." Suddenly Marshall slaps a pile of photographs on the table. They are from the surgeon's bureau, from his secret stash of images of fetid flesh and ulcerous parts of the female anatomy that were so vital to his early work, yet so abhorrent to those without medical training.

At the sight of them, Cutler turns ashen. "I am a surgeon. They are purely for research purposes."

Marshall says nothing, but only stares.

"Good God! A man would have to be sick and twisted to . . ." The surgeon trails off, realizing he has just tightened the noose around his own neck.

There is a pause and a further circuit of the table is completed before another savage question sallies forth. "Do you and your wife still have relations, Mr. Cutler?"

The inspector has gone too far. Cutler leaps up, fists balled. "How dare you?"

The constable rises, too, and presses firmly on the prisoner's shoulder, forcing him down again.

Marshall eyes him. "Any more of that and you'll be put in handcuffs, I can assure you," he warns.

Cutler, panting heavily, pauses for a moment and sniffs through his nostrils. With unseeing eyes, he looks straight ahead of him at the blank wall; then his eyes suddenly cloud with tears.

CHAPTER 28

Monday, October 29, 1888

CONSTANCE

Am I going mad? After the other night, I fear I may be. The face in the mirror, Miss Tindall's face, keeps flashing into my mind. She's trying to tell me something. I wish I knew what. I wish I could just find her, but then that terrible thought rears its head again: *Could* she *be dead and not Mrs. Cutler?* I shall try and act normal, as if nothing strange has happened, for Flo's sake, and for Ma's, and for my own sanity.

"Con! Con!" It's Flo's voice I hear, waking me from my half sleep. "Get up, will ya?"

I turn and blink toward the window, a rectangle of light behind ragged drapes. She's got her back to me and she's lifting up her long, loose hair so I can do up her stays. "You'd best stir your stumps, young lady," she tells me, just before she breathes in so that I can tighten the laces.

"I'll be ready in a jiffy," I say. I tie the bow, then heave my tired body off the mattress. I shiver. It's another miserable day, but I forgot to put my clothes in the bed, so they're all cold and damp. I dress hurriedly. I don't want to rub Flo up the wrong way any more than I have. She's ready before me and goes downstairs, leaving me alone in the room. I'm dressed now, but I haven't done my hair. It tumbles onto my shoulders. I pad to the window to allow more light into the dingy room. The trouble is, I don't think I dare look in the mirror again, not after what happened last night. I pull back the drapes, first the right, then the left, and that's when I see it, on the glass. Clear as day, it is. Written in the mist of the window are the letters *C,L,E,O*. I take a step back and look again to make sure my eyes haven't deceived me. *C,L,E,O*. "Cleo," I say to myself. "Cleo," again. It's a name, not a word. I think it's short for Cleopatra, the Egyptian queen, but it means nothing to me.

"Flo!" I call as I rush downstairs. "Flo!"

"What's up?" she asks, putting the kettle on the hob.

"Who's Cleo?"

She frowns and stands upright. "What you talking about?"

"Why did you write 'CLEO' on our window?"

"You're having a laugh."

There's a ringing in my ears. "You didn't write it?"

"What you on about?" Flo's getting crabby.

I shake my head and swallow hard. "Come see," I say.

So she tramps up the stairs and I follow. By the time I draw level with the window she's standing there, looking at it.

"Where?"

"There," I tell her, pointing, only there's nothing to look at, except a fogged-up pane. There's not even a circle where the letters could have been wiped away. "But I swear . . ."

Flo shakes her head slowly. "Dear, oh dear," she says, then she tuts. "You best be careful, Connie dear, otherwise they'll be dragging you off to the madhouse."

I can't protest, even though I want to, because I know what she's saying is true. "I'm sorry," I say. "I must've been dreaming." She darts me a distrustful look before she goes downstairs again. I feel wretched.

Flo suggests Threadneedle Street today. It's where the City bankers are. "Like Robin Hood, we'll be," she says with a giggle. "Stealing from the rich to give to the poor!" She's really up for it today, so I play along.

As we walk down Commercial Street, I see a

paperboy a few feet away on the corner. When I hear what he's saying, I have to stop.

"Ripper latest! Read all about it!" he calls.

Flo and I swap glances and I bring out a halfpenny from my pocket. "I found it on the pavement!" I protest, having to justify spending money on a newspaper. She nods and the boy hands me a copy of the *Star.* Across the front page are the headlines: ANOTHER RIPPER ARREST. DOCTOR QUESTIONED OVER FIVE WHITECHAPEL MURDERS AND WHITEHALL MYSTERY.

"Oh, my God!" I gasp. I can't contain myself.

Flo frowns at me. *"The Whitehall Mystery?* That's . . . ," she says.

She doesn't really understand why I'm so shocked. She's no idea what I've been up to and that I know all about this doctor they've arrested. I wonder if Miss Beaufroy has told the police that I dreamed about the sick lady, and that's why Mr. Cutler is now behind bars. And to think they're charging him with the Ripper murders, too. They must have evidence. Suddenly my guts heave; I double over and spew all over the pavement.

Flo looks around her. It's clear she's more worried that people will think I've been on the bottle. She wipes the vomit from my chin with her handkerchief—one she pilfered last week— and, putting her arm around me, she hurries me along, down the road.

"What's that all about?" she asks me as we stop in a doorway a few yards away. She's looking at me with suspicion in her eyes. "You ain't . . . ?"

"No, I ain't. No chance," I reassure her. "It's just my nerves."

She seems satisfied by my explanation. "Still, if this latest bloke is Jack, our worries is over, eh?"

"Yes," I lie.

We set ourselves up outside the Old Lady— that's what they call the Bank of England—and stay there till dusk. I'm offering lucky heather at a penny a bunch, only it's not lucky for some rich bastards. As I'm all sweetness and light, Flo nips by and helps herself to what's in their pockets. Most often, it's a shilling or two; in Threadneedle Street, she's more used to crowns. Today she lifts three in total. It's a good haul. As much as I hate myself for having any part in these shenanigans, at least we know the rent's taken care of till the spring and we won't have to hide when Sir William Sampson sends his bulldogs calling to collect it.

EMILY

It is proving more difficult than I thought. While Constance is receptive, she is not as malleable as I hoped she would be. That is why I am having to employ these rudimentary signs, as I would when teaching a child. By showing them, rather than simply telling them, they learn much quicker. As I said, I thought I was pushing at an open door. I was wrong. There is something in the way, something that is blocking her path to total understanding. On reflection, I think I know what it may be that is impeding the route to her enlightenment. She is not aware of the whole truth, a truth that I shall first tell you.

Even though my new lodgings off Russell Square were a good two miles away from Whitechapel, I found myself drawn to my old haunts. During my stay at the Cutlers' residence, a letter had been delivered to Mrs. Appleton's informing me of the date of the disciplinary hearing. It was to be held the following week at Toynbee Hall in the presence of none other than the Barnetts themselves. I could not pay for representation—a lawyer was out of the question—so, despite still feeling weak and dogged by a persistent hacking cough, I decided that my only chance of being acquitted of the crimes with which I was charged was to gather evidence in my own defense myself. Painfully aware that I was setting myself an almost impossible task, I decided I would begin just where my suspicions had first taken root, at St. Jude's.

Naturally, I chose a Sunday for my return. I knew that if I was fortunate, Dr. Melksham might be attending the class. This time, I would not let him escape. I would trail his movements after the pupils had been dismissed. If, as I suspected, he did not leave the church alone, but in the company of yet another drugged victim, then I would follow him and see for myself where he took his prey and, more crucially, to what end. The thought of what I might witness filled me with dread, but I knew that if I was to stand any chance of being exonerated, then this was the only course of action to take, albeit a potentially perilous one.

I arrived at St. Jude's on foot shortly after four o'clock on that fateful Sunday. It was a warm, sultry afternoon and the street outside the church thronged with strollers out for a pleasant promenade. A large crowd had gathered round a candy-striped tent erected at one end of the street where a Punch-and-Judy show was in full swing. The sound of children's laughter rang out around the spectacle. The irony of it struck me as I looked toward St. Jude's, just in time to see the first of my former pupils file out of the great front portico. I noticed, too, a rather grand carriage parked at the foot of the church steps. On both doors were emblazoned a coat of arms in red and gold. It was the same vehicle I had seen outside once before. I was convinced it had conveyed Dr. Melksham, and, alongside my general malaise, I suddenly felt sick to my stomach.

There was a bench near the church and it was here that I positioned myself, hoping to be as unobtrusive as any other Sunday promenader on that hot, hazy afternoon. I counted nineteen children leaving the building. There was no way of telling how many had attended class and I knew I could not leave until I had made sure that Dr. Melksham returned to his carriage alone. Part of me prayed that he would. I longed to be proved wrong in my suspicions. Sadly, it was not to be.

Ten minutes passed. Then twenty. Time was marked by St. Jude's bell. Half past four. Quarter to five. The sun, although not as glaring as before, had moved round and was now shining directly on me. My bronchial condition made the heat even more unbearable, and more than once, I was sent into a violent coughing spasm. Luckily, I had brought my trusty old umbrella with me and I now erected it to shade me from the direct heat. Thankfully, it also protected me from the gaze of anyone I might know. Mrs. Pouter, the butcher's wife, passed within ten yards of me and I was able to lower my impromptu parasol and escape her notice. So preoccupied did I become with avoiding being detected by my erstwhile neighbors and acquaintances that I might almost have missed any movement at the church portico, had it not been for the fact that one of the carriage horses, possibly bitten by a fly, let out a loud neigh. My head jerked up to see Dr. Melksham leaving the church via the front door. To my horror, he was shepherding a young girl inside his carriage. My stomach knotted. All I could see was the swish of her skirts and the toss of her golden hair as she was lifted into the gloom of the curtained conveyance. "Libby Lonergan," I muttered under my breath. I could not stand idly by and let this monster whisk her away from her home and her family to be used and abused as he or his employer saw fit. I had to act.

The coachman shut the door and climbed up to his bench. I looked down the road. A hackney cab was approaching. The meager shillings that remained in my purse had to be spent on the fare if I was ever to get to the bottom of this mystery and clear my name. My stomach lurched in a sudden panic. It was now or never. My arm jerked out into the road to hail the cab. I had to follow.

Poor Constance thinks I have, in all probability, returned to Oxford, forsaking my calling to educate the poor and thus abandoning her. But it was for her and all the other young girls like her that I took that cab that day. It proved to be my most terrible mistake.

CONSTANCE

The day has dragged and all the while I've been thinking about Mr. Cutler, and whether Mrs. Cutler is still alive. I worry that Miss Beaufroy's told Old Bill about my dream. Even if she did, Cutler can't have been arrested on such a flimsy say-so, could he? There's more to it. There's got to be. Then it occurs to me; what if I'm called to be a witness in court? To stand up in that box and tell everyone about my dream; I'd rather be in a coffin. My blood runs cold at the thinking of it.

We can't get home soon enough, even though that business with the writing on the window has rattled my nerve. Flo's feeling flush; so on the way home, we stop off to buy a slab of cheddar from the cheesemonger. It's Ma's favorite and we reckon she deserves a treat. It certainly puts a smile on her face when, as soon as we arrive back, we get out the pickle from last Christmas and start slicing the bread—even though it's a bit stale.

"Let's toast it," suggests Flo, pointing to the fire in the grate. We all agree it's a good idea and stoke the coals to make a good blaze. I then reach for the toasting fork and kneel down on the hearth rug. Flo hands me the thick-cut bread that she's sliced. It reminds us of when we were little and used to do this with Pa. The glow from the flames is warming and comforting and puts us all in a good mood. I pierce the bread with the prongs of the long-handled fork and hold out the first slice to the fire. I keep it near the flame for a minute or two, then turn it to toast the other side. It's golden. Just perfect.

"There you go," I say to Ma, handing her the first crispy slice.

Next it's Flo's turn. I do the same thing and the result is the same, too. I hold my slice to the fire as Flo cuts herself a thick wedge of cheese and slaps it on the bread; then I turn it. Another minute and I look to see if it's browned. It should have, but what I see shocks me so much, I let out a gasp.

"What's wrong, Connie love?" asks Ma.

I glance up at her, then back at my slice of toast, and shudder as I gaze upon a strange black oblong that is burned into the bread. All around the column the bread is golden, but there's this stripe of burn in the center.

Flo mocks me. "You took your eye off it!" she says. "Daydreaming again." I place the slice on my plate and cut round the burn mark. At least they don't expect me to eat it. I just stare at it, instead: a long, thin line that tapers toward the top. I think it means something, but I don't know what. And all of a sudden, I fear what the night will bring . . . again.

EMILY

Constance does sleep, albeit fitfully, so we shall leave her to return to my own story. For now, it is time to take you on a terrifying journey. My driver, a veteran with a kind, if toothless, smile, was under instruction not to lose the carriage. It was not hard to follow such a grand vehicle in these squalid streets. If anyone of any substance visited the area, most of us would hear about it, but it was being driven quite fast. That is not to say we were traveling at great speed, but with sufficient alacrity as to make me bounce around in the back of the cab. The exertion also triggered in me a bout of coughing. We had set off along Commercial Street, but had soon turned down Hanbury Street and onto Brick Lane. Past the brewery we trotted, under the railway arches, then we turned right into Mile End and I began to lose my bearings. We were venturing into unfamiliar territory and I wondered if my paltry coins would cover the fare.

Past tallow chandlers and potato merchants, we went, but soon the clapboarded shops became factories and storehouses. I was in two minds whether or not to tell the driver to halt when he started to slow down. I craned my neck out of the cab window to see what was happening. From the stench on the air, I guessed we might be near the docks. We were in an alley, bordered by workshops and warehouses. Despite the fact that it was nowhere near dusk, very little light penetrated the narrow passage. It lay in permanent shadow. It was the sort of place that was so familiar to me, and yet I had never been here before: the sort of cesspit where men either take their ease for free, or have a whore relieve them for tuppence. As it was the Sabbath, there was little noise, too. The shutters and pulleys were silent. I saw the cabman jump down from his perch. He put his face up to the window.

"The carriage has stopped over there, miss." He flapped his hand up ahead. I lifted my gaze to see it had parked across the mouth of the same alley at the far end.

"Very well," I said, opening the cab door.

The driver frowned. "Surely, you ain't wantin' to stop 'ere, miss?" he asked anxiously as I took his hand and alighted.

"I shall be perfectly fine, thank you," I replied in my naivety. I took out my purse and saw the driver's head swivel round, half expecting some vagabonds to jump out at us from the shadows. Thankfully, they did not and I proceeded to pay him. I counted out a few coins in the hope that I would not be deprived of every single penny I had. The cabman held out a grimy palm. I was not quite sure whether I proffered too much or too little; but as he tipped his hat, he gave me an odd look that exposed his gums. Was it of pity or pleasure? Either way, as the cab clattered off along the cobbles and out of sight, I felt a terrible sense of trepidation. The dread rose up from the pit of my stomach and seized me by the throat. My nerves allowed a cough to escape. I was on my own. There was no turning back.

CHAPTER 29

Tuesday, October 30, 1888

CONSTANCE

I wake and open one eye, then the other. I stretch out my hands in front of me, then wiggle my toes. I'm alive and nothing untoward has happened— not that I know of, at any rate. Strangely, I did not have any dreams last night. Or, if I did, I cannot remember them. Flo strides over to the window and I hold my breath as she draws the curtains. The panes are dirty with smog, but there is no writing, no words. We don't say a lot to each other as we dress. She's still a bit sulky with me.

Downstairs, over thin porridge, Ma suggests we return to the City. Threadneedle Street will be out of bounds to us today, because of yesterday. Someone will have reported us to the rossers, so it's best to steer clear. But there's always rich pickings to be had round Hatton Garden. We're just wrapping ourselves up in readiness for another day on the streets when we hear the clop of horses' hooves. But it don't sound like they're pulling your average dray cart or the rag-and-bone man's wagon, which you normally get round here. The clatter gets louder and louder till Flo can hardly hear herself speak and then it stops. All three of us swap glances as we listen to a cabman jump down, lower the steps and open a carriage door. In two seconds, there's a knock at our door. Ma peers out of the window and clasps her hands over her bosom.

"A lady!" she cries in a hoarse whisper.

Flo jerks her head and arches a brow at me. "It'll be for you, then, Con," she says, smirking.

I think of Miss Beaufroy, pull back my shoulders and answer the door. I am right. She is standing there in her finery, looking serious. I glance up to see faces pressed against windows on the other side of the street. They want to know who has come calling in a carriage. I want to know why. *It's bad news,* I think. I am right.

"Miss Beaufroy." I bob a curtsy.

"Constance. I am sorry to call on you unannounced." She pauses.

Oh, God! She wants to come inside, I think.

Reluctantly, I step back and open the door wider to let her in. Ma is mortified. She stands openmouthed for a second, then starts to cough as the cold, filthy air blasts into the room and invades her lungs.

Flo looks annoyed, churlish even. She stands her ground and does not return our visitor's smile as she walks in. Petticoats and stockings are hanging on the clotheshorse in front of the unmade fire. The room is a mess.

I invite Miss Beaufroy to sit, but she glances at the threadbare armchair and declines. I cannot blame her.

"What a charming home you have, Mrs. Piper," she tells Ma, who's plumping up the only cushion we have, in between coughs. I don't know why she had to say it when she clearly didn't mean it. It makes me feel wretched inside to hear her speak so.

"Thank you, miss, I'm sure," Ma replies awkwardly, nodding her head.

Miss Beaufroy's eyes slide along the bare mantelshelf—we still haven't put the clock back—and into the damp corners of the room. She peers into the kitchen with its earth floor as if she's never been in a poor person's home before. She appears quite curious, like someone who pays a penny to watch a sideshow at a circus, as if our ways are so very strange to her—which I suppose they are. Miss Tindall never behaved so. She never judged. Miss Beaufroy makes me feel uncomfortable.

"How can I help you, miss?" I ask. I'm probably speaking out of turn, but I'm squirming like a worm on a hook. I want to get this over with, for Ma's sake more than my own.

She fixes me with an uneasy look. "You have heard about Mr. Cutler's arrest?"

I blink. "Yes, miss." I don't know what else to say.

"I've been thinking about your dream. It's been troubling me. I say we should go and tell the police all about it."

"*What?*" I blurt. Part of me is relieved that I'm not the one who's nabbed this surgeon, but I don't want to get more involved than I already am.

Miss Beaufroy darts a scandalized glance at me. "It is most relevant, is it not?" She shakes her head. "Especially since his arrest. We must go to Scotland Yard this instant, Miss Piper." She is ordering me, not asking.

"*Me?*" I clutch my fist to my chest.

"Yes," she tells me firmly. "I am allowed to see my brother-in-law and you must accompany me."

From the tone of her voice, I know I have no choice in the matter. I feel so wretched I don't even dare look at Flo and Ma. I put on my bonnet, then reach for my woolen shawl. I pray that she won't ask me where my jacket is. Not now. I still haven't told Ma and Flo that she's paid for good clothes for me.

She looks me up and down. Again she makes me feel small; then she says, "Come along. There is no time to lose."

EMILY

As Constance and Pauline travel to visit Terence Cutler in the police cell in King Street, I shall take you back to where we left off, in pursuit of Dr. Melksham, in what I now know to be Limehouse. I looked down the alley. The carriage door was open. I sought shelter behind a large barrel. Straining my eyes into the murk, I could see an enormous warehouse door swing open and a man greet the doctor. His chestnut hair flowed from his crown like a romantic poet's. Melksham himself swept into the building alone, allowing the second man access to the carriage. Within a few seconds, the Poet had emerged with something in his arms. I cringed at the sight. Libby was now limp as a rag doll. She must have been drugged. I watched her being carried inside the building in the arms of this stranger. The door was then shut behind them.

Left alone in the shadowy street, I was in shock. I could barely believe what I had seen, but I knew that if I had any chance of exposing Dr. Melksham's vile enterprise, and, indeed, proving my own innocence, I had to take courage and see this through. The faces of my pupils—Molly Deakin, Gracie Arden and Maudie Dalton—flashed before my eyes. It might be too late to save them, but for Libby—inside that building, drugged and alone—it was not.

Keeping my back to the wall, I edged down the alley toward the door I had seen open. There was no one about, but then I heard a noise somewhere behind me. I turned, my heart in my mouth, to see two rats scuttle away from a pile of rotting filth and across the cobbles. I steadied myself, then carried on until I came to the building. It seemed quite anonymous, just like the other buildings in the row. An old factory or workshop, perhaps, although I thought it odd that all the windows seemed to have been boarded up. I reached the door. The paint on it was peeling and one of the planks had been damaged, but recently repaired. I put my ear to the wood. *Silence.* I could hear nothing. Slowly I turned the handle. The latch did not resist. It clicked softly and I pushed gently against the door to peer inside. It was a warehouse of some sort. Sacks and barrels were stacked high on either side of the door. Crates, too, all neatly aligned, although there was no clue as to what they contained. But of Melksham, or the Poet and Libby, there was no sign. There had to be a door. My eyes gravitated toward the walls, looking for an opening in the gloom. I could see none, until I spotted a railing. Moving forward, I suddenly realized there was a set of broad steps. As I stood at the top of them, the stink of the Thames flooded my nostrils. The staircase must lead to the river. This is where Melksham must have gone. I knew I had to follow.

I lifted my skirts and, carefully and quietly, began the descent. Reaching the bottom, I found myself in a wide passageway. To my left, there was light. I could just about discern the river beyond, but it is what I saw to my left that disconcerted me. Two large flaming wall sconces were bolted onto two pillars ahead of me. Between these pillars were double doors studded with brass. They looked new and completely out of place in such an outwardly dilapidated building. For a moment, I hesitated, listening. I could hear voices coming from inside the doors. Scanning the space, I sought out a hiding place and soon found one behind the stairs. I headed for its refuge and prayed that no one would see me.

From my new vantage point, I could take in this strange place that had proved so deceptive from the outside. The walls seemed freshly plastered. *And those torches!* It suddenly occurred to me that no one would go to the trouble of lighting them, had they not been expecting more company. The thought tightened the already-present knot in my stomach. I had to act fast, but what should I do? I knew I had to seek out the child. But once I had found her, what then? In all probability, she would be guarded. Even if she was not, I knew her to be drugged. I was aware, too, of the limits of my own strength and I certainly doubted my ability to carry the helpless victim. The truth was that I had to admit to myself that in all probability I would need to confront Melksham and his cohorts. How they might react to my intrusion was the real question, and the prospect terrified me. I realized all too late that this was a terrible mistake. I should never have followed the carriage. I should've gone straight to the police. But then again, would they have heeded my fears? After all, no one believed Josephine Butler when she first alerted the authorities to the paid abuse of children. And no one would have believed that members of Parliament, bishops and even royalty regularly raped young virgins, had their wickedness not been exposed by W.T. Stead in his series of newspaper articles. That was two years ago, when the shocking truth about child prostitution was laid bare in the press. There are laws now, thank God, but if no one implements them, then what will change? The same vile trade still exists, only now it is illegal, but that did not discourage the likes of Dr. Melksham and his ilk.

I was still debating whether to flee the scene to fetch help, when I heard footsteps above me. There were voices, men's voices. I crouched low and leaned into the wall. The footsteps drew nearer, and a moment later, two gentlemen emerged in a cloud of black silk and tobacco smoke. They were in full evening dress, and around their necks, they were wearing some sort of elaborate gold collar. The smell of the smoke unsettled my breath. I wanted to cough, but I knew that if I did, I would be uncovered. I buried my mouth in my sleeve and watched as the gentlemen were led through the double doors by two liveried servants, who had suddenly appeared from inside.

Just as the door closed behind them, I heard more footsteps and saw another gentleman appear, again in full evening dress with the strange collar. It suddenly occurred to me that I had stumbled across some sort of secret meeting, and before the evening was out, many more men would cross the threshold and disappear through the double doors. I was trapped and needed to make a move. It was no use trying to dash back up to the main entrance at the earliest opportunity. Nor was access to the dock of any use, as the tide was already high. Instead, I would have to stay put behind the stairs and wait until everyone had proceeded through the large doors. Only then could I make my own audacious entrance and appeal for the release of poor Libby. How her captors would react was anyone's guess. All I knew was that I could not leave her to their mercies.

It all sounds impossibly outlandish now. But at the time, I was so highly charged that if anyone had touched me, I swear I would've sent ten thousand volts of electricity lancing through their body. Fear and terror seemed to make me feel stronger. I believed I could've won a war single-handedly that night. I felt I could've slain all the demons in hell. My courage was my shield, my fortitude, my spear. Right was on my side, and there was little doubt in my mind that I would be victorious against these agents of darkness, these vile hypocrites, who now gathered to perform God knows what depraved acts on a young innocent. What a fool I was.

CONSTANCE

As the sky lightens, so the fog lifts. By the time we reach Fleet Street, I can see the dome of St. Paul's rising above the jagged rooftops. Miss

Beaufroy, seated opposite me, is in a most fretful state. Twisting and turning her handkerchief in her restless hands.

"You must tell them every detail of your dream. How you saw my sister lying sick in her bed with pleurisy and . . ."

She drones on, telling me what I already know—I'm the one who had the dream, after all—then she says something new.

"Put with all the other factors that have led to his arrest—" she says.

"*Other factors?*" I interrupt. I know she thinks me rude, but it's important. "What factors were they, miss?"

Miss Pauline leans forward, her eyes wide, as she reports what she has discovered, as if she's afraid someone else might be listening.

"They found my sister's diary," she tells me as we are driven along the Strand.

"A *diary?*"

She gives an emphatic nod. "Apparently, it details incidents and dates that are significant."

"*Significant?*" I repeat.

I have touched a raw nerve. She is on the verge of tears. "I do not know the details, except for the fact that they are incriminating."

I pause, trying to take in all the implications of what I've just been told. But Miss Beaufroy's voice soon fills my stunned silence once more.

"That's why I've called upon you again, dear

Constance. Now that it seems . . ." Her eyes reddened. "We need to find out what happened. Tell me. . . ." She reaches forward and puts her hand on my knee. "Have you had any more premonitions?" Her expression is so earnest that it makes me quake. Her eyes draw mine toward her with an intensity that frightens me. I have to tell her.

"I've had signs," I reply slowly, the words cleaving to my tongue.

"Signs?" she asks breathlessly. She fixes me with that intense stare of hers. "You must tell me."

So I do. I tell her about *CLEO* written on the windowpane and about the strange oblong shape burned into my toast.

"Do you know what they mean?" Her forehead is furrowed.

I say I do not and her whole body shudders as she lets out a great sigh. Her head switches to the window and my eyes follow hers. She looks even more forlorn as we clatter along the Victoria Embankment, past Cleopatra's Needle. Big Ben strikes nine o'clock in the distance. A few minutes later, we arrive at King Street Police Station.

EMILY

I return to the moment, to King Street, to see Constance and Pauline led into the visiting

326

room. The former has been subjected to a search. The latter has not, presumably because a lady would never break the law and help a prisoner escape. There's a table that is divided widthways in the middle by a low wooden board, so that nothing can be passed between the visitor and the prisoner. Apart from the table with a single chair at either end, the room is bare.

Pauline is invited to sit by a constable. Constance has to stand. One side of the room is taken up by a large grille gate and it is through this that Terence Cutler appears. The lock clinks; the gate rattles as it is drawn open. The prisoner is shackled and flanked on either side by officers. He is wearing his normal clothes, but it is clear that he has neither shaven nor slept since his arrest. He seems to have shrunk in stature, too. He is a tall man, but he seems smaller now, as if he has turned in on himself. He is told to sit, but when he offers his wrists to be uncuffed, the senior officer shakes his head. Despite his class, he is to be accorded no privileges.

"Pauline. Thank God you have come!" He seems to regard her as a link to the outside world and to his freedom.

"Terence." She is cool toward him.

"This is all a terrible misunderstanding. You have to believe me." He lurches forward toward the wooden board. One of the constables on guard reprimands him and he sits back again.

"I am listening," she tells him. Pauline has the measure of her brother-in-law. "But you must tell me the whole truth."

Cutler's eyes dart to her face, then to the desk; then he sighs, like a wayward schoolboy who has been caught stealing apples in the orchard.

"I am listening, Terence," she repeats after a moment.

The surgeon begins in a calm voice. "Very well," he concedes with a sigh. "A few days ago, I was informed that a brooch belonging to Geraldine had been found on the building site, near where the torso was discovered."

Pauline's brows dip in a deep frown. "*A brooch?*" she whispers.

"It was the one I gave her as a wedding present. It was engraved on the back."

"I remember it," she snaps. "But how did it come to be there?" Her voice is as urgent as her gaze.

Cutler shakes his head. "I knew that she'd lost it a short while back. We'd been for a walk on a Sunday afternoon along Victoria Embankment when she noticed it was gone. We retraced our steps, but we never found it. It must have been ground down into the mud."

"I see," says Pauline, more patiently this time.

"The police managed to trace me from the inscription on the back. I said it was Geraldine's, and then a few days later they returned and asked me to identify the remains."

Pauline lets out a strange whimper at the thought. Her expression is one of anguish. "You have seen the body!?"

Cutler nods. "I have."

"And? Please tell me it wasn't her." She has raised her hands and is clutching at her chest.

There is a pause, as if the surgeon wishes to tug at every fiber in her being before releasing her. "No, it wasn't her," he blurts. "It wasn't Geraldine."

I think Pauline will swoon. She suddenly goes limp and lowers her head to the table. One of the constables rushes to her aid, as does Constance, who puts her arm around her shoulder.

"Miss Beaufroy!" She looks up at the young constable. "Water," she says. But Pauline points at her reticule. "I have smelling salts," she says, and Constance rummages inside and pulls out a small vial. Uncorking it, she holds it under Pauline's nose and she quickly revives. Blinking rapidly, she straightens her back once more.

"I'm sorry. I didn't mean to upset you," says Cutler while Pauline composes herself.

Constance retreats, shifting her weight from one side to the other. She is listening intently, reading the situation, showing great perception. Yet, she does not contribute. She is worrying me slightly.

"I am most relieved to hear that you did not identify Geraldine," says Pauline, holding her handkerchief up to her mouth. "But I do not understand. . . ."

Both Pauline and Constance wonder, why should Cutler be arrested if he was able to confirm that the torso was not that of his wife? They are puzzled.

As if reading their minds, Cutler nods. "I can assure you I was most relieved, too. But I'm afraid the police do not believe me."

"Oh?" queries Pauline.

"They searched Geraldine's room. It was just routine, they told me, but they found a diary." He fixes Pauline with a stare. "Did you know she kept a diary?"

Pauline shrugs. "Not until earlier today. No, I did not," she tells him.

Cutler shakes his head. "Well, apparently, she did, and she wrote all manner of lies in it." He has suddenly become aggressive. His tone is aggrieved. He is a man wronged.

"What *manner of lies?*"

The surgeon swallows down his rising anger. He leans forward and lowers his voice, as if in a vain attempt to exclude the prison guards from his conversation. "Mainly about me. How I hated her." He rakes his fingers through his normally well-oiled hair. "She even accuses me of consorting with one of the whor . . ." He stops himself. "One of the women who was murdered."

Pauline's face, already pale, now drains completely. "The Whitechapel murders?"

Cutler nods. "The woman is mad, deluded!" He turns his head away, shaking it vigorously. His arrogance returns momentarily, as if Pauline's reaction has emboldened him. Constance moves forward and lays a hand on her shoulder to comfort her. Pauline responds by clasping it tightly.

"I do not know what to say" is all she manages.

It is then that Cutler remarks Constance, standing behind Pauline. He has noticed her before, but evidently chose to ignore her. It is only now that he inquires about her identity.

"Who is that?" He nods his head derisorily in Constance's direction.

Pauline glances round and beckons to her to stand nearer. "This is Miss Constance Piper," she announces. "She is my companion."

There is a slight pause before she adds: "And she is a spirit guide."

"What?!" Cutler's brows shoot up in unison. He snorts. *"A spirit guide!* Please don't tell me you have enlisted the help of a"—he smirks at Constance as he searches for a word to describe her—"a *fake* to find Geraldine. I credited you with more wit, Pauline."

I'm mildly offended by the rebuke. I see Constance is, too, but she is unbowed. She stands tall. Pauline remains remarkably composed. She tilts her head slightly. "You are hardly in a position to ridicule others, Terence. It seems to me you need all the help you can get—spiritual, as well as temporal—right now."

Cutler is calm for a moment; then his features harden. He lifts his eyes to address Constance. "So what do you see in your crystal ball, eh? Me, standing on the scaffold with a noose around my neck, most like!" he sneers.

I can tell his words wound her. But will she answer him? Does she have the courage I think she has? I will her to be brave.

"The dead woman suffered from pleurisy, sir," she tells him in an unfaltering voice.

The smirk is suddenly wiped from his face. *"What?"*

"I had a dream, sir."

Instead of the expected sneer, however, Cutler is intrigued. "Go on," he urges her.

"And in my dream, I saw your wife, lying ill in her bed carved with fishes. You and a doctor were in attendance. The doctor shook his head and told you that she was suffering from pleurisy."

He listens, spellbound, to Constance's words, but now he shakes his head. "My God," he says. "You are right. There *was* a woman lying in that bed."

"There was?" Pauline looks elated.

"And she had pleurisy," he adds.

Constance sways a little and steadies herself on the table. She has been vindicated. She is shocked that her dream was no ordinary dream; it was, in Pauline's words, a "vision."

"But it was not Geraldine," says Cutler.

"It wasn't—" Pauline does not have the chance to finish her question before Terence breaks in.

"No. It was your missionary friend." He shrugs, as if the incident were of no con-sequence, as if my illness and brush with death were a meaningless trifle to him. "She recovered well enough to leave us the following week."

Constance is confused. She leans toward Pauline. "Who . . . ?" But she is waved away by a firm hand as Pauline shakes her head at her brother-in-law.

"Even so, do you believe me now, Terence?

Surely, you must agree that Miss Piper is not a fake, after all."

Cutler switches back round to her, his face set in a scowl. "For all I know, Geraldine put you up to this. You expect me to trust you and this"—he sneers at Constance—"this charlatan!?" By turn, he appears both angry and wounded. "I am the victim here," he snaps. "I am the one being unjustly accused of these unspeakable crimes, and I am completely innocent." He brings up his cuffed hands, jabbing at his own chest, then bangs them on the table. It is the sign for the guards to step in.

"Enough now!" barks the older constable. He nods to the other officer and together they approach Cutler, scooping their arms under his and lifting him from the chair. He does not struggle, rather I see his back stiffen.

"You have a good lawyer?" asks Pauline as Cutler is led away.

"Not good enough," he replies ruefully, being escorted to the grille.

Time is running out. Constance remains holding back. I want her to act. I will her to ask the question of Terence. I send my thoughts to her in a great wave and suddenly she stirs.

"Mr. Cutler!" she calls.

"Have courage," I tell her.

The constables stop by the grille. One is jangling his keys. She persists as Cutler cranes his neck and turns his head to face her. "Mr. Cutler, do you know the name of your wife's friend? The one with pleurisy?"

"Come on, now," scolds the older constable as he bundles his prisoner through the bars.

"Turnbull. Miss Turnbull," he shouts as he is led away.

"Tindall," says Pauline quietly. "It was Emily Tindall."

The question is asked and answered. My faith is restored. Constance, however, appears in shock.

"Miss Tindall," Constance repeats in a feeble voice.

"What is it?" asks Pauline, sensing that all is not well.

Constance seems in a daze. She lifts her face. "I know her."

"You know Emily Tindall?"

"She is my teacher."

"The one you were telling me about?" Now Pauline's eyes widen at the seeming coincidence. The connection has been made.

An enigmatic smile graces Constance's lips. "Yes. Yes." She has grown flushed with excitement. It is gratifying to see.

Pauline, her face suddenly lit up, shakes her head. "But this is incredible. I know Miss Tindall, too. We practically grew up together!" She grabs hold of Constance's hands and clasps them tightly. "Do you know where she is?"

Such a reaction gladdens me. It is good to know that her affection for me is as deep as it ever was. I decide to act. Constance gives a little shudder, as if Pauline's question has, once again, triggered her fears for me. She seems anxious as she folds her woolen shawl close over her breasts. And as she does so, I make her feel my presence.

"Ah!" she cries out in pain.

"My dear, what is it?" exclaims Pauline.

Constance withdraws her hand from under her ribs and holds out her forefinger. Stuck deep into the fleshy pad is a darning needle. A red bloom of blood is already rising.

CONSTANCE

The pain comes sudden and sharp. I hear myself shriek and then I see the needle that's pricking my finger. I pull it out with my other hand and suck the blood that spreads in red rivulets down my palm.

"But you are hurt!" cries Miss Beaufroy.

"It's nothing," I tell her, clutching my finger. Ma must have dropped the needle on my shawl when it was on the chair, I tell myself. It is my own fault for not hanging it up. But then something else occurs to me. The idea sweeps over me, blocking all else out of my vision. My insides begin to twist and tumble. I know that a moment of great clarity is about to come upon me. Then I see it: the word written on the windowpane suddenly flashes before me, and the strange shape in the toast, too. I also remember that on our journey here, we passed a tall obelisk on the Victoria Embankment.

"That's it!" I cry.

"That's what?" Miss Pauline asks as I brush past her.

The constable looks alert and tenses. He can see something is wrong.

"The way out!" I say. "I need to get out of here."

Thinking I'm going to swoon, he acts sharpish, quickly unlocking the great clanking gate and rushing to open the door that leads to the main entrance of the station. I can hear my feet pitter-patter across the tiled floor in the hall, and my heart pound in my ears; then I'm out onto the steps and onto King Street. Behind me, Miss Pauline is calling, but I ignore her. Miss Tindall is the only person in the world who matters to me right now and I know she is near. I can sense her; I can feel her. Turning right from the police building, I break into a run, heading toward the river. In a few minutes, I'm dodging cabs and carts in Covent Garden; then I'm across the road and on the embankment.

I look straight ahead of me and there it stands, tall and mystical above the traffic, Cleopatra's Needle. Miss Tindall was trying to tell me something. The signs. They were pointing to Cleopatra's Needle. She will be there. She must be. I can barely breathe and my legs feel like lead. I pause for a second. There are people milling all around. Porters and boot boys, nannies, pushing perambulators, and gents in bowlers. Horns are blown; men shout. I think my head will burst, but as I take a breath, I turn to my right and see her. She has just passed me, walking in the opposite direction. For a moment, I am stunned. I blink, but she remains. I have to convince myself that she is real, that she is not a vision, that she will not disappear in a bright light when I approach her, as she did in Brick Lane the other night. I start to follow her.

"Miss Tindall!" I call. She does not turn round, but I recognize her hat and the way she moves and she's carrying her green brolly. It's her. I know it is. "Miss Tindall!" I call again, breaking into a trot.

We're heading toward Westminster and the pavement becomes more crowded. There's a barrow boy, selling fruit, and a cluster of people are queuing by his stall. I try and sidestep them, but a man shoulders me and knocks me back, sending me clattering into a crate of apples, which spill all over the pavement. I don't stop. I mustn't, but I feel a press of people around me. I crane my neck and I can still see Miss Tindall, only she's moving away from me fast. I can't lose her again. *Not now.* Now I need her more than ever.

"Miss Tindall."

Big Ben strikes ten o'clock as I near Westminster Bridge. I think I have lost her; then I see her hat bobbing along on the sea of humanity once more. She is turning left at the bridge. I hurry, pushing past a couple of ragamuffins, who want to get their hands in my pockets. They try to block my way. I stumble on a loose paving stone, then right myself. *Where is she?* I can't lose her. I spot her once more, only this time she seems to have risen slightly above the crowd crossing the bridge. What is she doing? I stagger toward her.

"Miss Tindall!"

She cannot hear me above the din. Wagons and omnibuses clatter across the bridge. Horses neigh. People shout. Breathlessly I draw closer and then, to my horror, she is gone. Frantically I peer along the balustrade of the bridge. There is no one, only a small huddle clustering up ahead. They are looking at something, or someone. With mounting dread, I take a few steps toward the spot where the others are gathering. Their heads are angled down toward the river, but it is not the water that draws their attention. A woman

339

has hoisted herself up over the balustrade and climbed down onto the parapet. For a moment, I freeze, trying to take in what is happening. I'm not sure if they're goading her to jump or coaxing her to come back to the safety of the bridge. My heart is about to burst. I edge closer, tears starting to well up. It can't be Miss Tindall. She'd never do such a thing. *Never!* I have to reach her. I just have to.

I make a grab for the balustrade and lean over. I see her. It is her. Her body looks so slight against the cold slate gray of the Thames. It's hard pressed against one of the cast-iron lamp standards above a pier. With her hands behind her, she's clinging on, but for how much longer? A sudden gust of wind blows off her hat and it falls into the river. Her hair is suddenly released like a mainsail on a ship and it flies and flaps like a brown flag in the wind. It's only then that I realize it's not Miss Tindall, I'm watching. It's not Miss Tindall who's standing on the parapet waiting to hurl herself off into the murky depths. It's some other woman—a lady scorned in love or life, who cannot see a reason to go on, like so many in this fetid city. My heart sinks. I've duped myself again.

I turn, sniffing away my tears, steadying the breath that is burning my poor lungs. Then something makes me retrace my steps. It's like a voice inside me, urging me not to abandon the woman. She may not be Miss Tindall, but she needs help, nonetheless. Behind her are the baying crowds, in front of her the blackest of rivers. Something tells me I need to show her she has a choice. I turn and elbow my way through the crowd, stamping on feet to make the people part. I draw close to her side. The way she's standing with her arms behind her back, clutching onto the lamp stand, reminds me of Joan of Arc about to be burned at the stake. She is perhaps the same age as Miss Tindall. Perhaps a little older. Tall, too, like her, and smartly dressed. She is a lady, I can tell, and then, as the wind whips round, she turns toward me and I catch a glimpse of her face. I can hardly believe my eyes. It is the face in the photograph.

"Geraldine," I mouth. "Mrs. Cutler!" I cry, my voice battling against the wind. "Mrs. Cutler!"

The sound reaches her ears and I see her suddenly tense. I call out again and she follows my voice. Her startled gaze latches onto mine. The crowd murmurs. The entertainment has taken a different twist.

"Here, take my hand," I tell her, reaching toward her.

Her chest heaves. "How do you know my name?" she shouts.

"I know your sister," I tell her. I think it's best not to mention her husband. "She is very worried about you." She is still, gazing down into the blackness. "Pauline," I say.

Her eyes grow round. *"Pauline,"* she repeats. I see her lips lift a little at the thought of her sister.

"She has been looking for you," I tell her.

"Looking for me?" She repeats my words slowly and deliberately.

"She wants to know you are safe," I say, stretching out my hand. "Here." I offer it to her and she grabs at it, holding it tight. Someone in the crowd puts a looped rope in my other hand. "Hold me," I tell the broad-shouldered man standing next to me. I stretch out toward her and gently slip the loop over her head and under her arm. At least now if she jumps, or slips, she will not drown. "Come now. Easy," I tell her. I force a smile and slowly she starts to move her feet, but there is green slime on the parapet and suddenly she loses her footing and slips. She screams. I scream. The crowd gasps.

"No!"

EMILY

Alarmed by Constance's erratic behavior, Pauline followed her out of the police station. She saw her skirt a bookstall before disappearing down Bedford Lane. In a panic, she hurried back inside the station to enlist the help of a constable, who, in turn, summoned a

342

cab. We join her as she travels along Victoria Embankment, past Cleopatra's Needle, toward the Houses of Parliament. As the carriage draws closer to Big Ben, however, Pauline, her eyes trained for Constance, notices something amiss up ahead on Westminster Bridge. A crowd is clustered on the pavement and now spills out onto the road, much to the annoyance of cabdrivers being held up. She alights from her own conveyance and walks along the pavement, when she suddenly realizes the cause of the congestion. There is someone standing on the parapet of the bridge, clinging onto a lamppost. Someone is about to throw him- or herself off into the Thames. The notion suddenly seizes her, drags her by the throat and pulls her toward the melee. She does not need my thoughts or direction to know that her sister is in need of her. She ups her pace; then as soon as she knows her voice will not be wasted on the wind, she calls out. "Let me pass, please! I know her. I know this woman!"

In an instant, she draws near. "Geraldine. Oh, my dear Geraldine. Please. Come to me!" she calls out. But the wind from the river flies up and pushes back her words so they are lost. Yet, it does not matter. Geraldine's gaze has already latched onto Constance. She has seen her and her despair melts away. Nobody hears it, but me. Nobody hears her whimper "Emily" as she reaches for her, her short cape flapping wildly around her head. My only sorrow is that she did not die that day. I wish she had. It would have been better for all.

CHAPTER 30

Wednesday, October 31, 1888

CONSTANCE

As I lie in the lumpy bed at home, I think I might be losing my mind. The books I read are full of women who have: Mrs. Rochester in *Jane Eyre*, poor Miss Havisham in *Great Expectations* and Mr. Collins's *Woman in White*. I think I am joining them. I am Alice down a rabbit hole. Colors are sharper. I see things differently. Shapes are better defined. Certain objects fall into clearer relief. It's as if my physical world is mirroring my mind. There is lucidity. There is enlightenment. I keep turning over the past few days in my head—my dreams, the strange happenings. Do I really have the power to see into the future, or have I imagined everything?

There are so many things that don't make sense to me. Why did Mrs. Cutler try to kill herself, and how did I manage to save her just in time? Did I lead Miss Beaufroy to her, or would she have found her, anyway? If the torso in the vaults isn't Mrs. Cutler, then who is it? Did the poor victim die by the same hand as the women of Whitechapel? And, most important, where, oh where, is Miss Tindall? There are so many questions that are whirling around in my brain, and yet I can't help wondering how I became involved in the whole terrible saga in the first place.

Or have I just imagined everything?

EMILY

We shall leave dear Constance to ponder, while you and I make our way to Whitechapel. Or, more precisely, to Miller's Court. It's only a few streets away from Constance's home in White's Row and it is where Mary Kelly lives with her lover Joseph Barnett. This Barnett is not a bad man, not truly bad, although he is inclined to drinking and subsequent violent behavior. He and Mary met when he was a porter at Billingsgate Fish Market. They began to cohabit shortly afterward and have lived in various rented rooms in the area. A few weeks ago, however, Joseph lost his job; since then, he and Mary have quarreled incessantly. Tonight, however, she is hoping they will not row, for she has some important news to tell him. Mary hopes it will please him.

Joseph has been tramping around White-chapel all day, looking for work. He's tired and he's had a couple of pints. Returning to the cramped and drafty single room he shares with Mary, he slumps onto the chair in the corner. She eases off his boots for him.

"There, there, my love," she soothes as she rubs his sore feet.

He reaches out and strokes her blond hair as she does so. It feels thick to the touch and coarse like rope.

There's a loaf on the table and a wedge of cheese. "Let's eat, shall we?" she says, heaving herself up from the floor.

Joseph cocks his head. "Bring it over 'ere," he grunts.

She goes to the table and, taking the long knife, cuts a thick slice of bread for him and a second, thinner slice for herself before putting both slices onto wooden platters. Next she cuts into the wedge of cheese and lays it on the bread. She hands the plate to Joseph and sits opposite him on the corner of the bed. He tucks into the food with gusto, as if it's his last meal. Mary, on the other hand, is more circumspect. She watches him for a moment and he feels her eyes on him. He looks up, his mouth full.

"What's up with you?" he asks. A sodden ball of crumbs escapes from his lips as he speaks.

Mary pauses. *It's as good a time as any,* she thinks. "I'm with child, Joseph."

For a moment, he says nothing, but continues to chew his bread and cheese. Then, looking her straight in the eye, he asks: "Is it mine?"

She's not sure, but she nods. "Yes," she tells him.

She thinks he'll be all right. It'll take a while, but she thinks he'll get used to the idea. But she's wrong. Suddenly he throws down the platter to the floor and leaps up from his chair.

"You stupid slut!" he screams at her, and slaps her so hard across the face that she's knocked back onto the bed.

Momentarily stunned, she rights herself and rubs her cheek. "It's yours, I said!" she protests.

Joseph paces up and down. "I don't care whose it is. Get rid of it!" He picks up one of his boots and hurls it at her. She swerves to avoid the missile and it hits the window, smashing the glass. It's followed, a second later, by a platter. It breaks another pane.

Huffing like an angry bull, Joseph stoops to pick up a leather bag from under the bed, then unhooks his coat from the back of the door. He hobbles on one foot as he wrestles to put on a boot. The other remains outside. He flings wide the door.

"Don't go, Joe!" calls Mary, launching herself

at him. But he pushes her back again onto the bed without another word and walks away.

She remains prone for the next few minutes, sobbing. Of course, they've rowed before, but not like that. She wonders if she'll see him again and her sobs grow louder. Soon they break into wails; meanwhile, all around her, the air in the room grows increasingly cold as the night air creeps in through the broken windowpanes.

CHAPTER 31

Friday, November 2, 1888

CONSTANCE

I sit in the tearoom of Brown's Hotel, dressed in my new smart clothes and surrounded by opulence and luxury. I am that different person again, the one who is self-assured, composed, knowledgeable. The East End flower seller is nowhere to be seen. My pale cheeks are subtly rouged; my lank hair swept under a stylish hat and my ragged petticoat is hidden underneath a full taffeta skirt. I am even wearing gloves to hide the telltale chapping on my hands. I fit in well with my surroundings. No one tried to turn me back at the door and out onto the street when

I arrived today. I am perfectly at ease among the coiffed and perfumed ladies and gentlemen of the West End who sit at the tables surrounding me.

Presently I am joined by Miss Beaufroy. I rise to greet her, a habit borne from years of being lowly and deferential. She looks a little drawn, a little flustered, too. She raises her hand to bid me to sit, then catches the eye of a passing waiter and orders tea for us both.

"My dear Constance, forgive me for being late, but I bring news." Her delivery is fast. She loosens the fur stole about her shoulders and lowers herself down onto her chair amid a waft of lavender.

"Mrs. Cutler?"

"Yes, indeed." She removes her gloves.

"How is she?"

"Well enough, but exhausted, of course." She shakes her head. "Her mind . . ."

"And Mr. Cutler?"

"He has returned to Harley Street, poor man. He seems to be bearing up, but obviously he has endured a terrible ordeal." She throws her naked hands up in a gesture of incredulity; then she leans forward toward me. "I have suggested that as soon as Geraldine is ready that she returns home with me to Sussex. Just for a few weeks, to rest. She has been through so much." She pauses reflectively. "We all have."

I wonder how Mr. Cutler will react to his wife.

Will he take her back after the way she has behaved? Could he find it in his heart to forgive her for those lies she made up about him in her diary that led to his arrest? The woman is so obviously sick in the mind that he could surely not be blamed if he shunned her or even had her committed to an asylum. I say nothing, but nod in agreement. We have, indeed, been through so much, and my own personal quest is far from over.

Tea arrives and Miss Beaufroy takes charge.

"Milk?" she asks.

"Please."

"Sugar?" The tongs are poised in her hand.

The old me wants six lumps. I crave the sweetness. "Two, please," I say.

She pours the brew in silence and I take the opportunity to raise the burning question that has been playing on my mind for the past two days, ever since I found out. "You say you know Miss Tindall, miss. Miss Emily Tindall?"

A quirk of her lips signifies fond memories. "Ah, yes," she says, handing me my cup. "Dear Emily. We were neighbors as children. We even shared a governess."

"Is that so?" I say, intrigued. I feel the blood draining from my face.

"And you?"

I know this can't simply be a coincidence. "She was my Sunday school teacher, first, then she became . . ." I trail off. I am about to say a friend, but that is not right. She was not a friend. She was—is—more. She was a mentor, an inspiration. She was a mother and a sister to me. I felt as close to her as the gloves on my hands, and still do, but since she disappeared, I have felt bereft.

"Yes?" Miss Beaufroy presses me.

"My private tutor," I say. I can't believe the words that have tumbled from my mouth, as if they have not come from me at all; it is as if they were put there by someone else. What would Flo say if she could hear me now? It's not me talking.

"Where do you think she is?" She takes a sip of tea.

I shake my head. "They told me at the church they didn't know. But I don't believe them. I can't," I say. I am close to tears. "Any more than I believe that you and I met purely by chance."

She places her cup and saucer back on the table and fixes me with an earnest look. "You think Emily has brought us together."

"I do," I tell her. "With all my heart, I believe that she guided you to me."

She nods, as if I have just commented on the weather or the price of a loaf. There is a tacit understanding between us. This is how it was meant to be. This is our fate and we are facing it together.

Miss Beaufroy stares into her cup, as if pictures

from her past are floating on the surface of the tea. "Emily and I were so very close," she begins wistfully. "Then I met a soldier, a dashing young officer." She smiles at the recollection. "We were engaged to be married. I fear my letters to her became less frequent when my fiancé was posted overseas. I wrote to him daily. He wrote to me, too." She pauses, her eyes growing watery. "Some of his letters only reached me after his death. He was killed at Khartoum, you see."

I'd read about the siege at the time and how General Gordon and his men fought and died heroes. "I'm sorry," I say weakly.

She does not notice, but carries on. "I retreated from the outside world." The wound is still open, I can see that. "I couldn't bear to speak with anyone, apart from my mother and Geraldine."

I nod slowly, showing that I understand. "She must have missed you very much," I venture.

She nods. "I know I missed her."

"So do I," I agree. And then it dawns on me. "It's almost as if she has brought us together for a purpose."

"A purpose?" she repeats.

"Because of our meeting, we saved your sister's life," I tell her slowly.

Miss Beaufroy puts down her cup and saucer on the table. "And her husband's!" she exclaims. "Yes, you're absolutely right."

It's true, I realize. Without our intervention,

Mr. Cutler may have been found guilty of murder and executed. "It's as if our mutual friend has been watching events unfold and guiding our actions," I say.

"*Your* actions, my dear." She pats my hand. "You are the one she speaks to in your dreams."

I, however, frown at the suggestion. A little shiver runs down my neck, as if a draft is caressing my skin. "But how can that be if she has not passed to the other side?"

Miss Pauline allows herself a smile. "But we know she has not." She shrugs. "Mr. Cutler told us that she recovered from pleurisy. You heard it yourself."

She is right. I did. Yet, still, I have that terrible feeling deep inside me. The dark thought is screaming on the edge of my mind. "But that was in the summer."

"And on her recovery, perhaps she returned to Oxford?" Miss Beaufroy's voice is so assured that I'm almost willing to accept what she says.

"That is most likely," I agree. "But why didn't she tell us?"

There is no answer to my question.

And there it is again, the doubt that nags away at my subconscious. I feel the fear as it creeps like a shadow across my face. "I worry that something has happened to her," I tell her. "Something bad."

Miss Beaufroy narrows her eyes. "Then there's

only one thing for it, my dear," she tells me with great conviction. "You must go to Oxford." She places her palm on my knee. "You must find her. Neither of us can rest until you do."

I swallow down my mouthful of tea. "I wish with all my heart that I could," I reply. How many times have I considered such a journey? I want to find Miss Tindall more than anything, but I know it's impossible. I don't have the money for a bed for the night, let alone the train fare. And even if I made it to Oxford, it would be like looking for a needle in a haystack unless . . . unless she guided me. Then, as if she is following my thoughts, Miss Pauline says: "I shall pay all your expenses, of course. And a fee."

"A fee?" No one has ever suggested paying me "a fee" before.

"For your talents. You have great"—she pauses, looking intensely into my eyes—"perception," she says finally. "If Emily is alive, you will find her."

It is a strange thing she has just said, like an admission that perhaps I am right. That all hope may be lost. "And if she is not?" I ask.

Do I see resignation in her look? "Then she will find you," she says softly.

I think she might have already—nevertheless, I swallow down my tea and with it my doubts. Miss Tindall is still alive, I tell myself. She has to be.

CHAPTER 32

Saturday, November 3, 1888

EMILY

In a private asylum in Hampstead, Geraldine Cutler sways to and fro in a rocking chair. Dressed in a simple robe and swathed in a woolen shawl, she sits in the conservatory. Her dark brown hair flows loosely down her shoulders, so that a casual visitor would not realize she is wearing a straitjacket and that her arms are restrained under her ribs. A nurse is in attendance just a few feet away. The doctor has ordered that in view of her mental fragility and her attempt to self-murder, his patient must not be left alone.

The autumn sun has made a rare appearance today and Geraldine Cutler is enjoying the rays. Lifting her face up to the light, she closes her eyes. She seems calm, contemplative even. There is not a trace of the anguish that was etched on her features only two days before as she relives the past few weeks in her mind.

She recalls walking out of her Harley Street home that August morning as she had done twice before in her marriage. Of course, she had returned after a day or so on both previous occasions. But this time, it was different. This time, she had evidence to back up what she had suspected all along and which she found impossible to bear. Her small private income meant that she could stay in comfortable lodgings until she could decide what course of action to take. And then the murders began. The first one was followed just three weeks later by another. The third happened the week after that; then there were two on one night. She was reading the account of the autopsy on the fifth victim, Catherine Eddowes, when she noticed a single sentence buried deep in a column in the *Star*. According to the report, the initials *TC* were tattooed on the victim's left forearm. And that's when it struck her, like a bullet. She lowered the newspaper. *TC,* she thought—the initials of her husband, her philandering, arrogant husband, who frequented the East End and regularly tended to women of the night. He'd thought she did not know. He'd thought she believed him when he told her he was working at St. Bartholomew's every Friday evening. But he had not bargained on her finding that envelope containing his fee. When she had confronted him, he had denied that he was responsible for terminating the lives of unborn children, but she'd known he was lying. With her own eyes, she had seen him leave the Whitechapel Workhouse Infirmary shortly before midnight. Then and there, she began to plan just how she would exact her revenge.

The diary was a stroke of genius, she mused. Written in retrospect, it covered a period of three months before her "disappearance." Among the tedious tea parties and general gossip that she recorded, she had managed to couch some incriminating tidbits.

July 10
A young woman of the lower class called in deep distress. She said she was a patient and asked to see Terence, but when I told her he was not here, she seemed most put out. I asked her name. She said it was Polly.

July 15
Yet another woman called asking for Terence. I must tell him not to give out our address to such women. It is not seemly to have such callers.

July 28
I am in a state of shock. While looking for some papers in Terence's study, I stumbled across several photographs of a most vile and shocking nature. They

were in his locked bureau, but I found a spare key and now wish to God I had not.

August 7
Terence did not return until the early hours this morning. He is working far too hard.

August 8
A horrific murder in the East End has put fear in the hearts of all women in the area.

That was the last entry in her diary, written from the comfort of her Chelsea guesthouse in early October. Martha Tabram's mutilation served her purpose so well. The day after her killing, she'd left Harley Street. The only problem had been how she could return to the house undetected to secrete the journal in her bedroom. It would, she calculated, be found by the police when they conducted a search after she had been reported missing. She still had her house key and had managed to slip inside, but she had almost been caught out. Terence had heard her on the stairs. He had ventured out of his room and onto the landing. She had cowered behind the door, not daring to breathe. Then he had whispered her name.

There was a tenderness in his voice that she had not expected. And when he did not see her, he had cried. She had not expected that, either.

Her next master stroke was to visit Whitehall and the site where the mysterious rotting torso was discovered. She knew the area well. Terence and she would walk regularly along Victoria Embankment. Her mission was to plant the brooch that Terence had given her on their wedding day. She thought she'd lost it a while back, but had found it only recently, snagged on the lining of a jacket. She had conveniently forgotten to mention the discovery to her husband.

As luck would have it, she'd heard that a journalist planned to set his hound on the site with the aim of sniffing out any of the remaining corpse that might be buried there. Mr. Waring's assistant had been very amenable. For the sum of three pounds, young Mr. Pugh had taken the brooch and "found" it close to the severed leg, which the dog uncovered. A little detective work on the part of Mr. Troutbeck, the coroner, had led him to Terence. She could not have wished for anything to go better than it had.

At around midday, the ward sister enters. "You have a visitor, madam," she tells her patient.

● ● ●

Geraldine Cutler knew that her husband would come. She had, of course, facilitated his visit. She had told the police that his incarceration was, in fact, a terrible mistake. They had read far too much into her diary, which had never been intended for anyone's eyes but her own. And as for the other so-called evidence—the brooch and the initials on the dead woman's arm—mere coincidence and purely circumstantial. Oh! How her poor, dear, blameless husband must have suffered. In light of her statement, he was freed on bail.

The meeting, or rather reunion, was her idea, too. Her doctors would never have agreed to it otherwise. They would have deemed it too upsetting for her, too psychologically disturbing. But she had insisted.

Terence Cutler had also been eager to see his wife, though for obviously different reasons. He had been questioned and considered that he could be trusted not to agitate or distress Geraldine in her present state of mind. So everything was arranged, under supervision, of course.

Geraldine turns toward the door to watch Terence walk toward her. Her heart leaps a little as he nears. She still finds him attractive, even after everything he has put her through. There is something in his bearing: that hint of danger she so admires in a man, that glint in his eye that makes her imagine he might draw a sword at any moment and fight for her honor. His sandy hair is made darker by the Macassar Oil, but now she notices streaks of silver among it. Had those been there when she left in the summer? She thinks not. Had her absence turned his hair gray? she wonders. She feels almost flattered at the notion that her disappearance could have had such a profound effect on his features. If it has done that to his physical appearance, what might it have done to him mentally? Terence has always reminded her of a swan—stately and serene on the surface, but underneath he is paddling frantically to keep his head above water. He has been damaged by her actions, most certainly, she can tell.

I watch as he approaches her. To my surprise, he manages a smile. I think it a magnanimous gesture, but there is more.

"Geraldine," he greets her.

"Terence." She meets his gaze.

He bends low and I think he is about to embrace her, when he suddenly recoils in horror. He had not been warned of the restraint. The doctor, hovering in the background, watches the reunion. Cutler frowns and turns.

"Is this necessary?" he snaps, pointing to the straps on the garment that are revealed beneath the shawl.

The doctor, now at Cutler's shoulder, veers away from Geraldine and addresses her husband out of the corner of his mouth. "A precaution, sir, given the circumstances."

The surgeon shakes his head. "I will take responsibility for my own safety, Doctor," he replies. "Remove it, if you please." The doctor gestures to the nurse, who carries out his bidding. Buckles are unbuckled, straps unstrapped; in a few moments, Geraldine's arms are free once more. Remaining seated, she stretches them out in front of her and wiggles her fingers, as if she has never noticed her limbs or digits before. It's as if they are something strange and new to her. Then she does something odd, I think. She holds out her hand for her husband to kiss. For a moment, he simply regards her. I wonder if he might shun her; yet he does not. Instead, he bends low, sweeping her hand up in his, and kisses it.

The nurse draws up a chair for him and he sits at his wife's side. They are almost touching. Almost, but not quite. Terence speaks first.

"How are you?" he asks in a guarded tone.

She nods and her eyes fill with tears.

Suddenly she is overcome. "Forgive me," she sobs. "Please find it in your heart to forgive me. I never meant . . ."

He turns toward her in his chair; then looking deep into her eyes, he wipes away the tears on her cheeks with his thumb and swallows back his own.

"I understand. The police are fools. They read too much into your diary. Let us not talk of it now," he tells her. "You are alive. I am free, for the time being. You need to rest."

"Yes," agrees Geraldine. "I am so very tired."

I shall leave them now, oddly relaxed in each other's company, saying nothing, but relishing the silence. It is time, however, to break mine. I have waited too long to tell Constance what I should have told her a while back. It has taken some time for her to come this far on her journey, but now I believe she is ready to hear what I have to say and ready to accept the burden of responsibility that I must place on her young shoulders. I pray she takes it willingly.

CHAPTER 33

CONSTANCE

So I am to leave for Oxford tomorrow. Once there, I am to find Miss Tindall, or at least seek her out. I've heard Oxford is a very fine city, with its dreaming spires and great libraries. It's not grimy like London, either. There's not so much soot in the air. And not so much fog, neither. All the buildings are made of honey-colored stone. Miss Tindall once told me that a lot of the undergraduates ride bicycles there. Ladies do, too. Can you imagine?

Anyway, that's why I'm in Petticoat Lane Market now, buying a big bag. Ladies would call it a *portmanteau*, I believe. That's French for coat carrier, I think, although don't ask me how I know. I don't speak French, but that's what's so odd these days. I seem to *know* things that I've never learned. Still, I'm glad it worked out all right for Miss Beaufroy's sister, Mrs. Cutler. What a to-do! Give Old Bill an inch and he'll take a mile at the moment. The police are so desperate to catch Jack, they'll start nabbing grannies next. If you ask me, I'd say that Mrs.

Cutler's a few bob shy of a quid. She was in a right state, but Miss Beaufroy says she's seen her in the asylum and that she's on the mend. She'll be taking her back to Sussex with her, in a day or two, so that she can recover in the fresh air. All's well that ends well, as the Bard would say. I only hope I'll be saying the same thing after my visit to Oxford. I only hope I can find Miss Tindall. And to think that Miss Beaufroy and I both know her so well. What are the chances? Of course, Miss Beaufroy believes that she's brought us together somehow. That she's willed us to meet. I believe she has, too, but, in a way, I also hope she hasn't, because I'm worried that can only mean one thing. . . .

Miss Beaufroy has given me five shillings for the market, so I'm planning on buying something half decent. Once I've bought my bag, I might even have enough left over to get Ma a little something—a scarf or even a pair of gloves.

It's Guy Fawkes and everyone's in a chirpy mood. Tonight there'll be bonfires and fireworks and Whitechapel's getting in the swing. Funny that—celebrating saving the Houses of Parliament from being blown sky high by a bunch of Catholics, nigh on three hundred years ago, with more bangs and crackles. Of course, there's food as well: a pig roasting on a spit and pies and jellied eels. Gingerbread, too, and hot roasted chestnuts on a glowing brazier and the smells are making my mouth water. I hold out my cold hands as I walk by the heat, but I've no time to loiter.

It's growing dark, so I better be sharpish. The fog's rolling in again and the traders are starting to pack up. The days are short in November. Short, dark days and long, dark nights. And *he's* still lurking.

"Penny for the Guy?" calls a crippled boy on the pavement as I pass. He's with another urchin, sitting by a huge doll that they've made of rags. It lies sprawled across a wheelbarrow, its newspaper limbs stuffed into filthy old trousers and its body covered by a ragged shirt. It's sprawled all higgledy-piggledy, like a grotesque old man in his death throes. It wears a cardboard mask, and its painted mouth is open with blood dripping from it. It's gross. Round its neck hangs a handwritten sign: *Jack the Ripper.*

"Penny for the Guy?" squeaks the gutter rat again as I walk past, trying not to look. I fix my eyes straight ahead, then narrow them. There's something going on at the far end of the street. A small crowd is jostling along. There are shouts. "It's 'im! It's 'im!"

I feel my feet quicken beneath me. More people are gathering around something or someone near the police station. My own curiosity pulls me along to the edge of the crowd. It's then that I notice the big woman standing on tiptoe next to me, straining her neck for a better view. It's Mrs. Puddiphatt.

"What's going on?" I ask.

She looks down at me, her eyes all beady. "Oh, Connie," she says as soon as she recognizes me. "There's a man with his face blacked up with soot. They're saying 'e's Jack!'"

EMILY

Terence Cutler is calling on his wife in the asylum for the second time. His visit yesterday went as well as he could have expected. He thought he might have been angrier with her than he was. After all, she was surely to blame for his arrest for murder, making up those ridiculous lies about him in her diary. But, after their reunion, he congratulated himself on his self-restraint. He still loves her, you see. He realized that in her absence. He had suspected it before, but on that night when he thought there was a grain of a chance that she had returned to him of her own volition, he knew it to be true. And although he also knows that she is mentally unstable, he still admires—in a perverse way—her intelligence and her ferocity. Pity and guilt are fighting inside him. Her entries into the diary, bemoaning his long hours away from her, opened his eyes to her loneliness. To think that his work blinded him to her feelings and needs. To think that he almost lost her!

Today he finds Geraldine much more alert, almost agitated. Her expression is engaging and her neatly manicured fingernails scratch at her own palms. He is glad to see there is no sign of the straitjacket as he sits at her side.

"Thank goodness you have come," she tells him. He notices she is wearing a little rouge today and her hair is swept back to accentuate her strong features. "I owe you an explanation," she goes on, suddenly clutching his hand in hers.

"Dearest, no. It is I who owes you one," Cutler says candidly. He lets out a long, deep sigh, as if he has not exhaled for the past ten weeks. "But not now. Later."

Geraldine shakes her head, then lifts her eyes heavenward, as if seeking divine inspiration. It is clear she is about to launch into a heartfelt speech. She inhales a long breath through her nostrils. "I was deeply unhappy." Now she looks in front of her, out of the large window and over the green, mottled heath that stretches before her. Then she corrects herself. "I am still deeply unhappy."

Cutler sucks in his cheeks and stiffens his back. "That is very evident."

Keeping her gaze ahead, and her face

expressionless, Geraldine tells him, "You see, I now have proof of what you do at the infirmary."

Cutler's brows shoot up simultaneously. Shocked, he switches round to meet her face. His eyes latch onto hers. He fears he has been caught out, but he must not beat the pistol. He feigns ignorance. "What on earth are you talking about, dearest?"

"Do you think me stupid, Terence? You denied it before, but I knew you were lying."

The edges of her mouth twitch slightly. *A smile?* She has taken aim and now she fires her salvo. "Your friend Dr. Holt has a loose tongue, especially if one offers him a bottle of whisky," she tells him flatly.

He arches a brow. After a moment's reflection, he says: "So that is how you came up with the name Polly. It was no coincidence."

She remains silent, her chin prominent, her gaze boring into his very soul. He, on the other hand, drops his head, then shakes it as he contemplates this act, or acts, of domestic treachery. Yet, he does not seem entirely surprised. At least her admission explains the presence of a carriage he had noted on more than one occasion when leaving the infirmary late at night. "I underestimated you, my dear." He struggles to suppress the hurt child in his throat that is fighting to sound resilient.

Geraldine, however, remains implacable. She

gives a little snort as she shrugs her shoulders. "You have to admit if the situation weren't so tragic, it would be almost humorous—" She breaks off, her eyes suddenly welling up. It is as if her hard shell has slipped to reveal a fragile belly beneath. As she turns to her husband, her lips start to tremble. "I cannot give you a child and yet you . . ." Clamping a handkerchief over her mouth, she looks away, although her attempt to stifle a sob fails. She has laid herself bare and spoken the unspeakable truth that has dogged their marriage for the past three years— the sullen greetings over breakfast, the cheerless welcomes after a hard day's work. The pendulum clock in the drawing room had so often been the only sound as they sat on opposite sides of the hearth. They had both known that it was ticking away the seconds of any hope that Geraldine might ever have of conception and yet nothing was ever said. And now it must be acknowledged. Her childless state is the reason for her unhappiness, the excuse for her behavior, the cause of all their problems.

Cutler's face falls and he closes his eyes. His own wretchedness at being discovered as an abortionist has tempered his muted anger toward her. Now he feels a surge of pity rush through him. His anger is drowned in a tide of compassion and solicitousness felt only once before—when he rid that poor waif of a wicked man's unborn babe on the operating table in Whitechapel.

"I . . . I am so very sorry. You were never meant to find out."

Geraldine dabs her eyes with her handkerchief. "I was devastated when I discovered what you were doing to those women, Terence. Don't you see that they are the cause of our misery, and your lust for them the cause of y barrenness?" Her voice burns like acid. "I had to get away."

He nods. He accepts her rationale. He is guilty. "Where did you go?"

"A guesthouse in Chelsea." She straightens her back. "I was there for more than a month before Polly Nichols was murdered."

"Ah," he says knowingly. "Jack the Ripper."

She coughs out a caustic laugh. "When I heard about the first murder and that the woman was"—she cannot bring herself to say "a prostitute"—"from Whitechapel, I wondered if you knew her." She switched back to face her husband. "I imagined you with her, Terence. I couldn't help it. I hate myself for thinking of it, but I could picture you with these . . . these whores." She is shaking her head. "Then when Dr. Holt told me that you had . . . that you had helped Polly Nichols. . . ."

Already wounded, he bows his head again. He cannot deny his weakness. He vividly remembers the night he got infected. His encounter had been a vertical affair just before their marriage. He had been anxious about their union and had doused his worries at one of the grubby taverns on a street corner, becoming almost senseless. He remembers very little of the sordid coupling, only that it took place in a back alley, up against cold, wet walls, and lasted a matter of seconds. Little did he then know that its legacy would stay with him for the rest of his life.

"And then"—Geraldine's reproachful voice brings him back from the fetid streets of Whitechapel to the moment—"And then when I found out that you kill other women's unborn children, when we cannot have one of our own . . ." Her shoulders heave in another great sob. "Well, it sent me mad with envy."

She has aimed her shots well. He cannot deny he had rid Polly Nichols of her unwanted child. He should never have trusted that drunkard Holt. He wants to double over so that he does not have to face her. It takes all his courage to lift his gaze and shake his head. "I am not proud of what I have done," he tells her, but he also wants her to know that, despite welcoming the extra income, there had been a smidgeon of moral rectitude in his actions. "You must understand that I believed I was helping these women out of poverty."

"What?" There is principled indignation in his wife's voice. "You are not above the law, Terence!"

He works his jaw. "Perhaps the law should be changed," he counters.

"What?" she repeats incredulously.

He shakes his head and tries to offer some justification. "Why feed another unwanted mouth when it so very often means that the older children starve?"

She is dumbstruck with anger. She has no answer. There is a long pause before she picks up on something he has said previously, as if she's been replaying his words in her head. "You *believed?*"

"What?"

"You *believed* you were helping these women? Are you saying you no longer perform abortions?"

Cutler sighs heavily, but still hopes to salvage the situation with his news.

"I have resigned from the infirmary. I will no longer carry out terminations."

Geraldine keeps him on tenterhooks for a moment, then nods emphatically, as if she has achieved a small victory. "I am glad of it," she tells him eventually. Her voice is a little sharp, but the edge on it is blunt. "May I ask what changed your mind?"

Cutler's mouth suddenly feels dry as he recalls the frightened child lying on the table in the infirmary. The image of her face remains with him still. "I realized that the poor and the vulnerable will always be exploited."

Geraldine inclines her head. "How true."

"But it's no use simply helping them," continues her husband.

"Oh?" She arches her brow.

"We have to address the root cause of the evil before we can be rid of it."

Geraldine lets out a derisory laugh. "You sound almost noble, Terence."

Her reaction spurs him on. His wife may have tried to take her own life, but he will not allow her to make a mockery of him, to laugh at him as if he were performing in a cheap sideshow. His jaw works and, this time, his fists clench as he shakes his head. "In your absence, I have been thinking a great deal, about us and our marriage. When you left, I was angry at first, as I have been before, but then, when you didn't come back after a week, I began to think that you'd left me for good. I couldn't blame you. Then that night, when I thought you'd returned, and I went to your room, only to find it empty, I was beside myself. I felt so lonely." He looks at her with a mixture of sadness and hope. "I realized that I really do love you. And despite every-thing, I still do."

Geraldine is silent for a moment, before she reaches for his hand and I see her expression switch unnervingly quickly once more. Her voice becomes thin and apologetic. "When I heard you had been arrested for those terrible murders, I instantly regretted that wretched diary. I was mad with worry for you. I couldn't bear to think of you in jail, and yet I couldn't bear to face you."

Cutler nods and suddenly grasps her hand. "And so you thought the only thing to do would be to end your own life."

Geraldine lifts his hand and kisses it lovingly, opening his clenched fingers and caressing his palm. He closes his eyes, relishing her touch; seeing that she has him thus enraptured, she speaks to him softly. "I, too, felt so alone. I was in despair. I could see no other way out." The tears are flowing again. "Please forgive me, my dearest," she asks. "Please."

After a pause, Terence opens his eyes, then reaches out to her and strokes her long hair. He believes her tears to be genuine. I have my doubts. She clasps his hand and holds it to her breast.

So now is the time. Moved by her melancholy

and the erotic power she still has over him, which he thought was lost, he must deliver his message of hope. All is not lost. "I do forgive you, my love, as I hope you forgive me, and what's more, I have a plan to help us."

Geraldine's head jerks up and she regards him with puffy eyes that are full of questions, as well as tears. "A plan?"

Her reaction is encouraging, but for the moment, he must tantalize without satisfying her. "I cannot tell you about it yet," he teases. "Suffice to say, I think I know how to make it up to you. All will be well." He gives her an enigmatic smile—the same smile that made her fall in love with him in the beginning of their courtship. "Everything will be well," he reiterates, taking her hand in his and kissing her palm.

I fear, however, it will not. But, for now, the moment has surely come for Constance to know the truth. It is time to execute my plan and reveal all. I shall seek her out in Petticoat Lane Market.

CONSTANCE

I stop by a stall selling leather bags. There's purses and cases and reticules of all shapes and sizes. The seller's Italian—all swarthy, with a cheeky grin. I catch his eye and he says I'm "*bella*." I suddenly feel coy and want to turn away, but then I spot a bag that looks just right—not too shabby, but not so new as to attract attention.

"How much?" I point to the black leather holdall.

"For you, *bella signorina*, just three shillings."

"Two." I suddenly feel bold.

"It is yours." He grasps it with both hands and delivers it with a gracious bow of his dark head. "Use it wisely," he adds, as if he's handing me something with magical powers, like Aladdin's lamp. I give a little chuckle, thinking it a strange thing to say. But then, I am growing accustomed to strange things happening.

EMILY

There she is. I see her with her new bag. Pleased as Punch, she is. I will let her savor such a feeling of elation for a while longer, because before I break into her short-lived happiness, I must ask something of you. I would ask that you take Constance's hand and walk with her as I lead her into the valley of the shadow of death.

CONSTANCE

I'm feeling so pleased with my bag that it puts a little spring in my step as I start back for home. I hang it over my forearm. It's a good-enough size to take a petticoat and a skirt, as well as my nightgown. Not that I've got that much to put in it, but there's enough to fill it. And there's my hairbrush, too, and . . . The brewery clock strikes four. Darkness is closing in. I must hurry back. I've so much to do before my journey. I turn down Crispin Street, leaving the clatter and clang of the market behind me. A wagon passes me along Artillery Row as I head toward Artillery Passage. It's quieter here. *Too quiet.* Suddenly I'm alone. I can't hear the market traders anymore, or the clatter of the poles as they dismantle their stalls. I think it odd. I take a few more paces and then it comes upon me—that same sensation that I felt before, in Brick Lane, the night I saw Miss Tindall. But this time, I'm not afraid, only wary and alert as if all my senses are rallying under me.

Nearby I suddenly hear laughter and voices chanting. "Remember, remember the fifth of November!" I turn to see a gaggle of ragamuffins run off shrieking and whooping with delight; then I nearly jump out of my skin. There's a blue flash and a crack and something explodes just in front of me. My head splits with the sound and my nose is filled with acrid smoke. The bang knocks me off balance, jerking me back, so that I hit my head against the brick wall. And that's when I see her. Just as the smoke clears, she's there, plain as the nose on my face.

"Constance." She's saying my name. *"Constance."* She's holding out her arms to me, like she wants to give me a hug.

"Yes," I reply. "I'm coming!" I rush forward and I feel her enfold me and I smell her smell and I suddenly feel so safe. The tears are streaming down my face. "I was worried you were . . ." I can't bring myself to say the word.

"I am here," she says. Softly she pushes me away, but still has hold of my hands, and she looks into my watery eyes. *"I am here, but I need you to listen to me."*

I can tell from her expression and her voice that what she has to say to me is important and urgent.

"I'm listening, miss," I tell her. "I'm listening."

"I believe you are," she says in a half whisper.

Emily

And so I tell her about Dr. Melksham, and how he abducted the girls who went missing and how he took them to a secret hideout in a warehouse near the docks. And I tell her what happened when I saw the last of the men arrive at the building. I watched with trepidation as they descended the stairs and entered through the double doors. A moment later, I heard the bolts slide across. They had locked the doors. That would have been my chance to escape, but then I thought of the reason for my being there, for perhaps even risking my own life. I thought of little Libby. If I went to fetch help—

and where would I find it—it might well be too late to save her from whatever unspeakable fate lay in store for her. I decided to act by myself. I edged forward from the shelter of the stairwell to suddenly feel a tug. My heart skipped a beat. I turned and realized the back of my jacket was caught on the handle to a low door. I freed myself from the latch and, to my shock, found the door was unlocked. Gently I eased it ajar, expecting to find a cupboard. However, when my eyes adjusted to the darkness, I saw before me a spiral staircase. My fortune seemed to have changed. Slowly I made my way up to the top of the stairs, not knowing where they might lead. Soon it was clear that the landing opened out onto a gallery. I was short of breath and the pain in my chest was almost unbearable. But it was then that I saw them.

A dozen or more men, all dressed in the same odd regalia, were standing on either side of a lofty room. It was clearly some type of vault that now appeared more like a sort of courtroom or temple. Large church candles were lit and seemed arranged in what appeared to be a precise formation, while the floor was checkered in black-and-white tiles. Painted on the walls were various symbols: an unsettling, all-seeing eye and a set square and compass. *A set square and compass?*

My mind darted to Mitre Square and I was suddenly reminded of the strange shapes carved into poor Catherine Eddowes's face. I grew cold.

At one end of the space, I could see a distinguished-looking man seated in an elaborate chair that appeared more like a throne. He seemed to be presiding over the proceedings, a ritual that beggared all belief. In front of him was some sort of altar. But it is what lay on the altar that horrified me most—the dear child, prone and seemingly lifeless.

At that moment, there was a loud rapping at the doors. Three times, they were hit, as if ceremonially, then they were opened. A blindfolded man, escorted by another, entered. He was dressed oddly, in a loose-fitting white shirt that exposed his chest. Round his neck was a noose. I feared for his safety. I was terrified I was about to witness an execution, but he did not seem agitated and made no attempt to escape. He was escorted by the man I had noticed before, the Poet, who guided him past the waiting assembly and toward the throne. Was he a prisoner? I could not be certain.

My anxiety mounted as the escorts introduced him to the man on the throne. "Here is a poor candidate in a state of darkness, Worshipful Master," one said.

From his throne, the "master" spoke in a loud, assured voice. "Bring him hither."

The "candidate" duly stepped forward. But candidate for what? It was then that it came to me. I must have unwittingly stumbled upon a Masonic lodge, a place where Freemasons meet to conduct their sacred rituals. It is a secret society, a brotherhood, where, they say, rich and powerful men meet to exercise illicit power out of reach of the law. There were rumors on the streets of Whitechapel that they were even involved in the murders—that Jack was a Freemason and that was why he had cut angular marks into Catherine Eddowes's cheeks and eyelids. *The compass and set square!* I'd taken little notice of the gossip at the time when I'd heard some of the women at church speak of "the Masons," but now I felt myself shake with fear.

The master addressed the prisoner again. "What is the predominant wish of your heart?" He was obviously reciting some form of litany.

After a prompting from the Poet, who whispered in his ear, the candidate replied in a clear, calm voice: "Light."

The master seemed satisfied. "Remove the blindfold," he ordered.

This the Poet did, and it is then that I realized, to my horror, that the candidate was familiar to me. It was Robert Sampson.

Reeling from shock, I saw him blink away the darkness to allow his eyes to settle on the altar directly in front of him. I observed closely as his expression changed from one of bemused compliance to horror as soon as he saw the child. His head darted up to the master, a stunned look on his face. His brow crumpled in a frown and his eyes were searching.

The master did not keep him waiting. Again his voice was formal. He spoke with all the authority of a high-ranking priest. "Before you are admitted into our brotherhood, you need to be cleansed of any impurities." He rose from his throne. "Step forward."

Robert, clearly bewildered, obeyed, approaching the girl on the altar with evident unease. The air was taut with anticipation. As the other men looked on, not a breath could be heard, until an official, whom I suddenly recognized as Dr. Melksham, stepped forward, carrying a red velvet cushion. On it was a shallow gold bowl. And a knife with a jeweled hilt. My head was spinning as I saw him approach Libby. Throughout her ordeal, she had remained senseless. Bending over her, the doctor rolled up the sleeve of her shift; then he reached for the ceremonial knife. The blade glinted in the candlelight as he held it aloft over her wrist.

● ● ●

I could no longer be silent. I knew I had to act. "No!" I screamed. I rushed forward and lurched across the balcony. "Get away from her! Get away!" All eyes rose to see me in the gallery and the order was given to apprehend me. I turned to run back down the stairs, but the pain in my chest was so great that I could barely move. I was only halfway down when I was caught and dragged roughly by one of the liveried men. As we reached the bottom of the flight, I saw my captor was none other than the man I had named the Butcher. Struggling in his brutish grasp, I was shoved along the passageway into the temple.

Inside there was uproar. Men were shouting, baying like wolves as I was hauled through their jeers to face the master. In among the mayhem, I searched for Robert. My eyes latched onto him as he remained standing at the altar by Libby.

"Please help me," I called to him. He simply stared at me.

"So we have an intruder," boomed the master. He stood glowering over me.

"Let her go!" I screamed. I tried to struggle free from the Butcher's grip, but the effort robbed me of my breath. I began to cough. "You murderer!" I croaked. I turned to appeal to Robert.

The distinguished-looking man raised his brow and directed a question to Robert. "You know this woman?"

"Yes, Father." He stepped forward toward me. "I do."

"*Father!*" I blurted. "What?" I fixed Robert with an incredulous gaze, but he ignored me.

"She is a teacher." That is all he said. He did not rush to my aid, or fight off the Butcher, or even tell him to unhand me. "She is a teacher" is all he could muster.

It was then that Dr. Melksham intervened. He approached the man I now understood to be Sir William Sampson. "Aye. A meddlesome one, at that. I knew she might cause trouble. She is the one I told you about, Worshipful Master, the one at St. Jude's."

Sir William nodded thoughtfully. "Ah, yes. Miss Tindall." The way he said my name chilled me.

I was feeling wounded and betrayed, knowing I could not rely on any support from Robert. Yet, from somewhere deep within me, I found the strength to speak again. "I have called the police. They will be here shortly," I lied.

Sir William darted a look at Melksham. He shook his head. "There was no need for that," he said with a smirk. He remained remarkably calm.

I did not understand, but he answered my

questioning look soon enough. "You see the police are already here, Miss Tindall."

I frowned. *"Already here?"*

He nodded and held out an arm. "Step forward, Chief Inspector Shepherd."

One of the men made himself known. He bowed first to Sir William, then to me. I knew him to be a high-ranking police officer. In an instant, I was both humiliated and defeated.

"I can assure you, Miss Tindall, that we had no intention of harming this child," the chief inspector tried to calm me.

"Only bleeding her," butted in Dr. Melksham, "so that this"—he pointed to Robert— "candidate can be initiated into our lodge."

My eyes widened. "You would drink blood?" I searched Robert's face for some sort of explanation. In the background, I suddenly became aware of a ripple of laughter from the assembly.

"Indeed not, Miss Tindall. What do you take us for?" Sir William was almost indignant. "It is merely used for the anointing."

"A virgin's blood," I muttered under my breath. I knew it was meant to signify great purity. I knew that some men even held that intercourse with a maiden could cure them of their vile ailments.

My vision began to blur and I thought I would faint at that moment, but Robert caught my eye and began to shake his head. "I did not know. I swear. The ceremony is so secret. . . ."

"Enough." His father raised his hand. "Too many secrets have been revealed tonight and we must decide what to do with Miss Tindall here."

At last, Robert intervened. He approached his father and lowered his voice. "Let her go, sir. She can be trusted to remain silent if we allow her to take the girl." He turned and regarded me with his piercing eyes as if willing me to agree.

"She will not!" countered Melksham. He had overheard Robert's suggestion. "She will go to the press and we will all be undone."

Sir William shook his head. "I shall make no decision tonight, gentlemen." He looked up. "Mr. Briggs!" he called. The Butcher stepped forward. "Miss Tindall will be our guest for the time being. I will decide what to do with her in the morning."

Briggs nodded his bald pate and grabbed me by the arm. He shoved me forward, closer to Robert. As I passed him, he managed to whisper, "I'll take care of the girl."

At the back of the hall was a small door. The Butcher pushed me through it. It was a closet, almost like a small church vestry. The only light came from the moon as it shone through a tiny window, high up in the wall. On one side of the room was a row of hooks, where cloaks were hung. On the other was a cupboard. I assumed it was where all the ritual paraphernalia was stored.

"You'll stay here the night," growled my jailer.

I knew there was little use in protesting. My only hope lay with Robert. His parting words led me to believe that he might be able to plead on my behalf. Then I thought of Libby. Even if Robert managed to rescue her, what about the others? What about Molly and Gracie? They, no doubt, were in some brothel, satiating the needs of well-to-do hypocrites—pillars of the establishment by day, and deviants with a lust for young girls at night.

I heard the key turn in the lock. I looked around for a chair. There was none, but there were several long cloaks or gowns hanging up on hooks. I took one of them down and wrapped it around me to keep out the creeping cold. I slumped down to the floor, settling myself in the corner, but I knew I would not sleep. Nor did my anger subside as the night wore on. Outside all was quiet. The Freemasons had all left, returning to their fashionable houses and their dutiful wives, but I knew my jailer remained. I could hear him snoring by the door. I wanted to cry out, but my chest hurt me so much that I could barely breathe. The intermittent pain I had experienced before now grew much worse, as if a weight was pressing heavy on my chest. I convulsed into spasms, vainly gasping for air. I felt as if I were drowning.

It must have been way past midnight when I could bear the pain of the coughing no longer. Heaving myself across the floor toward the door, I lifted my arm and started to bang on it, but my strength was so diminished that my fist could barely be heard above my convulsions. In the corner, I spotted a candlestick. I managed to reach for it and hit the door. *Once. Twice. Three times.* Then came a voice.

"Shut it!"

The Butcher was awake.

"Please, water!" I pleaded between coughs. "I need water."

"Shut it!" he shouted back.

Each cough made my body heave, and with each heave came a great wave of pain. Worse still, my lungs began to expel blood. I cried out in agony.

"Shut it!" came the voice again, only this time the door flew open. The Butcher stood on the threshold. I thought he might at last show me some compassion.

"Please!"

But instead of helping me, he stooped down, bent over and grabbed me by the throat. "Shut it, you stupid bitch!" he cried. I felt his grip tighten around my neck as he shook me. "Shut it, will ya?!"

The last thing I remember doing was battling for breath. My lungs were flooding. The last thing I remember seeing were his eyes, so full of hatred, as they looked into mine. The last thing I remember feeling was the cold plaster of the wall as my head was hurled against it and my skull hit it with a tremendous crack. My world flickered out of focus.

CONSTANCE

"No! No, it can't be true! No!"

"Connie? Connie. You all right?"

I feel a hand on my shoulder. A man's hand.

"It's me," says a voice through the blackness.

It's like I've been falling through the air and suddenly I land with a start. I try and shake away the clouds from my head. Then the voice starts again.

"It's me. Gilbert. Gilbert Johns." I look up through bleary eyes to see a familiar face looking down anxiously on me. "They've gone."

"Who?" I manage to ask.

"Them street Arabs with the firecrackers." I feel his big arms hook under mine and scoop me up. His large hands dust down my skirt and I'm jerked back to life.

"I'm fine, really," I say, smoothing my

own skirts, which have rucked up round my thighs.

"I'll walk you back home," he volunteers, and he crooks his arm. I hesitate at first, but feel woozy and take it so as to steady my shaky legs. I have to admit I feel safer with Gilbert. We start off and it's only then that I remember. I pull up short.

"What is it?" he asks. "You wanna sit down somewhere?" He stares at my face. "You look like you've seen a ghost."

I sway a little as I recall what has just happened. "Miss Tindall," I say.

Gilbert frowns and pulls me back toward him as I weaken. "Who?"

I suddenly feel alone again. A terrible sense of despair is gnawing away at my heart and I think it will break at any moment. I look into his eyes and see there is very little understanding in them. "She's gone," I tell him.

Gilbert shrugs. "You've had a bump on your 'ead. Let's get you 'ome." He takes hold of me once more, but I feel my knees buckle under me, so he gathers me up in his huge arms and somehow manages to carry me all the way back to White's Row. Just before we come to the door, I ask him to put me down.

"I don't want no fuss," I tell him.

Obligingly, he sets me gently on the cobbles and I walk the two or three paces to my own front door. The ragged drapes are already up at the window, but there's a candle glow beyond, so I know that someone's home. I turn the handle and open the door and suddenly there's an almighty racket.

"Surprise!" shouts Flo.

"Surprise!" chorus Ma and Mr. Bartleby in unison. They're standing in front of me, great smiles plastered on their faces; but as soon as Flo sees my expression, her mirth vanishes and, ignoring the other's merriment, she rushes up to me. "What's up, Con?" She puts her arm through mine.

"We thought we'd give you a good send-off," says a cheery Mr. Bartleby, his thumbs hooked through his braces, "before you went to Oxford, like."

Ma joins in, oblivious to my state. "There's Sally Lunn cake and lemonade . . . ," she clucks. Then she spots a bemused Gilbert loitering on the threshold. "Gilbert. Come on in and help us celebrate our Con's adventure. Has she told you, she's off to Oxford tomorrow?" She curves her arms in a great swooping gesture, like a mother hen marshaling her chicks around her.

I manage a few more paces into the room. "I'm not going," I say.

"She's taking the train," Ma gushes as Gilbert walks inside.

"What you say?" Flo asks me.

I summon up my last ounce of strength. "I'm not going to Oxford tomorrow," I manage to tell them.

"You what?" Mr. Bartleby's face turns gray.

"I'm not going to Oxford," I reiterate, only my voice has grown fainter. It's struggling to leave my mouth.

"Why not, Con?" asks Flo, her comforting arm around me.

"Because," I say, "Miss Tindall is dead."

CHAPTER 34

Tuesday, November 6, 1888

EMILY

It's strange to me how those who remain nearly always refer to those of us who have passed over as "dead," or, at best, "passed away." Yet, some of us are still very much alive, albeit in a different dimension. And for those of us who return, usually because our earthly lives were cruelly or unjustly cut short, we have often left unfinished business. We are the Returners, you see, the Revenants. We return to where we met our fate, and reach out to others who might continue what we aimed to achieve in our own lives. I have chosen Constance, but you know that already. What you do not know is how my earthly remains finally ended up on a building site in Whitehall.

My latest encounter with Constance did not go to plan. I thought it only right that I tell her before I told you just how it happened, but we were interrupted. I had not counted on Gilbert Johns being in the vicinity and scaring off the young louts who had given me my opportunity to reveal myself to poor Constance. I was only able to tell her half my sorry story; and because of this, she now languishes upstairs in her bed in a deep state of sorrow and despair. It pains me to see her sob so, but I shall reveal myself to her shortly, and she will be filled with hope once more. But first, I must fulfill my duty to you. Together we shall return to the asylum in Hampstead.

It has all been agreed. As soon as the doctors are of the opinion that Geraldine Cutler is no longer a danger to herself and fit enough to be discharged, she will go straight to Petworth to stay with her mother and her sister, Pauline. There, restored to the bosom of her family, she will be able to recuperate in the fresh Sussex air. Bracing country walks will be the best medicine, while a trip or two to Brighton might also work wonders. Terence agrees that such an arrangement will be beneficial to his wife. It also gives him the opportunity to set in train his plans.

Geraldine is notified of the proposal and is more than happy with it—but for very contrary reasons. Her sojourn in the asylum has given her a chance to formulate her own plans. She has long known that no one is above being corrupted and that a small inducement can produce very large returns. For half a crown, for example, she was able to bribe an orderly to smuggle a note to that nice Mr. Pugh, Mr. Waring's helpful assistant. He had proved his worth before when he had "found" her brooch in Whitehall, and would, no doubt, be invaluable again. Along with the note, she enclosed a letter, purporting to be from Pauline and countersigned by Terence. She knew that all those hours whiled away copying his signature would one day reap rewards. The letter, addressed to the senior consultant at the asylum, requested her release into the custody of another consultant known personally to the family. Sir Cuthbert Wilkinson was, after all, a personal friend of her late, and most eminent, father. Dr. Jacob Frankel, a Jew recently arrived from Vienna, and an expert in the intimate workings of the female mind, is happy to oblige.

So, on the eighth day of her incarceration, Geraldine Cutler is discharged, supposedly into the care of Sir Cuthbert, thanks to the masterly efforts of the charming Mr. Pugh, who poses as the eminent specialist's assistant. Expertly fielding any questions that come his way with the alacrity of a good county cricketer, his performance is a triumph. Within the hour, Geraldine is in a carriage, traveling away from Hampstead. Her conveyance does not, however, take her south toward her native Sussex, but southeast, through the ever-burgeoning suburbs of London and back to St. Bartholomew's Hospital and, unbeknownst to him, back to her guileless husband.

Once again, it is foggy, and the fog is much thicker here than in Hampstead. However, it is not so thick that she cannot see, quite clearly, the large Tudor gates of St. Bartholomew's Hospital. It is, nevertheless, very cold. For the past hour, Geraldine's cab has been parked outside and her driver is chilled to the bone. Were it not for the fact that this lady had paid him handsomely in advance for his services, he would assuredly have told her to "sling 'er 'ook." Or, at least, that is what he is thinking to himself as he paces up and down by his horse, rubbing his nicotine-stained hands and watching the London skyline as evening closes in. He lights himself yet another smoke, cupping his hands around the flame that flickers in the brisk easterly. He's just about to take that first luxurious drag when his passenger pops her head out of the carriage window.

"Quick about it, man!" she tells him in an odd voice, which is certainly not as loud as an exclamation, but not as soft as a whisper.

Alarmed, he looks longingly at his cigarette; then, in an act of defiance, he takes one long inhalation before he reluctantly snuffs it out with his thumb and yellowing forefinger and stuffs it back in his pocket. He heads to his perch, calling, "Yes, ma'am" as he goes.

His passenger is irate. "You see that gentleman over there," she tells him, pointing her gloved hand. The driver squints in the direction of the gate. A man is bidding the porter a good evening. He is well-dressed and carries a case. *A doctor, perhaps,* he thinks.

"Yer . . . ss," he replies.

"You are to follow him until I tell you otherwise." The driver hesitates and Geraldine rightly takes it as a signal that he wishes to up his price. "There's another crown in it for you if you hurry."

He thinks of all the cigarettes he could buy with that extra cash and nods his head in agreement. In another moment or two, he's climbed back onto his perch and they're off in hot pursuit. Not that the horse breaks into a trot. Terence Cutler sets a sedate pace. He intends to walk the two miles or so to

Whitechapel and does not wish to tire himself too soon. He begins south on Giltspur Street toward Cock Lane, then turns left onto Newgate Street, having no idea whatsoever that his progress is being tracked.

In half an hour, Cutler reaches Commercial Street. His wife is not surprised that, instead of coming home to Harley Street, he is taking advantage of her continued absence and has veered way off course. The traffic, always busy, seems to have come to a halt. It appears a horse has taken fright up ahead with dire consequences for its load. Timber is strewn across the street; the wagon is in pieces and the cartman unconscious. Geraldine decides it's time she made a move. Keeping an eye on her husband on the opposite side of the road, she jabs at the carriage ceiling with a stick, then cranes her head out of the window.

"Let me off here," she tells the driver. He's only too happy to oblige.

Geraldine Cutler alights gracefully onto a thoroughfare where grace is a rare commodity. At this hour of the day, Commercial Street is chock-full of working men and women. The nearby factories are disgorging their weary workers: weavers, ale tunners and soap boilers, all traipsing back to homes they cannot afford to heat. But Geraldine has no care for them. She is a woman on a mission, and her husband is still, mercifully, in her sights. In this, she is assisted by the fact that he is slightly taller than average and it's easier to follow his bobbing top hat in the crowds as he heads toward Christ Church.

Opposite the familiar landmark, he crosses the road and turns down the narrow thorough-fare of Dorset Street. Now that she is off the main road, Geraldine experiences, for the first time, a frisson of fear. This is no place for a woman of her class. She bows her head so as to remain anonymous; yet, if her deportment doesn't betray her, her clothes might well. She is diving into the swamp of the notorious rookeries, a hangout of cutthroats and villains, a quagmire of the doomed and the damned, where even the police dare not venture. And yet there is also something within her that is enjoying this illicit excursion; there is something thrilling in the fact that despite being only a few yards behind her husband, he has not the faintest inkling that she is metaphorically several steps ahead of him. At the asylum, he had the gall to tell her that he had changed his ways. She suspected he was lying, of course, and she was being proved right. He was obviously on his way to some Spitalfields whore! In the past, she would have credited her husband with a little more taste.

Nevertheless, she would not be dissuaded, despite the fact that this is a place of constant shadow. This Stygian district is most unsettling for her. Even before Jack was abroad, she was all too aware that the streets of Whitechapel were inviting only to those who had nothing to lose.

Up ahead is a gas lamp that throws out an eerie yellow glow onto the filth-strewn pavement. Under it, she can make out a figure, lolling on the lamppost. She holds her breath as her husband approaches the trollop. She hears the figure—a woman—call after him, her voice so rough it would rasp rough-hewn wood. The brazen hussy asks him if he wants for anything, and Geraldine sees, to her gratification and surprise, that he ignores her. "There can only be one explanation," she speaks aloud. "He has a special whore—someone who will do to him things that I could never imagine doing to him, lewd, depraved acts to satiate his lewd, depraved appetites."

Their courtship had promised much: a brush against a sleeve, a pat under the table, even a stolen kiss in the garden once. Yet, after their nuptials, reality had set in. Their lovemaking, although very formal at first, had rapidly become quite thrilling, but a few weeks after their marriage, Geraldine developed a fever and severe abdominal pain. Not wishing to compromise his own professionalism, Cutler had called in another specialist, who confirmed his worst fears. Despite the fact that he, himself, had experienced only mild symptoms, he had infected his wife with gonorrhea. Unbeknownst to him, the infection had spread not only to her fallopian tubes, but to her bloodstream as well. The specialist, a close personal friend and therefore an ally, was sworn to secrecy. Geraldine's suffering would be passed off as nothing more than a "female ailment." When intercourse became too painful, it stopped altogether, much to the relief of both parties. It was only when she consulted another specialist of her own volition that she discovered the truth. Terence had infected her. She confronted him and he denied that he had caused her sufferings. She, however, remained unconvinced. Yet, a man is a man, she would tell herself. It is only natural that her husband, deprived of his conjugal rights, should seek solace elsewhere, but she had not thought he would return here, amid the flotsam and jetsam of humanity that had cursed their union in the first place.

As if to echo her sentiments, Terence Cutler stoops low. He stops in front of an archway that leads off the street and ducks down into a flagged passage, disappearing out of sight into Miller's Court. Geraldine follows at a decent distance and catches sight of him standing outside a door to one of the lodgings. She supposes he will be there for a while, but she knows that revenge is a dish best served cold. She will bide her time.

Meanwhile, I shall return to White's Row to see how Constance is faring after her terrible shock. Come with me, please.

CONSTANCE

"But how do you know she is dead?" Flo asks me for what seems like the tenth time. She's perched on a chair by my bedside. The room is as cold as an icehouse and her breath comes out in puffs. She's tucked a blanket up under my chin, but the coarse fibers are scratching my neck. They prickle even more when I shake my head.

"Why won't you listen to me?" Her constant questioning is making me grow weaker by the second. "She told me herself." I can hear my voice grow thin as gruel.

Ma sits at the foot of the bed, her stooped frame swaddled in a thick shawl. "You've had a nasty do, love," she tells me, patting my feet. "Ooh, if I ever laid my hands on those louts." She balls her fists, but her anger spills over into a wheeze and sets her off, coughing again.

"Why don't you go downstairs and I'll light a fire?" suggests Flo. Ma, her eyes narrowing as she gasps for breath, nods and shambles off, leaving us alone. Flo gives me a look that's full of love, but there's pity in it, too. Her hand reaches out and gently she starts to stroke my forehead.

"You think I've gone round the bend, don't you?" I say.

Slowly she shakes her head. "I know you've changed," she tells me after a moment's reflection. "There's something going on in there." She taps my temple and smiles. "But I'm not sure what it is." I open my mouth to tell her, as I've told her a dozen times since yesterday, that Miss Tindall has passed over into another world. She's dead, but not as we know it. There's still life in her and she wants to speak to people through me. But poor Flo doesn't seem to have taken it in. "What is it? What's wrong?" she persists, looking deep into my eyes.

It's then that I feel her. Miss Tindall comes to me again. I don't see her, but she's in the room with me, I know she is. I can sense her. It's like a warm breeze fluttering in on a spring day, or the first ray of light at dawn. She loosens my tongue and then the words come.

"I'm a spirit medium."

Flo jerks back, like she's just been kicked by a horse. Her hands fly up and she pushes hard against her chair, tipping it backward. It's like I've confessed to being Jack the Ripper.

"A spirit medium!"

I find the strength to sit up in bed, easing myself up on my grazed elbows. "You don't believe me."

"A spirit medium! Gor, blimey!" She's looking at me all goggle-eyed. "Well, I never!"

I remain silent for a while, letting her digest the notion like it's a gristly piece of meat; then, when I think she's ready for more, I explain further. "You can't see Miss Tindall anymore, but she's here and she still wants to speak to people and she wants to speak through me."

Flo is still ruminating. I watch her in silence as she takes my words and chews them over. After a moment, she narrows her eyes and asks: "So how did she die?"

I sigh and the effort of it hurts my chest. "It's a long story," I tell her. I have neither the energy nor the inclination to divulge all the lurid details.

"Hmm," she replies. She is still not sure she can believe me. Just like Thomas the Doubter, she wants proof. It's something I don't have, but I do know someone who will not question my word. And I shall see her tomorrow.

EMILY

Now that I've seen how Constance is baring up, I return to Miller's Court to find Terence Cutler pausing before he knocks on the door to room

13. It's dingy, but he sees to his left that the passage opens out into a small yard. All around, there are noises—ordinary noises from ordinary people—voices, some raised; babies bawling; dishes clattering. A water tap drips away in the corner of the yard. It is a sorry state of affairs, he thinks as he looks at the windows round the corner. He sees a candle glow emanating from behind a torn piece of brown cloth that offers a modicum of privacy to the dwelling's inhabitant. As he looks, he spots two of the glass panes are broken. There's a hole bigger than a man's fist. Bending in, he puts his ear closer to the smeary window. Heaven forbid she is with a customer, he thinks. That would be most embarrassing all round. He waits a moment and hears no sound, save for—what is that?—the rake of a hairbrush through long hair perhaps? Taking his courage in both hands, he knocks. After a moment, the ragged muslin drape is drawn aside and a disembodied eye appears squinting through the broken pane. A woman's voice breaks across the jagged glass. "Who's there?"

This is precisely what Terence Cutler wanted to avoid, attracting attention to himself. His anonymity must be preserved. Taking off his topper, he lowers his mouth to the window. "An acquaintance," he says in a whisper.

The eye, which is large, blue and heavily

fringed, blinks; a second later, the door is opened wide to admit the unexpected visitor.

"Well, this is a surprise!" greets Mary Kelly. She is in a state of dishabille, wearing merely her shift in a room where the temperature can be only a little above freezing. The large bed that takes up most of the space is as disheveled as its usual occupant. The dirty sheets are all awry and Cutler recognizes the familiar fishy smell only too easily. A client has not long left.

There's a difficult pause; then she grabs a red shawl on a nearby table and holds it up to her ample bosom in a show of mock modesty. "Have a seat, sir," she says, waving a free hand toward the bed. She's cheery, as she is most times. "I didn't think to see you 'ere, Mr. Cutler. What can I do for ya?" Both her arms are suddenly thrust aloft as she twists her blond hair on top of her head and secures it with pins.

Terence loosens the scarf at his neck. He will keep his coat on if he doesn't want to freeze to death. He has not yet smiled at her, nor said anything, and this makes her a little fidgety. She reaches for her linsey frock, which is draped over the table, and climbs into it, jabbering as she does so.

"Caught me unawares, you did. Can't be too careful with Jack around, can you?" He does not respond to her question, but she persists in that sing-song Welsh accent of hers. "Just sorting myself, I was. That accounts for the mess. Lucky, you just missed one of my regular gentlemen."

He is studying her. She is young, perhaps a little younger than Geraldine. Quite pretty, too, for a Whitechapel whore. A fresh complexion is, however, marred by a purple bruise on her left cheek, as if it has been recently slapped. He sees her blush slightly under his gaze. He knows she has broken the unwritten rule not to talk about her gentleman to other clients. But Terence Cutler is not a client. True, he has come to ask for a service, but it is not the conventional sort offered by a prostitute.

"How are you keeping, Mary?" He throws a nod toward her belly, which she's squeezing into her dress.

"Oh, that," she says nonchalantly, patting her bodice. "We're doing all right." She shrugs and adds: "Considering."

Cutler detects a caveat. "Considering what?"

She sighs heavily and, turning her back toward him, offers him the row of buttons that needs doing up on her dress. He knows what is expected of him and his slender fingers get to work.

"Joe's left me," she tells the wall after a moment.

Cutler's hands drop and she turns to face him. "We had a row. That's how I got this." She points to the bruise on her face. "Walked out on me last week, he did."

Cutler stifles a smile. He could not have wished for better news. "So how will you support the child?" he asks, his face the model of concern.

Giving up on dressing, Mary slumps down by her visitor on the bed, her shoulders still uncovered. "I'll get by, I suppose," she says, patting her torso. "But it won't be easy. It never is," she says a little ruefully.

Cutler looks at her beautiful shoulders in the light cast by a candle on top of a broken wineglass on the bedside table. Her blond hair, swept up, shimmers in the glow. He wishes he could trace the nape of her neck with his finger. Instead, he says to her: "Mary, would you like me to check that everything is as it should be?"

She follows his eyes to her belly. For a moment, she is surprised; then she hugs herself and smiles. "Thank you, sir," she replies, suddenly strangely submissive. "I would like that."

Cutler reaches out to the row of buttons on the back of her dress, which he had just started to fasten. He unfastens them again and Mary pulls her arms out of the stiff sleeves.

"If you please," instructs the surgeon once she is back down to her shift. He is patting the bed.

She stretches out on the rumpled sheets, her arms by her sides. The doctor leans over her and begins to feel her swelling torso. Under his expert fingers, he can detect the mound of the uterus as it blooms. There is a fetus in there, sure enough. He feels a sudden jerk at his touch. Mary giggles.

"It's a kicker, all right!" She chuckles.

Six months, he would estimate. Seven, perhaps. The child should be born in early spring. That suits him well.

"Thing seems to be in order," he says after his short examination.

Mary takes a deep breath. "Good," she replies. He is not sure if she means it. He, on the other hand, is delighted. She rises from the bed and starts the lengthy process of dressing once more.

Cutler watches her struggle into her frock; then, just as she presents her buttons to him once more, he tells her: "I wish to put a proposal to you."

She turns her head slightly. Her hands are on her hips. She's been waiting for the catch, the compensation. In return for checking her bump, he would want a wank, at the very least, she thinks.

"A proposal?" she repeats, playing the innocent.

"Yes, a plan. A way out of your"—Cutler searches for the word while looking at her belly—"predicament."

Mary breaks away from Cutler's fingers and taps her abdomen. She is frowning. "You said it was too late." There is mild reprehension in her tone as she recalls how the surgeon refused to give her the abortion she so wanted.

Cutler nods. "It was too late for that." Thoughtfully he tilts his head. "What if I were to tell you that I had found someone who wishes to adopt your baby?"

Mary gasps audibly, then slumps back down on the bed. "Adopt 'im?" She pats her belly again.

"Yes," replies Cutler, enlivened by her—he thinks—positive response. "He, or she, would be taken care of—fed, clothed and educated— and you need never worry about their welfare again." He finds it hard to read her expression. It's one of shock, but, might he venture, relief also? He carries on. "Naturally, I would deliver the child, so you would have the very best care, at no charge. Then I would take it away and place it in the arms of a loving woman who has the deepest of maternal longings, but who has never been blessed with children

410

of her own." He pauses and dips his head to see if he can read her eyes.

Suddenly she turns to him. "Do I get to hold him before he goes?" There are tears in her eyes.

"Of course," he replies. "Not only that, but you would be paid for your pains, too."

"Paid?" Her voice is bewildered.

"I propose two guineas for your trouble."

He can see her calculating the numbers in that pretty head of hers. She need not work for two months or more. She could even buy some decent clothes, a new bonnet, eat out at a chophouse now and again.

"What do you say?" Cutler persists, watching for signs of agreement.

Another moment passes before Mary starts to shake her head, slowly at first, as if she is listening to an argument. The side for adoption is winning.

"Yes," she says finally, her face lifting into a faint smile. "Yes, I will give my baby away," she tells him. "It will be best for all concerned." And with that, she throws her arms around Cutler's neck. "Thank you!" she cries, as if she's suddenly released from her shackles.

The surgeon, although elated by her response, is taken aback by her exuberance and lets out a laugh. It's then that the ragged drape suddenly falls to the floor with a loud clatter. It's been secured to a piece of doweling that's somehow come loose.

"Good God!" Cutler leaps up from the bed. "What's that? Who's there?"

Mary lays a comforting arm on his and pulls him back down to the bed. "Don't worry about that, Mr. Cutler," she replies with a giggle. "That happens all the time," she tells him. And her bawdy laughter masks the footsteps that are retreating up the passage. Geraldine Cutler has seen all she needs to see.

Chapter 35

Wednesday, November 7, 1888

Constance

Miss Beaufroy is not expecting me. I'm standing nervously in the foyer of Brown's Hotel. The concierge alerted her to my arrival, and now, as she descends the stairs swathed in purple, I can see her puzzlement grow with every step she takes.

"Constance dear," she greets me, before detecting that something is amiss. She frowns. "But why aren't you in Oxford?" she asks, taking both my hands in hers. Searching my face for an explanation, she quickly finds it. "Something terrible has happened, hasn't it?" She bites her lip and withdraws.

"I fear it has."

Her gloved hand flies up to her face.

"Shall we walk?" I suggest. And so we do. She puts her arm through mine and we leave the hotel as sisters.

The day is cold, but crisp, and for once there is blue sky. We head toward a small square opposite the hotel that is bordered on all sides by trees and bushes. The berries on the holly bush are bloodred and plentiful. Pa would say that so many would be a sign of a harsh winter to come. A neat square of lawn lies at its center and there are beds, now brown and bare, that will, no doubt, be dressed gaily in spring. On each side of this square, there is a bench and we plump for the one farthest from the main entrance so that our conversation is less likely to be overheard.

"Your news concerns Miss Tindall?" Miss Beaufroy's brow is crumpled.

"It does." For the past few hours, I have been rehearsing my message; now that the time to deliver it is here, I find it does not leave my mouth easily. "I'm afraid . . ." I am choking with grief. "I'm afraid Miss Tindall has passed over."

Miss Beaufroy jerks away from me in shock. "*Passed over?* You mean . . . ? How do you know? Are you sure? But you have not been to Oxford! How can you know?" Questions tumble

413

out from her lips like a torrent. She rises, then sits again. She is distraught. Tears well up and brim over.

This time, it is I who take her by the hand. I become like a parent, addressing an anxious child. I look her in the eye. "I know because she told me herself."

"What?" Her brows lift. "You don't mean . . . ?"

It is so much easier explaining such things to a believer. Miss Beaufroy understands straight-away. "You have seen her?" she asks.

I nod. "She came to me in a vision in the street, yesterday."

Miss Beaufroy casts her gaze around her, as if she is suddenly seeing everything with fresh eyes. "But this is wonderful. I knew it. Oh, dear Constance, I knew you had the gift. I just knew it." She is like a child at Christmas, wildly excited and completely overwrought. "What did she say? Tell me, please." Her hands are clasped together in supplication. Of course, I do not refuse. I tell her the whole story: about the Sunday school and Dr. Melksham, about the disappearing girls, about the disciplinary action against Miss Tindall and about the fateful night she stumbled upon a depraved Masonic ritual that led ultimately to her death.

There is much to take in. I do not expect her to absorb it all at once. She asks many ques-tions, but I am able to answer them, with Miss

Tindall's help, of course. She is hovering around me, making sure I leave no pertinent details out. I do not tell Miss Beaufroy that she is present. I have no wish to alarm her, but my account of her last few weeks is rendered all the more accurate by having her close by. Yet, I save the last and most alarming piece of information until the end.

"There is one other thing," I say when Miss Beaufroy's exhausted expression tells me she thinks I have finished.

"There is more?"

I nod, dreading delivering my final message. "The torso at Whitehall . . ."

EMILY

Once again, I'd visited dear Constance as she slept. I had to finish telling her the whole, sorry truth. It was not easy to relate how they discovered my body the next morning.

"Won't nuffin' to do wiff me, guv'nor!" protested the Butcher, scratching the back of his bullish neck.

Sir William brushed him aside to look at my lifeless corpse. He bent down and studied my face; then I felt his warm fingers on my neck as he checked for a pulse. On finding there was none, he shot back up in a fury. He ranted at his henchman. "You bloody fool! How could you let this happen?"

Robert, standing by the doorway, seemed in a state of shock. Leaning low over me, he brushed my cold cheek tenderly, before he noticed the blood on the wall. "My God!" His father followed his horrified gaze. I had been hurled back with such force that my skull had cracked. A crimson smear remained on the plaster.

Sir William lunged at the brute. "You idiot!" he yelled, heaving him up by the collar.

Robert managed to pull him off. "It will serve no purpose, Father," he told him.

Coming to his senses, Sir William backed away and tugged at his waistcoat. "You are right," he said, straightening himself. "What matters now is how we dispose of the body. The quicker, the better."

CONSTANCE

Miss Beaufroy's eyes widen; then she shakes her head as she thinks of her friend dying such a lonely, terrible death. "Oh no! Dear God, no!" The color deserts her face. It looks all the whiter against her vivid purple coat. "What should be done?" she asks after a moment.

I have thought long and hard on the question. And, of course, I have sought—and received— guidance. There's a terrible pang in my heart. "A conviction for murder will not be possible," I tell her reluctantly.

416

She scowls. "But, surely, justice—"

I break her off. "We need evidence and there is none. Besides," I say after a pause, "who would believe me if I went to the police? A flower girl who claims she's in touch with the dead. They would say I was mad."

Realizing the futility of the situation, Miss Beaufroy's shoulders droop. It's as if she is standing on a cliff, about to throw herself off. I try and pull her back from the brink.

"There is something we can do," I tell her.

Her eyes latch onto mine. "Yes?"

"We can identify her remains, so that she can, at least, have a decent burial."

She closes her eyes, as if to try and blink away the vision of a naked, rotting torso on a coroner's slab. I see her swallow hard, but when her eyes reopen, I think the idea might have taken root. Her mouth lifts a little. "I would do it if I thought it would bring my dear Emily peace," she tells me.

"I know it would." I reach out for her hand. "She told me it would."

Miss Beaufroy nods. "If that is so, then, of course, I will. But how? You were at the inquest with me. There are no distinguishing marks."

I lift my hand to stop her. "Apparently, there were." Miss Tindall has told me about a childhood accident that left her with a scar just below her ribs. "Do you remember when you were playing in the wood on the edge of your estate? Miss Tindall was climbing an oak tree and she fell?" I ask.

"Good God!" The memory is triggered. "Yes," she blurts, clutching my hands to relive the incident. "I warned her against it. The bough gave way. It was rotten and she fell at least six feet to the ground. She tore her dress and cut her side. She was lucky she did not break a rib."

I nod. "But the injury left a scar, a small, crescent-shaped scar on her left side. The medical examiner must have overlooked it."

Miss Beaufroy takes a deep breath. She knows what she must do. "Will you come with me to the police station, Constance?"

"Of course," I reply.

We travel to King Street Police Station together. Miss Pauline makes a statement to the duty sergeant, who informs his superiors straightaway. Dr. Bond, the medical examiner, is summoned and Miss Beaufroy is escorted to the mortuary to identify the torso. I am allowed to accompany her, even though I have no wish to go. We both brace ourselves for the vile sight. That, and the smell, will stay with both of us for the rest of our lives. Dr. Bond tries to assist us as best he can, advising us to cover our mouths and noses prior to entering the room, but it is still the most

418

horrendous thing I've ever had to do in my life. Squinting through half-closed eyes, Miss Pauline asks if she might see the portion of flesh under the left ribs. Dr. Bond obliges and skillfully covers up the rest of the remains to show only a small area of decay. Yet, sure enough, the little crescent scar is there, clearly visible under the purpled skin, just below the ribs on the left side.

Miss Pauline shuts her eyes as soon as she is able, then turns and starts to sob. My heart goes out to her.

"Come," I tell her in a whisper, looping my arm through hers. "Remember, she is not there."

Leaving the mortuary, we return to the duty sergeant's office to find Inspector Marshall waiting for us. He stands up as we enter. He's been smoking a pipe and the air is thick with tobacco smoke, but I know we both welcome the fug of it after the stench of the mortuary.

"That can't have been easy for you, ladies," he tells us. "I am most grateful to you both." He points to a large, leather-bound folder. "Our investigations can now resume, thanks to you. We will make every effort to apprehend the fiend who did this to Miss Tindall."

"Like you have with the Ripper," I want to blurt. Of course, I do not. Neither Miss Pauline nor I have faith in his words, but we thank him, nevertheless.

EMILY

I am so very proud of Constance. She has handled herself extraordinarily well. She has also exercised her discretion, sparing Pauline the gruesome details of how my mutilated remains ended up on a building site in Whitehall. I fear I shall spare you no such details.

After Sir William and his son left me alone with the Butcher, another man, almost as brutish and muscular, arrived with a sack. My body was bundled into it and I was carried to a waiting wagon. The journey to the cat meat shop in Hanbury Street was a short one. Ironically, it lay opposite the place where Annie Chapman met her fate. We entered by the back. The room was cold, even though I could not feel it, although I could see the men's breaths wreathing their own heads when they spoke. There was no one else about. They locked the door behind them.

"On 'ere," directed the Butcher.

My body was dumped on the wooden chopping slab and I watched as the men took their cleavers and began hacking at my limbs. First my legs. Next my right arm. Then my left. Finally, and most brutally of all, the Butcher claimed my head, just below the bruising on my neck. As it left my body, it slipped back-ward, almost rolling off the table and drop-ping onto the floor, but the Butcher, perhaps through guilt, or remorse, accorded me the dignity of catching it before it fell.

All that remained was to distribute my mutilated body. My severed head, which had been saved from a fall, was, nevertheless, burned ignominiously. My torso, however, was wrapped in the remnants of my black dress and some old newspaper that was to hand. The rest of me was swathed in sacking. I was then loaded onto a wagon and taken under cover of darkness to the building site where Sir William Sampson was the main contractor. His men had easy access and knew the area well. My torso, one leg and an arm were secreted in various muddy recesses, while another leg was thrown into the Thames. And there I was to remain for several weeks.

CONSTANCE

Miss Pauline offered me a lift back to White's Row in her hansom, but I declined, preferring to walk through the City. I want to clear my head, unclutter my thoughts. After all, there are two people living inside me now. Granted, Miss Tindall is a guest, not a resident, but she can visit me at any time and I need to be prepared to act on her instructions.

From the police station in King Street, I head back east. My journey takes me along the Victoria Embankment, past the place where Miss Tindall's dismembered body had lain for all those weeks. The thought of it sickens me, even more now that I know what happened to her and how. To think that the men who caused her to die in such terrible circumstances, and who disposed of her body in such a despicable way, are still at large, fills me with despair. For a while, my footsteps are heavy as I trudge along the pavements, carrying the weight of the world's injustices on my shoulders. I am angry. How can anything be the same from now on? The omnibuses and carts and horses pass in a blur. Big Ben strikes the hour. Life goes on, and yet, for me, everything is changed.

It's almost three o'clock by the time I reach the City. I turn down Cornhill and into Mansion House Street to find they're putting out the bunting. Flags of blue, white and red festoon the route. It's then that I remember Friday is the Lord Mayor's Show. A big procession will leave from the Guildhall, taking in Ludgate Hill and Fleet Street, and go as far as the Royal Courts of Justice before returning. Thousands are expected to line the streets, like they do every year. There's a big meat tea in the Tower

Hamlets Mission Hall, and I recall Flo reckoning that if we couldn't get the food, at least we might see the entertainment afterward. But I'm in no mood for such frivolities. All I want to do is get home safe and go to bed.

CHAPTER 36

Thursday, November 8, 1888

CONSTANCE

The following morning, I go downstairs to find Flo already in the kitchen. She looks up from tending to the kettle on the hob. I can tell from her expression she's still mad at me.

"I'm sorry for running off like that," I say.

She looks up, brushing back a stray lock of hair off her face. "It's Ma you need to worry about. Started off an attack, you did, when you wasn't 'ere."

I feel wretched, thinking of poor Ma. "It's just that—"

"Save your breath," jibes Flo, showing me her palm. "I'm not sure what's going on in that head of yours at the moment, but you best get over it." I'm gladdened when I catch her lips twitch in a smile. "How about a nice cup of tea?"

"I could certainly do with one," I reply.

"So how's that Miss Belfry of yours, or whatever her name is?" she asks, pouring hot water into the teapot.

"Beaufroy. Miss Beaufroy," I correct her. "She's . . . she's not good." I do not volunteer more, but when Flo hands me a chipped cup a few moments later, she can tell that events have taken a turn for the worse.

"Streuth, you look peaky!" She clamps a palm onto my forehead to see if I have a fever. I haven't. She sits herself down opposite me at the table in the front room. "Lord Mayor's Show tomorrow," she reminds me. "Ma and me are going. You'll come, too, won't ya?"

I start to shake my head. "I don't . . ."

"Oh, come on, Con. It'll do ya good. The music, the flags, those old farts in fancy hats—not to mention the booze. There'll be free beer at the Britannia!" She's patting my knee and it's hard to refuse her. "What do ya say, eh, Con?"

I blow on my tea, watching the surface ripple like wind on a muddy lake; then I take a gulp. I feel the hot, soothing liquid trickle down my dry throat and instantly feel a little revived. "Maybe," I tell her after another sip, but inside I wonder how I can ever be happy again.

EMILY

Once more, we find Terence Cutler at break-fast. The table is laid with a white lace cloth as the surgeon takes tea, eggs and toast in the morning room. For once, he is in a good mood. For once, he has some positive news. Not only have the police dropped charges, but he also has something he can look forward to. He wonders how Geraldine will take it, or, if indeed, she is ready to take it at all. While their rapprochement has gone well, so far, he knows it will take time to heal the wounds mutually inflicted over the past few months. They have held hands, twice, and Terence has even managed to peck his wife on the cheek as he bid her farewell on his last visit before Pauline was due to take her back to Petworth. A month or so in Sussex will be just what she needs, after which she will return to Harley Street revived and refreshed. Who knows, he tells himself, they might even share a bedroom again? It's far too early in the healing process to return to the conjugal bed, of course, and besides, with his brilliant plan in place, the need to perform the act on his wife has become redundant, even if she would welcome him. She will have her child; Mary Kelly will have her food;he will be relieved of any pressure to perform.

Breakfast has passed off well and Terence is just dabbing his moustache to make sure no wayward crumbs have hooked themselves onto his bristles, when Dora enters to clear the breakfast detritus. He can tell straight-away, however, that all is not well. The girl is agitated and clumsy. A cup clatters sideways in its saucer; then a fork falls on the floor.

"Really, Dora!" chastises Terence.

"Begging pardon, sir," pleads the girl. Now on her hands and knees, she is mopping up the fragments of fried egg that were knocked to the carpet by the wayward fork.

"Whatever is the matter with you?" He will not tolerate this sort of behavior.

Still clutching the plate, Dora straightens herself. "I'm sorry, sir. It's just that Cook says her best knives have gone missing."

Terence is sanguine. "And why should that be of such concern to you, Dora, unless, of course, you have taken them?" He looks at her pointedly and she sizzles under his gaze.

"Oh no, sir!" She shakes her head like the child that she is. "It's just there were that many visitors to the house yesterday—the butcher, the baker and . . ."

"The candlestick maker?" Terence thinks his witticism is worthy of remark, but remembers it is lost on the servant. "So the knives were stolen?" he continues.

"Yes, sir." The girl nods, glad of a serious ear at last.

"And Cook has conducted a thorough search?"

"Yes, sir."

Cutler folds his napkin deliberately into a triangle and pats it down flat.

"Then you are right to be worried, Dora," he tells his servant. "With this Jack the Ripper about, we must all be on our guard."

The girl balks at her master's mockery and has just turned tail with a tray of empty crockery when there comes a loud and urgent ringing of the doorbell. She switches round, looking for guidance from her master.

"Don't just stand there!" he barks.

She deposits the tray and rushes to the door, the ringing persisting all the while. The source of this frantic bell pulling is Pauline Beaufroy.

"Miss Beaufroy," Dora gasps as the unexpected visitor marches into the hallway.

"Is your mistress here?" Pauline's eyes dart left and right.

Terence, by now on his mettle, ventures out of the morning room and into the hall. "Pauline! What on earth . . . ?"

"Is she here? Please tell me she is here!"

"Geraldine? No, I thought she was with you.

I thought you were supposed to collect her," he replies, shaking his head.

Pauline steadies herself on the console table and raises a forlorn hand to her brow. "I was, but she'd already left. She's gone, Terence." The realization that her sister has discharged herself from the asylum, and is now at large again, saps all her strength.

Temporarily lost for words, Cutler suddenly finds his voice. "No! No! This cannot be." He shakes his head, then brings a balled fist to his mouth to bite his knuckle. "How can this have happened?"

Pauline suddenly bursts into tears. "A man, an impostor, took her away!" she wails. Producing a handkerchief, she buries her face in it.

Embarrassed and angry in turn by both his sister-in-law's distress and her inadequacies, Cutler lays an awkward arm on her shoulder and guides her into the morning room.

"We shall find her. We shall hunt down this scoundrel," he tells Pauline, patting her on the shoulder, although just how he proposes to do this at the moment is anyone's guess.

CHAPTER 37

Friday, November 9, 1888

CONSTANCE

I sit bolt upright in bed. Flo screams. She sits up, too.

"What in God's name . . . ?" she shouts at me with eyes still halfway closed. In my panic, I've pulled the bedclothes off her and she yanks them back.

My chest heaves, and as I lay my hand on my forehead, I feel it is clammy with sweat, even though the room is bitterly cold. "Oh, God!" I say. "I think there's been another murder."

"What!?" Flo rubs her eyes. "Oh, Christ!"

I jump out of bed and pull on my pantalettes and stockings.

"Where are you going?"

Dawn is edging its way across the London skyline, but its progress is marred by thick fog and our room is still in darkness. I fumble to find my shift and frock.

"I'm going to Mary Kelly's house," I tell her.

"Mary! Oh, my God, you don't think . . ." Her hand flies up over her mouth.

I suddenly remember that she and Flo know

each other. "Let's hope not," I say as I tug on my boots. Within two minutes, I am out of the door and rushing along, heading for Miller's Court. The streets are muffled by the fog. The sounds of horses being harnessed, of carts being loaded, of warehouse doors opening—all the music of a new day in the East End—are deadened by the fog. Yet, despite the filthy curtain that's drawn across these parts, I know my way around and it doesn't take long before I'm in Dorset Street.

I narrow my eyes to see the archway up ahead that leads to Miller's Court. I've never been down the alley before—only in my dream—and I'm filled with a terrible sense of dread. In my nightmare, I saw a scene straight from hell. Blood was everywhere and at the center of my vision lay poor Mary, horribly cut. With every step I take, my heart beats faster. Only a few more paces and I will be at the passage. But then, just as I draw almost level with the entrance on the opposite side of the street, I see a figure appear from the archway, not ten yards in front of me. A tall woman. She's wearing a brown linsey skirt and a red knitted shawl over her head. My heart leaps. It's Mary and she's in a hurry; head down and walking fast, she seems not to notice me waving to her.

"Mary!" I call.

At first, she doesn't respond. I call again. "Mary!" This time, she looks round, pauses for a second to see who's hailing her, then waves back. But she doesn't stop. She just hurries on toward Commercial Street. I do not mind. I'm just relieved that I've seen her. My nightmare was clearly just that. A nightmare, not a premonition. I turn and head toward home. It's then that I see someone else I know. It's Mrs. Maxwell, the wife of one of the lodging-house keepers. I helped teach her little boy to read. I cross the street for a chat.

"Well, if it ain't Connie Piper," she says with a smile. She's carrying a basket of firewood. "What you doin' here at this time o' the mornin'?"

I return her smile, while trying to drum up an excuse. "Mary Kelly borrowed a bonnet of mine last week and I was wanting it back for the show today," I lie. Too late do I remember that Mary never wears a hat, but I think I've got away with it.

Mrs. Maxwell chuckles and shifts her heavy basket to her other arm. "Oh, bless you, you needn't bother going down there. Mary's already up and out. I saw her not a minute ago."

Again my heart leaps a little. "Really?" I think I must sound too relieved. She's just confirmed what I've already seen with my own eyes.

"Looking the worse for wear she was, an' all," adds Mrs. Maxwell, swinging her basket onto her hip. "She told me she'd 'ad a right night of it!" She tips me a wink.

I thank her for sparing me the journey into Miller's Court and we part. I see her enter her home opposite the archway and I begin to retrace my way back to White's Row. This time, there's a spring in my step. If Mary didn't stop to talk, it was because she was feeling the effects of drink. The explanation is simple. Perhaps I will go to the Lord Mayor's Show, after all. I'm hoping it'll take my mind off all the terrible things that've gone before.

"Well?" Flo asks anxiously as soon as I'm back in the house.

I throw her a reassuring smile. "It's all right," I say, walking toward her as she makes tea in the kitchen. "I saw her."

Her shoulders heave as she sighs with relief. For a moment, I think that perhaps she might believe me when I say I have premonitions, and that I've seen Miss Tindall since she passed over. I'm hoping she'll be an ally. But she spoils it all by saying: "You and your dreams, eh! What are you like?"

EMILY

There is a tension in the air, an anticipation mixed with fear. I sense it as I gaze at the crowds lining Ludgate Hill, waiting for the great Lord Mayor's procession to pass. It is cold and it is raining, but that doesn't seem to dampen the mood. The sky is generally gray, with the odd patch of blue appearing now and again between the sodden clouds. To get a better view, young boys have scrambled halfway up lampposts, as if they were ships' masts. Children straddle their fathers' broad shoulders. Women stand on tiptoe and wave flags, even though the procession has not yet come round the bend. Along one of the side streets, a brass band plays marches and small boys keep time, parading up and down, much to the amusement of the nearby onlookers.

Yet, for all this show and merriment, the people of London prefer to throw brickbats at their dignitaries rather than bouquets, and the Metropolitan Police's handling of the Ripper murders has made most figures in authority a laughingstock. The mounted policemen who line the route at intervals also come in for mocking from the common horde.

"Shouldn't you be looking for Jack?" shouts one wag to an officer.

Laughter erupts nearby. But it has been four weeks since the last murder—or so everyone believes. Four weeks since the fiend had his way with two women on the same night, and the investigation has made precious little progress since. The killer, it seems, has gone to ground. Perhaps he has left the country. Perhaps he has killed himself. Jack's been locked away in a dark room and the key has been turned. Everyone in Whitechapel wants to get on with their brutish little lives that are hard enough as it is without knowing there is a murderer in their midst. What's more, the Vigilance Committee is winding down and Mr. Bartleby has reassured Mrs. Piper that "Jack won't be coming back. Not now." Even the press is losing interest in the atrocities. Where once their entire column inches might be devoted to gruesome details and wild speculation about the fiend's exploits, now even politics and public health are given space in their publications.

In among the waiting crowd stand Constance and Florence Piper, together with their mother and Mr. Bartleby. They are all in their Sunday best, even though I know Constance wishes she had worn her more serviceable woolen shawl and stout boots. I do not let her know I am watching her.

Flo, resplendent in a new hat, stands next to her. Her fiancé was apparently unable to have time off work, but that does not seem to trouble her. She's humming to herself while eyeing up a handsome young sailor standing a few feet away. Her attention is reciprocated. Mrs. Piper is finding that the cold wind does not agree with her chest and coughs incessantly, while Mr. Bartleby dreams of sitting in the cozy, snug room of the Britannia, cradling a warming dram of whisky.

But we must focus our attention on the procession itself. The new Lord Mayor, Sir James Whitehead, is returning in a magnificent coach after being presented to Her Majesty the Queen and to the judges of the High Court in the Strand. Emerging along Ludgate Hill, the long and colorful cortege is headed by guards in blue-and-gold livery. Near the front comes the pompous figure of the city chamberlain, bedecked in ceremonial attire; a cocked hat on his head and epaulets on his shoulders. Dressed in a scarlet uniform, he sits astride a fine white charger. Yet, the crowd on either side of him does not cheer and wave as he progresses. Rather they shout and jeer at him. He is a figure of fun. "String 'im from a lamppost!" yells one bystander. The sentiment is applauded. The populace of London is hard to impress when there's a murderer on the loose. The new Lord Mayor, cocooned in his coach, fares a little better. As soon as the waiting horde catches sight of the procession, a cheer starts to ripple down the line. Flags and banners are raised.

"Here he comes!" exclaims Mr. Bartleby. Even Florence takes her eyes off her sailor to look at the spectacle. Constance manages a smile and starts to wave the flag that a passerby has given her. The crowd surges forward, but is kept back by the mounted police.

"Watch it!" Florence shouts as she's elbowed in the ribs. Constance feels bodies press about her as she's carried forward. She does not like the sense of helplessness. Switching to her left, she sees her mother gasping for air like a fish out of water.

Somehow, amid all this mayhem, two young boys manage to break through the cordon. Ducking and diving between legs and skirts, they head toward the front of the crowd. They're scruffy and impish and around their necks hang placards. Much to everyone's astonishment, they scamper out in front of the procession and begin to dance and lark about in front of the city chamberlain's steed.

"What the hell are they playing at?" Florence cries.

"They need a damn good hiding," replies an indignant Mr. Bartleby.

Just then, the horse takes fright at the boys' antics. The crowd is alarmed. The last thing they want is for the animal to run amok. The creature clatters backward, a wild look in its eye, but, thankfully, after an anxious moment or two, the chamberlain manages to rein in his mount. There's a collective sigh of relief from all those who were aware of what was afoot. Suddenly, though, the mob's attention is drawn to something else. In a moment, the waving flags are lowered; the cheering ceases; the band master's baton freezes in midair as he turns round to see what has happened behind him.

Flo, a full two inches taller than her sister, frowns and nudges Constance.

"What do them boards say?" she asks.

A hush is falling on the crowd as those nearest the front read what is written on the boys' placards. Constance cranes her neck to see as the last of the trumpet notes fade. She squints against the rain now slanting in her eyes. The raindrops blur her vision momentarily. She blinks them away and looks again. "Oh, my God!" she mouths as the gaiety, which had only a minute ago enveloped her, is replaced by an eerie silence.

"What is it?" urges Flo. "What do they say?"

Constance turns to her with terror in her eyes. There is no other way to break the news. "They say, 'Another Whitechapel Murder.'"

Of course, I know it to be true. I'd seen the carnage with my own eyes just before dawn that morning. I'd found myself once more in Whitechapel, in the dingy courtyard, just off Dorset Street. Why I was there, I could not be sure. I never can. I do not choose where I go, but I sense that something terrible has happened. For a moment, I stand outside the miserable lodging in the freezing cold. Of course, I cannot feel the fingers of frost caress where my skin once lay; yet I can still shiver, not through cold but through apprehension. I knew I ought to go inside; yet there was this inexplicable feeling of fear that was worming its way into my psyche. And then I noticed a faint glow coming from inside. Is Mary Kelly awake? Is she alone? I'd asked myself.

Through the broken pane, I'd peered inside—my eyes no longer needed time to adjust, for I can see in any light—and in an instant, it hit me. I could not believe what I saw before me. I was glimpsing into the mouth of hell. In my state, I am supposed to be immune from such horror, but how can I be when a woman's body has been so mutilated and degraded with such ferocious barbarity, as if executed by the very Devil himself? Blood on the walls, blood on the ceiling, blood soaking the bed, pooling on the floor; it was an orgy of blood—and body parts. And her face—her lovely face—slashed beyond any recognition. I will not say more.

The paperboys are parading now, in front of the stunned crowd, proudly displaying their placards as if they were hunters' trophies. No doubt the newspapers will report this most gruesome murder in lurid detail. They will delight in the severed breasts, one laid so meticulously under her head, the other on the table; the throat slashed from ear to ear; the flayed flesh and, of course, the missing uterus. All these gut-wrenching details will be pored over in minute detail. They are the stuff of the most ghoulish nightmares and fodder for the sickest of minds.

What their legions of readers will never know, however, is that Mary Kelly's womb was harboring an unborn child. And her attacker cut it out. Just where the fetus has gone, I cannot say. All I knew, as I stood aghast in that blood-drenched room, was that I could take no more. I left. It was the fate of an unfortunate rent collector by the name of John Bowyer to discover the sickening scene. Mary Kelly was behind with her rent and Bowyer was dispatched to obtain it. In the event, he found so much more than he'd bargained for. The sight will haunt him for the rest of his days.

CHAPTER 38

Tuesday, November 20, 1888

CONSTANCE

We're at the East London Cemetery in Plaistow, not too far from Whitechapel, but far enough. So many die in the East End nowadays that we're not allowed to bury our dead close to home. The churchyards are overflowing with corpses.

The fog curls around the headstones and licks at the mausoleums. I must confess that even I, someone who's in touch with those who've passed, find it an eerie place in this sulphurous light, even though it's near noon. I never liked churchyards when I was a youngster. They always gave me the creeps; then after Pa died, they gave me comfort. I'd sit for a while by his grave and just talk, grouse about this and that, moan about Flo and Danny, tell him about Ma, but never about Mr. Bartleby, of course. But then, perhaps he already knew. I used to tell him all the things that Miss Tindall taught me, too, about the pyramids in Egypt or the palaces of India or the wild beasts of Africa. Sometimes I'd recite poetry as well: Wordsworth or Shelley or Blake. Miss Tindall used to tell me I needed to escape from—what was it?—"mind-forged manacles"—that's what Mr. Blake called them, anyway. She said "ignorance is a prison" and that everyone should try and break free. The trouble is that now I've tasted freedom I no longer know who I am: a simple flower girl from the East End just trying to survive, or an educated lady who cares about all the poverty and injustice that surrounds me.

I stand within sight, but as far away as I can, from the memorial stone that has been laid in memory of Miss Tindall. Her parents are spectral figures, black ghosts in a blurred landscape, as they pay their respects. I thought they'd want to bury their daughter in their own parish churchyard in Sussex, but they told Miss Beaufroy that she always wrote to them with a passion about her work in the East End and would have wanted to be buried here among the people she cared for so deeply. She didn't tell me where she wanted to be buried. Perhaps it doesn't matter to her, just as long as she is laid to rest in a fitting and proper manner.

I've had no dealings with Miss Tindall's family. Miss Beaufroy thought it best that way, and so do I. She's taken care of all the necessary arrangements and sorted affairs with Mr. and Mrs. Tindall. I'm not sorry. For all my newfound knowledge and my manners, I'm still a simple soul at heart, not versed in the ways of registers and forms and all the etiquette that higher-class people observe when they're in mourning. They seem to like to make a great show. They wear their black weeds for months, sometimes sitting for hours on end in darkened rooms. They are not allowed to listen to or play music, not allowed to dance or sing. But I won't do that. I won't mourn Miss Tindall in that way, even though I'm feeling so alone. I'll remember her with love and respect. Every time I look at a beautiful sculpture, or pick up a book or visit a museum, I'll think of her and the riches she has given me. But still I'm so afraid she may have gone—that I've lost her for good.

She hasn't spoken to me since Mary Kelly's murder, you see. There's been not a word or a sign from her. Sometimes I think I've dreamed it all; she never really appeared to me in a vision and that all my premonitions, my strange sensations, were simply figments of my vivid imagination. The truth is, I feel incredibly alone. Miss Beaufroy has been thoughtful, so kind and understanding, but she will go back to her big house in the country tomorrow. I will go back to my hovel and still we'll have to beg, steal and borrow to pay our rent. While Miss Beaufroy takes tea with clergymen and politicians in her genteel drawing room, I'll be helping Flo pilfer, and will be scraping together pennies just to buy food. She can't understand me. How can she? We are worlds apart, whereas Miss Tindall was part of my world and now she's gone to another.

EMILY

There she stands, my Constance. A woman, yet still a child. She has come a long way since those first days when I returned to seek her out, but she still has much to learn. Of course, I owe her a huge debt of gratitude. Without her, my rotting torso would still lie anonymously in the mortuary. At least now my earthly body will enjoy the comforts of a proper grave. Yet, despite my ephemeral state, there is much I have failed to do. As I have told you before, I can only guide. I do not dictate how people behave. Man's free will does that, so despite my best intentions, evil still holds sway. It has dominion over so many, and, in particular, in Whitechapel.

I could not foresee what Geraldine Cutler did to poor Mary Kelly. God only knows how I wish I could have prevented her from wielding that knife. But the saying "Hell hath no fury like a woman scorned" is so true. Her rage and her jealousy blotted out all her reason and replaced it with a savagery that shocked the civilized world. She never confessed to her heinous crime, even though her husband found her bloodstained clothes and guessed. Instead, he saw to it that she was shut away quietly in the asylum in Hampstead, where she died three years later.

Robert Sampson was true to his word. He saw to it that Libby Lonergan was returned to her family, and a substantial amount of money was handed over to pay for their silence. The other missing girls, however, were not so lucky. Despite the illegality of it, like hundreds of English children, they remained in brothels for the rest of their wretched lives.

And as for Jack the Ripper? No one has been held to account, yet. Rumors are breeding like cockroaches, not just in Whitechapel and not just in London. All over the world, news of the killings has spread and so does the speculation. Jack is royalty; Jack is an American; Jack is a Jew; Jack is a physician; Jack is a Freemason. The mystery remains unsolved thus far, consigned to legend and endless debate. I fear several more women will be murdered in the East End in the two years following Mary Kelly's murder. No one knows how many will die at the Ripper's hands, but, for now, most pray that poor Mary is his last victim. Yet I know differently. You may not have heard of Catherine Mylett, or Alice McKenzie, or Frances Coles, but they, too, will all meet their fate in gruesome circumstances, not to mention another headless torso that will be discarded under a railway arch in Pinchin Street.

The truth is Jack the Ripper will always stalk the streets of London—and Paris and New York and every city in the world. He looms large at every ill-lit corner and in every narrow walkway. He sits next to you in a railway carriage and mingles in hotel lobbies. There isn't just one, single killer, but several, each determined to exercise the power that man has had over women since time immemorial; each one bent on satiating their perverted lusts, or wreaking revenge in order to ultimately, simply gain control.

Like any young woman, Constance will not be immune to such dangers, but if I can guide her safely through the maze of her existence, give her the confidence to right individual wrongs, fight injustices that seem small in the scheme of things, but are great to those affected, then perhaps my time on earth will not have been wasted.

Such is the nature of humanity; it is cruel and calculating and vicious, but in among the harshness and the dark iniquity of it all, a seed of hope must flourish. Granted, my own life was cut short before I could accomplish what I set out to do for the people of Whitechapel. However, as long as I can work through Constance, then this new life of mine, this second chance, will be as busy in the future as it was in the past, and, I pray, it will be as fulfilling in this new world as it was in the last.

Now that I have returned to this earth, to this part of London, in my altered state, I will see to it that, with Constance's help, I shall do just that. Together we will shine a little light into the darkest corners of existence and tend that seed. God willing, it will take root and bloom. It will not be easy. Many challenges will have to be overcome. Many obstacles will lie in our path. But I know that in our own small way, we can achieve great victories on behalf of the voiceless and the oppressed.

As Constance stands there, casting a forlorn look across at my headstone, her cheeks wet with tears, thinking she is all alone once more, I see her sadness and I hear her voice. I shall offer her my hand. Not now, but soon, and, if she accepts it, if she lets me into her life once more, then together we shall go on another journey. Let it be so.

Author's Acknowledgments

For introducing me to the extraordinary world of the spiritualist medium in late Victorian England, I must thank my longtime friend and expert on the paranormal, Lynn Picknett. Her study of Florence Cook, a fifteen-year-old girl who morphed into the materialized "spirit" Katie King at many a well-attended séance in England, piqued my interest.

I do not pretend to be a Ripperologist and, while every effort has been made to be factually correct, there are many facts that are still disputed among scholars. My thanks in this field must go to Ripper expert David Bullock, whose book *The Man Who Would Be Jack* I highly recommend. Of course, dozens of books have been written on the subject of Jack the Ripper. Ones that I particularly commend to you are Russell Edward's *Naming Jack the Ripper, The Complete and Essential Jack the Ripper* by Paul Begg and John Bennett, and *Jack the Ripper: The Hand of a Woman* by John Morris. By far, the best online resource is www.casebook.org, the world's largest public repository of Ripper-related information. Here you'll find—among hundreds of fascinating tidbits—newspaper and postmortem reports, articles and essays relating to the Whitechapel murders, as well as a photographic archive.

As ever, I am indebted to my editor at Kensington Publishing, John Scognamiglio, and to my agent, Melissa Jeglinski.

For spending many hours with me as I trawled around Whitechapel, I would like to thank my long-suffering husband, Simon. My thanks also go to my daughter, Sophie, and my son, Charlie, for their understanding when I forgot to buy any food or burned the dinner because I was so engrossed in the writing of this novel. Once again, my friend and fellow writer, Katharine Johnson, has lent her support, as have Carolyn and Barry Cowing. And finally I'd like to mention our little dog, Indy, who was always my constant writing companion and sometime (welcome) distraction, before he, too, "passed over" earlier this year.

Center Point Large Print
600 Brooks Road / PO Box 1
Thorndike, ME 04986-0001 USA

(207) 568-3717

US & Canada:
1 800 929-9108
www.centerpointlargeprint.com